REQUIEM OF SILENCE

EARTHSINGER CHRONICLES BOOK FOUR

Also by L. Penelope

Song of Blood & Stone
Breath of Dust & Dawn
Whispers of Shadow & Flame
Hush of Storm & Sorrow
Cry of Metal & Bone
Echoes of Ash & Tears

REQUIEM OF SILENCE

EARTHSINGER CHRONICLES
BOOK FOUR

L. PENELOPE

ST. MARTIN'S GRIFFIN NEW YORK

This is a work of fiction. All of the characters, organizations, and events portrayed in this novel are either products of the author's imagination or are used fictitiously.

First published in the United States by St. Martin's Griffin, an imprint of St. Martin's Publishing Group

www.stmartins.com

Library of Congress Cataloging-in-Publication Data

Names: Penelope, L., 1978– author.
Title: Requiem of silence / L. Penelope.
Description: First edition. | New York : St. Martin's Griffin, 2021. | Series: Earthsinger chronicles ; book 4 |
Identifiers: LCCN 2021008151 | ISBN 9781250148131 (trade paperback) | ISBN 9781250148148 (ebook)
Classification: LCC PS3616.E5387 R47 2021 | DDC 813/.6—dc23
LC record available at https://lccn.loc.gov/2021008151

First Edition: 2021

10 9 8 7 6 5 4 3 2 1

For Jared, who loves me

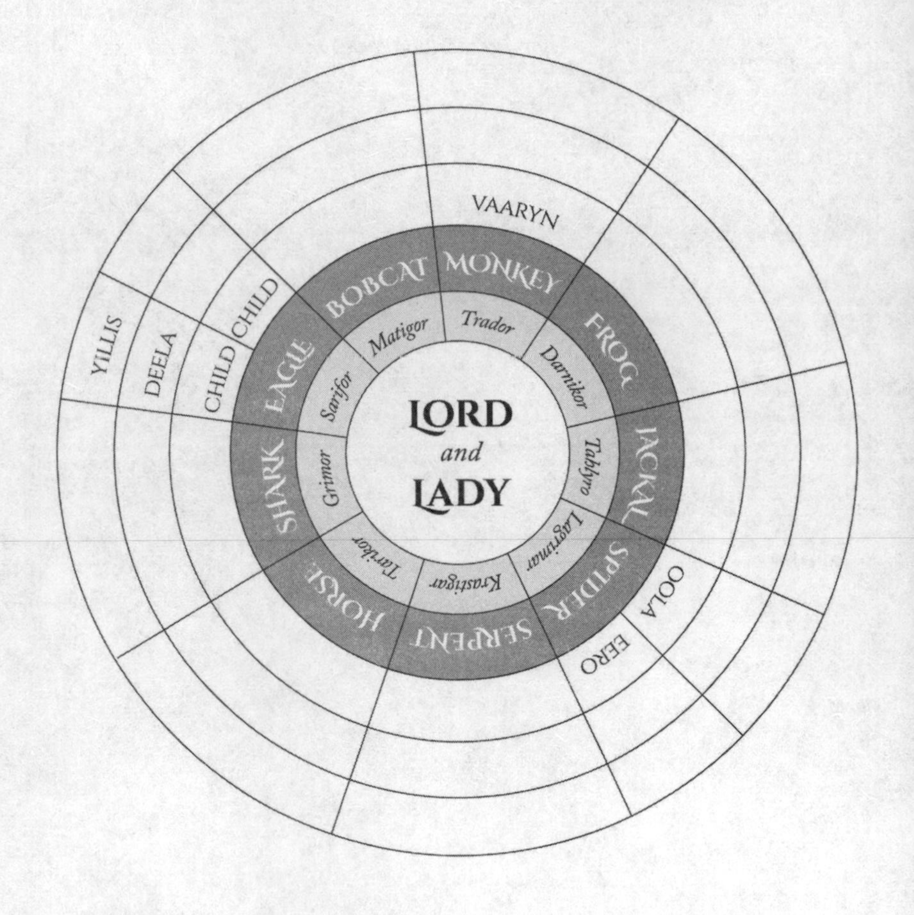

LORD
and
LADY
Trador
Darnikor
Tablyro
Lagrimar
Krastigar
Tarvikor
Grimor
Sarifor
Matigor
MONKEY
FROG
JACKAL
SPIDER
SERPENT
HORSE
SHARK
EAGLE
BOBCAT
VAARYN
CHILD
CHILD
DEELA
YILLIS
OOLA
EERO

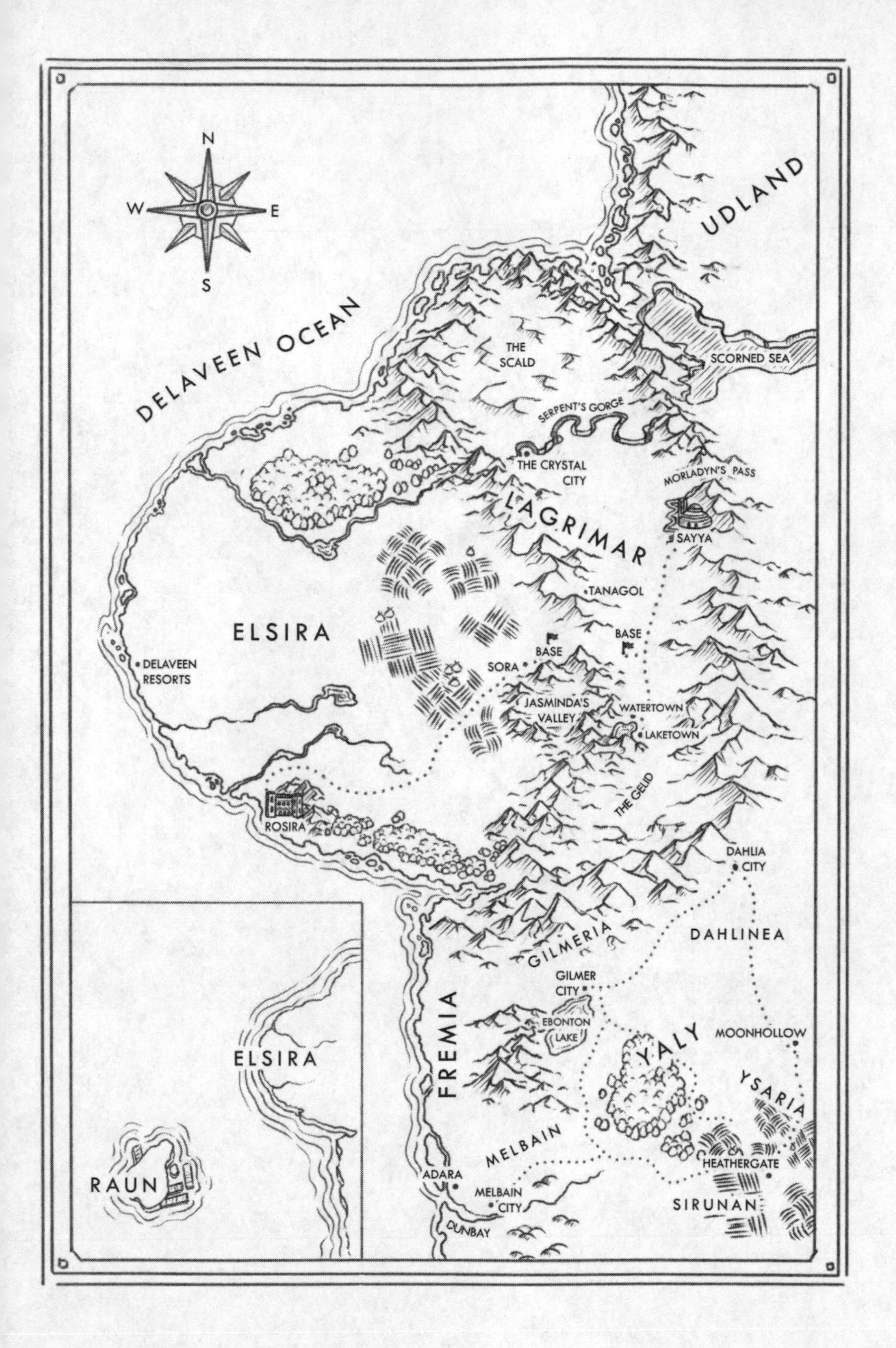

N
W
E
S
UDLAND
DELAVEEN OCEAN
THE SCALD
SCORNED SEA
SERPENT'S GORGE
THE CRYSTAL CITY
MORLADYN'S PASS
LAGRIMAR
SAYYA
TANAGOL
ELSIRA
BASE
BASE
DELAVEEN RESORTS
SORA
JASMINDA'S VALLEY
WATERTOWN
LAKETOWN
THE GELID
ROSIRA
DAHLIA CITY
DAHLINEA
GILMERIA
GILMER CITY
FREMIA
EBONTON LAKE
YALY
MOONHOLLOW
ELSIRA
YSARIA
MELBAIN
HEATHERGATE
RAUN
ADARA
MELBAIN CITY
SIRUNAN
DUNBAY

REQUIEM

OF

SILENCE

PROLOGUE

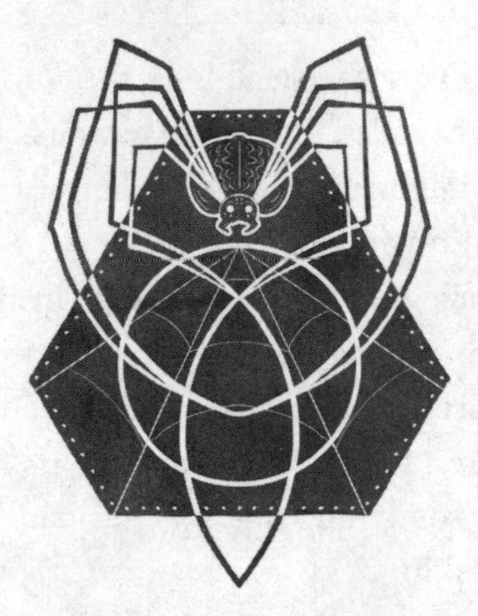

In the end, there will be silence.

Nothing but the warm embrace of the Flame and then . . . peace. The old man knows this and has waited for longer than he ever thought possible. He will wait a bit longer, for while he is old now, he was also old centuries ago. He suspects he will be old for centuries more before he can finally meet the Flame and be done with it all.

But even death cannot come before duty, not for one of his line.

The prophecy that came to him generations ago has never left the forefront of his mind. It seeped in and spread like a dye, staining everything that it touched: the one who walks in darkness will embrace the Light.

He stands at the mouth of a cave of his beloved Mountain Mother, staring at the world outside that has claimed so many of his kind. The rays of the sun pepper fevered kisses on his face. A harsh kind of love. He cannot become used to it. Outside is not for him.

Soon a visitor will arrive, one he has been expecting for a long time.

He thinks perhaps this visitor is the key to the prophecy. Darkness and Light rolled into one. He waits, and when the visitor arrives, the young man is haggard, but bears it well. His eyes are alight with charm and mischief.

The prophet has a moment of misgiving; however, this does not stop him from leading the visitor up a barely used trail, to a cave on the outskirts of the city where they won't be disturbed.

There he makes the greatest mistake of his life. There he teaches the visitor something that no Outsider should know. Even one with familiar skin.

Perhaps it was the prophecy that duped him. Or the fact that the visitor is only a generation removed from those who left the caves to live outside.

Had this seeker's fore-parent not left, he would have already known this secret. Could have known it, at least.

No matter now, the deed is done. The knowledge passed from prophet to man.

As the visitor's head bobs away down the narrow path, the prophet has another shudder of misgiving.

But surely the Mother would not have allowed him to do something that would harm his people. All he ever wanted to do was save them.

He watches the visitor's retreat and hopes that teaching him the Cavefolk secrets was the right decision.

He will ask the Mother about it soon.

CHAPTER ONE

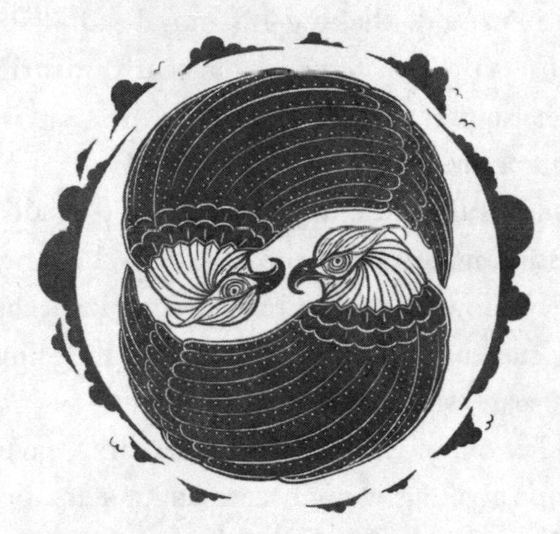

Where does solace hide when discord
warbles its tumultuous strains?
In silence or in sound, Harmony is found.

—THE HARMONY OF BEING

Queen Jasminda ul-Sarifor Alliaseen held a maelstrom of Earthsong within her. She found herself connecting to the stream of energy in times of distress, without any real intention of doing something with the power, but holding it inside herself brought comfort. She was on alert at all times now. She'd already been assassinated once, after all.

The current cause of her anguish was not the terrorists who'd taken her life mere weeks ago, nor the ongoing strife between Elsiran citizen and Lagrimari refugee playing itself out in the streets. These were on her mind at all times, but at this precise moment, it was the undervalets scurrying in and out of the royal suite who had her on edge. Usher, the king's valet and longtime friend, directed them as they brought in piles of clothing and shoes for inspection.

"No," the man said, shaking his gray head. "Not those—in fact, send those to the Sisterhood for charity distribution. He's nearly worn the soles off them."

The servant nodded and rushed off.

"That trunk is full, young man," Usher said kindly to another. "No use overstuffing, just place those vests in the other one."

Jasminda swallowed, taking in the organized chaos, a pulse of life energy rushing through her veins. "Is he going away for a fortnight or a year?" she muttered.

Usher led her out of the path of the servants, saving her from a collision with a young woman carrying a stack of shirt boxes that nearly reached her eyes. "His Majesty will require options. Prime Minister Buchanan has not provided us with an itinerary, so we don't know how many formal and informal dinners there will be, whether he's organizing a hunting carnival, wilderness explorations, or other entertainments. We must be ready for anything."

"Hunting *carnival*?"

"The elite of the south are quite fond of reveling after a kill. Rather intensely, as I recall," a new voice announced. King Jaqros Alliaseen emerged from the adjoining sitting room. "They do not even use the meat for food, they drape it over themselves and parade around taunting the birds of prey."

Jasminda shuddered, her face twisting in disgust.

"I know, I know, it's barbaric, but it's part of their culture, and it would be wrong to judge." Jack pulled her even farther away from the packing action to sit on the settee in front of the fireplace, now burned down to embers. The weather had turned colder with winter nearly upon them, but with all the activity the room had been warm all day and no one had stoked the fire.

"This is a terrible time for you to go off on vacation, you know," she said, crossing her arms. She didn't pout; she was constitutionally unable to do so, or so she'd always thought. But her husband was leaving on this ridiculous trip—where he would apparently be dancing while wearing raw meat and waiting for vultures to attack. And she would be left here for the first time to run the country on her own, stalked by her own birds of prey.

Jack gently untangled her arms and held her hands. "It's the worst timing ever, but Buchanan is an idiosyncratic old man. He believes in star alignments and makes decisions according to the phases of the moon. My invitation was not only last minute, it was apparently sparked by some sort of celestial event that we can only hope will induce him to give aid to his needy northern neighbors." He smiled. "But if not, I'm going to convince him to help."

"Maybe he can ask the stars and moon to end our drought."

Jack chuckled and brought her hands to his lips. Her shoulders softened. The invitation from Fremia's Prime Minister couldn't be ignored, especially when Elsira was in such a difficult situation.

"Or maybe the celestial beings can intercede with King Pia and ask her to stop this fecking embargo."

Jack's lips quirked. He raised a brow at her language and she rolled her eyes. She didn't normally curse, but desperate times and all. "I think we're going to have to handle that one ourselves," he said. "That last message from Ambassador Nirall was positive, wasn't it?"

She nodded. Both Jack and the Council had thought putting the situation with Raun on Jasminda's plate was a good idea. Not because of any skill she had with foreign relations, but because her younger brother Roshon was engaged to the daughter of the female king of Raun. And their new ambassador, Lizvette Nirall, had instantly created a rapport with the notoriously difficult leader. Jasminda herself was the weak link.

"Listen, I know you've been busy with the needs of the refugees," Jack said, "we all have, but if the embargo doesn't end soon, even Fremia's aid won't be enough. We need to get Raun back on our side and you're the best option for that."

"I know, I need to brush up on their history and culture and make some overtures, but honestly, if your brother made a misstep with them that caused this fiasco, there's little chance that I can fix it."

Jack sighed, shaking his head. "My brother was a great Prince Regent, but his people skills left something to be desired. I believe if you prove to Pia you understand and respect Raunian culture, you can smooth over whatever Alariq did to get us in this mess."

She nodded, though she wasn't convinced. Perhaps if Earthsong could create additional hours in the day, she would have time to handle every item on her to-do list. The drought, the embargo, the lines of hungry refugees waiting for food, the protests of Elsiran citizens wanting to push the refugees out of the country. She shivered, recalling the devastation that the fall of the Mantle had wrought when the defeat of the True Father changed their world forever.

A loud snap brought her attention back to the other side of the room. Usher had just closed the second trunk and the other servants were clearing out. Jasminda took a deep breath and pulled her hands from Jack's. They immediately felt cold, plus a chilly dread began to spread across her body at the thought of piloting this massive, damaged ship by herself for two weeks. The length of the visit was another thing predestined by astronomical forces.

She stood and Jack followed, tracking her with his gaze. He was worried and she didn't want him to be, so she tried to put forth an air of confidence she absolutely did not feel. Of course he saw through her.

"You can do this, Jasminda. You know how to handle the Council; most of them are afraid of your Song anyway. The Keepers will assist you as well. And if anything happens, maybe the Goddess will even step in to help."

She snorted, that wasn't likely. Goddess Oola had taken Her abdication seriously. As the only other person who'd ever been queen of Elsira, it would have been nice of Her to give some advice every now and then, but so far that hadn't happened. Jasminda could barely even find Her these days. No, she would have to do this on her own, as she'd done everything else for so long.

The trunks were carried down to the motorcade, which would transport Jack to the docks and his Fremia-bound ship. Jasminda held his hand as they followed the retinue of servants, winding their way through the palace and out to the vehicle depot.

A contingent of Royal Guardsmen was assembled outside, ready to accompany their king. Jasminda was glad to see Benn Ravel, Jack's former assistant and close friend, among them. It was a difficult time for him to leave his young family as well, but Jack had made an impassioned request and the man hadn't refused.

As Jack conferred with another Guardsman, Jasminda approached Benn. "This the first time you've been away from Ella and the girls?" she asked. He and his wife had recently adopted two Lagrimari orphans.

His somber amber eyes regarded her as he nodded. "Though I'm sure Ella can withstand anything, and my mother is helping, amazingly enough. But I still have this pain, just here, that won't let up." He covered his heart with a palm.

"I understand. I feel it, too."

"But they know what this trip means. What the aid would

mean for the country. They're proud of me, and that helps some." Benn's pained smile made Jasminda's heart clench.

"Thank you for going with him. I feel much better with you watching his back."

Benn sketched a short bow and headed to his vehicle.

A moment later, Jack was at her side again, wrapping strong arms around her. "I'll be back in a heartbeat," he whispered in her ear. "Maybe sooner." Her eyes began to tear, but she blinked them away. There were so many people watching.

She kissed Jack quickly, not wanting to linger, then tried to be as stoic as possible as the final checks were made and everyone began piling into the vehicles. Another kiss. A final wave. And then they were off, a caravan of autos heading away from the palace down the twisting streets.

She used her Song to follow them, sensing his essence, his reticence, and the worry he tried not to let her see. They were the rulers of a divided country that might not have enough food to last the winter, whose coffers were nearly empty and whose citizens were threatening ethnic cleansing. He was off to do his part to fix things and she had to keep the land together in the meantime. She strained to not lose her connection to her husband until he passed out of her range.

And so she sensed the messenger before the nervous young man arrived, panting from his race across the palace, a hand pressed to his side to try to ease the stitch that had developed. Jasminda healed the exhaustion with a silent spell so she could get the message more quickly.

"Your Majesty, there's been another attack."

Growing up in the isolated mountain valley, Jasminda had never been through one of the hurricanes that regularly assaulted the coast. Storm season was still several months off, but a part of her looked forward to experiencing one of the tempests she'd read so much about. What would it be like to withstand the effects of nature's fury? The onslaught of rain and wind strong enough to lift a man off his feet and cut a path of destruction through a city? How different would it be from life after the fall of the Mantle?

This morning, in the aftermath of a different kind of squall, the streets of the city were eerily quiet. The barely there hum of her town car's tires as they glided down the pavement was the only sound. Tinted windows hid her from view as she peered out to the empty sidewalks beyond. Fear hung thick in the air like smoke as her motorcade rolled along, unhindered by the light traffic.

She'd read that being inside the eye of a hurricane was similar. The most severe thunderstorms would pass and you would find yourself in the midst of a hushed landscape, with clear skies. Unnatural lighting from the turgid clouds would give a sickly, xanthous hue to the world. It was a false calm, surrounded on all sides by a towering wall of devastation. And it would pass, all too soon, the gale restarting just as intensely as before. No quarter to be found.

Her motorcade pulled to a stop on a quiet street in Portside, the neighborhood where, until recently, all foreigners had been sequestered. One of her two new assistants, Camm Bosa, stood on the sidewalk waiting for her to alight.

"Your Majesty," Camm said, bowing his head. He was an extremely capable young man in his early twenties, with dark reddish-brown freckles covering his face and a mop of unruly russet hair always looking ready to escape his head.

The street was hushed, with nothing obvious to cause alarm. Just a working-class neighborhood with well-maintained, mid-sized buildings. Concrete pavement in good repair; no trash littered the street. "Where was the bombing?" she asked, perplexed.

Camm winced. "This way. And it wasn't a bombing, not exactly." He began walking, long legs eating up the sidewalk. Jasminda's Guard, half a dozen towering men clad in black, fell into formation around them.

Halfway down the block, Camm stopped and pointed to a building, completely intact. The simple stucco facade painted in a faded coral.

"I don't see anything."

"Look at the windows, Your Majesty," Camm said. "The black smudges ringing each of them."

Now that he pointed it out, there was a sooty sort of smudging around the windows. Several had flower boxes bordering them, and Jasminda noted that all the flowers were dry and brittle. It was mid-autumn, still several weeks from the first frost, and the resilient jack-a-dandies should be doing well, even with the smallest amount of care.

Camm cleared his throat. "The Sisterhood bought this building last year, planning to turn it into a dormitory. They'd begun renovations, so the top two floors were vacant when the Mantle fell. Refugees began moving in a couple of weeks ago. According to the local alderman, there had been a few clashes with Elsirans on the lower levels. The fire inspector just completed his review and says the top two floors were smoke bombed late last night."

"Smoke bombed?"

"The devices are available in Fremia and Yaly. They produce smoke, but no fire. People who are sleeping never know what hit them. They just inhale the smoke until it smothers them." Camm looked a little green at the thought, and Jasminda could relate.

"How many dead?"

"Twelve. At least twenty others had lung injuries, but Keepers arrived to heal them."

The street was perfectly deserted, though movement caught her eye in the surrounding windows. Curtains fell back into place when she looked up.

"Where is everyone?" Her skin had begun to prickle with the feeling of being watched.

"Those in the building were evacuated just around back."

Camm led the way down a narrow alley. They emerged in an open lot that stretched to the next street. A rusted fence divided two properties, but at some point it had been flattened, leaving a tract of cracked asphalt and weeds that was currently full of people. Two Sisterhood ambulances were parked next to a handful of open-topped wagons holding miserable-looking Elsirans. Standing grouped together on the other side of the lot were the Lagrimari residents.

"That's not all, Your Majesty," Camm warned.

Jasminda had been headed toward the victims but stopped short. "What?"

"The bottom four floors were not immune."

"Do you mean they targeted Elsirans as well?" That hadn't happened since the initial temple bombing. Since then, the terrorists had been more precise in their execution.

"Well, the smoke bombing of the Lagrimari was partially thwarted. The constables believe those on the bottom floors were victims of a counterattack an hour or so later."

A gust of cold wind blew along with his words. "What kind of counterattack?"

"The temperature inside was simply . . . raised. No fire. And no smoke. Just heat, so intense that those who did not get out simply . . . cooked."

Nausea threatened, and this time it wasn't the wind that made her shiver. "Earthsong," she whispered. "The Sons of Lagrimar?"

A group calling themselves the Sons of Lagrimar had begun a spate of violence recently, answering each of the pro-Elsiran assaults with one of their own, twisting Earthsong to use it as a weapon.

"None of the Lagrimari will talk to me or to the constables," Camm said, "but that would be my guess. Ilysara is trying to get more answers." He motioned to Jasminda's other new assistant, a Lagrimari woman standing among the huddled victims, still in their sleeping clothes.

Ilysara broke off her conversation and approached, greeting Jasminda with a bow and Camm with a nod. "Your Majesty," Ilysara said in Elsiran, a language that she'd grown remarkably proficient with in a short period of time. She was several years older than both Jasminda and Camm, and had been some kind of recordkeeper in the True Father's harems.

"What have you learned?" Jasminda asked.

"The family I was just speaking with was awakened by a neighbor who arrived home from working a late shift and noticed all the smoke."

"Did any of them see who could have committed the counterattack?"

"No," Ilysara replied, frowning. "But a strong Earthsinger could have done it from a short distance away and not be seen."

"Anyone take responsibility?"

"The Keepers haven't said anything."

Jasminda nodded, biting her lip. For an Earthsinger to cause harm or death was incredibly difficult—for a *sane* Earthsinger, that is. A Song connected you to the life energy of every living thing, and purposefully taking a life while being a part of that connection was unnatural, painful, harrowing. It could easily drive you mad.

Jasminda reached for her Song and joined the infinite flow of life energy. She let it wash over her, filling her up, before reaching out to sense the emotions of those nearby. Fear, resentment, anger. A few shields keeping her out, those were other Singers. It could be that whoever perpetrated the violence had stuck around, but she had no way of knowing. If so, they were not feeling particularly guilty.

She sighed, releasing her power. "Everyone here has been healed who wanted to be?"

Camm nodded, and Ilysara pursed her lips. "The Elsirans who survived refused Earthsong healing," she said.

Camm shrugged. "You can't force someone to be helped."

Ilysara turned away looking sour. While neither had expressed any opposition to working with one another, Jasminda sensed that the two did not exactly get along. However, she could not possibly have chosen an Elsiran over a Lagrimari or vice versa—the optics would have been horrible, so she'd chosen one of each. Camm had come recommended by the royal event planner and was from an aristocratic family. Ilysara, with a few prematurely gray hairs at the temples of her short, kinky hair, had been identified by the Keepers of the Promise. She never spoke without careful consideration of her words, but her intelligence was nearly frightening. Jasminda liked them both very much.

"If they don't want healing, they won't be healed," Jasminda said with a sigh.

"There aren't many Singers willing to heal Elsirans anyway, given how ungrateful they are." Ilysara's eyes were flinty. Camm looked uncomfortable with the assertion, but wisely stayed quiet.

A commotion among the citizens caused Jasminda to turn as her Guard tightened its protective circle around her. She peered around broad shoulders to find two young men—possibly teenagers—one

Elsiran and one Lagrimari, tussling. They fell to the ground in a flurry of fists. Several cautious onlookers seemed ready to step in once an opportunity presented itself, but none did.

She could use Earthsong to distract them, pull them apart, or drop a wall of darkness around them like Darvyn was so fond of doing. But what would that solve? This scuffle was being played out on stages big and small around their land.

An elder Lagrimari man barked out some words she didn't catch, then grabbed the refugee boy by his collar and dragged him away. The cut on the boy's cheek was healed before their eyes by an unknown Singer.

The Elsiran was helped up by a woman who immediately began scolding him. Shouts and curses were traded back and forth in the respective languages of the two groups—though neither could understand each other.

Jasminda took a deep breath. "Get the constables to separate these people." Camm and Ilysara both nodded and pushed their way outside the wall of Guardsmen to go and defuse the situation.

Unity, when it came, would be hard-won, they'd all known that. But right now turning two nations, whose only commonality was an abiding mutual hatred for one another, into a unified populace didn't just look hard, it looked impossible.

CHAPTER TWO

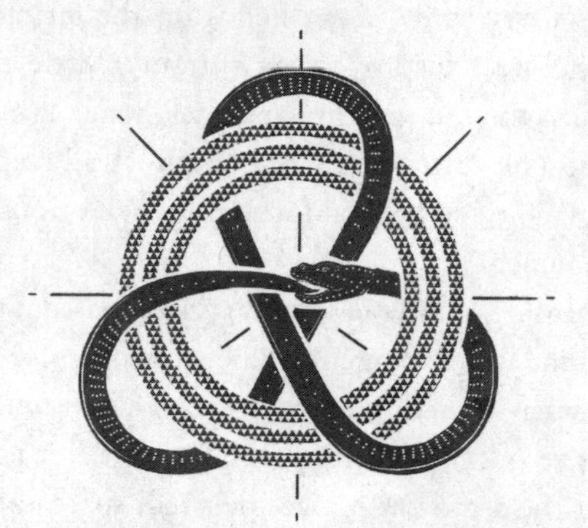

A road undriven leads nowhere.
All lives are journeys. Some will take
you across the globe while others
consist of only a single
step.

—THE HARMONY OF BEING

The squawk of a large black-and-white bird diving into the sea startled Kyara. Waves crashed in a soothing percussion, lulling her into a place just beyond consciousness, not asleep, but not quite awake, either. She yawned and straightened her back, slightly sore from sitting hunched over for who knew how long. The sand beneath her was warm from the sun, though the air had a jagged bite to it and a light wind had picked up, chilling it further.

The strange bird—they had no such creatures in Lagrimar, and she didn't know its Elsiran name—dropped into the water with a splash, then rose again on beating wings, a wriggling fish in its mouth.

She gave a wry smile, silent kudos for the talented predator, and rose to her feet, dusting off her bottom to little avail. Elsiran sand was much the same as the sand back home; it might sparkle subtly and be a bit softer to the touch, but it still crept into every crevice imaginable and held on for dear life. Her trousers and skin were not immune.

The sun was beginning to lower and she contemplated turning back toward the little cottage she'd been living in for the past few weeks. She wasn't exactly sure how Darvyn had found the place an hour's drive outside the city—his friend, the king, had likely helped—but she'd grown to love the small space they shared. It sat mere steps from the ocean, on the outskirts of a tiny town of artisans and tourists.

She and Darvyn had retreated there a few days after her execution had been interrupted. The house's sparse white walls and simple, comfortable furniture had brought her a peace she wasn't sure she deserved. Especially when she'd expected her last home to be a dungeon. But as lovely as it was, today she wanted to walk a bit farther, explore a little more, especially since the beach was deserted now that the weather had chilled.

Though she hadn't ventured into the town, Darvyn reported that his presence had not caused a riot or even elicited much comment. These folk, used to foreign tourists, seemed not to mind the presence of two Lagrimari among them. Still, Kyara had no desire to push her luck, and when the sound of voices rose just beyond the dunes to her right, she froze.

She would have turned around and retreated, had she not recognized the language as Lagrimari. Female voices chattered, too quiet to make out more than a few words. Children's laughter rang out as well. Now, curiosity won out over Kyara's desire for solitude.

She crouched and climbed up the small hill, hoping to remain hidden among the waist-high, wispy grass as she peered beyond. A small group of Lagrimari were seated about fifty paces away, the wind bringing their voices closer. Instead of facing the ocean, they sat looking toward a three-story building, teeming with construction workers.

Darvyn had mentioned this place to her the other day, a seaside inn, vacant for at least a year after the owner died. The Sisterhood was restoring it for use by the refugees.

The presence of the women and children made Kyara suspect that at least part of the building was inhabitable. The camps were being emptied as quickly as alternate housing could be found. A half dozen small children chased one another, squealing and laughing, remaining a safe distance from the construction and under the watchful eyes of the mothers. Just beyond them, a group of older children played carryball. Kyara flattened herself against the ground, observing, an ache of longing pulsing within her.

Near the women, a tiny boy began to spin, laughing riotously at his own antics. As other children egged him on, cyclones of sand started to twist and turn around him. Earthsong. A young woman who might have been his mother gasped when she saw it, her gaze darting toward the building and the workers, mostly Elsiran from what Kyara could see. The woman hurried to the boy and snatched his arm.

"No! No singing, not where they can see you."

Chastened, the boy nodded, and the small tornadoes died. The children all quieted, and the woman pulled him into her arms and squeezed, relief making her face go slack.

Kyara crawled back down the hill, oblivious to the sand abrading her skin. Part of her wanted to be able to walk up to them, introduce herself, and sit for a chat. The thought made her snort. She hadn't had a friend since she was eleven years old—and look how that turned out. She'd accidentally killed her.

One look at the Poison Flame, so recently liberated from the hangman's noose, and the children's easy laughter would turn to screams. She started back toward the cottage, heart heavy, when shouts behind her caused her to turn.

The ball the older children had been playing with flew in a wide arc over the small dunes, all the way to the water, where it splashed as it fell with a thud. At this time of day, the waves beating at the sand were frothy and white, rippling angrily as they came ashore. The ball disappeared into the jaws of the water, swallowed whole.

Kyara blinked, and in that time the body of a preteen boy came barreling across the sand. He raced through the wispy grass and down the incline, accompanied by the calls of his friends who trailed behind him.

"Taron, no!" a girl shouted. "Just leave it."

"But it's our only ball," another boy said.

"We're not supposed to go near the water. It's dangerous."

The commotion had brought the women to the hilltop as well, and Kyara stood frozen, not wanting to draw attention to herself. Taron raced across the beach on bare feet, but stopped short at the water's edge. The ball was nowhere in sight.

The boy's breath heaved in his chest as he scanned the water, panic in his eyes. His friends caught up to him, staring longingly at the rowdy waves.

"Leave it, Taron," the girl's voice came again, sounding sensible.

"We won't get another," a boy spoke up from the middle of the pack.

By the time Kyara had been this age, she was already in service to the True Father, quickly becoming his favorite assassin. Killing his enemies, and even his friends, when the mood suited him. She'd never actually played carryball, barely knew the rules, and so didn't understand the group's fascination with something so trivial as a leather bag filled with stuffing. But they all looked at the sea as if it had stolen their closest friend.

Taron was nearest to the water; he stood, hands on his hips, without taking his eyes from the writhing waves. "I can get it back," he said, and the determination in his voice caused the hairs on Kyara's neck to rise.

Without any further hesitation, he marched into the water, cursing at the cold as it swallowed his feet and legs. The women's voices raised in alarm, and several of them descended the hill in a panic.

Kyara stood locked in place. She should really go home to her cottage before she was recognized. She didn't know these people, had no connection to them. Then again, maybe she did . . . Maybe she'd killed one of their loved ones. Maybe they'd been there that day when the noose had been prepared for her and she'd been led over to it, ready to lay down her life in payment for her crimes. She had no way of knowing.

A surge knocked Taron off balance and his body disappeared beneath the frothy waters of the Delaveen Ocean. Screams rose up from the gathered audience and several women grabbed at the children rushing forward to go after him.

Kyara sank into her other sight, into her ability to view the Nethersong around her. The energy of death glowed in the adults, less so in the children. In the water, the glow of fish and sea creatures peppered the darkness of the waves. The largest form she sensed was about thirty paces away and sinking quickly, glowing brighter as death energy filled the young boy's body.

She couldn't reach him, not with her physical self. Like most Lagrimari, she couldn't swim and had never gotten more than her feet wet in the ocean. Diving in after him would be folly; however, standing by while he drowned was not an option, either. She was done with death—both causing it and witnessing it.

But she could keep him from dying—or at least staying dead.

Quieting her mind even further, she sank deeper into her Song, moving past her other sight until darkness once again filled her vision and the doorways appeared. She stood at the threshold of worlds, glowing arches of muted light before her. One led to the World Between and one to the World After.

In the water, Taron had been shining with Nether, a blinding brightness in a sea of dark. He was drowning and would soon pass to the World After, if he hadn't already. If she could catch him there before he got near the Eternal Flame, she could bring him back. She chose the softly glowing archway and stepped through.

The World After was nothingness. No light, no sound, not at first anyway. But she set her mind to locating Taron and found him easily. A recently discovered quirk of her power over Nethersong enabled her to navigate the World After at will. The boy appeared before her, lit from within, peering into the darkness, confusion marring his face.

"Taron," she called. He turned and stared at her uncomprehendingly. "I'm here to bring you back."

His brows descended. "B-bring me back?"

"Yes. You want to live, don't you?"

"Y-y-you . . . You're. . . ." He raised a finger at her and took a step back. His voice a mix of wonder and fear, unable to even identify her by name. "But that's impossible."

"No, it isn't. I've done it before. Did you hear about Queen Jasminda being poisoned?"

He nodded.

"She'd come here. To the World After. And I brought her back."

He blinked and dropped his arm. "Y-you brought back Queen Jasminda from the dead?"

"I did." Hundreds had witnessed the first time Kyara had stepped into the World After and returned with their queen—though virtually none had understood what they'd seen. She didn't know exactly how she'd been able to do it, crossing from the Living World was nothing she'd heard of before. Then again, she'd never known another living Nethersinger. Though she'd only done it once, she felt confident that she could repeat the action with this child. Perhaps bring him back to the living as often as it took until his body could be pulled from the ocean.

"Come with me, Taron. I'll help you go back. Do you have any family?"

He shook his head, and took another step away, looking around at the darkness that surrounded them. "Something's wrong here," he whispered.

Unease descended over her. "Yes. Something is. But we have to leave now. Take my hand."

"What's wrong with this place?" he asked, still peering around warily. She didn't know what he saw or felt, it must be something different than she did—maybe something only the truly dead could discern. But right now, it didn't matter. She didn't have long before his doorway would go dark and the path back to the living would close to him.

"Take my hand, Taron. It's time to go."

He shivered and looked at her again, gaze full of questions, then gingerly placed his hand in hers. She slumped with relief, then led him back to the glowing arch, pulsing in the infinite blackness.

Pulling the dead back through the archway was like walking

through thick, knee-high mud. It took effort and strength. It was nothing like the normal manipulation of Nethersong, but she focused all her energy on the task and dragged the boy through a darkness that didn't want to let him go.

Finally, they were through and shuttled back into their bodies. Her eyes were squeezed shut and she felt the sand on her palms—she'd fallen to her hands and knees at some point. Her lingering connection to Taron told her he was still unconscious. She sank into her other sight to find him still underwater, with every indication that he'd be back in the World After very soon.

But the light of his Nethersong was still dim. She began pulling the Nether from his body as he struggled and kicked in the water. If she could draw enough away, she could keep him from death for a time, and maybe he could break free of the waves and find air.

As she funneled death energy out of him, the Void took its place—neither life, like Earthsong, nor death, the Void was a mysterious energy that filled in the spaces between. Life, death, and the Void were the three forces at play in the world.

If the boy could get himself out of the water, one of the Earthsingers would be able to replace the Void with life energy and revive him. But that was a big *if.* It was likely the only Singers on the beach were small children. Still, one of them should be able to eventually manipulate the water and drag Taron out.

As she contemplated how difficult it would be to drag Taron from death a second or even a third time, a figure with the Nethersong of a middle-aged adult charged into the water. Kyara forced her eyes open to watch an Elsiran construction worker swim with sure strokes to where Taron was flailing. He grabbed the boy and swam, one armed, back to the shore. Cradled in Taron's arms, safe as a baby, was the waterlogged leather ball.

Other construction workers stood nearby, their concern evident, but Taron rolled over, spitting out the water in his lungs, aided by vigorous thumps to his back from the Elsiran man.

Two of the younger children ran up to him. The boy who'd created the cyclones closed his eyes, and within moments, Taron sat up, completely well.

His friend, the sensible girl, kneeled at his side as well. Her eyes were red-rimmed. "I couldn't find you in the water. It was so fast and strong." She shook her head, shivering with disappointment and shame.

Kyara felt bad for her. Darvyn had told her that manipulating water was difficult for an Earthsinger without a lot of practice. She hoped the girl wouldn't beat herself up forever for something she had little control over.

While the attention was on the boy who'd just been saved, and the cluster of Elsirans now being thanked profusely by the Lagrimari women, Kyara rose, preparing to slip away, hopefully unnoticed. But Taron's voice cut through the chatter.

"You're the Poison Flame," he announced. Everyone grew silent. A cold fear wafted off the Lagrimari—one she didn't require Earthsong to sense.

"Yes, yes, I am."

She held his gaze for a moment, then scanned the others. Some faces crumpled, others hardened in anger. Mothers grabbed their children tight and nearly everyone took a step back. The Elsirans didn't understand the words and looked curiously at the reactions.

No one said anything. The soft patter of worry and care were now silenced. Tears came to one woman's eyes.

No, Kyara didn't know these people, but they certainly knew her.

She took a deep breath, lungs still stinging, and inclined her head. "May we *not* greet each other again," she said, twisting the common saying.

She turned and headed down the beach, back to her cottage. Back to Darvyn, who should be home soon. Back to hiding, and solitude, and a quiet life by the sea that she did not deserve.

CHAPTER THREE

Responsibility is rain for thirsty roots
deep in the ground.
But if you are not careful,
it pours into unwatered mouths
and dribbles out,
overflowing
and wasteful.

—THE HARMONY OF BEING

The tray in Zeli ul-Matigor's hands wobbled as she planted her foot carefully on the uneven step. These rough, old, stone staircases were dangerous; she'd nearly twisted her ankle more than once on her daily trips up and down. Tantalizing aromas from the food under the silver cover made her stomach growl, though she'd already eaten. But she'd never touch a morsel on the tray. For all she knew, it was poisoned by the kitchen staff.

And with good reason.

After surviving the staircase, she passed through a dank hallway then entered a somewhat brighter antechamber where a trio of Royal Guardsmen looked up at her entrance. None of them changed expressions, so maybe she imagined their disdain.

What did they think of the short Lagrimari teenager who came this way every day bearing food for a man who'd harmed so many? If she'd still had her Song, she would know for sure—probably for the best then.

One of the guards unlocked the main brass gate leading to the dungeon. Zeli kept her head high, not looking into any of the cells she passed. There were truly vile people down here; it was only through weeks of practice that she'd managed to control the shaking in her limbs as she took this journey.

After deftly negotiating the familiar warren of passageways, she paused at the mouth of a shallow, narrow inner corridor, set deep in the heart of the palace's dungeon. The door to the only room in this section—a former storage space once used as a cell—was now back on its hinge. Weeks ago, it had been cracked into pieces and hung askew, the splintered wood appearing to have been kicked open from the inside.

Now the door was fixed, no doubt by the figure standing in front of it, peering inside the empty room. The Goddess Awoken was resplendent as ever in a flowing, white dress. Her hair was blown by an invisible breeze, power that crackled from Her like charged air just before a lightning storm. She was always connected to Earthsong, and Her strength was uncomfortable to be around.

Zeli approached, used to the faint buzz of magic whispering

across her skin. When she'd been appointed the robemistress of the Goddess—a position of high honor—shortly after joining the Sisterhood, Zeli had been overwhelmed by Her power. In awe at the very sight of Her. Now, she squeezed by the woman, set her tray down in front of the door, and slid it through the small hatch. Not a gourmet meal, but a quality one. Such a shame for it to go to waste, when ostensibly free refugees were standing in food lines for rations. The prisoner hadn't eaten anything even when he'd been here. But she still acted out this farce twice a day at the Goddess's behest.

A chill formed over her skin at the thought of the escapee somewhere out there in the world. The True Father, the immortal king who had tyrannically ruled Lagrimar for five hundred years. When the Mantle fell, the Goddess and Queen Jasminda had subdued him, drained him of his stolen Song, and imprisoned him here to await trial. And now he was gone.

Zeli was disgusted at herself for keeping the secret she'd been ordered to. No one but she and the Goddess knew of the True Father's escape. No one else knew the danger they were in, not just from the former king, but from whoever had been powerful enough to break him out of the dungeon and disappear without a trace.

"Did you need anything else, Your Excellency?" Her voice barely wavered.

When silence greeted her, Zeli turned to find the Goddess's normally bright eyes dim. She realized she'd never seen Her eat. Did She need food? Could Earthsong alone sustain Her or was it just another trick?

Zeli tried to rid herself of the traitorous notion, but it wouldn't leave her mind. She envisioned the Goddess locked away in a hidden chamber somewhere in the palace where no one could see Her stuffing Herself with sweet fruits and tubers and handpies and those Elsiran pastries with the creamy icing on top.

The Goddess didn't move to answer, so Zeli shrugged and headed to the exit. She hated these trips to the dungeon. They brought back bad memories.

Though this place wasn't nearly as bad as the fetid hole where she'd been held with dozens of other children, lightless and airless and overflowing with waste. That sobered her, causing the mutinous urges to flee. Joining the Sisterhood meant she would not be kidnapped or sold into servitude, she was almost certain of that. And if she wanted to do better than just survive—huddled with the masses awaiting their handouts—if she wanted to thrive here, she had to remember her place. Be grateful for the gifts she'd been given. Serving the Goddess was a great honor. Keeping Her secrets was just part of the job.

As she stepped through the doorway to the outer hallway, something brushed her mind. The Goddess had not yet spoken, but silently pushed Her will to Zeli, causing her to stop and wait.

"I need you to deliver a message to the queen." The Goddess's lovely voice hummed with a throaty purr.

Hope stirred. Could this be the day they would inform the queen and king about the missing prisoner? Perhaps a nationwide—no, worldwide—search would be conducted to bring the True Father back into custody, back where he couldn't hurt anyone else again.

"Tell Jasminda to meet me in the eastern gardens at her earliest convenience."

Zeli swallowed her disappointment. It was unlikely the Goddess would share the news with Queen Jasminda in the gardens where any gardener could overhear. Of course Earthsong could ensure they weren't spied upon, but the nonchalance with which She'd given the instructions didn't bode well.

Zeli squared her shoulders and nodded, then dipped into a wobbly curtsey—an Elsiran custom she still thought was silly. But it was how the Sisters greeted and took their leave of their betters, and Zeli would be a proper Sister if it killed her.

She spun around and swiftly left the dungeon, desperate for fresh air. Once back into the electrically lit, labyrinthine halls of the palace, where windows allowed sunlight to shine through, she took a deep breath.

Now all she had to do was find the queen. Being the Goddess's messenger was made much more difficult because the majority of the palace staff was Elsiran and as such did not speak Lagrimari. Zeli had been doing her best to learn the language, but with her duties she didn't have as much time to study or visit the tutors as she'd like. She'd picked up a bit, understood some of the common sayings, but was in no way fluent.

Her first stop was the queen's office, not that she necessarily expected the woman to be there—Queen Jasminda spent very little time in a place where she could actually be found—but at least Zeli could ask Ilysara and be sure to be understood.

The queen's two secretaries sat at side-by-side desks. The Elsiran man was busy with a phone call, and Ilysara was tapping away swiftly on a typing machine.

"Pleasant morning. Is the queen in? I have a message from the Goddess."

"No, *uli,*" the Lagrimari woman answered with a crinkle in her brow. "Her Majesty said she was going to the hedge maze to clear her head."

Zeli nodded her thanks and then took off in that direction. However, in the hedge maze all she found were the gardeners. Luckily one was Lagrimari—a former settler who spoke Elsiran. He asked his coworkers if they'd seen the queen.

"She was here earlier, Sister, but left. Not sure where she was headed."

Zeli beamed at being called a Sister, though in her light blue novitiate robes and white pinafore, she couldn't technically claim the name. Not yet.

She headed next to the dining room, then the music hall, and finally the Blue Library, known to be one of Queen Jasminda's regular haunts. But the queen was nowhere to be found.

Frustration bloomed. Zeli was tired and hungry and eager to be done with her errand. She wandered through the residential wing, a bit aimless, hoping to perhaps bump into the queen at random, when raised voices sounded from around a corner.

"She gave it to *me*," a male voice growled.

"No she didn't. My hand was closer."

Zeli rounded a corner to find two Elsiran boys wrestling for control of an object she couldn't get a good view of between their sizable forms.

"Let go! I just wanted a look. You're going to break it."

"I won't. Get off me!"

Standing just outside of elbow range, she raised her brows as the two fought. She couldn't get a good look at their faces, but recognized Sister Vanesse on the other side of them, a horrified expression on the woman's scarred face.

Zeli shook her head then placed two fingers into her mouth and gave out a loud wolf whistle. The boys froze; one had the other in a headlock, but they maneuvered enough to look over at her with matching pairs of golden eyes.

Now it was Zeli's turn to freeze, facing identical copies of the same person. Dark red hair, freckled noses and cheeks, slightly hooded eyes framed by thick lashes. She nearly stepped back in surprise, then recalled herself.

The twin with his arm around his brother's neck released him and they both stood up to their full heights, which was quite tall—at least to Zeli. They were big, but looked to be around her age, eighteen, maybe nineteen. And they held themselves a bit warily, far more cautious than most of the Elsiran elites she'd observed. But for all their size and stubbled jaws, they were still acting like babies—quite unlike reserved Elsirans.

On the ground between her and them was a small ceramic figure—was this what they'd been fighting over? She bent to retrieve and inspect it. The statuette bore the likeness of two smiling Elsiran children. The paint had dulled with time but the orange hair and eyes were still clear. The two wore old-fashioned overalls and were linked arm in arm. It fit in the palm of her hand and she gripped it, looking up at them.

The twin on the right looked chagrined. He smiled sheepishly and stuck his hands into a pair of worn trousers. The one on the left, dressed in finer, newer-looking clothes, grimaced and looked away.

The estate where she'd grown up had employed plenty of boys—pages and stable hands constantly engaged in roughhousing and mischief. Though these two were obviously not servants, they were still just as silly as any uncouth lad she'd ever had to scold for tracking dirt onto a freshly mopped floor or trying to steal an extra dessert. She pinned them with a glare that had caused many a young scamp to quiver.

The one on the right spoke first. "I apologize for our behavior, miss. My brother and I were just having a friendly debate regarding the possession of that figurine. Would you mind giving it back, please?" He grinned in a way that alarmed her, mostly because he appeared sincere. The other twin scowled, whether at her or his brother, she wasn't sure.

Sister Vanesse called out a few words in Elsiran and that's when Zeli realized that the boy had been speaking in Lagrimari. When they turned to answer the Sister, Zeli peered at their profiles more closely. The only way an Elsiran could speak Lagrimari was if . . . Well, she'd never heard of anyone except the king being able to do so. But Sister Vanesse was the queen's aunt and the resemblance between her and the twins made Zeli stumble backward a step.

These were the queen's brothers.

Mortified, Zeli dropped her head and held out her hand, palm open with the figurine presented. She kept her gaze on the ground as shame coated her skin. She would have never whistled at them like that if she'd known that these were the princes.

She was such an idiot. How could she not have known? She'd never seen them before, but had heard they were twins—there was no excuse. All her dreams of rising through the ranks flashed before her eyes, and she wondered what her punishment would be. Sister Vanesse was well-respected within the Sisterhood and had witnessed the whole thing. Certainly word would get back to the High Priestess about Zeli's indiscretion.

"Excuse me, Your Graces, I'm so sorry," she said, her voice thick.

"Oh, now, none of that," the one on the right said as she stared at his boots—which were scuffed and worn. "Maybe you should keep it, after all. Obviously we can't be entrusted with it." His hand enfolded her own, closing her fingers over the trinket.

She looked up, breath stuttering, to find him grinning in that welcoming way he had. Why did she find it so unsettling? The other one was still scowling, but shrugged when she looked his way.

"I'm Varten ol-Sarifor," said the cheery twin, "and this is my brother, Roshon."

Zeli looked down again to where their hands still touched. "Tarazeli ul-Matigor. Um, Zeli, Your Grace."

The scowling one, Roshon, groaned. "Please don't call us that. Drives me crazy. And sounds strange in Lagrimari."

She looked up to find him rolling his eyes. He was sort of rude and brusque, but that made more sense to her than Varten's kindness. She finally pulled out of his grip, her hand giving off sparks from the connection. The little statuette was warm now, as if it had absorbed the heat from his body.

"Will you keep it safe for us?" Varten asked.

"What is it?" she whispered.

"It was our mother's. Aunt Vanesse was telling us how Mama used to collect these things—it was some sort of fad when she was a teenager. Most of her collection was destroyed." His face gave the first hint of anger at this. "But our aunt managed to save this one. She said it reminded her of us." A grin slid across his face. "She failed to understand that you can't give a pair of twins *one* of anything." He chuckled, and to her amazement Roshon snorted in amusement as well.

Roshon said something rapidly to his aunt, who shook her head fondly. Sister Vanesse hugged both boys then gripped Zeli's hand and smiled warmly at her.

Zeli blinked. "I-I won't get in trouble for being rude to the princes, will I?"

Varten frowned and translated her question. To which Vanesse frowned—they really looked so much alike—and shook her head.

"No," Varten responded. "If anything, we'll get in trouble when Papa finds out we were fighting in the middle of the hallway."

Vanesse squeezed Zeli's hand again and then was off with a good-bye for them all. Once she was gone, Varten turned to her; she instinctively stepped back at the mischievous expression on his face. Now the *real* him would come out, all of that blithe sunniness no doubt hid a character intent on punishing her for interfering.

She swallowed then nearly choked when he leaned down and hooked an arm around her shoulder, steering her toward a side hallway. "Zeli ul-Matigor, House of Bobcats? Nice."

She shrugged against the weight of his arm. "I don't know much about the old houses."

"Neither do I, but it must mean you've got some fight in you. We should work out visiting hours for the figurine. Who do you think should get time with it first?"

Her lips curved into a smile in spite of herself. "Haven't you two ever shared anything before?"

Varten tapped his chin and pretended to think it over. His brother loped alongside them and lifted a shoulder. "Only everything we've ever had," Roshon muttered. He looked down at the chrome plated wristwatch on his wrist. Fancy. "I've got to go meet Ani now. Let me know what you decide." With a small salute, he nodded in her direction and then took off at a jog back to the main corridor.

Something sad flashed on Varten's face but it was gone almost too fast for her to be sure. His grin turned up a notch. "Now I'm not saying I expect any special treatment, but I would like to plead my case to claim the first time slot."

But Zeli was too curious to let the subject change. "Who's Ani?" she asked, watching him carefully.

The muscles in his face froze. "My brother's fiancée. Lovely young lady. Saved our lives once."

"Aren't you all a bit young to get married?"

He straightened, letting his arm fall away as that position required him to bend over to her diminutive height. Mock affront laced his voice. "We're eighteen today as a matter of fact."

"Oh, then happy birthday." Zeli was very proud to know that

she was nearly a month older, for all that she still looked like a child, nearly two heads shorter than them.

"You know . . . our sister is throwing us a party tonight—you should come."

Her mouth gaped. "Oh, I . . . couldn't. I'm not . . ."

"You are the custodian of one of our dear, departed mother's prize valuables. You're practically family now."

She shook her head, smothering a grin. She had no idea if the figurine she carried had any value other than the sentimental, and she had no desire for the job of custodian. Attending the birthday party of the queen's brothers was also not high on her list of things to do.

"Well, I'm very busy, I'll have to see if I can fit it into my calendar," she said, not looking at him.

"Of course, I know there must be a great many demands on your time, Zeli ul-Matigor, House of Bobcats."

Was he making fun of her? But a look up revealed a solemn expression. Still, she narrowed her eyes. "For instance," she said, stopping in the hallway. "Even now I'm on an errand for the Goddess Awoken. I need to find Queen Jasminda and deliver an important message. I've been looking for her for close to an hour."

His brow descended. "No one will tell you where she is?"

"Not exactly. My Elsiran isn't very good yet. There are some Lagrimari staff who've been helpful, but they're few and far between." And she hated having stilted, mimed conversations with Elsirans who already looked at her like she was an orphan dragged in off the streets. Which she was.

"Well, I can help you find her." He waited until she looked at him again. "I can help you with your Elsiran, too, if you'd like.

Papa, Roshon, and I have been working at the Sisterhood schools in town, but I could give you lessons . . . if you want."

"You will help me learn?" she said in self-consciously stilted Elsiran.

His face lit up like a sunrise. "Absolutely. I'll have you fluent in no time." He rubbed his hands together in a way that alarmed Zeli further. He seemed entirely too happy about this.

"Why?"

"What?"

"Why help me? Tutor me? It will take quite a lot of time. Aren't there balls or garden parties or underground cockfights or something you should be attending with the rest of the Elsiran aristocracy?"

He blinked, his face dimming. Several moments passed before he spoke. "I grew up on a farm in the middle of nowhere. I watched my father and sister be mistreated or ignored by nearly everyone we came in contact with because of their skin and their magic. I spent two years locked in a cell smaller than my closet here, with two other people. I'm not an aristocrat."

His words weren't accusatory, they were just a simple statement of facts, but Zeli's heart sped with shame all the same. She began to sputter an apology, when he stuck out his hand toward her, thumb up.

"We should shake on it."

She raised her brows in question.

"Our deal. I'll help you find my sister, and work on your Elsiran with you."

"How is that a deal? What do you get in return?"

He grinned. "I get to spend time with a pretty girl."

She rolled her eyes so hard she almost got a headache. If she thought he was actually serious she would have walked away—she was not interested in the flirtations of an insouciant Elsiran boy—but the glint in his eye made her stay. Coming from anyone else, she'd feel like she was the butt of some joke, but from him the compliment seemed offhand, like the effervescence of his frothy personality. And since the statement was patently ridiculous, she dismissed it, staring at his outstretched hand.

"What is 'shake on it'?"

"It's how they seal a deal in Yaly. They grab hands and shake them."

Why he would want to mimic the habits of the place where he'd been held captive, she had no idea. Yet she tentatively extended her arm in a similar manner. Varten's warm, dry hand enveloped hers and squeezed, pumping it up and down.

"Excellent. Now let's go find my sister."

CHAPTER FOUR

Foundation stones do not bear
more weight than they can handle.
If you have neither cracked nor crumbled,
then you are strong enough.

—THE HARMONY OF BEING

Varten ol-Sarifor snuck another look over at the girl walking beside him then snapped his head forward when she caught him. His cheeks heated; he hoped he wasn't blushing.

"What?" Zeli bit out. He shook his head and stuck his hands in his pockets—otherwise the traitorous things would probably try to reach for her again, and she wouldn't like it.

Funny, since he'd gotten back home and people started calling him and Roshon princes—he suppressed a shudder—folk were falling all over themselves to talk to him. Lads and girls who would have never looked twice at a farm boy from the Borderlands with a *grol* father were now fawning and sucking up and seeking to curry favor. Another shudder threatened to roll through him at the thought.

But Zeli ul-Matigor, House of Bobcats, was different. Maybe because she was Lagrimari and obviously viewed him as just another Elsiran boor, puffed up with money and privilege . . . But there was no light in her eyes when she looked up at him. In fact, what he saw now was more like suspicion, with her brow and nose wrinkled.

Shite. He was staring again.

“So the party starts at seven in the Winter Ballroom,” he said, trying to reroute her attention, and refocus himself. “Food, dancing, the whole thing. It will be a great time.”

She pursed her lips, then twisted them. Based on her expression, he shouldn’t hold his breath waiting for her to come, though he wanted her to—right now, more than just about anyone else he’d met since coming home. He wouldn’t stop to look into that too much, though.

“I-I’ll think about it.” She frowned, and he began preparing himself for disappointment. He was getting to be a pro at that.

They approached one of the supply rooms peppered around the palace. After days of exploring, he and Roshon had discovered the places where the servants stored things like towels, cleaning supplies, matches, oil, and more. There was generally one in each hallway, often attended by a staff person cataloging the inventory to keep thieving at a minimum.

“Let’s stop in here,” Varten said, opening an otherwise nondescript door.

A smiling young maid greeted him with a furious blush. “Pleasant afternoon, Your Grace.”

"Pleasant afternoon. Have you by any chance seen Usher?"

"No, but I can ring 'round." She picked up the phone and spoke to the palace operator, asking about the king's valet. After a few moments' consultation she hung up. "He's headed this way, Your Grace. You should be able to catch him in the gilded mirror hallway."

"Is that the one with the blue wallpaper?"

"No, Your Grace, that's the looking glass hall. The gilded mirror one has white wallpaper."

"Ah, of course. Thank you," he said with a small bow. He was learning his way around the palace, but the bloody place must have been designed by a cross-eyed architect. The maid erupted into giggles, her blush deepening to a level that looked uncomfortable.

Startled, and not wanting to cause her to suffer an apoplexy, he backed out of the room and closed the door to find Zeli scowling up at him. "What is it now?"

"Were you trying to give the girl a heart attack?"

"I didn't do anything. She must have some sort of medical condition," he said, leading them toward the proper corridor where, sure enough, Usher was ambling their way, his black suit crisp and perfect.

Zeli snorted in response, but Varten had no time to question her when the older man stopped, inclining his head at them.

"Hello Usher, we need to find my sister. Urgent Sisterhood business."

Usher's dark brown eyes took in Zeli's light blue robe and pinafore, then crinkled at the sides. "Her Majesty is in the Council Room."

"Oh, there's a Council meeting today?"

"An emergency one was called and just ended. She may be in there for a while . . . gathering her thoughts." His bushy brows descended and he looked like he may say something more, but thought better of it.

Varten thanked him, then headed off toward the Council Room. "That's Usher," he told Zeli. "He's the king's personal valet and very close with my sister."

"He's not Elsiran is he?"

"Um, no, I think he's originally from Fremia. He's worked here since before Jack was born. Why?"

Zeli shrugged. "Lagrimar was so isolated. I'm still . . . learning about the rest of the world." Her voice was soft and wistful.

This they had in common. The mountain valley home where Varten had grown up had been his entire world. Sure Mama had ensured their education included information about other places, world history and a few phrases in various languages, and they'd had plenty of books that let him travel in his mind, but his actual experience had been very limited. Up until two years ago at any rate. And that wasn't anything he wanted to repeat.

"So you think you might want to travel?" he asked.

She raised a shoulder. "Not much need for travel in the Sisterhood."

"But you do get time off. Vacations, right? Aunt Vanesse has been places with her partner, Clove. She told me about visiting Yaly and they're planning to go to Fremia and some island in the southern continent."

"Sounds nice," she breathed, a dreamy look taking over her face. Varten agreed. He had an itch to see the world as well, this time on his own terms.

Ani and Roshon were going to be sailing off soon . . . He stuffed away the tightness that took over his chest when he thought of it. He and his twin hadn't spent more than a day apart in their entire lives. They bickered and fought but were still two halves of a whole. But not for long.

And after Roshon was gone, then what? Varten hated living in the palace. He'd like nothing more than to go back to their mountain cabin, which was still being rebuilt after the fire that had destroyed it. He missed his farm, his goats, his life. He'd lost years in a prison and had come back to a world he didn't recognize. To a family he didn't recognize. Jasminda the queen, Roshon leaving, and Papa off trying to solve the world's problems.

And what did that leave for him?

They arrived outside the Council Room to find it manned by a Guardsman, who nodded at Varten before squinting at Zeli suspiciously. Varten placed his hand on her back both protectively and to assert that she was with him. He stared the Guardsman in the eye until the man's face blanked.

Beneath his hand, Zeli shivered. Was she cold? These marble hallways held in cooler air, and the heating system had a hard time sufficiently warming many of the rooms. Jasminda usually had a fireplace going wherever she was; hopefully Zeli would warm up soon.

He knocked on the door and pushed it open, finding his sister at the head of the table, several newspapers spread out before her. She looked up and gave a weak smile that barely cut through her obvious misery. He wouldn't wish the monarchy on anyone, least of all someone he loved.

"Are you all right?" he asked.

She ran a hand across her face and visibly tried to rally. "I don't have much of a choice but to be." She pointed to the papers. "No one's admitting to responsibility in the newest terrorist attacks, but editorials are filling the papers supporting them. We don't know who's behind them either—the Hand of the Reaper, the Dominionists, or some other group of disaffected Elsirans."

The Hand of the Reaper, the secret society that had blown up one of the temples a couple of months before, had gone quiet in recent weeks. But others had taken up their message of "Elsira for Elsirans" and called for the creation of a separate land for the Lagrimari refugees. Not Lagrimar, as it was a barren desert that could barely support life without the help of Earthsong. But not Elsira, either.

And whoever had attempted to assassinate his sister had yet to be found and brought to justice.

"Zann Biddel himself has penned a new piece," she continued, "which every paper has seen fit to print."

"He's the Dominionist leader, right?" Varten was trying to do a better job of keeping up with politics. For while they didn't interest him in the slightest, they were now quite personal. He leaned over her shoulder and began to read. "'As our beloved Elsira continues to crumble due to fiscal mismanagement and the diversion of resources to the interlopers who have flooded across our borders, the unfortunate perpetuation of racially charged violence will carry on. Every drop of blood shed onto our parched soil waters the seeds of the future. We are growing a stronger land. And if it must blossom from the pain of those who for so long sought to destroy it, then let that be the price. Nothing good comes for free.'"

He took a step back, shocked. "Zann Biddel wrote that?"

Jasminda nodded and Zeli looked horrified. She might not have gotten all the Elsiran words, but she obviously understood the sentiment.

Jasminda pulled out a pamphlet printed in Lagrimari—the refugee version of a newspaper. "And then we have the Sons of

Lagrimar, who claim what they're doing is self-defense. Of course a lot of the refugees are listening."

"I can understand why," Zeli muttered.

"What does the Council say?" Varten asked, looking around the now-empty room that still radiated discomfort from the contentious meetings it usually held.

"'Instead of constantly visiting these scenes of devastation, you should be working on our foreign affairs as the king is,'" Jasminda said, in a nasally voice mimicking a fancy Elsiran accent. She snorted. "A few weeks ago both Jack and I were interlopers, now he can do no wrong, while I seem to do nothing but . . ."

She cracked her neck and sucked in a deep breath. "So what do you need, little brother? And your friend?"

"This is Zeli ul-Matigor, House of Bobcats, sender of messages from the Goddess Awoken."

"Yes, I know," Jasminda said laughing at him.

Zeli curtsied awkwardly and kept her head down. "The Goddess requests for you to meet Her in the eastern gardens at your earliest convenience."

"So will She just be there waiting all day or . . . ?"

Zeli spread her hands, eyes wide. "It's very possible, Your Majesty." Perhaps she was nervous in the presence of the queen because her arms shook slightly though the room was as warm as summer.

Jas sighed. "All right then. Why not? Perhaps She'll finally give me some advice I can use." She began gathering up the newspapers and stacking them into a pile. "Where's your other half anyway?" This to Varten.

"With his other half." He tried to keep his voice light, but didn't think he did a terribly good job. To sell his nonchalance, he pretended great interest in the contents of one of the other newspapers.

"I see." Jasminda's tone didn't change, but he could tell she was unconvinced. He wracked his brain for something that would forestall a follow-up question. "I'm going to help Zeli with her Elsiran," he blurted out. "Tutor her, you know."

His sister's gaze was shrewd. She peered at him, certainly unfooled by his subject change. But she let him get away with it and leaned around him to speak to Zeli. "Do me a favor, try and keep this one out of trouble."

Zeli's brows rose. "That might be a tall order."

They shared a smile and Varten felt both put out and gratified. Smiling meant less misery—at least it should. He was convinced that if you smiled enough it must chip away at some of the pain.

When Jasminda rose and stretched, Zeli spoke up. "Um, Your Majesty, might I ask you a question before you go?"

"Certainly."

"In Elsiran law, can you be . . . punished for following the orders of your superior? For instance, in the military, if a commander instructs his subordinate to do something . . . wrong, would that person face reprisal?"

Varten's attention narrowed on Zeli. Jasminda hugged the papers to her chest and looked into the distance, thinking. "Military law differs from civilian law. As far as I can tell, there are very few circumstances in which a subordinate would get into trouble for following orders."

Zeli's gaze flicked back and forth between them. "But civilians could?"

"Well, yes, the law is the law and short of royal decree, if one doesn't follow it, they are responsible for the consequences."

Zeli seemed to fold in on herself in a way that poked at Varten's innate protective instinct. But before he could ask her what she was so concerned about, a bell began to chime. All three of them looked up toward the ceiling of the Council Room—it sounded like the bell was directly above them, but of course, there was nothing there but the ornate decorative carvings filled with swirls and flowers.

A reflection glimmered in the corner of his eye. Varten turned to find something like a heat shimmer rippling the air in the center of the room. Everyone else's gaze was locked overhead to the same location. The undulating air took on a golden gleam that brightened until it shone like a precious gem. The ringing continued as the mirror-like apparition solidified then shattered, revealing a dark hole.

A shadow slid through, separating itself from the pit of inky blackness to fly into the room. Fear dried Varten's eyes out; he blinked a dozen times, not believing what he was seeing. This couldn't be happening again. Not here.

Two more shadows wriggled out of the hole—a darkness that could only be a portal to the World After. Roshon, Darvyn, and Kyara had witnessed a similar attack back in Yaly by angry wraiths intent on seeking revenge and destruction.

Zeli's screams unlocked his rigid muscles. He nudged her and they backed out of the room. He couldn't tear his eyes away from the shadow creatures and reached behind him for the doorknob, missing it twice before grabbing on and wrenching open the door. Jasminda was still motionless, staring at the nightmares flying around the high ceilings. Varten pushed Zeli out, then followed her into the hallway.

"Jasminda!" he yelled, and his sister darted out after them and slammed the door shut.

The two Guardsmen posted on either side of the door stood at attention, their pistols at the ready. Varten and Zeli backed down the hall, away from the Council Room, gazes glued to the door.

Just as he suspected, the shadows didn't let something as simple as a wall stop them. All three shot through the plaster and wood as if it was air. Two of the creatures disappeared into the Guardsmen. The third veered toward Jasminda, but bounced off her as if she was covered in invisible armor.

The last shadow hovered for a split second before apparently seeking an easier target and darting in Varten's direction. He braced himself for impact, knowing he couldn't outrun a spirit who had escaped the World After. Shutting his eyes tight, he winced, waiting for the blow to come as the specter invaded his body. But it never came.

Instead, a prickling energy floated across his skin. When he opened his eyes, the Goddess Awoken stood in front of him, between him and the spirit. Her white dress billowed in an invisible breeze. The power coating Her was so thick even he could feel it. With Her back to him, She raised an arm above her head and tightened her fist.

The shadow spirit floating before Her appeared to shiver, convulsing and quaking in what might have been fear or pain had it been alive. A crackling light flashed from the Goddess's closed fist, darting into the center of the shadow, illuminating the creature from within and causing it to fade.

Jasminda shouted, tearing Varten's gaze away. She now faced off against her own Guardsmen, except they were no longer her Guardsmen. In the places of the two Elsirans pledged to protect her, two Yalyishmen stood on either side of the door. Both were of the Daro race, pale-skinned with icy blue eyes. Their heads were shaved and even their clothes were different: the gray shirt and trousers of the servants of the Physicks. But it was obvious they weren't in their right minds. Both growled like vicious dogs, and the one on the left was actually slavering.

Hearing about the attack from his brother and the others had been one thing, but seeing it happen in front of him was totally different. Even Jasminda looked shocked—it wasn't that they hadn't believed the reports, it was just that after the Physicks' headquarters had been destroyed, no one expected this to happen again.

As one, the wraiths leapt forward, charging Jasminda, who knocked them back with a blast of her power. The sound of rushing wind gusted by, lifting the men off their feet and crashing them into the far wall. The Goddess rose into the air and landed at Jasminda's side. The two women took defensive positions as the men righted themselves with superhuman speed and stood poised for another attack.

"Go!" Jasminda yelled. Varten didn't need to be told twice. The two powerful Earthsingers had things well in hand; there was nothing a non-magical person could do here other than be harmed. He shot a glance at Zeli, whose eyes were wide with fear.

"This way," he said, motioning down the hall. Zeli shook herself and they both took off, racing away to what Varten hoped was safety.

CHAPTER FIVE

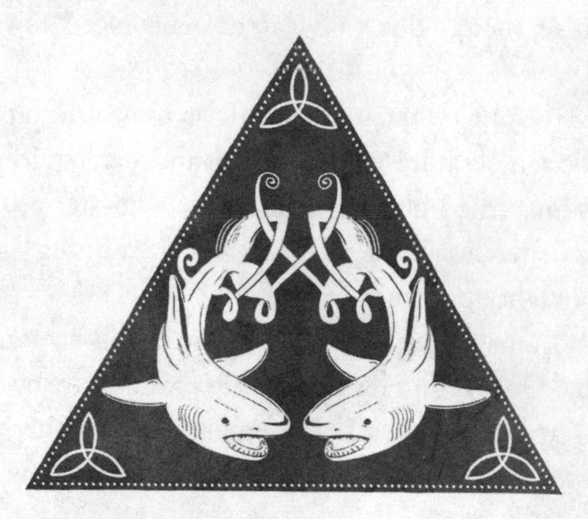

What's hidden within you is blinding.
A startling, radiant reminder of all
that has come before and is yet to be.
Its concealment will not last.

—THE HARMONY OF BEING

"Any ideas?" Jasminda asked as she and Oola forced the enraged wraiths back again and again with blasts of air.

"I have not done battle in many years and never against ones such as these."

"How did you stop that thing?" She motioned over her shoulder to where the faded, graying shadow was still locked in place, hovering in the air.

"Before they take hosts, spirits are vulnerable. But it is temporary. I created a cage of Earthsong—pure life energy that the spirit must drain with Nethersong. But feeding a constant stream of energy will maintain it, though it is costly."

Oola was intense, some strain showing in Her eyes. "We need to immobilize them," She said as the men raced toward them again.

"I've got the one on the left." Jasminda took a deep breath and dropped the temperature of the air around her wraith, freezing him. His skin turned blue, and his movement stopped midstep. But seconds later he shook free and began running against the wind she brought up to keep him back.

They had amazing speed and strength and seemingly endless stamina. Oola spun Her target into a miniature cyclone then threw him against the wall. He emerged from the huge dent in the plaster unfazed. Undamaged. Of course, he was already dead.

Lightning had little effect on them nor any other natural phenomenon either of them could conjure in the palace. Jasminda was in the midst of ripping the marble tiles from the ceiling to smash against the men, when the sound of bells clanging began again inside the Council Room. Her attention momentarily diverted by the noise, she paid for it dearly as a wraith crashed into her with immeasurable force. Her skull cracked against the ground, and several bones broke from the impact. She managed to tilt her head away in time to miss the fist that punched straight through the carpeting and into the cement below. The wraith pulled his arm back and did not bat an eye.

The clanging, in a different tone from the bells that had marked their arrival, grew louder and the man on top of her reluctantly stood—as if compelled by the sound. Jasminda lay heaving, pain radiating from her head, neck, and back, while Oola stood stoic as ever watching as the two wraiths slumped to the ground.

The spirit shadows flew out of the bodies and the third, hovering shadow gave a final shiver then darted with the others back through the closed door of the Council Room. A moment later, the ringing stopped.

Jasminda lay on the ground, directing Earthsong to heal her various wounds. Exhausted, she rolled to her side to find her two Guards lying unconscious. Their bodies and clothes had transformed back to normal, but they were far from unscathed. All of the injuries that she and Oola had inflicted on the wraiths had been borne on the bodies of the hosts. The Goddess Awoken was already healing the men of the internal and external damage they'd taken during the fighting.

More Guardsmen came running up with their leader, Captain Bareen, in front. Jasminda stood as Oola faced the men.

"All is well," Oola said calmly. Jasminda cautiously opened the door to the Council Room in order to be sure. Blessedly, the portal was closed and the room was empty and silent as a tomb.

"I was demonstrating something to the queen," the Goddess continued, "and got a bit carried away." She motioned toward the devastation evident on the walls and floor, tapestries ripped and hanging off the walls, and debris everywhere.

The two Guardsmen who had been the unlucky hosts for the spirits blinked, appearing confused. One held a hand to his head, while his partner looked around at the damage to the hallway in obvious shock. Neither seemed to remember their ordeal.

"These men will have the rest of the day off in appreciation for their unwitting participation in my demonstration." Oola smiled beatifically, dazzling everyone present. Jasminda bit her tongue and kept from rolling her eyes.

"Certainly, Your Excellency," Captain Bareen said. "Lenos, Erseen, you're relieved."

The men saluted and then walked away. They would need sleep after being healed of such severe injuries.

"Captain," Jasminda said, "please alert the steward to the need for repairs in this hallway. And I'm sorry for alarming you."

"No apology necessary, Your Majesty." He bowed and then led his men away to inspect the mess.

Jasminda gave Oola a hard look that the woman brushed off. "Come, we must talk," She said.

They ended up in the eastern gardens after all, having moved through the corridors in silence. In fact, none of the servants, staff, or aristocrats they'd passed on the way had acknowledged either the queen or the Goddess Awoken at all. Considering the state of Jasminda's dress—dirty and torn—that was a good thing. Oola must have diverted everyone's attention with Her Song. Of course, She still looked perfectly put together.

Once in the garden, one of Oola's favorite spots, which overlooked the city with a view of the ocean beyond, the Goddess sat lightly on a stone bench. Jasminda remained standing. Oola's gaze tracked the progress of a lone ship a ways off. Not many were docking in the port due to the embargo by the king of Raun and her allies.

"An attack of this kind inside the palace is unique," the Goddess said, breaking their silence.

"Yes, so why keep it quiet?"

Oola pursed Her lips. "Knowledge of it would only serve as fodder for your enemies."

"I don't know about that. I think the Guard should be aware; they'll need to prepare. And I'll have to call Jack back. He'll want to be here."

"And what of Fremia and their aid?" Oola's expression was guileless, but Her words stopped Jasminda midstep.

"Someone just attacked us *inside* the palace using undead warriors. You don't think we should alert the *king*?"

"What good would that do?" She tilted Her head, eyes glinting in the sunlight.

Words wouldn't come so Jasminda simply stared. Oola turned back to the water. "It is my belief that sharing information with others who can do nothing about it is useless. Jaqros has no ability to fight the wraiths. Knowledge would only give him additional worries. What he is doing now is necessary, is it not?"

Jasminda blinked.

"Telling him would just be to make yourself feel better."

Her fists clenched. "He will want to know," she whispered.

"And he will know when he returns."

Jasminda spread her arms apart. "And what if there is nothing left to return to? We could barely hold our own against three spirits! I'm telling Darvyn, at least. Do you think that the Physicks—or whoever this is—will not try again?"

"I am certain they will try again." Oola was quiet for a long time. Jasminda resumed her pacing, needing to work off the energy still rushing through her limbs from the attack. She was both wound tight and completely worn out and feared if she stopped moving, she wouldn't start again for a long, long time.

Oola's voice cut through her racing thoughts. "While it's clear the Physicks were involved in this, I do not believe that they have any desire to attack us."

Jasminda spun around to face Her. "Who does?"

"Who always has?"

"The True Father? But he's in the dungeon, powerless. How could he possibly . . ." Her heart grew heavy as a dark expression crossed Oola's face. "He *is* still in the dungeon?"

Oola took a deep breath. "No."

A bone-deep chill took over Jasminda's body. "No?"

"He escaped. With help. Magical help." Her ancient gaze returned to the ocean, appearing unusually troubled.

Jasminda's mind buzzed with this new information. "When?"

"Six weeks ago."

Her heart nearly stopped. "What?" Breathing turned shallow as she struggled to comprehend. "And so you thought I could do nothing about it and didn't bother to tell me?"

"I have been looking for him." Oola's head tilted up. She still wasn't looking at Jasminda.

"I take it you haven't found him, have you?"

"Not as of yet."

Breath rushed in and out of her chest. She spread her arms apart. "There are other Singers who could help you look. Maybe working together—"

"He is not in Elsira. And there are none else alive connected to him as I am. None strong enough—not even you or Darvyn—to do what *I* must do."

Jasminda rubbed her eyes and crossed over to sit on the bench beside Oola. She was a deflated balloon, sagging and empty. Fear and anger and a sudden rush of hopelessness assaulted her. "We may not be strong enough, but we could link. We could become stronger together. Why don't you trust anyone?"

"It is not about trust!" Oola snapped, for the first time appearing as if She was losing Her temper. "It is about responsibility and Eero is mine."

"But his actions affect all of us. We can't keep this quiet because it will happen again!"

"And so we tell the country? The world? Incite fear and chaos? How will people prepare for spirits overtaking them when even the land's most powerful Singers had a difficult time fending off three?"

Her eyes shone and Her voice rose with each word. Jasminda fought not to shrink back away from the intensity and anger.

Oola leaned forward. "His actions are because of *me*." She pointed a finger at Her chest. "*I* will find him."

Jasminda swallowed. "And we will all deal with the consequences."

"Such is life." Once again Oola was calm, poised. Staring out at the sea. "My brother has set his sights on this land and as you say, more trouble is coming. It is far easier to take over a broken, weak nation than a unified, strong one."

Jasminda leaned back, allowing the cold stone of the bench to seep into her clothes. "The unification is difficult. The people. . . ." She shook her head.

"The people," Oola repeated. "Yes. Well, I had hoped for more."

Jasminda couldn't help but feel that the censure was personal, that she herself had failed. "I'm sorry, I've been trying. We're all trying. The divisions are deep and being stoked by strong voices." Zann Biddel and his editorial came to mind.

"You cannot force harmony, people must choose it of their own free will." Oola's voice was weighted with hidden emotion. "A referendum must be set to allow the people to choose between unification and separation. All may vote as they see fit—both Elsiran and Lagrimari—and that will put an end to it."

Jasminda stared, shocked. A vote? "But the Council will never—"

"The Council does not have to approve. The ruling monarch may call for a public referendum of any issue that she sees fit to at any time, Council be damned. That is the law."

"But I'm not certain—"

Oola waved her off. "Then become certain. Eero will not stop until he is defeated. I sense this attack was a trial run and that he is still gathering his strength. There will be more once he has done so. If it is possible for us to unite, the time must be now. Call for the referendum. Hold the vote as quickly as possible. Do not give the people time to overthink it."

She stood suddenly and walked to the cliff's edge, white gown billowing out behind Her. Jasminda considered Her words. "And what do we do the next time we're attacked?"

Oola rose into the air on a current and spun toward the ocean. "We fight." Her voice was just an echo as She swiftly disappeared into the sky.

CHAPTER SIX

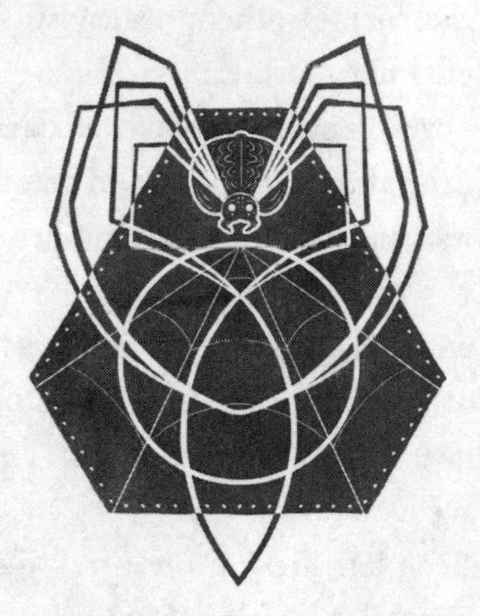

A wrong note can be replayed,
an instrument brought into tune.
Dissonance may echo
but not
forever.

—THE HARMONY OF BEING

You wake on a stone floor, colder than you have ever been in your life. The same dirt-encrusted trousers and tunic you've been clad in for weeks are stiff, nearly frozen to your skin. Every part of you aches from where it's been in contact with the unforgiving, icy stone.

Not long ago, you slept in a lush and lavish feather-filled bed fashioned by the finest artisans in all the land. A headboard inlaid with precious jewels, sheets of the finest silk, a warm body or two on either side. Now you are alone. You know it before you open your eyes.

The constant presence of others nearby was always soothing, and you are decidedly not soothed.

You peel your eyes open to survey the dark room. A barred metal door leads to a dim hallway. Your breath turns to steam, barely visible before you. It's like your new prison is in the center of a block of ice.

There are no windows, no way to tell the time of day or see where you are. Just an endless box made of stone, a pile of straw that might once have been some sort of mat, and a rusted bucket. The indignities have no end.

But food has been left for you on a tray just inside the door. Simple fare. A thick slice of bread and some sort of stew. You haven't eaten in so long—a weak protest against the audacity of your imprisonment—and yet you don't feel hungry. Did they force you to eat at some point? Heal the worst indications of your starvation? They have magic, whoever *they* are, your new captors.

You have your suspicions about their identities. Only so many have access to the type of magic that broke you out of your last prison—a day ago? Longer? You were not unaware of their existence, though they continually disrespected you by not asking permission before invading your land and killing your people with their experiments.

Little went on in your land without your knowledge. But you turned a blind eye because they were powerful—and while you were also powerful, their power was different. Untainted, though in its own way just as insidious.

But now you are weak. Not just of body but of mind. You've been stripped of everything, not only your robes and the accoutrements of power, but the power itself. The Songs. They'd been gained with such difficulty.

You are reminded of the impotence of your youth when you lusted after so much. A woman who wanted nothing to do with you. A magic you were not born to handle. And when you could not have one you stole the other, biting into its sweetness, allowing it to drip from your lips like honey. Like an addiction.

You recognized the monster in yourself even as you could not stop it. You counted the horrors wrought even as they seemed like they were happening outside of your body.

What body you have left is skin and bones now. Emaciated and fragile and nearly useless.

That thought makes you struggle to a seated position, pain flaring from every possible place. You are worthless. Powerless. Dragged from one prison to another like so much baggage. But those who brought you here must want something. They must want *you* for something.

A purpose.

One that will be made plain soon enough.

The meal on the floor is cold. Impossible for it to match the standards you were once used to. But food will nourish this sad body. Give you strength for whatever they will ask of you.

And so you crawl over to the tray and scoop at the cold stew with the gritty bread. A loose plan formulating in your mind.

For these people have power, magic, resources. All things you lack.

All things that can be taken.

They come for you on the third day.

You've spent the time eating everything you've been given and pacing the length of the small, frigid cell to keep warm and get your muscles working again. The time for sulking is over. Plans must be made.

Food is delivered by some magical means—the tray appears twice a day, and once you've cleaned your plate, it disappears into thin air. You suspect this is done to unsettle you. Earthsong cannot accomplish such things but blood magic can, so you catalog it, filing the information away for a point in time at which it will be useful.

The two men who retrieve you are solid walls of flesh. Bald heads tattooed with some sort of insignia. Their vacant, unintelligent stares mark them as servants.

They don't appear to be armed, but you aren't certain. And anyway, you have no desire to resist. Indeed, you must disguise your eagerness to finally meet your captor.

Lanterns cast tiny pools of light along the hallways of the dungeon. You can barely see your feet as you climb long staircases, bringing you into the main level of a castle that has seen better days. It is even colder up here; wind whistles through the corridors, sneaking in through gaps in the mortar of the stones. You enter a wide atrium where an entire wall has fallen away, revealing the surrounding snowcapped mountains.

Eddies of snow gather along the remains of the ruined wall. The guards lead you to another staircase. Its crumbling condition makes climbing perilous—one misstep and you would tumble over the edge and disappear into blackness. You gird yourself and step carefully.

The room they escort you to is a parlor—all walls intact—where a roaring fire has been built in a fireplace as tall as you are. The flames battle the bitterness of the cold, but don't appear to be winning.

The fire crackles. The wind hisses. You miss the ability to take in your surroundings in more detail, to identify the people nearby and their emotions with Earthsong. Now you rely on your mundane senses. The scents of dust and smoke obscure what else might be there.

They push you onto an ancient wooden chair that surprisingly does not fall apart under you and there you wait. The delay is long enough to communicate that this is a power play. Everything is a game. This you understand perfectly well.

A woman finally enters. Her warm skin tone reflects a mix of races, making her most likely Yalyish. In your land, children have always taken after one parent. Singer or Silent. Dark-haired or ginger-haired with nothing in between.

But here the blend is more even. Hazel eyes, canted lightly, head covered with a bloodred wrap so you cannot see her hair, but her brows are a muddy brown. Her long robe is in the same red as her hair covering. She appears to be in her fifties, which could mean anything. You yourself appear only thirty, a tiny fraction of your true age.

She settles on a sturdy, cushioned bench perpendicular to you. When she raises her hand, a glass of ice-blue liquid appears in her grasp. She takes a long sip before focusing on you. "I am Nikora. Do you mind if I call you Eero? *True Father* sounds so formal, does it not?"

You do not want to be called Eero, so you remain silent.

She smiles, with unnaturally white, sparkling teeth. "Ydaris told us so much about you. It's nice to finally meet."

Your nose flares at the mention of your former second-in-command. Ydaris served her purpose, you always knew one day her own agenda would win out. You simply thought you would end her before the reverberations of her betrayal managed to touch you. Pity that.

"We're so grateful you could join us. As you have no doubt discovered, you will not be able to use blood magic during your stay. Feel free to try if it makes you feel better. Some people have to learn thc hard way, and I have a feeling you are like that. Hard-headed." She smiles as she says it, taking away some of the sting, but you don't appreciate her tone.

While in your cell, you did everything you could think of to draw blood. You used fingernails, the rough stone walls, the edge of the bucket, the bars. You scraped yourself with every object there, but your skin was impervious. Biting your tongue had achieved nothing, either.

Nikora's all-knowing grin seems to be aware of your thoughts. A few weeks ago you would have drained her of any power she had and ordered her execution. Now you simply bide your time. They may think they know what you can do, but they are wrong.

"Generations ago, this castle belonged to Saint Dahlia and the original Physicks. Sadly, after she progressed from this world and we established our headquarters in the city, the place fell into disrepair. But it is isolated and it is secure, and if anyone cares to look for you, they will not find you here."

She laughs as though she's said something funny, and sips at her liquid. You continue to stare, unwilling to be unsettled by her performance.

"You must be dying to know why we've brought you here. One prison for another?" She lifts a shoulder. "We think you can help us, Eero. And we know we can help you."

You pitch forward slightly, intrigued in spite of yourself.

"For a long time you wielded a great deal of power. Dark power. Power you had no business having. Then it was taken from you."

She leans forward, setting her glass on the side table, all seriousness now. The shrewdness in her gaze sends a chill through you, unmatched even by the icy wind.

"Wouldn't you like to get it back?"

CHAPTER SEVEN

We are aglow.
Incandescent, filled with glee
the shadows only memory until
the sun drops down beneath
the confines of our view.
Tomorrow starts anew.

—THE HARMONY OF BEING

The midafternoon sun did little to warm Kyara as the wind picked up from the west. She hurried back to the cottage, slipping on the silken sand. Once inside, she stamped her bare feet and rubbed her hands together to bring some warmth to them.

Today, she'd gone south on the beach instead of north, mostly to avoid the inn and the refugees from yesterday. What would she do with her time when the weather turned too cold for her to walk the coastline and stare at the ocean all day? She was free for the first time in her life, and had no idea what to do about it.

Suddenly, her senses went on high alert. She hadn't perceived a sound, but some change in the air prickled her awareness. Then Darvyn stepped in from the bedroom and a smile stretched across her face.

She relaxed instantly. "I didn't know you were home." But tension thrummed through him.

"We finished checking the soil at the refugee camp, so I decided to stop in and get a change of clothes for the twins' party tonight."

Guilt wrapped around her. She'd shared a prison block with Roshon, Varten, and their father, Dansig, for weeks after being captured by the Physicks. In that time, she'd bonded with the family. She should go to their party and share in the joy of freedom, but the idea of being around so many people . . . Also being in the palace again, where she'd been a prisoner and then, briefly, a guest—it was too much.

She shook her head. "Please tell them I'm sorry that I won't be there. I know they won't understand but . . ."

"It's fine. They'll understand . . . But there's more." His hands squeezed a bit of fabric between them. A cravat, if she wasn't mistaken. Part of Elsiran formal wear.

"What?"

"I received a call from Jasminda." He motioned to the telephone that had been installed in the cottage shortly after they'd arrived. "It's confidential, but I'm sure she knew I'd tell you."

"As if I have anyone to tell," Kyara joked, growing worried.

His expression was bleak. "Wraiths attacked the palace."

Her jaw dropped. "But . . . we . . ."

"I know. There were only three of them, but Oola and Jasminda together barely held them off. Then they just went away. Oola wants to keep it quiet though, as to not spread panic. Jasminda said there was more bad news, but she will only tell me in person."

"So the Physicks' Machine wasn't destroyed? Or somehow they've found another way to open the portal?" Her voice pitched higher than normal with the memory of the wraith attack she'd witnessed.

Darvyn crossed the room with rapid steps to embrace her. Kyara hadn't realized she was shaking until she was pressed into his arms. "We'll find out," he said. "We'll figure it all out."

The destruction those spirits had created back in Yaly was burned into her brain. Now it was coming here. Something had told her that a quiet life of solitude would never be possible, but she'd hoped. A fat lot of good hoping did.

She pulled out of Darvyn's arms and looked into his dark eyes. "I wish that I could come with you tonight, but I'm still not . . . ready. Not to go back to the palace." Or around other people at all, truth be told. She'd been in a self-imposed exile since arriving here, and even this new disaster could not pull her from her solitude. She'd never imagined herself a coward before now, but perhaps that's exactly what she was.

"I'll let you know what I find out."

"You think you'll be home tonight?"

"Of course, but it might be late."

"If it's easier for you to stay in town, I'll understand. It's rather a long ride and—"

"Kyara." His tone was sharp, his gaze serious. "I am *not* spending a night away from you."

She blinked in the face of his fierce declaration.

His hands gripped her shoulders gently. "I spent too long away from you, not knowing where you were or what was happening to you. I won't do it again. Not unless it's unavoidable. Understand?"

When she'd been captured, she never thought she'd see him again. In fact, she'd thought him dead and that their next meeting would be in the World After. It had taken two long months for Darvyn and her to find their way back together. She didn't want to do anything to risk it, but couldn't help feeling that she was somehow holding him back.

"All right. I'll expect you back late," she said lightly. "I hope there won't be any more attacks before then."

He frowned. "Oola seemed to think this was a test, and that makes sense. Opening the portal seemed fairly difficult in Yaly, when the Physicks were at full strength. I know we dealt them a blow even if we didn't wipe them out completely. Let's hope that they'll need even more time to regroup and mount another attack."

"Between the queen, the Goddess, and the Shadowfox, I know Elsira is in good hands." She tried for a smile, but failed.

Darvyn snorted and shook his head. "Between the new terrorist attack yesterday and this? I don't know." He ran a hand across his shortly cropped hair. "Fighting the True Father was one thing, but here we have to fight the people for our very right to exist. It feels different. Harder." His shoulders slumped and she pulled him close again, this time trying to offer comfort as well as receive it.

They held one another for a long time until Darvyn pulled back. "The driver is waiting. If you change your mind about the birthday party, just call Jasminda's secretary and she'll send a car for you."

Kyara nodded. Darvyn had showed her how to use the telephone, but she didn't imagine she'd ever need to. His face turned grim, like he could read her thoughts.

"Pity you'll miss out on the sunset," she teased, trying to

lighten the mood. After watching the sun fall beneath the ocean on three consecutive days, Darvyn had failed to see why sunsets so fascinated people. She'd tried to share what enthralled her, how the colors that bled across the water were so vibrant, never the same twice, but it never moved him the way it did her.

"Would you like me to stay until it's set?" he asked. He would if she wanted, this she knew and was grateful for. But she shook her head, attempting a smile.

Darvyn kissed her very thoroughly. She allowed herself to linger for just a few moments in his embrace and then pulled back. He needed to be on his way.

"I'll see you tonight," he said.

And then he was gone.

She was glad that the cottage was relatively small. Larger than a Lagrimari dwelling, especially one meant for two people, but not so large that she felt lost in it. Not so large that the loneliness pressed in against her from all sides. Could she even be lonely when it was what she preferred? What she explicitly asked for?

A knock on the door had her whipping around. Did he forget his key? Even though this seaside town was supposed to be safe, Kyara insisted on using the locks and keys provided, never feeling too secure.

She wrenched open the door to chide him and stopped short, finding not Darvyn on the step but a short Lagrimari woman with a shorn head. Her delicately canted eyes were turned down at the corners, giving her a sad expression.

"So you decided to knock this time?" Kyara said irritably.

Mooriah smirked. "I do know how to be polite."

Kyara shrugged. "If you truly understood politeness, you would stop coming here every day and would have listened to me the first time I told you no."

Mooriah crossed her arms and leaned against the doorjamb.

"How long have you been waiting?" Kyara asked.

"Five hundred years."

She snorted; she should have seen that one coming.

An automobile drove slowly down the road, a beat-up jalopy, not one of the sleek town cars the crown provided for Darvyn. Still, she didn't want to incite the curiosity of the neighbors by hanging about in the doorway. "Come in and close the door then."

Not feeling like entertaining the nuisance of an unwanted guest, Kyara marched over to the couch and plopped down on it. Mooriah made herself at home in the armchair to her left, and they both looked out the picture window to the sand and surf beyond.

"I used to wish for this," Mooriah said softly. She wore an unfashionable, drab dress with long sleeves, something similar to what she'd been wearing in the visions Kyara'd had of her in the World After—or wherever she'd been after having her Song drained by the Physicks. How the woman had managed to travel to the Living World was still a mystery—Mooriah had been vague, promising answers only if she got what she wanted.

Kyara sat rigidly. "You can keep coming here, because I suppose you have nothing better to do, but my answer won't change."

"What makes you think I have nothing better to do?" Mooriah asked, cocking her head.

"Because if you did, wouldn't you be out doing it? You wouldn't come back from the dead to darken my door every day, or walk right in whenever it pleased you."

Mooriah's gaze turned a bit sadder if it was possible. "There are a great many other things I could be doing, I assure you. But I know that I have a responsibility. And I am endeavoring to remind you of yours."

Kyara took a deep breath. "I don't have any responsibilities anymore. By design."

"You need to learn to use your power. Now more than ever. The attack this morning? The wraiths? That is just the beginning. The prophesied events are upon us."

"How do you know about the wraiths?"

Mooriah merely blinked at her, and Kyara huffed in exasperation. "Why don't *you* teach me then? You're the only other Nethersinger in existence, for seed's sake."

Mooriah tilted her head. "Do you want to do it here, so close to so many? How many people could you kill if you lost control of your power?"

Kyara gritted her teeth; the woman was right. "Well then, we can go somewhere without any people."

"Like the eastern mountains? Inside the caves that have been protected for millennia from power like ours? Exactly what I've been asking you to do."

Kyara stomped her foot like a child. "I don't trust the Cavefolk."

She'd fallen into a trap of theirs before and Darvyn had paid the price. He'd nearly been killed by Murmur, an elder of the Cavefolk, who'd also wanted to teach her to better control her power.

"Their method worked, didn't it?" Mooriah asked. But that was the wrong thing to say.

Kyara stood abruptly. "Get out of my house and never come back. I will *never* let Darvyn be hurt by me or anyone else—not if I can help it. If you think that you can use him as bait—"

Mooriah held up her hands. "I mean him no harm. And neither did Murmur. He would have helped him if you couldn't have."

Kyara shook her head, staring the woman down.

"And we are *not* the only two Nethersingers in existence."

That stopped Kyara short. Mooriah looked up expectantly, anticipating Kyara's reaction. "If you won't do it for you, then do it for the child who, unless she's trained, will be far more destructive than you could ever be. Do you want that on your conscience? When you could have helped her learn control so that she won't bear the guilt you do."

Kyara's burning eyes blurred. Mooriah had struck a nerve, and it seemed the woman knew it. Fire raced up her throat as she thought of herself at eleven, wandering the Great Highway alone, a mounting stack of bodies already behind her.

"There is another?" she said through clenched teeth.

Mooriah nodded.

"A child?"

She nodded again.

"And why did you not tell me before?"

"It took me time to locate her. But she needs help. Your help. *Our* help."

A dam within Kyara broke and a rush of emotion burst forth; she barely held it back. "I want to meet her."

"Then write down this address."

CHAPTER EIGHT

We are harnessed to one another,
connected by the chorus and the verse.
Bonds strengthened when we choose to rehearse.
For practice is the key to Harmony.

—THE HARMONY OF BEING

"I'd expected the Shadowfox," the driver said as Kyara settled into the backseat of the town car idling in the driveway. He was an older Lagrimari man and almost entirely bald, except for a few stubborn patches of white clinging to the sides of his head.

"Sorry to disappoint," she said, shutting the heavy door. Nerves racked her as he turned in his seat to study her. She tensed, waiting for a gasp of shock or horror, but he didn't seem to recognize her.

"Not disappointed. You're a sight more pleasant to look at." His grin was gap-toothed as he turned back around to put the car in gear. "Erryl's the name," he said as they pulled onto the dirt road.

"Kyara. Thank you for the ride."

"It's my job."

"You're a settler?"

"Aye. Been here since the Sixth Breach. Learned to drive from some Sisters a while back and helped with their deliveries. It's peaceful work."

The ride was serene, and Erryl remained quiet as they headed toward the city. The sun had dipped below the horizon and dusk painted the surroundings with a glowering pall. The winding road bordered the ocean on one side with a seemingly endless stretch of browning grass on the other. As they crossed into the city proper, a fenced-in field full of flickering light stole her attention. She leaned forward for a better view. It had been nighttime when she'd left Rosira, so she hadn't noticed whatever this was the last time she'd been on this road.

Fragments of glass stuck out from the ground at even intervals—mirrors. Rows and rows of mirrors, some big and some small, extending far into the distance.

"What is that?" she whispered in confusion.

Erryl looked over at what had her captivated. "Cemetery. Elsirans bury their dead and mark the grave with a mirror over the head of the deceased."

"Why would they do such a thing?"

He chuckled. "They believe their loved ones can use the mirrors to view the Living World. They want to give them something to look at before they join the Eternal Flame."

It was bizarre, as many of these Elsiran practices were, Kyara was finding. But the automobile zipped past the cemetery and into the outskirts of the city. The colorful houses they passed seemed to mock her with their gaiety and beauty. Rosira was a nearly picture-perfect city, at least for its citizens. Anyone not like them, whether they looked different, spoke a different language, or possessed magic, had been unwelcome in this land for a long time.

Erryl pulled to a stop in the middle of a row of tall, narrow houses, their stucco exteriors painted in bright colors. The greens and yellows and oranges of the buildings made the quiet, well-kept street feel very homey. It reminded her of the Windy Hill neighborhood back in Sayya, though far more beautiful.

"This is the address?" she asked, staring out the window.

He turned back to her again, brows raised. "It's what you gave the dispatch. Is it not what you expected?"

"I don't know quite what I was expecting." A refugee camp, she'd supposed. What sort of Lagrimari child would live here?

"Do you want me to wait?" Erryl asked.

She was about to refuse, but then thought better of it. "Yes, if you don't mind. I don't know if this will take long or not."

"Not a problem. I'll be right here."

She exited the car, still gaping up at the house. The street number Mooriah had given her belonged to a pale green house with flower boxes under the window—empty now since the weather had turned. As she approached, the front door opened and two constables exited.

They stood on the front stoop replacing their billed caps atop their heads. A sandy-haired woman appeared in the doorway, eyes red and face tear-streaked. She dabbed at her cheeks with a handkerchief as she spoke to the men. Kyara wished she understood the Elsiran words, but whatever was said did little to comfort the woman. A crime must have taken place here, perhaps a robbery? They must not be uncommon in such a nice neighborhood.

The men ambled down the stairs, eyeing her suspiciously where she stood next to the town car. Kyara clenched her jaw until they passed. They piled into a boxy, wagon-like vehicle parked on the corner and drove away.

When she turned back to the house, the woman in the doorway was looking at her sadly. She raised a hand in greeting and Kyara, surprised at such a simple kindness from a stranger in obvious distress, did the same. Then a small Lagrimari girl appeared at the woman's side. She, too, was crying and a pang hit Kyara's heart.

The child's gaze caught on Kyara, and her expression shifted. Her jaw dropped and she detached herself from the woman to dart out the door.

"It's you!" the girl cried. Kyara took a step back, her legs hitting the car door. This child obviously knew the Poison Flame.

"Are you here to help us find my sister?" the girl asked, racing down the steps to her side. Confusion made Kyara's skin tighten.

"Ulani!" the woman called, coming down after the girl. She was not Elsiran and she certainly wasn't Lagrimari, yet she appeared to be caring for this child. She spoke in rapid Elsiran, in firm but even tones, before giving Kyara an apologetic look.

Ulani shook her head and grabbed Kyara's hand with small fingers. The exchange was lost to Kyara, but the hand in hers shocked her so much she wasn't sure how to react.

"What's happened to your sister?" she finally asked.

"She got nabbed. By a lady."

Kyara's heart nearly stopped as a sense of dread overtook her. She did not believe in coincidences. "A lady? What did the lady look like?" She spoke around the sudden dryness in her mouth.

"Little and bald-headed. She wasn't mean or angry. She felt like a thistle plant." The girl tilted her head, thinking. "The kind with the pretty, purple flowers."

"How so?"

"Prickly."

A lump formed in Kyara's throat. The description was somehow apt. "Was she wearing an ugly, black dress?"

The little girl stared up at her and nodded. Her eyes were slightly different colors, one lighter than the other, though it could have been a trick of the light. It was full dark now, gas lamps forming pools of illumination on the street.

"I know you," Kyara said, suddenly remembering this girl and her odd eyes. "You hid under the table, while I . . ." Her mouth snapped shut. She had killed this girl's father right in front of her.

She looked down at their clasped hands, then back up, incredulous. Ulani's expression was solemn. "You saved us from the nabbers and were helping the Keepers. You'll help find Tana." The last wasn't a question.

A ripple of shame moved through Kyara, throwing her off balance. The children in the warehouse—this girl and her sister had been among them. So strange to have encountered her twice before and now again. She swayed before righting herself again, something like fate settling across her shoulders.

Ulani spoke to the woman, whose expression changed from puzzlement to hope. She motioned for Kyara to follow her back into the house. With a tug on their joined hands, Ulani led the way.

Once inside, they entered a well-appointed sitting room just off the entry. Kyara perched on a couch next to the little girl, who had yet to release her, while the woman disappeared momentarily before returning with a loop of black wire that she put around her neck. When she next spoke, a tinny sound rang in her voice, but her words were in Lagrimari.

"This is an amalgam translator. They aren't being made anymore, and aren't even legal here, but I have a friend with connections who was able to get me a few. They don't last particularly long, so I've only been using them in emergencies, but I think this counts as one."

Kyara agreed.

"My name is Ella Farmafield. My daughter has told me who you are and that you saved her life. You have my gratitude."

Daughter. That was good. There were many Lagrimari orphans needing families. Kyara tried to pull her hand from Ulani's grip, but the child wouldn't budge.

"Did she also tell you about the first time she met me?" Kyara asked.

Ella looked at Ulani, who turned her head away, unchastened.

Kyara sighed. "In Lagrimar, I was known as the Poison Flame. I was an assassin for the True Father." The woman's eyes widened; her posture stiffened.

"I was controlled by a blood spell that forced me to follow directions or face . . . extreme pain." She did not like to dwell on the spell or its consequences.

"You were nearly executed, but you saved the queen's life, isn't that right?" Ella's voice came slowly as if she was remembering.

"That's true."

"And you are no longer practicing your former occupation?"

Kyara snorted. "No. I never will again."

"Well, then. Ulani believes you can help us, and though she's small, she can be quite wise. If you can help find my other daughter, then that is really all I care about." Her spine straightened, and she looked Kyara in the eye. "You know who took Tana? Because the constables refuse to take the kidnapping of a Lagrimari girl seriously." Bitterness tinged her voice.

"Yes. I think I do know who took her and where they've gone. Does Tana have a Song?"

"No." Ella shook her head slowly. "She said she was born without one."

Ulani shifted beside her. Ella's eyes narrowed. *"Uli?"*

"Tana doesn't have a Song like everyone else's, but she has *something.*"

Kyara nodded. "Do things ever die around her? Turn black?"

The girl bit her lip and shrugged a shoulder. "Grass under her feet sometimes. Plants. She doesn't do it on purpose though." She shot a nervous glance at her mother, who frowned.

"And the woman you saw, did Tana look like she was going with her willingly?"

Ulani nodded. Ella blinked away tears furiously. "I thought she was happy here," she whispered.

"It's not that," Kyara advised. "I don't think that Tana was unhappy, just the opposite. I'm sure that she left to try and save you."

Ella's brow furrowed. She swiped at the falling tears, and Ulani launched across the room to plant herself on her mother's lap, embracing her. "Save us from what?" Ella asked.

"Have you ever heard of Nethersong?"

"No, what is that?"

"Just as Earthsong is life energy, Nethersong is death energy. There are some of us, a very, very few, who are born with the ability to manipulate it. I am one. The woman who I believe took Tana is called Mooriah. She is another. Tana may be the only other Nethersinger alive. Our ability is dangerous, hard to control. Accidents happen. It is very easy to kill everyone you love without meaning to. How old is Tana?"

"Eleven."

"When I was that age, I hurt people I loved, too, for the first time. I'm not sure if the power is dormant before then or if there's some other reason, but Tana was probably scared. And

Mooriah preyed on that fear and convinced her to go train to learn to control it. She will take her to the eastern mountains bordering Lagrimar."

Ella mulled over her words. "But why so far away? What's in the mountains?"

"The Cavefolk."

Surprise made the woman's breath hitch. "There are still Cavefolk around? I'd thought they died off centuries ago."

"Almost all of them did. There are only a handful left. And deep in the mountain, they have protections against Nethersong. Mooriah says a Singer can train without fear of harming anyone there."

Ella wrung her hands together and bit her lip. Ulani lifted her head from where it was buried in her mother's neck. "Mama, we have to go and find her."

"Well, yes, of course. Can you take me there? If she has to train, she shouldn't do it alone."

Kyara swallowed. "There's another reason that Mooriah wants her to learn to use her power. A prophecy. A war coming where Nethersingers will be needed to fight." Thoughts of the wraith attack in the palace made her shiver, but she squared her shoulders.

"I will go and find her. I don't know that it's safe for you to come. The Cavefolk are . . . unpredictable. Neither they nor Mooriah would hurt Tana—they need her. But they don't need anyone else." She hoped her meaning was clear without scaring them.

Ella closed her eyes and took a deep breath. Her lips moved silently; she appeared to be whispering a prayer. Kyara remained quiet until she was done. "This morning, Saint Siruna sent me a sign," the woman said, eyes still shut. "Remember the egg with the two yolks, *uli*?"

"It made you sad, Mama."

"It did, because I wasn't sure what it meant. Now I believe I do." She opened her eyes and appeared resolved. All uncertainty banished.

"If she has to train, fine. If she's needed for some grand purpose, all right. But she's eleven, and she's my daughter, and she's not going through this alone. I'm going, too." Her tone brooked no opposition. Kyara sat back, impressed. It must be nice to have such a mother.

"And me, too," Ulani spoke up, jutting her little chin into the air.

"I'm sure that Grandmama would love a visit with you, since Papa is out of town," Ella said softly.

Ulani shook her head stubbornly and crossed her arms. Ella met Kyara's eyes with an exasperated gleam. "We'll talk about this later."

Ulani's mulish expression didn't change, and Kyara suppressed a smile. She didn't expect the conversation to go extraordinarily well.

"We'll have to find a way out east," Kyara said.

"I will make some calls. I'm not sure we'll be able to find transportation before morning though." Ella's voice was thick with worry.

"Mooriah will not hurt Tana," Kyara reiterated. "And she is formidable. Nethersong is more powerful than you can imagine. I can't conceive a scenario where the girl will come to any harm in her company." She kept to herself the fact that the woman could no doubt kill anything around her for kilometers if she so chose. Ella might not find it a comfort.

No, Mooriah would not allow the child to be injured in any way, but stealing a little girl, no matter her reasons, was unforgivable. If the prophecy was coming to pass and Nethersingers were needed, would she truly force a child to fight? Given the ruthlessness of the Cavefolk, Kyara already knew the answer.

Manipulations and deceit were exactly why she'd refused the woman in the first place. Why she had no love for the Cavefolk. And now this.

Kyara wished she could ignore Tana's plight and return to her cozy cottage by the sea, but how could she leave an eleven-year-old girl to deal with those vipers on her own? Mooriah had done her job well and pushed Kyara's back against the wall very neatly. But Kyara had a lot of fight left in her and an aversion to being handled in such a way. She would not walk away, but she would not give in easily.

Mooriah would need to answer for what she had done.

CHAPTER NINE

A whole split into parts
does not corrupt, unless the
parts lose their integrity
and weaken once apart and
soon forget
their nature is not many
but one.
Complete.

—THE HARMONY OF BEING

Jasminda strode into her office, her evening gown billowing around her. She was pleased that everyone she'd gathered was already here. Nadette Gaviareel, the royal event planner, stood with perfect posture behind a straight-backed chair at the small, round conference table in the corner of the room. Next to her stood Camm, Ilysara, and Darvyn. *Two Elsirans, two Lagrimari, and one half-breed,* Jasminda thought to herself with a chuckle.

"Your Majesty." Nadette gave an extremely proper curtsey. "The guests have already begun arriving to your brothers' birthday party, and there are still some details that I would like to check on and make sure of."

It was as polite a way of inquiring as to her reason for being here as any. Jasminda crossed the room and took a seat at the table. The others did the same, except for the planner. "Your staff is impeccable, Nadette. I'm quite sure you've already checked everything twice. The twins will live if the ice is delivered late or the decorations droop. I need to talk to you about something very important."

The woman raised her brows and sat, clasping her hands before her on the table. When they'd first met during the planning of the royal wedding, she and Nadette had butted heads, but Jasminda had come to respect the woman. Certainly she was a frivolous aristocrat, but she truly wanted the best for Elsira. She had recommended Camm for the assistant position, and that morning Camm had pointed out that Nadette held a degree in public relations from Adara University. Jasminda had requested the woman stop by her office before the party started, along with Darvyn and her two assistants.

"I'm putting together an . . . advisory board," Jasminda began. "Tomorrow we will be announcing a public referendum on the subject of unification versus separation. The vote will be held in ten days. I want to create a media campaign to influence the results."

Silence reigned as several pairs of eyes blinked owlishly.

Camm and Nadette shared a glance, but it was the assistant who spoke up. "Your Majesty, the palace must be seen as an impartial party during referendums." He shifted uncomfortably.

"Otherwise how would people have confidence that the results will be properly carried out?"

"There are few in the land who do not already know my position on the matter," Jasminda replied. "The other side has been waging media warfare practically since the Mantle first came down. Unification needs a strong voice. I realize it can't be mine, and in public I will do my best to appear objective. But you must understand that I, above all people, have a personal stake in the results of this vote. My family could be split down the middle if the Lagrimari are forced out into a separate territory. My very existence here could be questioned."

Camm swallowed and nodded. Ilysara's expression was grim.

"So why hold the vote in the first place?" Darvyn asked, leaning forward. "You are queen. Can't you just . . ." He waved a hand in the air. "Make things happen?"

Jasminda smiled wryly. "Wouldn't that be nice? But this is an issue that is tearing the people apart. Our constitution has a host of barriers to granting blanket citizenship to the Lagrimari—or any other group. And the Council is as divided as the people. The Goddess is not often helpful, but She does know Her way around the law. This vote is really the only way to answer the question once and for all, and quickly. In instances like this, the will of the people can supersede all else. Whatever the Elsiran citizens and the refugees seeking asylum decide will be the new policy going forward, and I think we need to advocate strongly for unity."

She turned to Nadette, who sat frowning, a faraway expression on her face. "I suppose I should ask your politics on this before we go forward. Are you pro- or anti-unification?"

Nadette focused and blinked rapidly. "Pro-unification, Your Majesty. I think what the Lagrimari people have suffered has been horrific. This land is big enough for us all."

Relief flooded Jasminda. "So will you help me?"

The woman tapped her finger on her lips and then pulled out a small, leather-bound notebook and pencil from her pocket. She began scribbling rapidly. "I'm thinking a multipart series on life under the thumb of the True Father, printed in the largest newspaper with audio clips on the nightly newsreader's reports. Tear-jerking stuff: mothers and children separated, man's inhumanity to man, that type of thing." She stared at her notes, underlining a word. "I'll contact Hazelle Harimel, she's an influential reporter."

Jasminda groaned internally. "That woman hates me. Every piece she writes is another log on the fire for those who want to burn me in effigy."

Nadette nodded absently. "So imagine if we're able to sway her and turn her to our side? What we really need is to humanize the refugees, draw the people in viscerally to their plight."

While Jasminda was glad the woman was on board and seriously contemplating the options, she balked internally at the idea that the refugees weren't automatically thought of as human in the first place. However, Ilysara tilted her head, considering. "What about photographic essays on the war orphans and those who survived the camps and the mines? I know some refugees who managed to transport a box of photo negatives from Lagrimar. If we can get them developed, I'm certain there will be some engaging photos there."

"Yes, that's excellent," Nadette replied. The two women continued trading ideas on how best to tug on the heartstrings of the Elsirans, and hopefully push public opinion toward unification.

The phone on the desk across the office rang, and Camm jumped up to get it. Darvyn leaned over to Jasminda. "How can I help?"

"I know you're not a Keeper of the Promise any longer, but you still have friends among them, right?"

He nodded.

"We need to take the pulse of the refugees. They will get an equal vote and I know they have not exactly felt welcomed here."

"I'll get some people on it. When do you expect Jack back?"

Jasminda blinked. "He'll be in Fremia for two weeks."

Darvyn looked stunned. "He's staying after this morning's attack?" Her gaze darted to the other two at the table. "They can't hear us," he said. He must have sung a spell to dampen the sounds of their conversation.

"Oola said that we should keep the attack quiet. So as not to cause alarm."

"Quiet, yes, from the public but from Jack as well?" He was incredulous and sat back, rubbing the back of his neck. "That is Her playbook, it doesn't have to be yours. He would want to know."

"You're right, he would. But he would rush back and not be able to do anything. She's right about that. We need Fremia; the wraith attack this morning is an Earthsinger problem."

"If what I saw in Yaly will be repeated here, it will be a problem for everyone soon enough." He took a deep breath, face still grim. "This is your choice, but for the record, I think you should tell him."

Jasminda nodded sadly. He was probably right, but so was Oola.

Camm approached the table. "The Chief of Constables has arrived."

"All right, I'll see him in Jack's office. Thank you." She turned back to Darvyn. "I'll need to talk to you afterward about the other new development." He frowned again; she had little desire to tell him of the True Father's escape, but he needed to know.

As Camm left the room, she rose, motioning for the others

to stay seated. "I'd like regular updates on your progress. Pull in whomever you need that you feel you can trust. We don't have much time."

The women nodded and Darvyn's expression held both worry and disapproval. She swept out of the room, his doubts following her.

The Chief of Constables, Lennard Floreen, was a man of average height and build. He was clean-shaven with short-cropped hair and a distinct lack of freckles, unusual for an Elsiran. He bowed when Jasminda entered the room and held himself erect with a posture honed in the military.

"Thank you for coming, Chief Floreen. I know that with all of the unrest in the city, your time is even more valuable than ever."

"I am honored, Your Majesty. How can I be of service?"

She took a seat in an armchair and motioned for him to do the same in the chair next to her. Camm entered with a tray of water and tea and set it on the coffee table between them. He poured Jasminda a cup then retreated to the corner when Floreen declined a refreshment.

Jasminda cleared her throat. "The monarchy does not generally concern itself with the day-to-day running of the city, however, we are in unprecedented times, are we not?"

"Certainly, Your Majesty."

"As such, I would like to *suggest* a city-wide curfew, due to the rise in terrorist activity. I know the aldermen are against it, but I believe it's in the best interest of the citizens and for the safety of all. As your men would be responsible for enforcing and maintaining it, I wanted your input and to see if this is something you would consider influencing the aldermen on."

Floreen was a no-nonsense man, it was clear in everything from his posture to his hair to the shine of his boots. He was not an aristocrat, like the group of elected aldermen who ran things in Rosira, but his word held sway with them.

"It would require significant overtime hours, Your Majesty, and we've been advised that the budget would not be able to accommodate such. Curfews are generally unpopular, and the force will encounter resistance. The extra pay is much needed for the additional effort and to uphold morale."

"And if the funds could be found?" That was a big "if" considering the state of their coffers, but lives were at stake.

"Then I would be in favor. It would improve our ability to keep the people safe."

Jasminda was formulating a plan that would doubtless decrease her already tenuous popularity. She was certain that some among the elite would call for her head on a pike, but her reputation had never been important to her.

"Excellent. I'm glad to hear it. These have been difficult times for us all." She sipped her tea, considering how to broach the next topic delicately. "You are receiving the briefings from the Intelligence Service, I trust?"

"Yes, Your Majesty. Daily."

"And so you're aware that Zann Biddel is a person of extreme interest in the terrorist attacks."

He narrowed his eyes slightly and nodded. "I am."

"There has been, as of yet, no firm evidence of his involvement, though all signs point to it." She stirred her tea, though she'd added no sugar or cream, stalling. Politics and gamesmanship were not her forte. Jack may have been able to do this delicately, but of course, he would not approve of this at all. "I should speak plainly," she finally said.

"That would be appreciated, Your Majesty." A hint of a smile graced his lips but was gone almost immediately.

"The Intelligence Service has not been able to find the evidence we need to get Biddel off the streets. And people continue to die. You and I have not spoken personally before, but as a representative of the law I want to know if there is a way that you could help us find justice for all of the victims."

His jaw tensed, and Jasminda stiffened. She called Earthsong to her to reveal his mood and emotions, but he was a brick wall. She got a faint wisp of curiosity and a thread of respect for her boldness, but that was it.

"You would like me to arrest Zann Biddel?"

"Yes, I very much would. And I personally don't care if you have to make up a crime, fabricate a witness, and conjure evidence in a counterfeiter's laboratory in order to do it, the blood on his hands is thick and flowing. But I would never impugn your integrity with such a suggestion."

The faint smile appeared for longer this time before he squashed it.

"I understand that my candor may not be particularly regal," Jasminda said.

"I believe that frankness is much lacking in our society, Your Majesty." His fingers drummed against the hat that sat on his knee. He looked into the distance for a moment while Jasminda worried if she'd just made a huge error in judgement. She did not dare peek at Camm to see his expression.

Chief Floreen finally met her gaze, Earthsong still revealing nothing of his emotions. "I lost my niece in the temple bombing," he said gruffly. "She was just nine years old. Dreamed of joining the Sisterhood."

He cleared his throat as grief funneled through a crack in the armored shell he kept around his heart. The intensity of it struck Jasminda like a blow to the chest. She took a deep breath to hide her reaction.

"I would like to see the bastard responsible drawn and quartered." He pulled himself together, straightening even more until she thought his spine would crack. "But I won't break the law to do it."

He held Jasminda's gaze as nerves flittered in her chest. She nodded, respecting his decision and went to set her teacup down.

"However, our grand land does have a great many laws." A true smile graced his lips, transforming his face from severe to slightly less severe.

"Yes, you're quite right, Chief Floreen. I have become a scholar of our legislation in recent weeks. It is both vast and fascinating."

"Indeed."

"I'm glad we were able to come to an agreement on this."

"It's been my pleasure, Your Majesty." He rose and bowed before exiting the room.

Camm came over to grab the tea tray and she caught his grim expression.

"You think I went too far?" she asked.

He paused, considering. "I think it's a distinct possibility."

She nodded and dismissed him, staring around the room, full of Jack's things, and missing her husband.

"Sometimes going too far is the only way," she said to no one in particular.

CHAPTER TEN

A corner is a good place for shadows to hide.
It is also a
good place
to shine a light.

—THE HARMONY OF BEING

Meet me in my sitting room, immediately!

The mental message was strong, urgent. It nearly pushed Zeli from the chair where she'd been sitting cloistered in a corner of the busy kitchen. She popped up, slamming the textbook she'd been trying to study shut, and almost crashed into a maid bearing a stack of dirty plates from the ballroom.

Normally, she found the palace kitchen comforting. It reminded her of the estate where she'd grown up. She understood the workings of kitchens, even one on such a grand scale as this one was largely the same, but there had been no comfort to be found today. The terrifying aftermath of the morning's attack still reverberated through her limbs. She mumbled an apology to the maid and hustled off toward the western wing of the palace.

Sounds of revelry from the Winter Ballroom mocked her as she passed. The twins' birthday party was in full swing. The Goddess had informed her that they were all supposed to go on as if nothing out of the ordinary had happened. As if spirits from the World After had not attacked Queen Jasminda and the Goddess Awoken only a few hours ago. No one else knew and that was how it would stay. More secrets. Her life was uncomfortably full of them.

And how was Varten going to stand in front of all those people coming to wish him well? She wanted to peek in and catch a glimpse of him, but was too afraid. Though he'd invited her to his celebration, she certainly wouldn't fit in at an aristocratic affair like that.

Instead, she rushed to follow her summons, heart beating nearly out of her chest with every step. What did the Goddess want at this hour? It couldn't possibly be anything good.

She arrived to find the door to the grand office assigned for the Goddess's use ajar.

"Come in and shut the door," an ominous voice echoed. Zeli did as she was bid and stepped a few more paces into the room, trembling.

The Goddess's back was to her. She stood beside a wooden desk, inlaid with gold filigree. The designs and swirls always drew Zeli's eye, but the woman's rigid posture and stiff shoulders raised pulses of alarm. Slowly She turned. "What do you know of this?"

Zeli tore her gaze away from the Goddess's deceptively placid countenance to regard what She held in Her hand. A small, leather-bound book. Zeli frowned. "I have no idea, Your Excellency. What is that?"

The Goddess eyed her for a long moment, probably peering into her soul. She wouldn't dare lie, so the woman must be satisfied, but the silence held. Zeli's palms began to sweat under the intense scrutiny.

Finally, with what appeared to be reluctance, She beckoned Zeli forward. "I found this on the desk this evening. Is this not where you usually answer my correspondence?"

One of Zeli's duties was to pen responses to the many letters that flooded the palace mailroom addressed to the Goddess Awoken. An Elsiran acolyte dealt with the letters in her language, but since Zeli could read and write, she managed quite a large volume of mail. The literate among her people were few, but apparently enough to fill bags daily. The Goddess Herself only answered a small number.

"Yes, but it wasn't there earlier when I did the mail, Your Excellency." She gripped the skirt of her robe to keep her hands from trembling. Stepping closer, she noticed that the little book was thick, with the ragged edges of the pages peeking out. It looked old, well-worn, the cover cracked and paper yellowing. A leather strap was wrapped around it, tied in a neat bow.

"When was the last time you were in this room?" the Goddess asked.

"This morning before breakfast. Before the . . . incident." She swallowed, her throat thick with dread. All day she'd darted her gaze around, certain that vicious shadows were swirling in the corners of her vision.

"And you saw nothing amiss then? No one who struck you as odd as you approached or left? No strange feelings?"

She shook her head silently. She'd noticed nothing. While the Goddess's face remained undisturbed, the energy swirling around Her was active. Zeli had rarely seen Her take on an expression other than serenity or slight amusement. But now She was shaken. Her hand quavered slightly as She held the book up. She seemed to notice and dropped it onto the desk, then stepped away, as if afraid it would hurt Her.

That was it! Zeli realized with a start. The Goddess actually seemed afraid. The indications were subtle, but Zeli had spent quite a bit of time with Her over the past months and had never witnessed Her such. Even when She'd stood facing down angry spirits filled with malevolent power, She hadn't appeared truly afraid.

A trill of anxiety rocked Zeli. What in that little book could frighten a deity? "Your Excellency, is the book dangerous?"

The Goddess sighed, a world-weary sound that also surprised Zeli. "It is a journal. A diary, a very old one, its origination—as old as I am. How it came to be here is a mystery, and the knowledgc inside . . ." She closed Her eyes on a long blink. "I have no doubt the pages contain secrets hidden for centuries that are likely best left that way."

She turned, looking to the window and the gardens beyond. Lights had been strung up among the trees, illuminating the paths in the darkness.

"Place it in the vault with the other thing. Ensure that both are safe. I do not . . . I do not want it near me." Her voice almost broke there.

Zeli's anxiety ratcheted. Certainly merely holding the book could not be hazardous. The Goddess had said so, but She, as it turned out, was not as infallible as everyone believed. This realization scared Zeli. She edged toward the desk and picked up the journal gingerly. It was just a book. Soft, weathered leather, inlaid with a border of vines. The strap tying it was loose, but she didn't dare peek insidc.

"Directly to the vault. Lock it away and ensure the caldera there is safe."

"Yes, Your Excellency."

Though the royal vault was perhaps the safest place in the country, Zeli still had to check on the other powerful object stored inside every few days to ensure it hadn't been molested or stolen.

She tucked the journal against her chest and hovered, waiting. "Is that all, Your Excellency?"

"Yes, *uli,* that is all."

Her voice was strong again, dismissive, as if the last few minutes hadn't happened.

But even though it appeared Zeli's secret thoughts were safe for the moment, a new fear creeped in. If this book was enough to make a goddess afraid, what in seed's name could be written inside?

The Winter Ballroom had been decorated to live up to its name; Varten stood with a group of young men under a cluster of paper snowflakes hanging from the ceiling next to a pile of what smelled like soap shavings masquerading as snow. He'd been starched and creased into a formal suit, something he hadn't counted on when the idea of the party was first broached. His hair was flattened with heavy pomade, and he felt entombed in the vest and jacket.

Every young aristocrat in Rosira had wrangled an invitation. They were gathered in thickets like weeds on the dance floor—not dancing—and snickering smugly at the tables. Lads and girls who didn't know the twins at all chattered away in their posh accents, cutting their eyes at one another with judgmental glances.

Varten was doing his best to play his part. To act as though the world was the same place it had been yesterday, before he knew that some unknown enemy was intent on sending wraiths into the palace. But Jasminda had insisted that telling anyone—even Roshon—would only spread panic. He wasn't sure how long he could keep a secret like this from his brother. As it turned out, he hadn't even seen his twin until he'd stepped into the ballroom tonight.

He'd gotten a glimpse of Roshon and Ani earlier, but now a small phalanx of blue bloods had Varten penned in. Sons and grandsons of Council members, governors, aldermen, and anyone considered "old money."

"If you ask me," Hyllard Dursall said around a mouthful of birthday pie, "the umpire should be fired and never allowed to judge a match again if his vision is so poor. My father lost nearly seven hundred pieces on that game and flew into a terrible rage."

"I thought your father had sworn off betting on swivet games after the finals last year. Didn't you have to sell your boat?" the son of some distant cousin of Jack's asked.

"We still have the boat." Hyllard's already slightly bulging eyes protruded even more at the perceived insult. "We don't keep the crew on staff, that's all, but we can go out on it whenever we want. We're thinking of buying another, if you must know."

"From where? Raunians are the best shipbuilders and won't sell to us now."

"They have perfectly good shipbuilders in Fremia."

"Well, my father is buying an airship," Godriq Norilos added.

"Same style as the king's, just a larger model." Whispers of disbelief filtered through the group. Godriq looked smug, having successfully one-upped the others.

The mention of airships caught Varten's attention. "When you get it, maybc I'll take it up for a turn," he said easily. "Clove's been teaching me to fly. You know she came in second in the Yaly Classic. Who's your flying instructor?"

Godriq looked peeved. There weren't many airship pilots in Elsira, as they all well knew. And little chance Clove would want to help any of these snobbish horse's arses. Varten hadn't even been trying to play their little competitive game, he'd barely been paying attention, but found he was good at it. His position as "prince" had rocketed him to the top of the hierarchy of this group, and every lad here wanted to be his best mate.

The group kept getting larger and larger as people wandered over, itching to be in his orbit. Especially since Roshon was nowhere to be found.

Varten loved a good party, or at least, he had loved the idea of a party—having not been to one in so long. When he was younger, Mama had sometimes taken them to stay with friends on a farm near the town where they bought supplies. The family had four children close in age, and he and Roshon had played with them and celebrated more than one Breach Day at their home. Until the year Jasminda had accompanied them, instead of staying home with Papa, and suddenly none of them were welcome anymore.

In the valley where he'd grown up, with only books and magazines to teach him about the wider world, he'd imagined a palace party quite differently. In his mind, these beautiful, rich, well-dressed people with access to the best of everything were truly happy. Their smiles were real, rooted in the depths of their joy at being so privileged. But here the laughter and gaiety were brittle porcelain masks barely concealing disdain, posturing, and emptiness. Varten found their concerns petty and meaningless on the best of days. But today, he could barely hold himself back from screaming.

Godriq, Hyllard, and the others had changed the subject back to the latest swivet match and the terrible umpire. Varten didn't know anything about the game played almost exclusively by the rich, so his attention wandered again. He took a few steps back to peer around the knot of bodies surrounding him to the doorway for the thousandth time that night. The chances that Zeli would come were slim, but he couldn't help hoping.

Was she holding up any better than he was? Was her body on constant alert, searching the darkened corners of the room? The dim lighting in the ballroom could easily hide shadows. Jasminda had claimed Oola believed another attack would take some time, but no one truly knew. He hoped his exterior didn't betray the anxiety ratcheting inside him.

A swath of purple silk and beading filled his peripheral vision—a girl, smiling wide with bright teeth, had appeared at his side. "I'm Claudette," she said, offering a genteel curtsey. "I just wanted to wish you a happy birthday, Your Grace."

He nodded politely. "Thank you so much. My brother and I appreciate you coming to our party to help us celebrate." *Even though we have no idea who you are.*

He resisted the urge to loosen the bow tie surrounding his neck. The band started another song, one that seemed to capture the attention of the guests, though he'd never heard it before.

The girl before him—Cosette? Clavette? He'd already forgotten her name—was looking up at him expectantly. He smiled and raised his eyebrows. Was there something else he was supposed to do?

"The band is lovely, Your Grace. They're playing the most popular dances tonight."

"You don't need to call me Your Grace," he replied hastily.

"Oh, but I do," she said, laying a hand on his arm, fluttering her lashes. "You are a prince of Elsira now."

The proprietary feel of that hand made him cringe internally. He turned back toward the lads, who were earnestly debating the merits of two famous swivet players; he wished he knew enough to rejoin the conversation. A movement in a gloomy corner of the room caused him to jerk, but it was just a butler emerging with another tray of hors d'oeuvres. His movement dislodged her hand, but she just stepped closer to him.

He smiled, more forced this time. "Just because my sister was made queen, doesn't mean that I'm a prince."

Godriq paused, mid-rant. "Of course it does. What else would it mean?"

Varten shrugged and widened his practiced grin. "Don't you think things mean more when you work for them?"

Nothing but blank gazes met him. He stifled a laugh. "I mean, inheriting's nice, too."

He jumped when Colette, or whoever, grabbed his elbow. "Are you certain you would not like to ask me to dance, Your Grace?"

He chuckled to drive away the tension in his jaw and pulled away from her firm grip again. "Sorry, I don't even know these dances." The few couples on the dance floor performed elaborate steps to the syncopated music.

A Lagrimari servant came over with a tray. Varten greeted the man in his native tongue, but the pushy socialite shooed him away, a look of disgust on her face.

"You don't like scallops?" Varten asked.

Her lip curled. "I don't like the help. Seeing *grols* in the palace, it's a disgrace."

Varten stuffed his hands in his pockets, his face growing taut. "*Grols,* you mean like the queen?"

She paled and clutched the jewels around her neck. Nearby, conversation stopped. He honestly had no idea what he sounded like, but judging by the way everyone had suddenly grown tense, he hadn't hidden his ire. "No, I . . . Queen Jasminda isn't like the rest of them. Neither is the Goddess. You know what I meant."

He grew very still, feeling almost as if he was turning to stone. "Because the rest of them are, what? Like my father? I'm not sure how you managed to come here forgetting that my brother and I are half *grol,* but please allow me to remind you." He leaned closer and lowered his voice. "I may look like one of you, but I'm not."

He hadn't yelled, but he hadn't managed to hide the venom pouring out from deep within. The girl reddened and scurried away, teetering on her high-heeled shoes. When he looked up, the lads around him were all gaping at him like he'd grown another head.

Roshon was suddenly at his side, a hand on his arm, pulling him away. "Your face looks like a tomato. What'd she say?"

"The same shite everyone here is probably thinking."

They escaped the ballroom and went out into the hallway. Dressed identically, somehow Roshon seemed to appear more comfortable in his formal wear. The music was just a low hum on the other side of the wall and Varten's emotions began to settle. He ran his hands over his face. "Who thought this party was a good fecking idea?"

Roshon raised a brow. "As I recall, when Jasminda first brought it up you said, and I quote, 'That's a good fecking idea.'"

Varten shook his head and turned away. That felt like a lifetime ago.

"You don't have to go back in, you know."

"It's our party." Varten crossed his arms.

"Yeah, so we should be having fun."

"Well, you've been hiding out somewhere with Ani the whole night, so I have to pick up the slack." Did he sound bitter? He was having a hard time reining it in right now.

Roshon sighed and leaned next to him. "You don't have to do everything everyone asks. Jas meant well with this, Sovereign knows she did it for you. But if it's not your thing, just tell her."

"But she worked hard on it."

"*Someone* worked hard on it, but not her personally. She has *people* for things like this, you know."

"And all the money . . ."

"Jack's rich, remember. Don't worry about all that."

Varten shrugged and slid down to sit on the floor. His brother joined him. They sat in silence for a while until Varten wasn't vibrating with cold anger. Roshon studied him closely, and Varten worried that his secret was written on his face. But when his brother spoke, it wasn't what he expected.

"So have you decided whether or not you're coming with us? Ani has a shipment she needs to pick up in Fremia next week. We might leave as soon as Firstday."

Varten blinked. He got the sense that Roshon truly wouldn't mind him coming along on Ani's ship as they sailed the seas smuggling and trading and whatever it was Ani did for a living. The idea of always being the odd man out held no appeal, but that would be true whether he stayed or left.

"What about the wedding?"

Roshon let out a groan. "That's turning out to be a problem.

Looks like it might start an international incident. Ani's mother insists the wedding be in Raun. And Jasminda is equally adamant that it be here."

Ani's mother was the king of Raun, a small island nation to the west. Considering she was also responsible for the trade embargo, this could get dicey. "Do you think Jas really cares, or is this a political thing?" Varten asked.

"I don't think Jas *does* political things, that's more Jack's domain. She said that since we'll be at sea most of the time, the least we could do is have the wedding here with family. If it's there, she wouldn't be able to go—at least not while the embargo is happening."

"Seems like they could use this as a way to come together." Varten scratched his chin.

Roshon shrugged. "If King Pia is anywhere as stubborn as Ani—or Jasminda for that matter—then I doubt things will work out anytime soon. We may have to elope."

"That may cause a war."

"Don't think I've forgotten you haven't answered," Roshon said, nudging him.

"I'm neutral, like Fremia," he said, holding his hands up. "But no, I don't want to be the third wheel as you start a new life."

Roshon's face fell. He began turning the golden cuff link at his wrist. "You're still thinking of joining the army?"

"Seems like a good way to be useful." Varten didn't have any better ideas. There was always university in Fremia, which would at least allow him to see somewhere new, but he wasn't as studious as his sister, and didn't want to be locked away in a classroom for years. The army held some appeal, or maybe the foreign service, so he could travel. With all the recent upheavals, Jack and Jasminda needed folk they could trust abroad, too. Enemies, both magical and not, were all around. Someone was going to be needed to fight them off.

"I'll figure something out, don't worry about me." He brought a smile to his face; it was almost easy to do.

"Hmm," was Roshon's response.

The door to the ballroom swung open, releasing a torrent of sound. Ani marched out and spotted the twins. Her short, blue hair was almost in her eyes. The ball gown she wore was in the traditional Raunian style, a thin, sort of wispy material that wrapped around her, leaving a swath of torso bare. Scandalous by Elsiran standards, but Ani didn't care. She wasn't wearing her prosthetic hand tonight, and the scar tissue at the bottom of what remained of her arm made Varten hold back a wince. She said she didn't remember the pain, but he couldn't help feeling at least a little responsible since she lost her hand the day his family was captured and imprisoned.

"What's wrong? Too many spirits?" she asked.

"Are they serving spirits here?" Roshon's brows rose.

"They should be, given how much of a snooze the party is. No offense." She pulled a silver flask from her bosom and grinned mischievously before settling beside them.

"None taken," Varten said. They passed the flask around, but the burning liquid did little to improve Varten's mood. Fortunately, neither Roshon nor Ani pressed him for conversation. Melancholy swelled within him and he battled it, knowing he really should get back inside the ballroom.

Something moved in his periphery again and he whipped his head around, half-expecting to see a shadow wriggling its way out of the wall. But it was a person rushing along the intersection between hallways. A familiar, shortish figure in a light blue dress running as if a wild dog was chasing her.

He leapt to his feet.

"Where are you going?" Roshon asked.

"I'll . . . I'll be right back," he said, already jogging away.

CHAPTER ELEVEN

Deny, refuse to comply.
Close eyes against the tyranny
you cannot bear to be.
You will not mirror that which you
don't see.

—THE HARMONY OF BEING

Varten raced to catch up with the distant figure he was certain was Zeli. Though she had such short legs, she was speedy when she wanted to be. It took him the length of two entire corridors before he reached her as she entered an unfamiliar narrow chamber in a part of the palace not much trafficked.

The lighting was dimmer here, the walls and decorations older. This place must be deep in the heart of the building where it butted up against the mountain. He reached out to touch her shoulder and she shrieked and spun away, clutching something to her chest.

"I'm sorry," he said, holding up his hands. "I didn't mean to scare you. But you were running so fast."

Her normally vivid skin tone was ashen; she looked almost as scared as she had this morning. He had the urge to comfort her and bring her in for a hug, though she was so squirrelly he wasn't sure she'd appreciate the gesture. As it was, she looked at him with shaking, fear-filled eyes.

"A-aren't you supposed to be at your birthday party?"

"It was a bore. You didn't show up." He grinned, but her expression didn't change.

"I'm on a mission from the Goddess," she stammered.

"A secret mission?"

She frowned and looked around the empty hallway then down at the bundle in her arms. She seemed . . . lost, and her expression made him determined to give aid in whatever way he could.

"You don't have to tell me. How about I just walk alongside you, like a guard, while you finish your mission." He lowered his voice. "If a wraith shows up, they can take me and you can run for help."

This seemed to startle her. "You think they'll come back so soon?"

He shrugged. "Even if they don't, I'll need to practice guarding people if I'm to join the army."

"You want to join the army?"

"Well, I need something to do. Papa wants me to finish school first, but he's not around to teach me anymore and Jasminda has better things to do. I've never been to proper school anyway, and I wouldn't know how."

She considered, then started walking again, a little more

slowly. He fell into step beside her. She was still hunched over her bundle, which, now that he was able to get a closer look, was a book.

"I've never been, either," she said. "To school. Though my mistress taught me to read and write, mostly to amuse herself."

"The Goddess taught you?"

"No, my former mistress. I grew up on the estate of the Magister—he ruled our city and its territories. His daughter and I were the same age, and I was her personal servant." Pride rang in her voice. Varten wasn't surprised. She seemed to take her job very seriously.

"So what is it that you have there?" he asked, motioning to the object she clutched like a safety line.

"Are you sure no one will miss you at your party?" She eyed his formal suit dubiously.

Varten shrugged out of his jacket and tossed it over his shoulder. "It's my party. I should be able to take a break from it if I want to."

She looked at him like he had a cat on his head. "This is for the vault."

He rubbed his hands together. "Ooh, the vault. I've never been to the royal vault before."

Zeli shrugged. "It's not much to see. Metal doors half a pace thick. Lots of locks and combinations."

"And She's entrusted you with all of that?"

She nodded; Varten grinned, impressed. "Well you must be very special then." She dipped her head, embarrassed. Varten got closer. "So what's the book about?"

"I don't know. I haven't read it. The Goddess found it and it . . . It made Her uncomfortable."

Varten picked up on her distress and shared her worry. "What kind of thing could do that?" She looked up wide-eyed. That was answer enough.

He peered closer at the leather-bound book. "She didn't say what was in it?"

"No, She barely wanted to touch it. Though She said it wasn't magical. Just words on paper."

"Words on paper can be magic enough," he mused. "Maybe we should have a look." Zeli's eyes were in danger of bursting from her face and running away entirely. "I mean, aren't you curious?" He could tell she was by the indignant look she wasn't quite pulling off. "What's the harm of taking a quick peek?"

She wavered, then tightened her arms and shook her head. "No, it isn't our business."

But Varten had seen the chink in her armor. "I suppose you're right. The Goddess Awoken always has our best interests at heart. She never tricks or manipulates things in order to get Her way."

Zeli appeared surprised at the bitterness in his voice.

"Not like She let my sister die or anything." Varten hadn't been there for Kyara's execution, but he'd seen the newspapers and heard the radiophonic newsreaders. Jasminda had collapsed, poisoned, something the Goddess should have been able to prevent easily, but hadn't, all to test Kyara's power or some such.

"I'm betting the *situation* this morning isn't the only secret She's keeping."

Zeli stopped walking entirely, her jaw dropping. After a long moment she spoke, voice wobbly. "Maybe She gave me this task to test me?"

"She's been known to do that before. She tested my father—that's how he came to this country in the first place." It was also why they'd ended up in prison, but he restrained himself from mentioning it.

Zeli swallowed. They continued walking until they arrived at an intersection. Down the hall was a small door, nondescript but guarded by two Royal Guardsmen. The vault must be somewhere through there. But instead of approaching, she made a turn and dipped into the side hallway; this one looked to be for servants. She stopped in an alcove.

"I don't know. She told me to put this in the vault with the—" She cut herself off.

"With the what?"

"Something else powerful and dangerous that needs to be kept away from everyone." She shook her head. "I should just do what She said."

Varten tapped his lips in thought. Zeli's stance was relaxed, not as rigid as before. "You're right. You'll want plausible deniability in this type of situation."

"Plausible what?"

"My brother and I believe that one should ask for forgiveness instead of permission."

Her confused expression lasted a moment longer until Varten plucked the book from her hands. Her eyes widened and her mouth opened into an *O*. Varten danced around her, fleeing down the hall, not knowing where he was going but hearing her feet race behind him.

He tried a few doors, all locked, then finally one at the very end of the hall opened. He found himself in a sitting room, one that hadn't been in use in quite some time. White sheets covered the furniture, making it seem that the place was full of lounging ghosts.

The smell of dust hung thick in the air. There was no switch on the wall for electric lighting, but a bookshelf held two oil lamps. He pulled out the pack of matches he always kept in his pocket and lit the lanterns, while Zeli watched from near the door.

"You can honestly say you had nothing to do with my actions," he said. "*That's* plausible deniability."

She shook her head as he uncovered some of the furniture, then sneezed as the dust caught up to him. He revealed two armchairs and a side table. The fabric smelled musty, but he tested one of the chairs, which was still springy.

"You don't even have to look. I'll just take a quick peek and you can stay right over there. Afterward, we'll make sure it gets into the vault." He settled into the chair with one of the lamps on the table next to him and carefully unwrapped the book. It fell open to a place in the middle, well-worn pages covered in neat handwriting.

It was a journal, written in dark, fading ink. The pages were thick and hearty, handmade, and very old. He flipped to the front, seeking a name or identifier of the journal's author. Grinning, he read the inscription. "'A gift from the heart to my beloved.'" It was only signed "O." Hmm, the mystery increased.

He looked up to find Zeli's eyes on him. She'd inched closer. He bet if he read far enough she might make her way over here as curiosity gripped her.

The first few pages contained sketches of simple machines and bodies. He scanned a few more pages until Zeli was seated beside him, craning her neck. He shouldn't tease her too badly; how could they resist taking a peek? So far he'd seen nothing he imagined would make the Goddess uncomfortable.

Taking care with the old parchment, he flipped toward the back—he always read the end of a book first to know what he was in for. He stopped on a page filled with writing, but with one word larger than the others, outlined over and over again.

BLOOD.

Zeli gasped.

"Can you read this?" he asked.

"I can read. It says 'blood.'" She sounded affronted.

"But it's written in Elsiran."

She frowned. "No, it's in Lagrimari."

He squinted at the words, clearly written in the language that his mother had painstakingly taught them all to read. They'd learned to speak Lagrimari from Papa, though he hadn't known his letters in order to pass on reading and writing to his children.

"But the written languages aren't the same," he said, heart beating faster.

"They're not," Zeli said. "But the characters are. This is sort of like an old-fashioned version of Lagrimari. It's not particularly easy to read but—"

"It's understandable." Varten felt the same way. It was like wading through the classic literature Mama had made them read. Jasminda had loved the stuff, Roshon hadn't particularly cared one way or the other, but Varten hated it. He'd struggled through the lessons, always resenting having to learn something so archaic.

"That doesn't make any sense," he said. "It shouldn't be possible." Zeli's gaze was tense. She scooted her chair closer for a better look at the book. Now they were knee to knee and she draped herself over the arm of his chair to read.

"Here," he said, giving it to her.

She shrank back. "Plausible deniability."

He chuckled, shaking his head. "You learn fast."

"That, I do."

On the opposite page from the ominous, underlined word was an outlined sketch of a man's body, a circle in the middle of his chest with arrows pointing in and out. Varten traced the text below it with a finger and read.

"'The question of whether there is, in the body, an internal organ such that separates the Silent from the Songbearers has been definitively answered. There is not. The Song then must be deduced to have manifested in some other sphere, perhaps from the combination of bodily humors or some other esoteric blend of forces.'"

He met Zeli's perplexed gaze with one of his own.

"'Regardless of whether its source is physical or energetic, the removal of a Song from a Songbearer requires a fleshly severing of the aethereal from its bodily form. Its restoration cannot be undertaken by simply reversing this process, though true mastery of the replacement methodology may provide a future procedure to that end.'"

The last words dissolved into breath. "Does this mean what I think it does?"

She didn't respond, but the truth was in her wide-eyed expression.

He was almost too scared to put it into words. "Is there a way to restore lost Songs?"

CHAPTER TWELVE

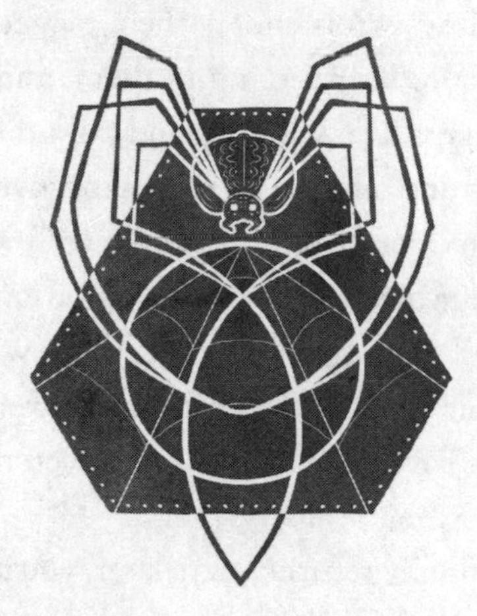

Power rests in action
acts in resting
brings the shallow world to heel with its perception
runs nipping at your heels for its protection.

—THE HARMONY OF BEING

You are given warmer clothes that hang loose on your emaciated frame. A thick coat of gray, matted, stinking fur. Wool leggings. Boots a size too large for your feet. Accepting them makes you feel vaguely ill.

Not even in your youth were you ever brought so low as to tolerate hand-me-downs. But to rise again, sometimes we must first fall. So you accede to the garments because they keep out the biting cold.

Instead of the prison cell, you are brought to what was once a lavish guest room. Now it is in tatters like all else in this place. But it has a fireplace crackling with heat, and you stand before it, warming yourself for hours.

Echoes of wailing winds moan their ragged songs. You rub your hands together to keep feeling in them, and don moth-eaten mittens so your fingers do not cramp and fall off from frostbite. At least that's the warning one of the guardians gives.

The waiting game continues. Regardless of your captor's words, you don't cease your attempts to draw blood and conjure. Just a drop is all you need to be free. Every creature with blood flowing warm through their veins can harness its power with the proper education. But you have been cut off from even that.

Now, but not forever.

When Nikora finally returns, days later, you are ready. You rise to face her, belly full and mind sharp. If she sees the resolve darkening your eyes she does not let on.

"Come with me," is all she says. The guards step aside, letting you out of the room that is just another kind of prison.

Only a small part of the building is even moderately livable. The castle was cut into the mountain, so the rough-hewn rock walls have stayed secure. But the man-made parts of the structure have submitted to age and decay. Large sections of roof are missing, in addition to many walls. You cross a courtyard where crumbling spires loom overhead, threatening to fall at any moment. The heavy furs buffer the chill in the air, but you miss the warmth of your desert land.

Finally, after negotiating a set of decaying stairs completely open to the elements on all sides and held up by hope more than any visible architectural buttress, you pass through a shallow cave to reach a top level with no walls at all.

There is no exit from what is essentially a platform hovering in midair except the cavelike hallway you stand in, barred with an ancient iron gate.

A fine layer of snow carpets the stone ground where at least a dozen men sit chained together. They all wear tattered army uniforms, the green of Lagrimar. But they have been given no furs, no boots. Still, they all have their limbs intact. Frost has not bitten their skin away.

You peer more closely to find they are members of the Wailers. You recoil. Their necks are bare.

"You have uncollared them!" Your voice is far more powerful than you intend. Rage explodes inside, bringing a modicum of heat to your skin. "Are you mad?"

Nikora raises a hand. "They are no danger to me. Or you," she adds. "We have ways of subduing them." The Wailers sit side by side, rocking slightly, vacant expressions on their faces.

"What did you do?"

These men belong to you, only *you* may do with them what you wish, and it would be wasteful to allow them to freeze to death here. But not affixing the blood magic collars that prevent them from accessing their Songs is lunacy.

"Collared, they could not heal themselves of the effects of the cold and the hunger," Nikora explains patiently. "These Singers must not be allowed to die, yet we have few resources to waste."

"But without their collars what keeps them here?"

The Wailers had always been a nuisance. The Singers, whose Songs were spared to be used for battle, had to be controlled via complicated blood spells that could be invoked only by their regiment's commandant, the Cantor, or the king.

"They are meek as mice," Nikora says. "Whatever you did to

them leaves them barely able to do more than follow orders. And before your thoughts race too far ahead, these men cannot be used to harm me or any of my people. Gentlemen, lift your sleeves."

As one, the men lift their right sleeves. A small wound of crisscrossing lines has been cut into each of their forearms.

"It won't counteract your blood spell, but it keeps us all safe. In case you had any ideas of manipulating them against me."

You feign ignorance, but disappointment claws at you. "And what do you want me to do?"

Nikora raises a brow. "I want you to give their power to me. Take their Songs and put them into a caldera so that I may use them."

You jerk back at the audacity of her statement. "And why should I do that?"

Her smile is a brittle, delicate thing. "Because if you don't do it voluntarily, I will force you. You are not the only one who understands compulsion blood magic."

You force a chuckle. "Do you think I cannot withstand the pain of a blood spell? Do you think I have not spent hundreds of years inuring myself to that particular weakness—the one thing any of my people could have used against me?"

Her eyes darken. "And you think that pain is all we can conjure?"

Her tone is merciless. The Physicks have spent centuries studying magic and innovating it. You are still using the primitive spells you were taught generations ago. It is very possible—nay, probable—that they have come up with something that you have no defense against.

"I cannot make a single caldera from all of their Songs, not unless I absorb them first."

"Fine then, a dozen calderas." She waves her hand impatiently.

"Why have a dozen weak ones when you can combine them into a single, more powerful Song?"

"Wielded by you?" She raises a brow.

"I have the unique experience to do so."

Nikora scoffs. "You can control these men's Songs with your voice, correct? Their blood spells are already attuned to you. So you control them, and my spell controls you. It's all the same to me."

You stiffen. "So, you plan to carve a blood spell into me so that you can control the blood spell *I* carved into *them*?" You chuckle, derisively. "That's many levels of separation from the original spell. The results might be . . . unpredictable."

Her smug look melts away.

"And since you're familiar with blood magic," you continue, "I don't need to remind you what that sort of dilution of intention can do. Controlling this many with the blood is a delicate proposition. To do it once removed, and with an unwilling intermediary . . ." You spread your hands and shrug. "It took me nearly eighty years and hundreds of men to perfect the method of control. Not all of my generals could do it. But please, be my guest. You will definitely need more than these few. Working out the kinks in your method will kill ninety percent of them before you even begin to master control."

You watch her carefully, taking in the micromovements of her expression. She doesn't give much away, but you are used to watching people for dissent or agreement and see when she begins to understand your words. She's probably been experimenting with your people while you've been imprisoned. Perhaps she began with more men and these are all who are left.

"So what do you suggest?" she says through gritted teeth.

The cold of your cheeks aids in holding back a smile. "An alliance. I need not be your prisoner if I can be your ally."

She narrows her eyes. “Do you think me stupid? I could never trust you. You were far too powerful for too long to be able to ‘ally’ with anyone.”

“But here I am at your mercy. For food, clothing, all the amenities of life, I require you and your people. Not a position I am used to being in, certainly. So I can liberate their Songs for you. Then whatever it is you wanted them to do, I will do—with the benefit of centuries of mastery.”

She tilts her head in thought. “If I allow you the use of blood magic *and* their Songs, you would be back to conquering, and I would not get what I want. No, you must do your part without magic of any kind. Command them to do what we want using the blood spell already in place. Then we will see if you are a worthy ally.”

You grimace internally, disappointed to be limited in such a fashion, but finding her a worthy adversary. There are still ways to turn this to your advantage.

Nikora nods almost imperceptibly at the guard standing just behind you. He grasps you around the waist in a painful hold and Nikora produces a bone-white knife from inside her coat. One of her steely hands grips your wrist and you freeze—her touch burns and you realize you may have underestimated her.

She carves a mark into your forearm and the blazing fire of the knife’s tip makes you wonder if it was dipped in poison. There are ways to use poison in blood magic, but you never bothered to master them. The low, guttural words she speaks are in the language of the blood. A spell of obedience and restriction from causing harm. Not sealed with pain, but with a string of words you do not know. Alarm courses through you.

“There, now we are allies,” Nikora says, releasing you. “You control the Wailers and do what I instruct you, or you will suffer.”

Her tone is perfectly pleasant but her eyes are hard. "Pain is only the beginning of misery. And since you are hardheaded, I suspect that you will quickly discover that. Afterward, we will see."

You grit your teeth as she spins away. Yes, we will see. For nothing, no blood spell, no enemy, no foreign type of magic will stop you from reclaiming what is rightfully yours.

Back in the parlor, a moderately effectual fire roars. You are seated on the chair that creaks under your sleight weight. Nikora lounges on her bench, clad in red as ever, sipping a steaming cup of tea.

Your cup sits on the table next to you, too hot to drink. "What do you want me to command the Wailers to do?" You have always believed curiosity to be a weakness, but right now, knowledge is strength.

"What do you know of the Physicks, Eero?" She seems to know the use of that name irritates you, though you strive not to react.

"None of the emissaries you sent ever deigned to seek an audience with me," you reply tartly. "I found Ydaris when she was little more than a child, and offered her a chance at more than you all ever did. I know you create medallions that can mimic Songs, that your amalgam magic combines Earthsong, Nethersong, and blood magic."

Nikora grins enigmatically and sips her scalding tea. "We are an order both ancient and holy. When our patron, Saint Dahlia, walked the earth, she met many from all over the globe. She was a proponent of health and her followers were the first physicians. But after her passing on, the Physicks were lost. We did not understand why when we worked to banish illness and promote life and health, death had to constantly intervene. And so it was proposed that we stop it." She pauses, expectant.

"Stop what?"

"Death." Her eyes sparkle mischievously. "There is a way to live forever. To become one with the spirits who hover at the edge of dreams. All we are searching for, all we have ever been searching for, can be found via the wisdom of those who have already passed over. The portal we will open to the World After will allow us to commune with the spirits and discover the secrets of eternal life."

You had thought her cunning and wily, but perhaps she is just mad. "Impossible."

"Oh, quite possible. We have gained many insights from individual spirits over the years, enough to know that they can avoid the Eternal Flame and exist indefinitely in the World After. While the Flame still pulls the majority of the dead into it, a few resist. It is difficult, but mastery of the technique will provide an important link in the chain of immortality."

"Did you not try such a thing before with disastrous consequences?"

She looks surprised that you know anything, but your sister insisted on visiting you daily, telling you the news of the day, including what had happened when the Physicks had first attempted to commune with the spirits.

"We learn through trial and error, that is the way of knowledge." Nikora spreads her arms. "The first spirits who answered our call were angry. We are refining the technique, seeking to assert a larger degree of control over them when they arrive."

"And how will the Wailers help with this?" It's all madness, but your curiosity has been piqued.

She motions to one of the tattooed attendants standing by the door. He leaves briefly and returns with another man in tow—this one dressed similarly to Nikora, wearing a billowing red robe. Dark, fathomless black eyes peer at you curiously from a milk-pale face.

"Bring it over here, Cayro," Nikora says, and the newcomer approaches bearing a large wooden box. You scoop up your teacup to avoid it being knocked over as he sets it on the table.

The box is adorned with an image of a waterfall carved into the lid. Cayro steps out of the way as Nikora leans forward to open the box reverently and pull out a glass jar. Inside the jar is a bit of what looks like scorched, shriveled leather.

"This is all that is left of the great power of the Physicks. All that remains of the Great Machine, the source of Dahlia's breath."

"In her name do we work," Cayro intones.

"By her grace do we prosper," Nikora whispers, lifting the jar and pressing her forehead to it, eyes closed. "Saint Dahlia's flesh. A bit of her left behind and holy enough to catalyze the power of the machine."

Revulsion swamps you as you regard the contents of the jar more closely. It is actually the remains of a hand, four grotesquely curved, blackened fingers, mummified in some way.

Nikora opens her eyes, gazing adoringly at the disgusting remains of her goddess. "The Great Machine preserved the flesh, extended its power, focused and amplified it. But we can still perform certain rites with the flesh alone—though each attempt will sacrifice more, and there is little enough left. That is why it is imperative that we succeed quickly."

You shudder at the zealotry evident in her voice. A gaze at Cayro standing stiffly beside her reveals nothing in his expression. Is he as much of a fanatic as she?

"So you want me to control the Wailers and use their Earthsong to tear open another portal into the World After? What about when the angry spirits come through?"

"We do not know that is what will happen."

"You have the evidence of it happening before, do you not?"

She places the jar back in the box and closes it, much to your relief. “In our excitement to test the process, the summoning spell did not contain enough precautions. The next time, we will be better able to control the spirits.”

You have your doubts about that, but do not voice them. “Teach me how to summon them. Perhaps I can help to strengthen the spell.”

Her eyes narrow. “I will teach you your part, the part requiring Earthsong. That is all you need to know.”

“As an ally,” you begin, teeth clenched, “I must have information in order to hold up my end of the bargain.”

“You will know what you need and no more.” Her eyes flash.

The spark inside you rises, longing to lash out, unused to being suppressed for so long. But you lean back. Force yourself to relax. Take a breath, sip some tea.

Playing this her way is against your nature, but you have been patient before. Nothing worth having comes easily.

You shrug. “Very well then.” The words sting coming out, but it is all a means to an end. Breaking the chains she thinks she’s bound you in will be sweet.

CHAPTER THIRTEEN

Our footsteps are a map
for others to follow.
Walk well.

—THE HARMONY OF BEING

Kyara left Ella's home with a vow to return at dawn. The woman had secured space on a Sisterhood transport leaving for the eastern army base the next morning. On the drive back to the cottage, Kyara wondered how she could discourage Darvyn from coming with her. She didn't think it was possible, but didn't want him anywhere near the Cavefolk again. Her options were few.

The cottage was dark when she entered. Good, he was still in town. She located the carpetbag he'd acquired for her when they left the palace. She didn't have many belongings, just a few donated dresses, an extra pair of shoes, a nightgown, some toiletries. Still, it was more than she'd ever really owned in her life.

The last item she packed was a small, wrapped bundle, but she wavered for long minutes before deciding to place it into the bag. The coldness of the stone inside radiated out through the soft fabric to chill her hand. It wasn't exactly something she could leave behind, though its oddness both frightened and enticed her.

The bundle had been left in her bedroom in the palace before she'd left, with no note or instruction, though as soon as she'd approached and felt the Nethersong pulsing within, she'd known it must have come from the Goddess Awoken.

When she'd dared to look inside, she'd found a caldera. Embedded within the red, gemlike stone was a small object, though she couldn't identify what it was. Calderas could be created from anything: a lock of hair, a bit of jewelry, a broken shard of pottery—she'd once witnessed the Cantor create one from a discarded shoe. She'd guessed at the purpose of this one, given the large quantity of Nethersong it held. In all likelihood, this was what the Cavefolk had called the death stone.

The Physicks had been searching for the death stone, wanting to harness its power, and now she had it, but did not know what to do with it. Shaking off the strange feelings it evoked, she buried the bundle under her clothing. The thing was too dangerous to remain here, so she'd keep it with her until she knew more.

Her packing complete, she sat at the rolltop desk situated next to the picture window and pulled out a sheet of paper. She was going to embrace her cowardice and write Darvyn a note to let him know where she'd gone. Certainly he'd be upset when he returned home that evening to find her explanation, but there would be nothing he could do. He could not track her with his Song and even if he did come to the mountain, he couldn't sing inside the caves. When she returned, he would either forgive her or not—she just hoped he would be able to.

Now she just had to figure out what to say.

She'd never been a wordsmith; though she loved to read, she had very little experience writing down her own thoughts. The pencil in her hand shook, causing the letters to waver as she tried to compose words that matched her feelings. She was on her second attempt when the front door opened, taking her by surprise. Darvyn was back far too soon.

Guilt squeezed her chest. She didn't have time to hide the note and so merely turned the page she'd been working on facedown.

"How was the party?" she asked, trying not to appear guilty.

Darvyn looked exhausted. "I don't think the twins enjoyed it very much. They were both absent for large portions of the evening. I had a long chat with Clove and Vanesse, though. They're talking of traveling, heading down to the southern continent for a while, once things settle a bit more. Whenever that is. Sounds nice though." He scrubbed a hand down his face. "I'm surprised you're still up."

He pushed off the door and crossed the room to her. She stood to greet him properly with a hug and kiss. She scented something perfumed and vaguely soapy on his clothes, but underneath, the familiar smell of his skin grounded her. Home. This felt like home, like something she didn't want to leave. But she had committed to this trip and must see it through, for Tana's sake if nothing else.

"There's more, of course." He led her to the couch and relayed what had happened during his two meetings with Queen Jasminda. "The last thing she told me, what she hadn't wanted to say over the telephone . . ." He paused, looking pained, then took a deep breath. "The True Father has escaped."

A vast hollow space opened up within her chest. She blinked, unseeing for a long moment before focusing back on Darvyn. "It really is beginning, then," she finally said.

"What?"

"The war. Murmur said that the living, the dead, and those in between will battle. He saw the vision centuries ago and has been waiting for this day. The dead have returned and our great enemy is somewhere out there. Those two things cannot be unconnected."

"No, I suppose you're right. The True Father must be involved somehow."

The cavity in her chest yawned wider. Bottomless. A great weariness overtook her at the thought of the journey before her. But with the True Father out in the world once again, it was more important than ever that she hone her skills. She hated to admit that Mooriah had been right.

Darvyn squeezed her hand, bringing her back to the present. "We should go to bed," he said. "Let's hope the war does not begin before morning."

Kyara nodded and allowed him to pull her to her feet. He entered the bedroom ahead of her and stopped short. She murmured a curse when she saw what had caught his attention. She'd left the lamp on low and the carpetbag still sat on the bed. Having been so concerned with the note, she'd lost track of time.

He turned slowly and fixed her with a stare full of hurt that melted her insides. "Are you leaving?"

Oh, she was so stupid. What must this look like? "I'm coming back," she rushed to say, moving to him and grabbing his arm. "I—I just—"

"You've decided to go with Mooriah."

She swallowed. "Yes."

His shoulders loosened. "Why didn't you just tell me?" He

looked back toward the desk. "Were you . . . Were you going to leave a *note*?"

Kyara didn't answer; her mouth hung open wordlessly. "I don't like good-byes," she finally whispered.

Darvyn scrubbed a hand down his face again, groaning softly. "What makes you think a good-bye is necessary? We're leaving in the morning, I take it? I'll just make some calls before we go to alert the others that I'll be away. It's too late to do so now."

She tightened her grip on his arm. "You can't come."

His muscles turned to stone.

"Darvyn, we're going inside the mountain. Mooriah is determined for Murmur to train us. You can't sing there; remember what happened last time?"

A vision of Murmur's power pushing Darvyn out of a cliff opening, his fall to the toxic waters of the Poison River below. Carcasses and mummified creatures along its banks telling of its deadliness. Darvyn's labored breathing as he pulled himself to the shore and then stopped breathing altogether. She shivered.

"Mooriah may trust the Cavefolk, but I don't. And I don't want you anywhere near them again." She shook her head and took a step back.

Darvyn's stare was full of dismay. He cupped her cheek in a palm. "When I got you off that table in the Physicks' headquarters, I made a promise to myself that we wouldn't be separated. I couldn't keep it when I was collared while you awaited execution, but I bloody well sure am going to keep it now. When I said that we weren't sleeping apart, I meant it." He released her face and crossed his arms to match her stance, digging his heels in.

Kyara's jaw tightened as he continued. "I know I can't sing in the caves, I understand all of that, but it doesn't matter. If you're going, I'm going, too."

"But what about your work here? The refugees, the queen's plan for unification? You can't just up and leave with no notice."

"Who says I can't? I'm not a Keeper anymore, I choose what I do now. There are others who can help."

"I just mean . . ." She took a breath. "It's dangerous, and I can't have anything happening to you." Her breathing was getting more difficult, she stuttered and almost choked on the words. "I can't risk you."

He pulled her to him, touching their foreheads. "I feel the same way. Which is why I can't let you go off to train with strangers you distrust by yourself."

"But you'll be powerless there."

"Are you saying you don't *want* me to come?"

Her jaw trembled; she tried to breathe deeply. The thought of being without him for so long was terrifying, but she'd lived a whole life before she met him. If she told him she didn't want him, maybe he would listen and back off. But she couldn't give voice to the lie.

"I didn't think so," he said.

"It doesn't matter what I want, I won't *let* you come."

He tilted his head back and grinned, reminding her of the first time she'd seen him in a small, darkened pub a world away. She'd felt it even then, this pull. It hadn't gotten any weaker.

"You'll disable me? Knock me out and sever my connection to my Song?"

She pressed her lips together. He knew very well she'd never do that again.

"I know how to go east." His voice was gentle. "I remember where the crystal city was, at the edge of Serpent's Gorge. If you try to leave me here, I'll go back there. Wander through the caves until I find you. You can't leave me behind so easily."

"You don't understand," she began.

"No, I think I do. I understand very well. I lost you twice." His dark eyes flashed, all mirth gone from them. "I won't do it again. It would be different if you truly didn't want me there, but barring that, you're going to have a hard time getting rid of me, Kyara."

The pendant around his neck glinted in the low lamplight. He'd had it soldered back together, the two halves of the Master of Jackals sigil that had brought them together. Responsible and courageous, the Jackal was. Just like Darvyn.

He leaned toward her, capturing her lips. Relief bled through her worry for him. He was the Shadowfox, but stripped of his Song in the caves, he was just a man. And she would have to ensure his safety. No matter what the Cavefolk or anyone else tried to do, she couldn't allow him to come to harm.

Not when he was all she had.

They rose in the predawn hours and got ready silently. Kyara packed food for the journey, while Darvyn made his telephone calls, organizing things during his absence. Soon enough Erryl arrived and drove them back to the city. He dropped them off once again at Ella's townhome.

Little Ulani's face when she met the Shadowfox was priceless. Her joy cut through the pall of gloom and worry for her sister, and for that, Kyara was glad.

"You decided to let her come?" Kyara asked Ella, as Ulani fawned all over Darvyn.

"She told me she had a dream that she needed to be there when we find Tana." Ella shook her head. "If it was any other child I'd think she was making things up to get her way, but Ulani doesn't lie. She often knows or senses things that I can't explain. I'm not sure if it's because of her Song or something else, but I told her she could come. Honestly, I don't want either of them out of my sight."

Kyara pursed her lips. "She won't be able to sing in the caves, but I will watch out for her, too." Ella gave a grateful smile. Kyara wasn't certain of the wisdom of allowing a small child to join them, but it wasn't her call. Darvyn would help protect them until they crossed into the mountain, then it would be on Kyara's shoulders.

Erryl drove them all to the Eastern temple before bidding his farewell, and the small group boarded a Sisterhood transport headed east. Ella had arranged passage through connections of hers within the organization. She seemed to be quite a resourceful woman.

As the kilometers went by, even though apprehension tied Kyara's stomach in knots, the view of the countryside kept her calm. She'd never seen this much of Elsira, having only glimpsed a tiny bit from overhead in the airship ride from Yaly. Since then, she'd been either in the capital or the seaside cottage, but the beauty of the land took her breath away.

She could almost understand why the people here were so afraid of their country being taken over by outsiders and why they kept such a tight hold on it—every bucolic meter of rolling hills and farmland was precious, even as the scenery before her crisped and languished, preparing for winter.

They rode in a small bus with seating for twelve, with the remaining seats occupied by Sisters. The women chatted to themselves, occasionally looking curiously at the motley group of foreigners sharing the ride. But no one was hostile.

Eventually, Ella began a friendly conversation with a couple of the Sisters, which lasted much of the rest of the trip. She hid the strain of not knowing exactly where her daughter was fairly well, though Kyara could see it was taking a toll.

Their final stop was an army base in the shadow of the looming mountains, where a dozen soldiers observed them stoically. Kyara disembarked from the vehicle with some trepidation, but a young man approached Ella and greeted her warmly. They began a rapid-fire conversation.

Darvyn leaned to speak in her ear. "Ella's husband was a soldier here and has secured us a ride to the foothills along with additional supplies."

"Her husband is friends with the king, right?"

"Yes. Benn is with Jack now visiting another country's leader."

"Then she must have many worries," Kyara said, her heart aching. Husband out of the country, daughter nabbed and taken away—Kyara's respect for the woman doubled.

Along with the soldiers marching about, intent on their tasks, refugees were still straggling into Elsira from Lagrimar. And surprisingly, though it really shouldn't be so, a steady trickle of travelers were heading in the opposite direction. No doubt these Lagrimari had grown weary and disillusioned with Elsira and were now willing to face whatever remained in their own land. Likely there would be warlords or strongmen who'd risen in the wake of the True Father's departure.

Kyara wished them luck. She had no desire to go back. Then again, she didn't have a true desire to do much of anything. She turned at the sound of her name being spoken by the soldier talking to Ella. He passed the woman an envelope, and she frowned, looking down at it. The writing on the envelope was a childlike scrawl, written in Elsiran.

Ella's voice was uncertain; Darvyn translated. "It's for you. She thinks it's Tana's handwriting."

"For me?"

He nodded and passed the envelope over to her. She ripped it open to find it empty except for a small, black stone humming with a hint of Nethersong.

"Mooriah made a caldera," Kyara said, voice biting.

"A message?"

"A way to find them." Certainty filled her as her jaw clenched. Mooriah knew Kyara would come for the girl.

She sighed deeply. "I need a knife."

CHAPTER FOURTEEN

To witness joy without jealousy,
celebrate without resentment,
applaud without lament,
is to harmonize in tune with the ultimate
accord.

—THE HARMONY OF BEING

Zeli's steps grew slower as she reached the entrance to the Blue Library. Two soldiers walked by, locked in conversation. She stopped suddenly, then turned to stare at the tapestry on the wall, pretending an intense interest in it. When the men's footsteps receded, she released the breath she had been holding.

The fear was stupid, she knew. She was often sent on errands taking her all around the palace, and sometimes around the city. No one would look twice at her coming to the library. But the weight of what she was doing, added to the secrets she was already keeping, was immense.

When she entered the room, Varten was already there, bouncing on his toes with anticipation. For the past three days, they had been meeting together—usually in that old, dusty parlor in the unused section of the palace. The night of the birthday party, when Varten had stolen the journal from her and begun reading it, the revelations he discovered set both of them on this uncertain path.

"Do you think this is what the Goddess was concerned about?" Varten had asked that night as they reeled from shock.

Zeli's body had jerked at the thought. "I hope not. Why would She be? Restoring our Songs would be wonderful. It would change everything. Go on, keep reading."

He flipped the ancient pages carefully. "This is all about experiments, I think. The author has theorized about restoring Songs, and spends a long time trying to get it to work."

As his finger traced the text, Zeli watched him, her mind too busy to focus on the words on the page. In concentration, he looked different. Serious, almost scholarly as he frowned down at the antiquated language. Still not like a prince—though she had no idea what a prince should look like. Once upon a time she'd thought she'd known, but *that* prince had turned out to be a monster.

"There's mention of the cornerstone of the Mantle—and of obelisks." He looked up. "Kyara told us of an obelisk she encountered in a strange city in the desert. The buildings were all built by ancient Earthsingers out of sand and glass."

Zeli tilted her head, intrigued.

"Apparently, these obelisks focus Earthsong and can also help to combine it with blood magic." He read on silently, and Zeli grew impatient.

"What? What does it say?"

"More formulas. Equations." He flipped another page. "He talks about meeting an emissary from the south. Another Earthsinger. Here, listen to this: 'The young man, Gilmer he calls himself, has the strength of a Second. This land has not seen a Singer so strong since the days of my grandparents. Already, he has taught me much, helping to refine certain techniques that the Cantors struggled with. He says mere curiosity has brought him here, but I am not so certain. I hope he can aid my quest and help me find a way to correct the mistakes of my past.'"

Varten lifted his head and they shared a look of wonder. "There's a lot more here. It will take some time to get through it all. I don't think all of it is written in order, either, which is . . . kind of odd."

"If the writer really found a way to restore lost Songs, why haven't we heard of it before? He was doing experiments, but must have failed." False hope was worse than no hope at all, and she couldn't bear this kind of disappointment.

"Maybe." Varten tapped his chin. "But he seemed confident that he was on to something. This guy was really smart, obviously, and he spent a lot of time on this, from all appearances. If we can figure some of this out, wouldn't that make all the difference in the world for the Lagrimari?"

Zeli was dubious. "Whoever he was, he had his Song and was way smarter than us. And the Goddess said whatever was in here was best left unread. She—"

"Didn't even read it. Are you sure She knew what was in it? What if you went back to Her and told Her—"

"Told Her what, that I disobeyed Her and read the journal when She told me to take it straight to the vault?" She shook her head. Visions of being sent back to a refugee camp, standing in line for rations filled her head. Varten pursed his lips and sat back.

"You're right though," Zeli said. "Her reaction to the journal was really strange. Sometimes . . . I'm not sure about Her sometimes," she whispered, hunching down, ashamed to have even said that much. Worries about the True Father on the loose had never left her—the promise she'd made to keep his escape quiet haunted her. And now, hiding the wraith attack from everyone—none of it felt right.

"If there's a chance to restore the Songs of the Lagrimari, isn't it worth just about anything, even the Goddess's wrath? More Earthsingers could give us a fighting chance against the wraiths at the very least. It would give the Lagrimari options."

He was right. Zeli knew he was, but fear still raced through her veins. "We have no idea of how to do it."

"I think we need to go through this journal with a fine-toothed comb. Study it and everything it references. Find out about this Gilmer from the south—that must be Fremia or Yaly. I didn't even know there were Earthsingers there. Then again, I didn't always pay attention to all my history lessons." He looked a bit abashed.

"This is crazy. I don't think we can do this on our own." But if she got on the Goddess's bad side, she could very well lose her position in the Sisterhood and kiss her future good-bye.

"What if we find something in here we can take to the Goddess or my sister? Something real that could help?"

Zeli took a deep breath. "All right. We'll read this very carefully and see what we can find out."

"The Singer from the south, what was his name again?" Varten asked, looking up from the large book he'd been reading. More like it were spread all over the library table before them. Zeli squinted in thought and tapped her lips. He fought to wrench his attention away from her mouth and not be distracted by her skin and her scent and her presence beside him. What they were doing was serious and he needed to focus.

"Gilmer," she replied. "He's the traveler who came and shared knowledge with the journal's author. And then disappeared again."

"And this would have been after the erection of the Mantle, right?"

"Yes, I think so. The author talks about how he wishes the others were still around to help, so I think it means that he was the only Singer left in Elsira after the Mantle went up and trapped everyone else in Lagrimar."

"What do you think happened to him?" Varten asked. "I wonder why nothing of him remained?"

"You mean stories or legends? Maybe more of him persisted than we know," Zeli said. "Have you found anything about a Singer named Gilmer anywhere in all of these? Or any other Singers at all?"

"No." He shut the large, musty history text he'd been scanning. It probably hadn't been opened in decades. "It's like once the Mantle went up, magic disappeared from Elsira until the First Breach. There's nothing in any of these books about Earthsong."

Since most Elsiran writing wasn't in the peculiar script of the journal that could be understood by readers of both languages, Varten would read from the Elsiran texts and Zeli would take notes. Visions of teaching Zeli to read Elsiran swept Varten's mind. It would give them a reason to keep meeting after all of this was over.

She pushed her notebook away to lean her forearms on the polished wooden table. "We might have to start—" But whatever she was going to say was swallowed up when the door crashed open.

Varten jerked around to the entrance, then relaxed to find it was just Roshon. "Fancy meeting you here," his brother said dryly.

"Told you I was helping Zeli with her Elsiran."

"Welcome, please be seated," she said in formal Elsiran, playing along. It wasn't a lie, they had been working on her language skills while they studied the journal.

Roshon looked around skeptically at the towering shelves stuffed with books. This place was Jasminda's fantasy, but it wasn't filled with the type of reading material that either of the twins preferred: comics or detective novels.

"Oh, you found him," Ani said from the doorway. She entered and stood next to Roshon.

Varten froze at her appearance. He blinked rapidly then produced a smile. "I wasn't hiding."

"Weren't you?" Roshon asked, sharp eyes focusing on him intently.

Had he been avoiding his brother? A thread of guilt wormed through him. The thing was, he really liked Ani. He didn't have any problem with her being his new sister. In fact, he was the one who had pushed Roshon to challenge for her and issue the Raunian version of a proposal in the first place. She'd been in a bad situation, about to become the apprentice and future fiancée of a truly vile man, and Roshon had been her way out. And though the two hadn't seen or spoken to one another in two and a half years, as soon as her ship had docked in Rosira, and they'd gotten through some initial missteps, she and Roshon had become closer than ever. Inseparable.

Varten was just preparing himself for the inevitable by pulling away. He was surprised Roshon had even noticed.

Ani paced around the room, peering at the shelves and the books scattered on the tables. She wasn't wearing her prosthetic today, but apparently didn't need it, using her maimed arm adeptly, pushing books out of the way to get a look at what was beneath.

"So, I wanted to tell you," Roshon said, "we'll be leaving on Firstday."

Two days away. Varten swallowed. "Oh, okay."

"We're going to postpone the wedding for a while, you know, to avoid a war." Roshon spoke in Elsiran, probably for Ani's benefit as, of the many languages she spoke, it was the only one they shared. Varten turned to Zeli, hoping she was keeping up. She nodded at him encouragingly.

"Makes sense," he said.

Ani had made a small circle around their table. She was the kind of person who couldn't sit still for any length of time—the opposite of Roshon, but maybe that was why they liked each other.

"Hi, I'm Ani," she said to Zeli.

"Oh, right, you guys haven't met. Zeli, Ani."

Zeli smiled and stuck out her hand for a Yalyish-style handshake. "Pleasant to meet you." Ani chuckled and they shook hands. Zeli didn't display any visible reaction to Ani's missing limb.

"How do they greet each other in Raun?" Varten asked.

"We don't. Unless it's someone who owes you money, and then it's usually with a blade." She grinned, the tattoos on her forehead and chin stretching slightly. Then she continued on her circuit, moving off to the other side of the room, casually inspecting the wall art and the morning's newspapers stacked neatly on a table.

"We, ah, wanted to know," Roshon began. "That is, the offer's still open. For you to come with us."

Zeli turned to him and whispered, "You're leaving on Firstday?" Panic flared in her gaze.

"No, I . . ." he said, flustered. Zeli reined in the terror in her expression, dropping her head to stare at the floor. Varten cleared his throat. "Thanks, but I think I'll stick it out here. I'm not sure a life on the sea is for me." He spoke to his brother, while watching Zeli's reaction from the corner of his eye. She didn't lift her head, which had him worried.

"Are you certain?" Ani called out from across the room. "We were going to catch the Festival of Frogs in Dunbay on our way south. You haven't really lived until you've seen a trained racing frog wearing a tiny diesel flyer shoot through the air above your head. It's hysterical."

Varten and Roshon shared a look of incredulity.

"One year, Father and I bought an army of frogs from Sirunan to enter," she continued. "The best ones are raised and trained in Gilmeria, but we didn't want to spend that much. Anyway, our team made it past the first round, solidly in the middle of the pack. We would have made it farther, only Father lost a bet and all our diesel went to a very lucky Udlander." She crossed back over and settled next to Roshon, leaning against a table. "I've always thought I'd make a good frog racer, if I wasn't sailing, you know?"

"So, wait, you're saying the frogs—" Varten began, but Zeli straightened abruptly and cut in.

"Did you say Gilmeria?"

A loose thread in the carpet had snagged Ani's attention. She nudged it with the toe of her boot. "Yeah. One of the commonwealths of Yaly."

Zeli turned to Varten with a wide-eyed expression. "Would that have anything to do with someone named Gilmer?"

"Saint Gilmer is the hunter, I think. The commonwealths are all named after their saints. But there's a lot of them and it's confusing. You know the Gilmerian Rumpus starts next week, too. I wish we had time to get up there and check it out." Ani tapped her chin. "I wonder if we can sneak it in, just for a day . . ."

Zeli had turned ashen; Varten reached over to touch her arm and ensure she was all right. She didn't draw breath for a few seconds.

"What's the Gilmerian Rumpus?" Varten asked, as casually as he could manage. Fortunately, Roshon was watching Ani and not either of their reactions.

"Basically the biggest party on the continent. Only happens once every ten years. People come from around the world to honor Saint Gilmer with three days of feasting and hunting and dancing and general madness. And it's the only time anyone can access the Gilmerian Archives, which are supposed to hold all the saint's knowledge. You know, we once had a passenger, a scholar from Fremia, whose grandfather had won access to the Archives during a Rumpus. The old guy had found something in there that led to him inventing the first salt engine. I didn't believe him at first, but Tai looked it up and it was true."

"That's . . . amazing," Varten said, still gripping Zeli's arm. He thought she might faint.

"Well, salt engines were notoriously inefficient compared to solar or even diesel"—she shuddered—"but the tech was a big leap forward for its time."

Zeli leaned into him, and for a moment, Varten was distracted by the warmth and closeness. Then he heard her whisper that Ani was talking too fast, and he translated for her.

She sat back, pulling away from their contact. "So . . . the saints. They are real?"

Ani shrugged. "Doesn't everyone believe their gods are real? I don't know if Myr ever walked the seas like the legends claim, but there must be some truth to the myths. Look at the Goddess. A few months ago, who could have predicted She'd be real enough to touch?"

"And this Rumpus starts next week?" Varten asked.

Ani jogged over to the table with the newspapers and riffled through them until she found the one she was looking for. "Yeah, just saw it here. A group of Yalyish musicians, expats living here, are headed over to play at the celebration. This article says they're raising money in Portside for the trip down." She came over and tossed the paper on the table in front of them. Varten scanned the brief article.

Ani leaned next to him, tapping her fingers against the end of her abbreviated arm. "The partying is supposed to be legendary. I'd hate to wait another ten years to see it, but I just don't think my seller will stick around." She returned to Roshon's side and lay her head on his shoulder, frowning in annoyance at the circumstance.

"It's okay," Roshon said. "The frog thing sounds . . . interesting."

She elbowed him, good-naturedly. "Until you've been hit in the face with a flying frog, you can't judge." He held up his hands in surrender.

Zeli stared at the newspaper, though she couldn't read it. With great effort, Varten pulled his attention away. He didn't want his brother to suspect that he and Zeli were doing anything other than studying the language, both for his and Ani's safety and another reason that Varten couldn't share. Roshon had a new life at his fingertips, a plan for his future. The only things Varten had for himself were the journal and the hope that he and Zeli could restore the lost Songs of the Lagrimari. It wasn't a life plan, but it was something no one else in his family could lay hold on, at least for now, and he wanted to keep it that way.

"Is no one else hungry?" Ani announced just as her stomach growled.

Roshon snorted. "That reminds me, we'll need to stock something other than jerky and dried seaweed on the ship."

"Picky, picky," she muttered.

"Lunch sounds good to me," Varten offered, nudging Zeli. "Let's go see what they have ready in the kitchen." She looked up and nodded quickly, then rose. He knew that she just wanted to learn as much as she could about Saint Gilmer and the Rumpus, but it would have to wait until they were alone again.

CHAPTER FIFTEEN

The passing days turn tart to sweet.
But pluck too soon for
bitter tastes.
Leave it too long, the fruit will burst
there on the vine.
Keep the right time.

—THE HARMONY OF BEING

Jasminda pressed her fingers to her temples. She should be able to heal her own headache, but as of yet she had not been able to, not with this one. The voices rising in the auditorium only made it worse. Some part of her wanted to silence them. She could use Earthsong to do that, couldn't she? Perhaps utilize Darvyn's trick of solidifying the air around her to block out all sound?

She opened her eyes a fraction, hoping the harsh overhead

lighting didn't spear her brain. Gripping Earthsong to her like a lifeline, she tried again to ease the pounding in her skull—to no avail. Perhaps her ailment had some other source, maybe it was all in her mind.

Voices dripping with bitterness rose, buoyed by strong emotion. Their elegant Elsiran speech grated against her skin. What was this force that had entered her body, making the language sound like arrows nocked and ready to be unleashed on an unsuspecting target?

She opened her eyes fully, ignoring the pain, to survey the packed assembly hall. Three-fourths of those attending the community meeting were Elsiran, many of them well-to-do in starched shirts or fashionable, expensive dresses. Though the rougher clothes and careworn faces of working folk were liberally interspersed.

The Lagrimari refugees sat on one side, separate from the rest. It made sense for them to be close together for the sake of the translator, but she still hated to see it.

Jasminda shifted her attention to the stooped and bent old man standing in the aisle. A glittering gold watch chain glinted in the light against his patterned vest. He clutched a gold-tipped cane in his hands. The man droned on and on, but she attempted to tune back in. Fortunately, one of the city aldermen, serving as moderator for this meeting, interrupted. "Master Banios, you have had your say, sir. We have heard your complaints, now it is time to allow someone else a chance to speak."

"But you are not listening, and *she* is not listening." A gnarled finger pointed in Jasminda's direction. She coolly raised a brow. "This infernal curfew is making me lose hundreds of pieces a day. My boys can't make their nighttime deliveries and our business is suffering. Not to mention the hit being taken by the pubs I own. Times are lean enough and it just isn't right to punish us all."

"Thank you. I think there's time for another comment?" The alderman turned to Jasminda, who nodded for him to continue. She would stay for another citizen's tongue lashing. She'd only come to this community meeting because it was something that Jack would do. Hearing from the people was exhausting and she wasn't convinced it was productive. She'd hoped that the discussion would center more on the unification and referendum, but it was the curfew that had people up in arms.

The Lagrimari who had spoken up hadn't been bothered by the inconveniences associated with the new restrictions. They at least understood the purpose—to protect the lives of everyone, Elsiran and Lagrimari alike. She held herself back from rubbing her temples again. Seated as she was on the stage of the auditorium in the assembly hall, she did not want to be perceived as weak or in pain. When the next speaker began, a sliver of dread snaked down her spine. She recognized that voice.

"Your Majesty and honored guests. My name is Marvus Zinadeel, and I am the owner of several businesses in Rosira and throughout Elsira."

Her jaw clenched and she focused her bleary eyes on him. Her grandfather was haughtiness personified. His full head of hair was white at the temples, but still reddish-blond everywhere else. His lean form was rod straight, as if he'd never bent an inch in his life. Standing next to him was a woman who must be her grandmother; Jasminda had never laid eyes on her before. Her oval face and prominent chin favored Aunt Vanesse. Silver streaked her auburn hair. Jasminda saw little of her own mother in the woman's face and was grateful for it.

After the coronation and wedding, Marvus Zinadeel had made many attempts to contact her, but she'd denied every one. She would never forget their one meeting—before she'd become queen—and the coldness with which he'd treated her. The utter disregard from both of her mother's parents during the lonely years she'd spent writing for help after the disappearance of her father and brothers.

There was a standing order to not allow them on the palace grounds but they could not, of course, be kept from a public assembly. Her grandfather eyed her with barely leashed contempt and sketched a shallow bow.

"We are in a time of civil unrest and economic downturn," Zinadeel said. "We cannot afford the cost of this curfew. After only a few days it is becoming untenable."

Unwilling to hear any more, Jasminda stood suddenly. The alderman stumbled, though he'd been standing still and she was a good ten paces away from him. As she approached his podium on the stage, he stepped to the side, flustered.

"Master Zinadeel, have there been any attacks in the days since the curfew was enacted?"

Her grandfather pursed his lips. "No, Your Majesty." Though he said it with as little reverence as possible, it still cheered her to hear the words pass from his lips.

"Well then. The cost is minor compared with the human lives that have been saved. Lives on both sides of this conflict. I think that is proof enough of its efficacy. Surely you can spare a few coins for human lives?" She barely avoided adding the word "grandfather" to that. He'd had no desire to claim her, and she would not deign to claim him in public, either. The gossip column writers would have plenty of fodder today.

His nose flared and his eyes widened. "The cost is high, maybe not in human life, but what good is life without thriving? That is what you are asking the people to do, Your Majesty. Cease their thriving."

"Who exactly has been thriving in this land? You, certainly, but who else? The rich and powerful have been doing quite well and a few days or weeks of curfew is unlikely to change that. There are thousands upon thousands of our citizens unable to afford even the goods you carry in your stores. Their lives have value. Do you care so little for them?"

Anger burned hot within her, feeling like a firestorm waiting for an outlet. The pain in her head was completely consumed by the rage in her heart. Her grandfather appeared taken aback by the venom in her voice.

Yes, the curfew had unintended consequences, she recognized that, but she also knew that no one else had died senselessly in the days since it was enacted. And it was only a temporary means to an end. The first step in the plan to unify these people and make them one harmonious country.

She pulled her attention away from her grandfather to survey the gathered audience. Putting her shoulders back, she adopted her most queenly voice. "The curfew stays for as long as the city government deems it necessary. I suggest all of you adversely affected make the necessary adjustments to your schedule. Our focus should remain on the survival—and thriving—of *all* within our land." She eyed her grandfather icily and he stared back, indignation in bold relief in his features.

She left the stage and waited in the back as her Guardsmen gathered. They led her through a side exit of the assembly hall and onto the street. A small crowd had gathered there along with some members of the press. Flashbulbs popped and cries rang out, people calling her name and shouting questions.

"Your Majesty! Hazelle Harimel, *Rosira Daily Witness*," a high-pitched voice called out. She paused and turned. This was the reporter Nadette had planned to contact. The woman's wide-set face and snub nose lent her a youthful appearance that was belied by a head of graying curls. Something in the glint of her eye put Jasminda in mind of a battle-ax, unyielding and splintery.

"Do you believe the curfew will help or harm the unification you seek, Your Majesty?" Her voice held an unpleasant tone, obsequious on the surface, but unkind.

"How would it harm unification, Mistress Harimel?"

"Without the refugee presence, the curfew wouldn't be necessary. People are losing money, livelihoods are at stake—how long do you think it will take for Elsirans to connect those dots?"

Jasminda's eyes widened. "That's absurd. The only person connecting those dots is you. Both peoples have had casualties due to the violence."

"Violence that would not have occurred had the refugees not been pouring into our land."

"Violence that the curfew is aimed at addressing," she said through clenched teeth. Then she nodded regally and motioned for her guards to continue moving.

She waved at those gathered as she approached the town car that would bring her back to the palace, but she was not in the mood to talk to any more reporters. Obviously Nadette's plan to win the woman over was not working.

"Your Majesty! A word, if you please?" A strident voice cut through the clamor and a hush descended on the crowd. Jasminda turned to find her grandfather standing amidst those exiting the hall, a solid post with a sea of people parting around him.

Cameras swiveled in his direction as the reporters recognized him. Murmurs reached her ears, whispers of "Zinadeel" and "alderman." Her grandfather had recently announced his intention to run for an open seat on the city's ruling body. He was highly favored to win his race in the spring. If the queen snubbed a candidate for public office, it would likely be a top news story. Especially since it was not exactly a secret that he was her grandfather. She had never publicly mentioned their estrangement and while she knew it was an occasional topic of the gossip columns, she was loathe for it to become front-page news. To snub him now with all these witnesses would make that a certainty. So as much as she did not want to speak with him, she resigned herself to the situation.

Her grandmother peeked around from behind her husband, whose larger form effectively hid her. Jasminda turned to a member of her Guard. "Please let Master and Mistress Zinadeel through. We'll talk in the car."

Jasminda did not generally use the longer limousines when she was alone, but today she wished there was more space between them as her grandparents piled into the vehicle on the bench across from her. Once they were situated and the doors closed, she fixed them with an icy glare. "You had something else you wished to say?"

Her grandmother stared openly. She was still quite beautiful, but Jasminda would never forgive her not only for what she'd done to her mother—cutting her off without a thought—but to Aunt Vanesse, who bore the burn scars this woman had inflicted upon her.

And her grandfather had tried to take everything from her: her name, her parentage, her home. There was nothing these people could do to get back into favor with her. They should be ashamed to even step foot inside this car.

"Your Majesty," Zinadeel started, somewhat mockingly. "We were dismayed to be denied entry to our grandsons' birthday celebration." He paused, apparently expecting some type of answer.

"I see. Was there anything else you wished to share?"

He looked aggrieved. His wife appeared crestfallen, but if the woman thought she was getting anywhere near the twins, especially after what she'd done to both of her own daughters . . . Jasminda fought to wrangle her temper under control and continue to appear regal.

Zinadeel cleared his throat. "I wanted to reiterate to you the negative effects of the curfew on your family's business interests. I'm hoping you will intercede with the aldermen."

"My family?" She chuckled. "My family has no business interests. My father volunteers with the Sisterhood to aid the refugees. My brothers have taken no trade. My aunt is a Sister. My husband is king, as I'm sure you're aware. That is all the family I have."

She clasped her hands in front of her as he regarded her. "Didn't you have paperwork to that effect drawn up?"

A tremor crossed his face, but otherwise he made no visible reaction. His voice was low. "Your brothers are my only heirs. And likely all there will ever be. They will inherit all that I have built. It is in *their* interests that I bring you my concerns."

Her grandmother looked back and forth between them, practically vibrating with nerves. Jasminda breathed deeply, even as steam flowed through her veins. Her brothers would inherit. Her brothers who could meld seamlessly into Elsiran society with their red hair and amber eyes. She loved her brothers dearly and wanted nothing but the best for them, but that did not stop the rage from building.

"I see." She was determined to let nothing show, just as he was doing. The idea that they shared any blood was abhorrent to her, but she would not crack. "Well, your message has been received. Loud and clear. Now if you'll excuse me, I must get back to the palace."

She knocked on the glass to alert the Guardsman standing there. He turned to open the door.

"Jasminda!" her grandmother called out.

She held a finger up to stop the Guardsman. "Only my family and friends may call me that. To you, I am *Your Majesty.*"

"We just want to see our grandchildren." Tears filled her eyes; her voice was pleading.

Jasminda's skin hummed with barely contained fury. "And here is one before you. Do you see me? I think you do and that is the problem, for I don't look the way you want me to." She smiled coldly. "I will not subject my brothers to you. And if you try to contact them, you will feel every bit of the wrath and pain that my mother felt, every bit that I felt all those years when you could have helped and didn't. The fact that you dare to come to me and talk of inheritance." She scoffed. "Leave your wealth to the Sisterhood if you want, my brothers will be well taken care of. None of us want or need anything from either of you. You will *never* be our family."

She nodded to the Guardsman, who opened the door. She would not meet the gazes of her grandparents, regardless of who else was watching. After a long moment, they exited the vehicle, leaving behind the scent of expensive cologne and disappointment.

The trip back to the palace seemed longer than usual. Jasminda worked on restoring her equilibrium, dousing her anger, and getting her breathing under control. The old pain from years alone, surviving as best she could, stroked the edges of her awareness. But she could not give in.

Back at the palace, she exited the town car to find Camm waiting for her.

"Whatever it is, can it wait?"

"It's good news. I think it will cheer you." He searched her face, no doubt noting the strain evident. She straightened and nodded for him to continue as they entered the palace.

"Zann Biddel has been arrested."

Jasminda stopped in the vestibule and spun to face him. Camm nodded, smiling slightly. "He was caught crossing the street in the middle of the block, outside of the crosswalk."

"Jaywalking? Really?"

"Yes. A bicyclist nearly ran into him. It was extremely dangerous and very illegal." His eyes danced.

She sucked in a breath, solemn, though joy began to seep through. Bless Captain Floreen for his attention to legalities. "Well, we certainly can't have a dangerous jaywalker who may cause all manner of traffic imbroglios out on the streets."

"Yes, Your Majesty. As I understand it, the paperwork is very involved and could take some time to complete. Floreen has assured me he has a constable with incredible attention to detail handling the forms. They could take days before being sent to the judge." Where the man would no doubt be released for such a small crime.

"I do appreciate someone who takes extreme care with their responsibilities." Aware that they were blocking the entry, she began walking again. "I want you to know that all I am after is justice. I just want the attacks to stop."

"I understand, Your Majesty." The disapproval he'd felt earlier had lessened, but she could still sense his worry.

"And you will tell me if you ever think I'm losing sight of it?"

His expression froze with obvious indecision.

"Please feel free to tell me. With Jack gone . . ." She took a deep breath. "It's good to have pushback. To be challenged. Jack isn't here, neither is Darvyn. Speak up if you think you must. I do not pretend to be infallible. I'm doing my best, just as we all are. And I feel . . ." She wasn't able to put into words the mix of anger, fear, bitterness, and overwhelm she was experiencing. "A good leader has those around her who tell her the truth. We will all be better for it."

"Yes, Your Majesty," he said, smiling faintly. "I will consider myself free to do so."

She nodded once. "And Camm? Thank you. I did need some good news today."

CHAPTER SIXTEEN

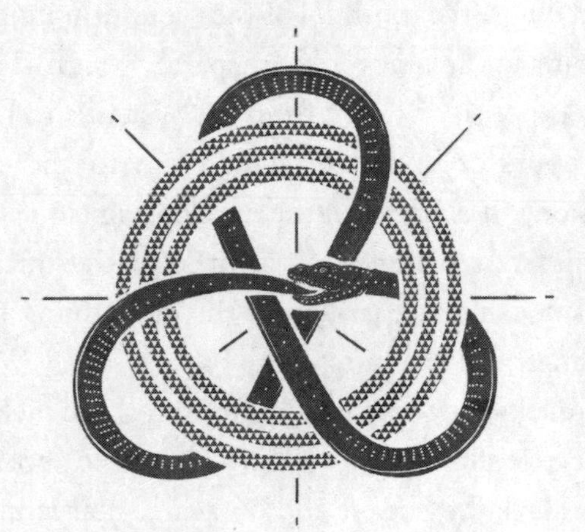

Follow the stars or your art or your heart,
find answers that speak to your inner spark
and let them lead the way.

—THE HARMONY OF BEING

The caldera Mooriah had left for Kyara was a map—of sorts. When she applied a drop of her blood to the tiny, black stone, she was thrust into a vision. A journey unfolded in her mind like a memory. It was as if she had walked the trails before: a narrow, rocky path leading to an opening in the mountain. And then through the twisting tunnels, deeper and deeper inside until they ended at the cave city.

When Kyara came back to herself, Ella had marveled at the magic of it, but didn't appear surprised. Apparently, she knew a thing or two about blood magic. The group piled into an army vehicle driven by the young soldier who'd first greeted them. Kyara directed them north and as far east as they could go, until the dirt road petered out in the foothills of the mountain range. They were dropped off in an area covered in sparse, tough shrubbery. The landscape was not so different from the foothills in Lagrimar.

Several hours of hiking brought them to the cave entrance from her vision, an opening in the unrelenting stone that had been cut into a perfect rectangle. What little of the interior that was visible was smooth and sparkled in the day's dying light. Beyond was an impenetrable blackness.

The knapsacks they'd picked up from the base included battery-powered electric flashlights, which entranced both Kyara and Ulani. They clicked them off and on again, marveling at the convenience and easy operation. Darvyn finally plucked hers out of her hands, shaking his head and smiling.

They entered the mountain, their steps echoing on the smooth, but uneven, cave floor. When she'd last been here, she'd heard the Cavefolk calling her—low whispers inside her head had led her to them. This time, as she adjusted to the atmosphere and smell of the tunnels they walked through, the whispers were silent. But anticipation hung in the air. Murmur and the others knew she was coming, she could practically feel them waiting for her.

Long hours later, Kyara's legs were sore and her emotions on edge. Ella seemed to be having the hardest time with all the walking, but to her credit she didn't complain. Kyara wished that someone could heal the woman's blisters, visible during breaks when she'd take her shoes off to rub her feet. Ulani tutted and fretted over her mother in the most adorable way, but could do nothing to help.

The map's vision was a constant in Kyara's mind, guiding them through the maze of tunnels. Sometimes they would hear the trickle of running water, sometime the flutter and patter of some kind of animal. But on and on they walked into the heart of the mountain.

Finally, the darkness surrounding them steadily lightened until it was bright enough that they turned off the flashlights. Before them a doorway opened onto an upper ledge that looked out onto the city of the Cavefolk. The enormous cave had to be the size of the glass castle of Sayya. Walkways of stone crisscrossed the open space, with staircases rising and falling at intervals along the way.

She stepped through and up to the ledge, taking in the vast, wondrous space again. How had it been constructed? How many people used to occupy this place, and what was life like when it was a full and bustling city?

Darvyn, who had been bringing up the rear of the party, made a sound of alarm. Kyara spun around to find him still in the entryway, having not crossed the stone threshold onto the ledge the rest of them stood upon. When he tried to move forward, an invisible barrier held him back—one much like the Mantle that had once separated the two countries. He could not physically move past it. Kyara went back to him, easily crossing the space that restricted him. But even when she held his hand, though she could pass easily, he could not.

"This is some kind of spell," she said. "I wonder if there's another way into the city?" The map had only showed her one path, but obviously there must be more than one way to enter. There were pathways all over the place. But would any of them allow Darvyn through?

A melodious voice behind them broke in. "Who *are* you?"

Kyara spun to find Mooriah standing there, tilting her head. Rage mushroomed within at the sight of her. "This is Darvyn, you know him!" Kyara shouted. "And how *dare* you! How dare you take that child and force us out here?"

A visibly agitated Ella was talking rapidly in Elsiran, doubtless asking where her daughter was, but the ancient Lagrimari woman ignored both her and Kyara. "You are Lagrimari?" Mooriah asked Darvyn. "*Both* your parents?"

Darvyn jerked in surprise. "I never knew my father."

"Hmm." Mooriah's gaze never left him. She waved a hand at Ella. "Tell the woman her daughter is fine. If she would just be quiet for a moment, I will take you to her."

Darvyn narrowed his eyes and translated. Ella fell silent, eyes burning holes into Mooriah.

Kyara gritted her teeth. "Darvyn's mother said his father was a man made of light," she said. "Everyone always thought she was mad." Kyara had known his mother when she was a child, and had loved her the way she'd never had the opportunity to love her own.

Mooriah shook her head. "No, she spoke true. His father must be why he cannot pass. His kind are not allowed in the city."

Darvyn straightened. "You know who my father is?"

"No. But I know *what* he must have been."

"A man made of light?" he asked slowly.

"Yes."

Kyara inhaled sharply. "Like Fenix?"

For the first time, Mooriah seemed discomposed. A wash of pain coated her features at the mention of the strange man they'd met in Yaly. The one who had been imprisoned like Kyara had been, only he'd been there for hundreds of years. He'd been an Earthsinger, but not quite human, with glowing flesh brighter than the sun.

Fenix had disappeared into a portal torn between worlds to a place unknown, but had promised he would return.

"My father was like Fenix," Darvyn repeated, testing the words on his lips. "And why can't people like him—us—enter the city?"

Mooriah's lips twisted. "Because Fenix was a fool." Her tone was wry, but held great affection. "He made mistakes that resulted in his being banned, not only him but all of his kind. Which, apparently, extends to you. I did not realize."

Kyara looked back and forth between them. "Can Murmur lift the spell that bans him?"

"Perhaps, though he may not have the power to any longer. It's an old spell, and there are so few of them left."

"Well, we can't just leave him out here." Her voice grew louder. The reality of what they were here to do was weighing on her; without Darvyn's calming presence, she feared she was finally going to fall apart.

"There is nothing for it." Kyara wanted to slap the calm from Mooriah's round cheeks.

Ella was brimming with tension. She wasn't wearing the translation device and as such was unable to follow the conversation. Ulani looked on with wide eyes, watching the argument unfold.

"I've seen the men made of light, too," the little girl whispered. "Sometimes."

Mooriah appeared startled and crouched down to her level. Ella gripped Ulani's shoulders, holding her tight against her legs.

"And what did these men do?" Mooriah asked, intently focused on Ulani.

She shook her head. "Watched."

"Hmm."

"You took Tana," Ulani accused, crossing her arms and scowling.

Mooriah rose, lifting her chin. "With good reason. And there is little time to waste. If you do not want to wait here," she directed to Darvyn, "there is a campsite on a ridge aboveground not far from here. It's where . . ." She trailed off then cleared her throat. "You can stay there." The melancholy in her voice reminded Kyara of their first meetings, when she'd known Mooriah only as the Sad Woman because of the despair that hung around her.

Darvyn appeared resigned, and Kyara's anger muted. "I'll come to meet you tonight," she said around the lump in her throat.

He smiled, then kissed her. "And I'll be waiting."

Mooriah gave him directions to go through a different tunnel from the one they'd used before. He took a flashlight and stared back at her.

Conscious of both Ella's and Mooriah's urgency, Kyara traded a long look with him before taking a deep breath and stepping back through the doorway to the cave city.

Mooriah unerringly led the way down to where the Cavefolk were gathered. They carefully navigated the towering staircases cut into the rock and the angled pathways leading to the bottom level of the vast underground city.

The temperature dropped steadily as they descended. "Why do they stay on the ground where it's so much colder?" Kyara asked, donning the brown army jacket that she'd found packed in her knapsack.

"The gardens are on the lowest levels, where the soil is oldest and most fertile," Mooriah answered.

"How do plants grow with no light?" Ulani asked.

"There is light, not from the sun, but from the Mother herself. She provides." Mooriah motioned all around them to where the cave softly glowed from bright rocks embedded in the walls. "The firerocks—their brightness is enhanced with the blood and they illuminate our world."

At the word "blood," Ella shot an alarmed glance at Kyara. The woman had donned her translator amalgam and glared viciously at Mooriah whenever her gaze settled in that direction. "I have much I wish to say to you," she'd told the woman, "but I don't want to drain the translator with my rage. Just take me to my daughter."

Mooriah had appeared, if not chastened, then at least contrite. "Much depends on the girl," she'd said. Not an apology, Kyara noted.

"What happened to the rest of the Cavefolk? Why is this place abandoned?" Ella's tinny voice rang out now.

"Many left, favoring the Outside, in the years after the Founders came and made the land more hospitable and life-giving. Over time, the population dwindled as fewer wanted to maintain the old ways."

Mooriah stopped walking; Kyara realized they had reached the entrance to the Cavefolk meeting place. Just like the last time she was here, she sensed five beings, their Nether as abundant and fresh as those newly dead. Bright as stars, they shone in the field of black with the strange light of death energy. But this time, a sixth light shined in her other sight. The Cavefolk were hundreds of years old, which is why they had amassed so much Nether, but this last light was from a Nethersinger—Tana.

Mooriah paused at the entrance to the cave. "Their appearance is shocking, but they will not harm you." Kyara sincerely hoped the woman spoke true. She didn't believe that Murmur would hurt the children, but he could try to use Ella for some purpose the way he'd used Darvyn. She would have to make sure that didn't happen.

Once duly warned, they all stepped through the entryway. The five Cavefolk sat around a fire. Their bodies were colorless, with sagging translucent skin showing the veins and muscle beneath.

Kyara had known what to expect and still had a hard time facing them.

During the short journey, Mooriah had told them the five remaining Cavefolk were Murmur's family group—his wives and husbands, a vestige of a former age when many of the Folk were polyamorous. They spent most of their time in communion and meditation with the Mother. They ate only every few weeks and slowed the processes of their body with blood magic. That was how they'd managed to survive for so long.

Tana sat on a low rock just behind the oldest, most colorless man. "Mama!" She launched herself up and ran around the circle to greet her mother. Ella welcomed her child with open arms.

"I'm so sorry, Mama. I know you were worried when I left, I know I shouldn't have gone without telling you, but look, I've already begun to learn." She spoke at a rapid clip and tugged Ella's hand closer to the circle. "Watch." Without letting go of her mother, she pulled a patch of moss out of the pocket of her dress.

"Tana, no!" Mooriah warned, but the dark green fuzzy texture of the moss was already turning black in the girl's palm. Ella gave a pained cry and wrenched away to hold her stomach with both arms.

"Mama?" Tana looked down as her mother collapsed onto the ground.

"You must never touch someone while using your power child." Mooriah's voice was censorious but soft.

Ulani dropped to Ella's side and clutched her arm. Tears welled in the girl's eyes. "I can't use my Song." Her voice was hushed with terror. "I can't heal her."

Kyara's jaw tightened. She looked to the Cavefolk, whose eerie translucent eyelids revealed the pale orbs beneath. She sank into her other sight and witnessed the Nether growing within Ella's body. It started at her hand, where it had been joined with Tana's and shot straight to her heart.

Kyara pulled the Nether from the woman rapidly, drawing it out, but without Earthsong to heal her, there was little more a Nethersinger could do. The Void took the place of the Nethersong, but Void was neither life nor death, it was simply the space between. Opening her eyes to the cave again, she spoke to Mooriah. "We need to get her out of here. Outside the mountain so Darvyn or Ulani can help her."

But Mooriah simply knelt, calm as the raindrops, and plucked something from her pocket. It was a sliver of white, long as her forefinger with a pointed, sharp edge. She pricked her palm and used the blood to draw a mark on Ella's hand. The squiggly line was a symbol, Kyara didn't know of what, but once the blood touched her skin, Ella's moans quieted.

Mooriah whispered a string of words too low to hear, and Ella's body softened. Kyara's other sight revealed the static of the Void steadily receding and, surprisingly, the darkness of Earthsong overtaking Ella's body.

Mooriah casually wiped the blood off the little sliver with her skirt, then replaced it in her pocket. Everyone monitored Ella until the woman fluttered her lids before opening her eyes. She took several deep breaths before sitting up. "What happened?"

Tana was frozen in place, having not moved during the entire ordeal. Ulani wrapped her mother in a tight hug and thrust her face into her neck. Ella patted the girl's head. "I'm all right, *uli*. It's okay."

Tana crossed her arms protectively in front of her and backed away toward the far wall, looking at her mother and sister with dread.

Kyara turned to the Cavefolk, gaze honed in on their leader, Murmur. "You taught her this trick, but not its consequences?"

"I'm all right, Tana," Ella repeated, reassuringly. She beckoned the girl toward her, but Tana remained motionless. Finally, Ella dropped her arms, her expression an excruciating mix of pain and comprehension.

"Is this how the training works?" Kyara spat out. "Done halfway without any precautions?"

"Tana has been with us less than a day. She is eager to learn." Murmur's voice was surprisingly strong given his advanced age and appearance. The other Cavefolk never moved or said a word.

"This was why I didn't want to come. Your methods are suspect at best, dangerous at worst." She turned to Tana. "Do you know who I am?"

Tana tore her gaze away from her mother and looked at Kyara fully for the first time. "The Poison Flame?"

"Yes. I brought your mother and sister here and we're going to take you home again." She shot a glare at Mooriah.

"I can't go home," the girl whispered, shaking her head. "Look what I did. What I will do again. It's why I came in the first place. I felt . . . Something is happening to me and I can't control it."

Kyara inhaled deeply. She didn't trust the Cavefolk or Mooriah, but something needed to be done about Tana and her Song. She wished she was able to train the girl effectively.

"I need to learn," Tana said, echoing her thoughts. "I want to be like you." Kyara startled.

"Why would you want to be like her?" Murmur asked gently.

"Because she is strong and fierce. She's afraid of nothing. She stands up to those who do harm and she saves others. She's a hero."

Kyara's jaw dropped; her throat began to thicken. Hearing

those words from Tana's lips cracked her heart open. She couldn't bear to let the girl continue thinking her someone she wasn't.

She squatted down to face her. "I'm not any of those things, *uli*. I'm afraid all the time, and this power. . . ." She shook her head. "It is terrible. I'm sorry that you must share its burden."

"This power is a gift," Mooriah declared, stepping up beside her. "That is why you are both here. You are to learn control over it and mastery of it so that you may go out and save your people. This is what you have been called to do. It is your purpose, one chosen by the Breath Father for you."

Kyara stood, patience thinning. "I don't know anything about the Breath Father, but if he gave us this power of death, then what kind of deity is he?"

"A mighty one," Mooriah said gravely.

Kyara crossed her arms, defiant. "Fine. She can stay and be trained. And I will stay and protect her."

"So you want to continue to be selfish and holed up by yourself, squandering your gift." Mooriah's voice brought an additional chill to the air. "You are a force, and she will be, too. Both of you will be needed if you plan to have a land left to live in." The harshness of her tone made goose bumps spring up along Kyara's skin.

"I have kept the watch from the World After for many, many years. I could not see much of the Living World, but what I did would leave you cold. Nethersingers born and slaughtered over and over again. Few managed to survive their births." She glanced over at Tana. "Though, a handful did. Those who were bound as children by other hands. They would live sometimes. But when the bindings wore out and there was no one around to restore them, they would go the way of the rest. Slaughterers to be slaughtered." She spread her hands apart.

"Her power is bound?" Kyara asked.

"It was bound. Now it is leaking out. When yours began to emerge, you were lucky that Ydaris and the True Father kept you alive and trained you."

"Lucky?" Kyara spat out the word. "It was not luck for those I was forced to kill."

Mooriah waved away that little detail. "You learned some skill, but true mastery eludes you. That must change."

"I don't want to know any more. I don't want any more death. Train Tana, she is eager to learn."

Murmur slowly rose to his feet, drawing everyone's attention. "Both of you will be trained or neither will."

Kyara's head snapped back. "What about the prophecy?"

"I would ask you the same thing. Will you really allow the child to fight alone?" He shook his head. "Both or neither."

A roiling heat rose within her with nowhere to go. She took a deep breath to steady her. Tana squeezed her arms around herself tighter. Kyara caught the movement from the corner of her eye. The girl looked small and alone. Frightened, not of her surroundings or the strange, ancient beings present, but of herself.

Kyara closed her eyes on a long blink. *Could* she allow this child to face the battle ahead alone? She saw so much of herself in the girl and recalled the brutality of her own training. Though she did not trust him, she was certain Murmur's training would not be so merciless. She did not want this, not even a little, but her protestations had been pointless from the beginning, she recognized that now. She hung her head and gripped her fists tightly at her sides.

"Can you at least allow Darvyn entry into the city?" Her voice creaked with strain.

"The spell keeping him out is ancient and was settled into the mountain by the force of our people when we were strong. Now that we are weak, we cannot undo it."

"Why is it so important that people like . . . like whoever his father was not come here?"

"Did Mooriah not tell you?" He seemed genuinely surprised.

"She said Fenix made a mistake. Why punish an entire group of . . . beings?"

"Fenix disrespected the Mother to such a degree as to throw into question the trustworthiness of the entire race of Bright Ones."

"He didn't know," Mooriah said quietly, staring at the ground.

"He tried to take a piece of the Mother with him as a trophy. Thievery is not permitted. No stone not freely given can be removed. That is one of our most sacred rules. He broke it, through ignorance or not, and his kind were punished."

"That's rather harsh, don't you think?" Kyara asked.

"Harsh it may be, but that is the way it is . . . was. I cannot change it now. Perhaps if you beseech the Mother, she will alter it herself."

Kyara didn't believe the mountain cared a whit about Darvyn, regardless of whether or not he was the love of her life. "Well, you must at least promise that you won't harm anyone else while we undergo training. No more bait, no more tests . . . of any kind. I won't have you tossing this girl's mother off a cliff just to see if she can save her."

Ella gasped and took a step back. But Murmur had the nerve to chuckle.

"What's funny, old man?" Kyara asked, seething.

"Your precious Darvyn was in no danger, child."

"He nearly drowned in Death River!" Rage exploded from her, unwilling to be controlled.

Murmur wisely sobered. "Very well, I vow it. None here will harm another living being as part of your training. Does that make you feel better, child?"

"Not really," she grumbled.

"The war I warned you of is upon us," he said. "There is little time to waste. If you two do not master your power and help fight for the side of the Living, your world will cease to exist."

Ella's eyes were wide; she held Ulani against her. For her part, Tana did not appear to be affected by this dire pronouncement.

"The dead are coming, Kyara." Murmur gazed at her, unblinking. "And right now, the three of you are all that can stand in the way of the extinction of the human race."

CHAPTER SEVENTEEN

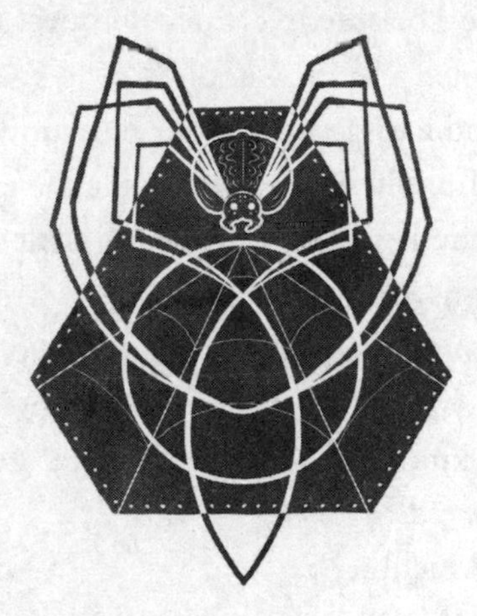

While safety is harmonious,
and eternal,
and ethereal,
and ubiquitous,
it is not guaranteed.

—THE HARMONY OF BEING

Once again, you follow Nikora through the castle. Usable rooms are often far away from one another. You tuck this information away for when you escape. They cannot martial whatever forces they have effectively with a layout such as this. You do not know their numbers, having only seen a handful of servants, Nikora, and her subordinate, Cayro, but they must be few.

This time she leads you up to a rooftop surrounded by crumbling stone. You briefly wonder if it is safe up here or if the stones will fall away and leave you tumbling down into the swirling abyss of white below. The weather is calm, thick flakes of snow fall lazily, but a storm here would be devastating. When you have your power back, you will be sure to create a tempest to level this castle once and for all.

Nikora cradles the disgusting jar of human flesh to her bosom as she would a child. She is a zealot, you can see the fever in her eyes. Faith has made her weak as it does all men. You have never made such a grievous error.

In the corner of the roof lies a tarp covered with a soft sheet of snow. She removes the tarp with a flourish to reveal smoldering ashes of some kind. You see melted metal gears, wood that is blackened and charred.

"Was this the Machine?"

The light of pride shines in her eyes. "Yes. Our greatest achievement. The Great Machine combined the magics of Earthsong, Nethersong, and blood magic and imbued the result—quintessence—into a physical object. Power to the powerless, strength to our kind."

The light in her eyes dims as she looks toward you. "Now there is only a finite amount of quintessence left in the world and we have no way to make more." She squeezes the jar containing the petrified remains of a deity. You fight to keep from rolling your eyes.

"And you believe we can use the Songs and the quintessence that you have gathered?" You try to prod her along. The cold bites at your exposed skin; you wonder if she feels it.

"We are draining Nethersong from our slaves the way we have since times of old. The Wailers will provide the Earthsong, and blood is readily available." She eyes your arms, and you take an alarmed step back.

"Oh yes, my dear Eero, your blood is necessary. Since you will control the Earthsong, we will require a sacrifice from you."

Your jaw clenches. "And where will this sacrifice go? What will be done with the Earthsong and the blood and the Nether?"

She gazes toward the mountain peaks that surround the castle. Soft clouds cap the summits in the near distance, though visibility is low due to the snowfall. Her expression is difficult to read, but it appears as though she is coming to a decision. When she focuses on you again, the fever is gone from her eyes, leaving only determination.

The rattling of chains behind you causes you to turn. The other Physick, Cayro, is at the head of a group of servants leading the Wailers. Manacled together hand and foot, your men shuffle along like mindless, brainless automatons. Which you suppose is what they are. They have no free will, it was all subsumed by their programming. But there are only twelve of them.

"I will not tell you all, Eero, only what you need to know. You think you hide your desires from me, but I see through you," Nikora says.

When you turn, she has grown quite close, within spitting distance. The damaged flesh on your arm burns at the thought of harming her even only with spittle on her cheek. The pain you can ignore, but along with it comes a flash of despondency, a fleeting sense of despair that makes you almost stumble. You know it is the work of the spell she carved into you—not just physical pain then, it lays a mental tripwire that would be impossible to disregard.

"Follow my instructions exactly," she says, "and you will live to see our rise. Perhaps then, we will become the allies you claim you seek."

Her wariness is warranted but still vexing to you. However, you comply. It is the only way forward at present.

She walks you through the spell, indicating that she will perform the blood magic portions herself. Working together to do magic usually requires linking, but since the Physicks have no inborn Song, they have devised another method using the blood. Ingenious really.

When she gives you leave, you speak the commands to control the Songs of the Wailers. Not being able to feel the rush of Earthsong flowing through you is difficult. The delightful sensation of the power at your command was yours for so long, its lack is a vast canyon of emptiness within you.

The many complaints of the people from whom you liberated the power filter to your consciousness, released from the stronghold of memory, but you brush them aside. Their petty quibbles are of no import. They never were.

Now you must satisfy yourself with witnessing the Wailers as they look to the sky, eyes clouded over with control. Your control, wielded as deftly as ever.

You describe to them what must be done, how they must tap into the source energy of all life and pull it into themselves, then focus it on the bit of withered, dead flesh. Nikora says that the hand is not entirely dead. The flesh of their goddess lives on in some small way that can be felt with Earthsong.

The Wailers do not speak, but they obey. They pour their combined Songs into the meat inside the jar, making the glow brighter. Before your eyes the muscle regains some rejuvenation, some small part of itself. What is this madness?

Nikora stands holding onto her medallion, chanting. The language of blood magic falls from her lips in unfamiliar ways. You take note, try to commit to memory all that she is saying, though she speaks quickly and softly. She thinks it's too soft for you to hear, but she doesn't know you as well as she thinks she does.

In her other hand, she holds a red stone—a caldera filled with Nethersong from these unseen slaves. She jerks her head, and Cayro grabs your arm, wrenches your sleeve up, and slices you again. You falter in your commands to the Wailers, and Nikora glares at you.

Maintaining control of the Wailers requires talking them through each step, without ceasing, even if that means repeating the same command over and over again. "Steady," you repeat as more of their power flows into the desiccated flesh, now plump and whole again. "Steady."

Your blood now collected from the fresh wound in a small sponge, Cayro squeezes it onto the caldera Nikora holds. With reverence, she places the bloody stone into the jar with the remains of her goddess's hand.

Light continues to bleed from the flesh. It soon becomes blinding. The jar shines even brighter, until it is a blade, sharp as steel, piercing your eyes. You shut them, but the pain persists. It claws its way into your head, tearing at your flesh as it burrows.

Then it is gone.

You open your eyes and when they adjust to the normal light of day, the air high above the jar is shimmering. Nikora's voice cuts through the haze in your mind left from the pain. "The portal is opening. We must say the words together to control it."

She repeats them to you. This spell, in the language of the blood, reminds you of something, but you're not sure what. Even as you bristle at the thought, you obediently recite the words in time with Nikora.

The shimmer becomes a golden light, and you wince, just before it tears a hole in the sky. Columns of dark shadow flow through eagerly, like a nest of snakes chasing their prey.

Nikora's chant changes; you clumsily hurry to follow suit. These are the words to close the portal. More spirits slip through before the tear slams shut. You count at least six that have gotten through to the Living World. They whip over your head like a dark wind.

One darts for you, but Nikora lifts her hand and a sizzle of lightning-like energy shoots from her palm, repelling the shadow. The spirit changes direction and heads toward the Wailers.

"Protect them!" she cries, and even as you instruct the Wailer to defend himself, he is entered by the spirit. His skin changes color, body changes shape until he is someone entirely different—a bald man of middle years with a blocky tattoo marring his head, like that of the other servants.

You are agape. Your sister had relayed this fantastical story, but to see the possession in person leaves you awestruck.

The other spirits have found hosts in Nikora's guards, though she remains untouched. The transformed Wailer snaps his chains with no apparent effort and roars. A half-dozen men and women in red robes run up to the platform from inside the castle. Their quick arrival indicates they must have been waiting just out of sight for this very thing to happen.

Cayro joins them, barking orders. They all raise their arms and shoot bolts of sizzling energy toward the creatures, who have taken on the bodies of bald, tattooed guards. Your sister theorized these are the dead who have been mistreated, the blood slaves and others. But the wraiths are not without their defenses. One leaps out of the way, jumping higher than any human should be able to. Another avoids the shot of energy by twisting unnaturally, bending back at the knee until his body is parallel to the ground. A third lifts an arm and, with a flick of his wrist, tosses one of the

Physicks racing toward him into the air and right off the roof. Another wraith is hit by the blast, and stunned momentarily, but does not go down.

You command the remaining Wailers to freeze the feet of the wraiths, sinking them into the stone to hold them in place. To bind their arms with tight bands of air to keep them at their sides.

But it only works temporarily. Their incredible strength and whatever magic they possess allow them to break free.

Amazingly, Nikora is attempting to speak with them, even as her fellow Physicks battle them. "We seek only knowledge," she says, holding her hands up as in supplication. "Secrets of the World After. We have brought you here, not to fight with you, but to learn." She raises her voice to be heard over the din.

While she has proven herself to be an opponent deserving a modicum of respect, her plan is foolishness. Appealing to the better natures of vengeful spirits is getting her nowhere. More Physicks make their way onto the platform to defend her as her companions fall due to injury or death.

The Wailers attack with ice, rocks, wind, fire—it does no more than slow the wraiths for brief moments. What is fueling their power? Certainly not Earthsong or blood magic. Which leaves only Nethersong—fitting as they are creatures returned from the world of death.

"The Nether, can you manipulate it directly?" you ask Nikora. "Can you blast them with Nethersong instead of Earthsong?"

She holds her medallion again and shoots out another blast of energy, a purplish stream of power that seems to absorb all light. The wraith she hits, rears back, howling. Until now, they've done no more than emit animal-like grunts and growls, but this sound of pain brings you great joy.

She continues pummeling the wraith. It jerks and shakes and

disappears inside a cloud of dust. The body crumples to the ground and the black smoke-like form shoots into the air.

The other Physicks focus their power, changing tacks and shooting Nethersong into the remaining wraiths. One by one, the spirits are expelled and hover overhead, darting around, searching for another host. But the Physicks blast them before they can take hold of anyone.

"We must open the portal again to banish them," you say. Wearily, Nikora nods.

You all repeat the spell to reopen the portal, and the other Physicks help direct the spirits to it with carefully targeted peals of Nethersong.

Finally, they are gone and the portal is closed again. You sag, breathing heavily, more from the exertion of mental energy than anything else. The Wailers are almost all drained. It will be at least a day before most will be able to sing again.

Nikora and the Physicks look deflated as well. The carefully cultivated sheen of superiority she reflects is tarnished and dim. Cayro stands, breath heaving, face no longer impassive but full of rage. Four Physicks are dead, killed by wraiths. A few of the ones who became hosts still breathe, though they remain unconscious.

In the jar, the hand is shriveled again. One of the four remaining fingers reduced to a stub. Nearly one fourth of the remaining power of Saint Dahlia has been expended in this experiment. Nikora stares at the jar with pained eyes, doubtless grieving the loss. But you see something altogether different. Possibility.

Learning to do this all on your own may be difficult, but once you are able to control these spirits, a powerful army will be at your disposal. One that would be nearly impossible to defeat.

All creatures can be mastered, controlled, dominated—even the dead. You simply need to discover how.

CHAPTER EIGHTEEN

Deaf to the strains of freedom
blind to the path from pain.
Like children, ever needy
we seek what is already ours to claim.

—THE HARMONY OF BEING

Zeli's feet whispered across the terrazzo flooring as she approached the Goddess's office. Since discovering the journal, the Goddess had spent far more time than usual in the office pacing the floors or staring out of the windows or hovering over the novices as they responded to correspondence. It was as if She was waiting for something to happen in that room.

Zeli did her duties to the best of her ability, delivering trays of food that would never be eaten to the dungeon and seeing to the Goddess's needs in whatever way she was asked. She didn't speak at length with anyone other than Varten for fear of saying too much either about the wraith attack that still hung over her head or the secret journal they were studying.

Some of the other Sisterhood acolytes would tentatively try to strike up conversation. Chatting with them would be a good way to practice her Elsiran, but she always demurred, blaming the language barrier. The more people she talked to, the more one of her secrets might slip and it was hard enough being around the Goddess, knowing the woman could read her emotions and intentions, see her guilt, excitement, frustration, and fear. She was also worried enough about what would happen to Varten when they were eventually discovered and didn't want to risk bringing anyone else into this.

Standing in the threshold of the room, Zeli took a deep, calming breath. Her emotions could call attention to her if the Goddess were paying attention, so she endeavored to wrangle them under control. She had always been a little nervous in Her presence; that hadn't changed. The reasons why were now different, but surely *She* wouldn't know that. Earthsingers couldn't actually read minds.

And the other reason her heart stuttered more often than not these past few days? Why her breaths were just a little more difficult to draw into too tight lungs? Certainly that could be blamed on the musty smell that had permeated the secret room. Though she'd scrubbed the place from top to bottom.

The racing in her chest must be a reaction to mildew or dust—though if she was honest, she'd admit she hadn't smelled either in days. No, when she was there, sitting shoulder to shoulder with Varten, heads bent over the book or their notes, all she smelled was his unique scent. And if her blood felt thick in her veins the whole while, and she spent the other hours in her day watching the clock until their meeting time, there was a reasonable explanation; she just hadn't figured it out yet.

Zeli squared her shoulders and entered the Goddess's office. At first she thought the room was empty, but a door in the corner she hadn't ever noticed before was slightly ajar and two voices could be heard, one male and one female. The door was hidden in the paneling of the wall. She wasn't certain where it led, perhaps to a closet or an adjoining chamber that the Goddess simply had never used before.

Concern filled her, causing her to approach slowly. Once, she had been caught alone in a room by a young man. She'd been frightened, unable to call for help. Her thoughts went to the Elsiran acolyte normally at the desk at this time of day, but suddenly nowhere to be found. Fear for the other girl gripped Zeli as the terror she'd felt all those months ago washed over her. However, as she drew nearer to the doorway, the Goddess's melodic voice flowed out, putting her mind at ease.

Zeli turned to leave when the words she was hearing registered.

"What is it, exactly, that you want?" the Goddess asked.

"What I always wanted, dear sister. Equality." The answering voice was like a snake slithering over gravel. Zeli froze, her blood turning to ice. Another flashback, this one from eleven years before slammed into her—she was immobilized on a stone table in the glass castle of Sayya, Lagrimar's capital city. Fear took root in her chest like an evil rose. A robed figure swished away and as she stared at the ceiling, tears streaming down her cheeks, the masked face of the True Father hovered over her. She didn't remember the words he spoke, but his grating voice was forever burned into her memory.

During the king's stay in the dungeon, he hadn't uttered a

single word. Zeli had been able to imagine the thin, russet-haired man lying on the cot safely behind bars as just another Elsiran. He'd worn no robe, no mask, no jewels. No bell ringer announced his every step and movement. No speech sullied the silence.

But now the voice coming from this hidden room in the Goddess's office was the same one that featured in her nightmares. For years after she returned from giving her Song in tribute to the king's thirst for power, she would awake in the middle of the night, skin slicked with sweat, writhing on a pallet between two other servants, screaming silently. Grasping at her chest, willing her Song back into place.

This rasping voice belonged to the one responsible for hundreds of years of her peoples' terror. Her own dread and night frights. This was the Goddess's brother, Lagrimar's dictator, the True Father.

Slowly, feeling came back into her limbs, though she didn't move a single muscle. The two spoke casually. The Goddess's tone was nonchalant. Like this was just some errant family member off on a vacation and not a fugitive wanted for countless unspeakable horrors to generations of her people. Zeli struggled to focus back in on the conversation.

". . . did you not say you wished to see me free?" the True Father was saying.

"If you could manage it without harming anyone. If you could find the light of goodness within your nature. I believe it is still there. What would you do with your freedom, I wonder?"

Zeli's jaw dropped in horror. She backed away instinctively and ran into a chair. How could the Goddess speak so to him? Of . . . freedom?

Zeli didn't understand what magic this was. Certainly the True

Father was not in the room with Her Excellency, though she didn't dare move closer to check.

"When will you return?" the Goddess asked.

"When it is time. When I can reclaim what is mine."

Her breath caught; she had heard enough. She left the room on quiet feet though she no longer really cared if she was discovered. Once she'd prayed the political deadlock between the Council and the Keepers on how to proceed with the True Father's punishment would continue so no one would discover the king's disappearance before the Goddess located him. But she didn't even know who she'd been praying to.

Surely not this woman in there chuckling with Her beloved twin. Hoping for his *freedom*. That was not the Goddess the High Priestess had taught them was infallible. And if *that* wasn't true, then what was the point of the Sisterhood that she'd planned to pledge her life to?

If the True Father was returning, then there was little point to anything at all.

Zeli's rushing feet slowed as soon as she was three corridors away from the Goddess's office. Her run turned into a shuffle, and a gauzy film dropped over her eyes. She had no idea where she was going. She managed not to bump into anyone but couldn't say if any of the people she passed greeted her or not. Her mind was still in that room, ruminating on what she'd overheard—she couldn't tear it away. Her hopes and future disintegrated in front of her blinded eyes.

Could she question Her Excellency? Reveal that she'd caught an earful of this traitorous conversation? And what then? To many, the Goddess *was* Elsira. The Elsirans worshipped Her. The Lagrimari were in awe of Her. Those who didn't believe in Her were trying to eject the Lagrimari from the country.

Her people had nothing now but the favor of the Goddess and the charity of others. They needed more. They needed their Songs back.

She shook herself and turned, getting her bearings before slowly making her way to the old corridor near the vault entry. She had yet to see so much as a servant in this wing. Still, she used caution, peering at her surroundings carefully to ensure no one saw her sneak into the parlor they had claimed as their own.

Varten had arrived early. He sat at the table they'd uncovered, his back to her, broad shoulders hunched taking notes on a pad as he studied the journal. He turned at her entry and then did a double take. What must she look like? Concern furrowed his brow as he began to rise, but she held up a hand and crossed the room to sit beside him.

"What's wrong?" he asked, searching her face.

Zeli took a deep breath. But nothing came out. Was it all really over? She closed her lips and pulled the wretched ribbon from her hair, letting it fall onto the ground.

Varten watched her with wide eyes.

"It's all a lie." She blinked but the tears fell anyway. Varten pulled her into his arms as she began to sob.

She'd come to this land for a new life, a new start away from the corruption and misery of Lagrimar, but what did she find here? More deception. The hope of her people placed in someone who didn't deserve it.

Crying was a weakness that shouldn't be tolerated, but she was empty, so empty and sad and tired of standing up alone. Of trying to be strong. Finally she pulled away, sniffing. She closed her eyes as Varten dabbed at her cheeks with a handkerchief, and then she sat back some more, out of his reach. Gathering the shreds of herself together as she'd always done.

There was good, even in this. And she would find it.

"You haven't spoken to your sister yet, have you?" she asked, blinking. "About the Rumpus?"

Varten cleared his throat. "No, she's been so busy. I don't think she's slept since Jack left. I can let Usher know that it's an emergency though. She'll make time."

"No." Zeli crossed her arms and took a long breath. "I don't think we should tell her about the Gilmerian Archives. I don't think we can trust anyone anymore."

He frowned.

"Not that Queen Jasminda is untrustworthy," she hurried to add, though at this point Zeli didn't even trust herself. "It's just that . . . the Goddess . . ."

Varten leaned forward, looking like he might touch her, but she jerked back. She couldn't focus on his hurt expression; she just held herself tighter, keeping all the pieces of herself together when they wanted to float away, like little kites tired of being trapped in the form of a girl.

"I overheard the Goddess talking with someone. Someone who wasn't there. Someone who hasn't been here in a long time."

Varten shook his head. "I don't understand."

She twisted her hands; she was mucking this all up. "I've been sworn to secrecy, and I don't want you to get in trouble."

"I'm a prince, remember? What kind of trouble can I get into?" His lips curled.

"Trouble with the Goddess."

The smirk dropped from his face. "You can tell me. If it's a secret, I will keep it."

She swallowed, gripping her arms even tighter. "Not sure about this one. It's a whopper."

"You don't trust *me*?" His voice didn't quite mask his hurt.

"Right now, you're the only one I do trust." She discovered the words true as she spoke them. *I trust him more than myself.* "It's just that keeping this particular secret might not be the best thing to do. It might be wrong."

The slight wavering of the lamplight made his eyes seem to glow. She stared just over his shoulder so as not to be distracted. "What if we can't trust the Goddess? What if She has Her own agenda that isn't in our best interest? What would we do then?" Her voice was a whisper.

"What did She do this time?"

"Telling you might put you in danger."

"I don't care. Tell me. I'll accept whatever comes. You shouldn't bear it alone."

New tears burned behind her eyes at his fierceness. She shouldn't tell him, but this secret had bored a hole inside her. She could hold it in no longer. "Six weeks ago . . . the True Father escaped the dungeon."

The words settled in the air, and she felt immediately lighter. But she'd burdened Varten. His brow creased, but he stayed silent.

"It looked like he had help, magical help of some kind. Since then, She's claimed to be looking for him, but said he was far away. Too far to hurt anyone here. And She won't let me tell anyone, not the queen or the Guard or anyone."

Her throat threatened to close up, but Zeli continued. "I don't know if keeping Her secret was the right thing to do. I feel like I've been doing something wrong, and the guilt . . ." Her voice hitched and she struggled to breathe.

Varten looked like he wanted to leap from his chair, but stayed across the invisible barrier she'd created.

"Just now, when I went to Her office, I overheard the two of them speaking. They were using some kind of magic so he wasn't actually in the room, but Varten, She was laughing with him. Joking. They sounded like any other brother and sister, not like . . . what they are." She blinked away the moisture in her eyes and struggled to steel her spine.

"And because of that you don't think we can trust Jasminda?" Varten asked quietly.

"Can she stand against the Goddess? The most powerful Earthsinger ever known?" Zeli shook her head. "What if the Goddess doesn't *want* us to get our Songs back? What if Queen Jasminda does something and the Goddess stops her, or hurts her?"

Varten startled. "Do you think She would do that?"

"Didn't She already let Jasminda die? She's capable of anything." Zeli had worked with Her for months and knew for a fact the Goddess wasn't the same as a normal woman. The power, the long life, they had made Her distant, strange, and cold, not like someone with a conscience, or at least one Zeli recognized.

"So what should we do now?" Varten asked.

What she was about to say might be a mistake, but she kept going. "I think we should go to Gilmeria."

He stared back, urging her silently to continue.

"The journal's author implied that Gilmer helped him figure out how to restore lost Songs. And everything we've learned about the Gilmerian Archives indicates that it contains a full record of Saint Gilmer's travels around the world. What he did in Elsira must be there. The exact way to restore Songs could be in the Archives."

"So you want to go to the Rumpus? And try to get into the Archives?" he asked. "Ani made it sound like there was a contest of some kind—only certain people can gain access."

"It might be the only hope for the Lagrimari. The True Father is coming back; those wraiths were the first wave and he gloated about returning to his sister. There are still some Lagrimari here with their Songs. He wants them, will always want the power. Our only hope is for all of us to regain our Songs and fight back. We can't trust the Elsirans or anyone else."

Varten's eyes shined even brighter than usual. She hoped he hadn't taken offense at her comment about Elsirans. But then she realized, his expression was one of pride.

"You really want to do this, Zeli? Seems a little out of character."

She almost smiled, he'd teased her endlessly about being so cautious, especially in the face of his bravery, but everything she'd hoped for—a future in the Sisterhood, having a place and a home and family—it was all gone now, as sharply as the laugh of the siblings she'd overheard. Like dust through her fingers.

With her Song, she could make her own future. She wouldn't be at the whims of fate or the powerful. *She* would be powerful. Her Song hadn't been noteworthy, but it was strong enough to help her rule her own destiny. Strong enough to fight back.

She pursed her lips and nodded grimly. "It is the last thing I want to do. I don't even know if we *can* do it. But we have to try, because staying here and waiting for the True Father to attack us again and drag us back into slavery isn't an option."

Fear threatened to overwhelm her. "If we do this, we can't tell anyone. I don't want to risk the Goddess's retribution on anyone else. We'd have to do it alone," she whispered. "Travel somewhere we've never been before, join the contest to enter the Archives, and win."

"The odds seem terrible, but that doesn't scare me," Varten said. What did scare him, she wondered?

"So you'll come with me?"

He leaned forward; unconsciously she found herself doing the same. "Of course I'll come with you. We're in this together. We'll find a way." He reached out and squeezed her hand quickly, then let go.

He looked so earnest, she had to hold herself back from reaching for him. Her breathing restarted, faster than ever. They were partners now, joined for as long as this journey took, and committed to where it would lead. A pang of guilt hit her—as much as she needed his help, she hated to bring him down with her.

The space between their chairs was only a pace wide, but suddenly stretched to the width of an ocean. She had to be cautious. There was no reason to believe that Varten would betray her, but she hadn't believed it of the Goddess Awoken, either. Her judgement was the thing she lacked confidence in, even now.

How easy it would be to depend on him the way she had always depended on others for safety and protection. His arms were strong and warm, and she could feel herself getting lost in them even in the brief minutes he'd held her while she cried. But if she was going to go out of her comfort zone and make this journey, she had to go out completely. They were friends and partners, but he was not her savior.

However this ended, she no longer believed that her salvation could be provided by others. No prince was going to rescue her. Not this time, not ever.

CHAPTER NINETEEN

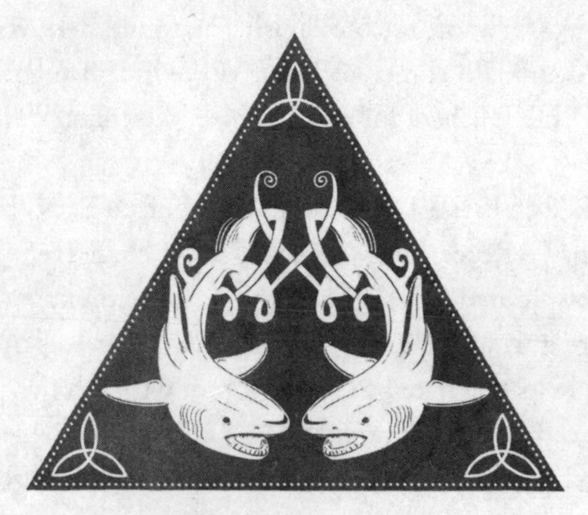

Come nearer, watch close.
Listen well, touch more.
Taste the scent on the air.
Bear witness to our unity.

—THE HARMONY OF BEING

"It is late," Murmur announced, staring into the fire. Kyara wasn't certain how they kept track of time down here in the cave city without the sun or watches or clocks of any kind, but she did feel tired. They had walked much of the day to get here and the emotional upheavals had been fierce.

"Our training will begin in earnest on the morn. I take it you will go to find your beau tonight, Kyara?" The ancient man's description of Darvyn nearly made her smile.

"Yes. He will not like to spend the night apart."

"Very well. You may see if he is able to unbind the child. Her bindings are loosening on their own, but speeding the process would aid in her training."

"But Earthsong has no effect on Nethersingers."

"She was bound by a Bright One. They are Earthsingers but also something more." This confused Kyara, but she nodded at him.

"Come," Mooriah said, "I will show you the way."

Ella tapped the wire loop device around her neck and removed it, shaking her head. From her expression it was clear that the amalgam's power had run out. She spoke to Ulani, who appeared distressed.

"What's wrong?" Kyara asked.

"She only has one left," the girl said.

Tana spoke up, speaking to Murmur. "Can you give her one of the stones? Like what you gave to me? Will it work on her?"

Murmur nodded slowly and Mooriah crossed over to him, retrieving two small black stones that had appeared in his outstretched hand. They were bits of the walls of this cave or one like it. Pieces of the Mother.

Mooriah handed the small calderas to Ella and Ulani, who accepted trustingly. Kyara held her breath as they closed their eyes. A stone like the ones they held had imparted the Cavefolk language to her when she was here last. With their eyes closed, Ulani was smiling and Ella looked perplexed. The calderas gave visions and hopefully each was viewing something innocuous that would simply transfer the magic and not some horrific display of ritualized murder. Kyara shivered.

Cavefolk society and culture had involved blood sacrifice on a large scale. The offerings had been voluntary and considered a great honor, but death was death, and these people were dealers in it as much as she was.

The Folk were not natural Nethersingers, but blood magic had close ties to death magic. While in service to the Cantor, Kyara had learned some blood spells. The scars all over her body were evidence of the cost of that knowledge. With a gasp, both released the stones at the same time and opened their eyes.

"That was intense," Ella said in Lagrimari. She held a hand to her throat and spoke again. "What is . . . ? What am I saying? How did I do that?"

Ulani threw her arms around her mother and squeezed. "Mama, you can speak like us now!"

Ella swallowed, blinking rapidly. "Yes, darling, I guess I can."

Begrudgingly, Kyara acknowledged that the Cavefolk had given the woman a gift—to be able to speak to her children in their native language—in addition to understanding the Cavefolk. The visions didn't appear to have frightened either of them, which was a blessing.

"Thank you," Kyara said to Murmur. The others all repeated their thanks and then they were off.

Mooriah guided them through tunnels embedded with sparkling stones, which reflected back the moonlight from an opening somewhere far above.

"Did the Cavefolk create the caves? Did they dig them out of the mountain?" Ella asked as they ascended a gentle incline. Now that her daughter was back with her, she spoke to Mooriah with tight civility.

"No, the Mother provided. Blood magic was used to call upon her when the population grew and more dwellings were needed. They are created by her hand."

The wondrous views around them could not have been a natural occurrence. Kyara supposed the cave city *could* have been man-made, over hundreds of years of mining and digging . . .

perhaps. It was an incredible feat no matter how it had been achieved.

After nearly an hour, they ascended a gentle incline and emerged in the crisp night air, on a wide ledge high on the mountain. The space was ringed with a natural rock border that offered limited protection to the unfortunate or clumsy. Darvyn sat before a small ball of fire hovering just off the ground. He stood, grinning as they approached, then hurried over to embrace Kyara. Tension and worry she didn't know she carried melted away with his touch. Her eyes closed and she lived inside his hold for as long as she could.

When he pulled away to greet the others, she opened her eyes and nearly swooned due to the height. The ledge overlooked the Elsiran countryside, where distant trees were losing their clinging leaves. A lustrous moon illuminated the land.

Behind them, hidden by the gnarled peak, was Lagrimar. A pang actually went through her at the thought of her homeland. A cold winter would be descending on the desert, not as frigid as the temperatures promised on this side of the mountain, but bad enough. Who had stayed there and what would become of the refugees headed back?

She retreated from the edge and the steep drop down. "Be careful where you step," she called out to the children. Ella kept her daughters close.

Kyara turned back to Darvyn and went to sit beside him at the fire. "How have you been holding up? Sorry you insisted on coming along?"

"Never sorry, not when I get to see you. Even if it is just once a day." He grinned again and pulled her near, kissing her all too briefly.

Sadness clung to her where his hands wrapped around her

waist. "Well, now I know the way. We also wanted to see if you can unbind Tana. The Cavefolk are unable to unlock her magic, but they say it was done by a Bright One. You're the closest thing we have."

Darvyn turned to Tana, who looked up at him shyly. "I can't sense her with my Song. I'll try again, but Nethersingers are invisible to my power."

The girls took a seat around the fire and Darvyn inhaled deeply, staring in Tana's direction, brow furrowed and eyes soft. Then he shook his head, eyes clearing. "I see nothing. No binding, no Tana, nothing. I'm sorry, I wish there was something I could do."

Tana looked dejected but just nodded, appearing used to accepting whatever hand fate dealt her. Kyara's heart broke. She squeezed Darvyn's hand, knowing he hated to disappoint the girl as much as she did.

"We'll try—" but whatever she had been going to say was interrupted by a ringing sound, as if the temple bells in the city were chiming. Everyone jumped up in alarm. She and Darvyn stood protectively in front of Ella and the girls, backing them toward the cave entrance.

The already bright moonlight rose to a blinding level as a glimmering, golden ripple tore the air. The radiant disturbance became a hole—a portal—through which daylight was visible. The thought of wraiths was foremost in her mind. *Not yet! We're not ready!*

The ringing sound grew louder and more intense. Then it was gone and the night was as quiet and dark as ever with only the flickering firelight and the glow of the moon to see by. The sudden change in brightness made Kyara blink rapidly to clear the searing impression the portal had left on the backs of her eyelids. When her vision settled, a gently glowing figure stood at the edge of the ledge, balanced on the short rock barrier. He rapidly dimmed, revealing the form of a man.

"Fenix?" Mooriah said from somewhere behind them. Darvyn sucked in a breath.

The strange man they'd met inside the Physicks' stronghold stood before them. He wore a light-colored tunic and loose-fitting trousers made of a strange, shimmery material. His skin was the color of sunset in a dust storm, no longer illuminated from within but a shade unlike she'd ever seen. His eyes were a shiny, bright gold, full of swirling colors.

He nodded in greeting at her and Darvyn, giving a slight smile. Then his gaze passed over Ella and the girls and appeared to get stuck on Mooriah. His expression teetered and Kyara could not define the emotions she saw on his face. He quickly muted them and stood still as Mooriah made her way toward him.

"What are you doing here?" she asked, her voice accusatory.

He gracefully leapt from the rocky border onto the ground, but still stood two heads above her, forcing her to look up. "It is today. The first frost."

She gasped.

"You'd forgotten." His smile was rueful. "I came every decade as promised. Well, every decade I was able." His gaze shot to Kyara before he swallowed and lowered his head. "Even when I was too late and you were gone."

Mooriah's jaw worked, shifting from side to side. "You were always a fool." But her tone held no malice. She reached up to touch his cheek, tentative, fingers quivering. She stroked him once then dropped her hand, curling her fingers.

"How are you here now?" Fenix whispered. He took a step closer to her and she stiffened, then relaxed a fraction.

"The prophecy is coming true. I am needed."

Fenix nodded. "Yes. I saw the ones who first tore the hole between worlds. The Physicks. They did not know what they were starting."

They stared at each other for a long beat, so long that Kyara felt awkward, like she shouldn't be witnessing whatever was happening. She sensed a pained history between the two. But both appeared to get themselves together with a little shake.

Fenix looked Mooriah up and down. "So you returned. I had a feeling you would not go easily into the Flame. Whose body did you take?"

Kyara froze. It hadn't occurred to her to ask exactly how Mooriah had come back to the Living World. But Kyara, too, had witnessed the spirits brought by the Physicks from the World After take over bodies. Had she thought Mooriah different? Were there other ways the dead could come back to life? Perhaps she'd given it little thought because the spirits she'd seen in Yaly had been angry, set on revenge, and using incredible power. In comparison, Mooriah seemed . . . normal. Annoying, to be sure, reckless and foolhardy, but not a vindictive, vengeful creature.

Mooriah brushed away Fenix's question. "She was just an old hag I found in a prison. One who had tormented my descendant. She will not be missed."

Mooriah had descendants? Kyara looked at the woman again with sharper eyes. Caught in avoiding her own guilt, she hadn't asked Mooriah about a great many things. Hadn't wondered more about her life. That had obviously been a mistake.

Fenix turned to Kyara and Darvyn. "When you saved me, I made a promise to return and bring aid. Though, in that, so far, I have failed. My long-awaited homecoming was not as I'd hoped. I could not convince anyone to come and assist this world."

Mooriah snorted. "Your brethren always cared only for observing."

Fenix firmed his lips, disappointment evident. "I have not given up all hope. Not quite yet."

"There are only us three to stand in the way of the army of the dead and their dominance. She is untrained." She pointed to Kyara. "And she is bound." She motioned to Tana.

Fenix's gaze passed Kyara to settle on the younger girl.

"None here are able to unbind her," Mooriah said. Fenix took a few steps toward Tana, but Kyara blocked his path. He tilted his head in silent question.

"What are you going to do?" Sure, he had helped them escape in Yaly, but she still didn't know who or *what* he was. "Where is it you come from, and what power do you have?"

Fenix blinked before bowing to her. "I apologize. Our introduction was in haste as we were both prisoners. I regret that I was unable to communicate with you during our incarceration. But it was not within my power at the time."

He folded his hands before him. "Your ancestors, the two who came from my world and made this land their home, they were of my people. From the world on which we originated, at least. That place was destroyed and we were scattered across the worlds, using the portals to travel and find new homes. I am one of the observers sent by what's left of those who govern us to keep track of our people. History tends to repeat itself and we would prefer not to be left to the random hand of fate for survival as we once were.

"I came here many centuries ago to do research on the land and progeny of the two who settled here, the ones called the Founders. Virtually all of Elsira and Lagrimar are their descendants. However, the occupants of this land were less than welcoming." His mouth twisted in a grimace.

Kyara's mind went blank for a moment, then restarted. Her current dizziness had nothing to do with the height. Other worlds? Besides the World After and the World Between? Of course she'd seen him disappear into a portal and arrive via one just now, but how many were there? What were they like?

She shook her head and blinked. "And—your power?"

"Our powers manifest differently on different worlds. In each place, the source is the same. Refugees from our dying home all took small pieces of the source with them, to sustain them. But for reasons we don't yet fully understand, what we can do is always slightly different."

He raised a hand and a glowing ball of light materialized in it. "Earthsong you call it here. The collective life energy of all beings. So simple." With a twist of his hand, the ball of light transformed into a blooming flower of some variety she'd never seen before. Next to her, Darvyn leaned forward, enthralled.

The flower transformed again, into a tiny, black puppy—floppy-eared, with copious amounts of fur. Ulani gasped then squealed in delight.

"Is that an illusion?" Darvyn whispered.

"This is life," Fenix said simply. He knelt and set the puppy on the ground. It yipped, and then ran straight for Ulani's legs. She scooped him up and cradled him to her chest. Ella's jaw had unhinged as she stared at the little wriggling creature lapping at her daughter's cheek.

"But Earthsong cannot do such things," Darvyn said. "Create life from nothing."

"Not from nothing, life from life, from energy," Fenix corrected, rising. "And there are a great many things possible with Earthsong that are only limited by the capabilities of the Singers currently alive. I am not, strictly speaking, an Earthsinger. One must be born here to claim that. However, the way my power expresses allows me to manipulate Earthsong."

Darvyn looked like he had more questions, but seemed a bit overwhelmed. He'd likely need some time to think this over and process it. They all would.

"But then at some point you were captured by the Physicks?" Kyara asked, now in awe that such a thing could occur.

Fenix lowered his head. "I was careless. By that time Mooriah was gone—I'd forgotten how short lives are here—but when I returned, I would check on her descendants. It was during one of those times, when I was lost in my own mind, lamenting the way things had turned out, that I fell into a trap a child should have seen through. I paid for it with many years of my life powering the Great Machine for the Physicks."

He took a step closer to Kyara. "So you see, it is because of both of us that this threat has appeared on this land. I will do whatever I can to rectify my mistake and help."

"But didn't you banish all the spirits the Physicks allowed in?"

"The seal between the worlds was already weak; they cracked it open. Otherwise, Mooriah would not be here, either. The door has been opened, we wait now only for someone with ill intent to take advantage of that."

"That has already begun." Mooriah stepped to his side. "It is why I brought them here to train."

"But why was Tana bound? And who did it? Someone like you?" Kyara was still trying to wrap her mind around it all.

"Yes, it was one of my fellow observers, no doubt," Fenix replied. "We are meant to monitor only and not get involved, however, when one of us senses something catastrophic approaching—the creation and existence of one of your kind can be felt by us—then in order to stop tragedy, we bind the child. However, it does not last forever." His expression was apologetic.

Like Tana, her power had expressed at age eleven. What would it have been like if the bindings were permanent? Would she still be in the harem? One of the *ul-nedrim* guards keeping the women and girls safe?

"I can unbind the girl," Fenix said. He looked to Ella, who had an arm around each of her daughters and was dodging an over-eager puppy tongue. "It will not cause her any harm or pain."

Ella's eyes were wide. She hadn't spoken at all during Fenix's revelations, but appeared just as struck by them as the rest. Tana eyed the puppy suspiciously, but was otherwise impassive; a lifetime of disappointments had likely made the girl wary of hope. Kyara understood the feeling.

"As long as she isn't harmed," Ella said. "It's what she came here for."

Kyara nodded at Fenix. "Fine, then. Do it."

He bowed respectfully, and perhaps a bit amused, before approaching Tana. He knelt before her and inclined his head. "May I hold your hand, please?"

Tana held out a trembling hand. Fenix smiled and it was beatific, a glorious beaming that brought to mind calm blue skies and warm spring days. "Best close your eyes."

She did so and at first nothing happened. Kyara held her breath, waiting, hoping she hadn't made a mistake in supporting this. Then Tana began to glow. Ella startled, her grip on Tana's shoulder tightening. But almost as soon as the glow hit her skin, it was gone.

Tana's eyes grew big when she opened them. A huge smile filled her face. "I feel it," she said excitedly. "It's like . . . I'm not quite sure what it's like, but it's wonderful!" Her breathing had sped up as her excitement increased.

Kyara used her other sight to sense the girl's Nether. The bright glow of the Nethersinger shone in the darkness. But shockingly, it was growing stronger and stronger. Tana was drawing death energy into herself rapidly.

Where was it coming from? She shuttered her sight, watching for the reaction of the others, before sinking into it again, realizing that she could sense Fenix and he was quite odd. He didn't have the bright light of death energy of an adult, nor was he nearly invisible to her like a powerful Earthsinger. He was . . . normal. Just as he'd been in real life, fully visible.

He smiled at her, noting her shock. She wasn't quite sure how to react. But then Tana pulled even more Nethersong into herself, capturing Kyara's attention again. "Tana! Don't draw it all in at once." She could sense the girl's lack of control, she just couldn't figure out where the death energy was coming from or what the effect would be.

"She's drawing it from everywhere in small amounts, equally distributed throughout her range." Fenix answered her unspoken thought. "Every living thing around her will lose a small amount of Nethersong."

"And then be filled with the Void?"

He nodded. "But being so small, their own life energy will eventually replace it. They will be healthier and stronger for it."

That was possible? Why hadn't she ever thought of it before? "She's still taking on too much, too fast." What would she do with it all? Especially having never learned even a modicum of control. "Tana, stop!"

Then Mooriah was there, bright as the sun in her other sight.

The woman approached Tana and it looked as though their lights merged. The shining star that Tana had become dimmed as fast as it had grown, transforming back to something more like normal.

The girl was just a girl, with a tiny amount of Nether, and she was breathing heavily. Using her regular sight again, Kyara watched her try to catch her breath. Mooriah stood next to her, swaying gently. She met Kyara's gaze with an expression of slight exasperation, which somehow made everything better.

Tana grinned like she'd just won a race. "I like it!" she said, giggling, a sound never before heard from the child's lips.

Kyara sagged, leaning against Darvyn. "Well, it's obvious we have a lot of work to do."

CHAPTER TWENTY

Enjoy ever-deepening camaraderie
with those whose voices rise in chorus.

—THE HARMONY OF BEING

Varten packed very light. He couldn't risk someone seeing him walking around with heavy luggage in the palace and asking questions that might get back to Jasminda. But he wasn't sure what he'd need. Gilmeria was south of Elsira, but in the northern part of Yaly, abutting the mountain range separating the two countries. Temperatures there would be frigid, far worse than in mild Elsira.

He figured he would just have to buy additional clothing and supplies once they got there. Fortunately, money wasn't a problem. He had a full wallet and a virtually unlimited line of credit at the Bank of Elsira, money that he would be able to access in Yaly, when needed.

So he made his way to the docks with just a small knapsack. Roshon and Ani were leaving this morning, so he had a good cover story for being down there. Papa had risen earlier and was already at the busy port when Varten arrived, staring up at a Raunian-built ship named the *Rapskala* with misty eyes.

"You'd think after seeing your faces every day of your lives it wouldn't be so hard to go without." His throat sounded clogged.

Varten stuffed his hands in his pockets, flustered by his father's display of emotion. While Ani and her two-person crew did their final checks, Roshon came down the ramp to stand on Papa's other side.

"It's not a long trip," he said. "Just two months and we'll be back." He was happy, happier than Varten could remember seeing him.

"So long as you two don't elope," Papa chided, bringing Roshon into an embrace.

"No promises." Roshon pulled away and turned to Varten.

"Stay out of trouble," they said to each other in unison. Roshon shook his head, and Varten gave a half smile. He hugged his brother one more time, then stepped back.

Roshon looked at them both, then nodded and made his way up the ramp to the ship's deck. The invisible string that connected the twins grew taut. Varten knew it wouldn't snap, but it tugged at his chest and constricted his heart.

Papa wiped a tear from his eye and the two of them stood in silence until the *Rapskala* pulled out of its berth and headed off into the endless ocean.

"Two months isn't so long," Varten offered.

"No, I suppose not." His father looked up, grim. "And you are certain you don't want to come with me?"

"I am. This is the best idea you've had in years. The refugees need healers. Translators. They need *you*. I will be fine."

Papa was headed up north to one of the new settlements to volunteer and help the Lagrimari adjust. Varten wanted to help, but he wasn't an Earthsinger. He could always teach or translate, but was inevitably met with suspicion and fear by Lagrimari who viewed him as just another Elsiran. The effort of breaking down the walls of distrust with kindness and humor shouldn't have been taxing, but it was. Just another reminder that no matter where he went, he didn't truly belong.

"Things are changing, but they always would have eventually," Varten said. "They're good changes. We all just need time to get used to them. You won't be that far away. The refugee community in the north is what, an hour by auto? I live in a palace, Papa. I'll be fine." He grinned, hoping to put his father at ease. He couldn't lie to the man, since Earthsingers could sense it, so he injected all of his sincerity into his words.

Papa squeezed him into a tight hug. They were of a height now, and a similar size, almost. The old man's hair was fully gray, though it hadn't been two years earlier, and he still looked just as strong as he was in his son's memory. A couple of years in prison would change anyone's hair color. Varten was surprised his own ginger locks hadn't shifted a shade or two. But he'd been altered in other ways.

Papa stepped away, a serious expression on his face. "This is the beginning of you all starting your own lives. Roshon off on an adventure. And you—I know that you will figure things out in due time. All I want for you is to live. Promise me you'll do that? Live as much life as you can."

Varten swallowed and nodded. "I will, Papa." Guilt punched him in the gut. Should he tell someone about this trip?

He'd told Jasminda that he was going with Papa up north, and she'd seemed relieved. Papa believed he was staying here with his sister. Telling either of them about the journey could not only put them in danger if the Goddess truly was untrustworthy, it could give them both false hope about the possibility of restoring Songs. For even if he and Zeli managed to access the Archives, there was no guarantee the answer they sought was even there. Best to keep quiet until they had something real to share.

After giving the retreating ship one last look, Papa said his final good-byes to Varten and went to catch his bus. Varten settled onto a bench, out of the way of the bustle, watching it orbit around him.

The port was peppered with people from all over the world speaking in their languages, haggling, yelling, commanding, and laughing. He breathed in deeply, closing his eyes to take in the intermingling smells. The salt water and brine, a sour odor that he couldn't quite place, aromas of spices and different foods wafting in from the market just a few blocks away. He'd sat there only a few minutes when a familiar scent threaded its way through the rest.

Varten opened his eyes to find Zeli before him. She was no longer in her Sisterhood blue robe and pinafore, having exchanged it for a simple gray frock. Her hair was in dozens of thin braids hitting her shoulders.

Varten grinned. "Nice disguise."

She looked down at herself a bit self-consciously. "I took it from the Sisterhood charity bin. I suppose I am a poor Lagrimari refugee, so it's not exactly stealing."

"No, not stealing at all."

She looked around, dubious. "You said you had a plan for us to book passage? Why couldn't we get a ride with your brother anyway?"

"Roshon may not be an Earthsinger, but he knows when I'm lying. There'd be no way we wouldn't have to answer a thousand questions a day about what we were doing."

She pursed her lips and nodded. Varten tore himself away from her to look back at the ships. Because of the embargo, port traffic was light. Still, he'd seen a few vessels that looked promising.

"Booking a trip on a regular passenger vessel would leave too much of a paper trail," he continued. "We'd need to show identification and fill out all kinds of paperwork. If we want to be sure not to be followed, we'll just need to find someone willing to take us on for the right price. Check out berth twenty-two."

Zeli turned in the direction he pointed and her eyes grew big. The ship he'd scoped out was a luxurious-looking vessel, a yacht, no doubt a pleasure craft for someone rich. They had plenty of space, he figured, and might not mind taking on a few extras for the right price.

"Come on," Varten said, rising and moving quickly. Zeli kept up with his pace, though he remained mindful of her shorter legs. A middle-aged, brown-haired sailor stood at the ramp to the yacht when they approached, a stack of crates at his feet.

"Hey there," Varten said. "Do you accept passengers?"

"Go away," the man said gruffly in accented Elsiran.

"I was just—"

"I said . . ." The man looked up sharply, then his gaze locked onto Zeli. She stiffened and slid closer to Varten. The sailor tilted his head. "Passengers, you say? Not sure my boss would take kindly to that, but he doesn't have to know everything, does he?" He winked and grinned exclusively at Zeli.

"Ah, that's all right, mate," Varten said, sliding a protective arm around her. "Wouldn't want to risk you getting in trouble or losing your job." He backed away, pulling her with him.

"No trouble at all," the sailor said, laughing rudely. "How much for her?"

Her small, trembling hand gripped his back. "She's a person, she's not for sale," Varten said through gritted teeth.

"I mean, how much are you paying her? We could use someone to scrub up, empty the latrines, things like that."

"We're not looking for work," Varten said, still moving slowly backward.

"*Grols* have strong backs, there's lots of work to be had here, and they don't charge much. I can offer five pieces a week, plus a finder's fee for your trouble."

Two more sailors appeared on the yacht's deck, both large and grizzled. Their cold eyes looked at Zeli like property, just another good to be sold. One of the men grinned in a manner that made Varten suspect scrubbing toilets wasn't the only work they would expect of her.

He swung her around. "Let's go."

"Aye, not so fast there. We're offering good money for honest work."

Varten snorted, looking over his shoulder at the men. The two on the deck were headed down the ramp to stand side by side with their coworker. The move seemed aggressive, and he hoped the sailors wouldn't try to chase them. Varten hadn't been in many fights and knew he couldn't take on all three of them.

A Lagrimari man appeared by their side with a wrench in his hand. He didn't say anything but glared at the sailors. He was maybe thirty, clean shaven with a bald head.

The sailors stared back, then a call from the deck of the yacht grabbed their attention. A man in a captain's uniform stood looking at the scene. "I'm paying you to get the ship ready, not to converse with ruffians." The captain stared down his nose at them and the sailors complied, the first one leering once more before going back to his duties.

Varten turned to the Lagrimari man. "Thank you."

The man raised a brow, likely at Varten's command of the language, and then nodded his head. "Someone over there wants to meet you."

Varten tensed. It wasn't impossible that he'd been recognized, though he would have expected it more in an environment full of aristocrats than here on the docks. The man led them down a few berths to a small fishing ship where two more Lagrimari stood, a man and a woman.

Zeli gasped. "Yalisa?" She began running toward the woman, who grabbed her in a bear hug. "I can't believe it's you, are you all right?"

Yalisa was quite possibly the most beautiful woman Varten had ever seen. Her skin was luminous, and her short hair was a small puff.

"Your hair, did they make you cut it?" Zeli asked, patting the woman's head.

Yalisa smiled. "It's good to see you, too, *uli*."

Zeli wrapped her in another embrace, resting her head on Yalisa's shoulder. Varten looked on in wonder at Zeli's obvious joy.

Yalisa smiled at him over Zeli's head. "And who is your friend?"

Zeli finally pulled back, wiping her eyes, but didn't let go. "Oh, this is Varten. Varten, Yalisa, I've known her almost all my life."

Yalisa nodded in his direction as greeting. "This is my brother, Eskar-yol." She pointed to the man who had come to help them. "And this is Lanar-deni. We met a few days ago in the camp." They were all of a similar age, though the second man was prematurely gray and looked taciturn by nature. He nodded solemnly. Knotted locks threaded with silver and tied back in a queue reached his midback.

"I didn't know you had a brother," Zeli said with surprise and turned wondrous eyes at Eskar.

"I was sent to the camps as a child and then recruited into the army. Been in Elsira since the Seventh Breach." Eskar's voice was soft and scratchy. He seemed like a man of few words.

Tears welled in Yalisa's eyes as she looked at her brother. "We met again in the refugee camp after the Elsirans took Sayya. I barely recognized him."

Eskar gazed at his sister fondly. "Well, my face is forgettable, yours, however . . ."

Yalisa shook her head and lifted a thick green scarf to cover her hair. The air off the ocean was chilly, especially for Lagrimari used to a desert climate. "What are you doing here, *uli*?" the woman asked Zeli.

"We're trying to get to Yaly. We . . . that is . . ." Zeli looked back to Varten, distressed.

"Seeing some of the world?" Yalisa asked conspiratorially. "I understand. It's just what we're doing as well."

The ship they stood in front of was older. It appeared to be of Elsiran build, and had been well-patched. "Whose ship is this?" Varten asked.

"Won it in a bet against a drunken fisherman," Eskar replied, looking proudly at the vessel. "Taught the man a valuable lesson about how smart *grols* actually are."

Varten grinned. "Where are you all headed?"

"We're not entirely sure," Yalisa said. "We want to sail the continent, see other countries, go where the winds take us."

"We've plotted out stops for fuel and supplies though," Eskar hastened to add.

"Yes, yes, we don't plan to be hungry ever again if we can help it." There was joy on Yalisa's face, mixed in with sadness. "And what is in Yaly?"

"We want to see the Gilmerian Rumpus." Zeli seemed almost shy to admit it. Neither Yalisa nor Eskar had heard of the Rumpus, so Zeli explained what she knew of the celebration, leaving out, of course, their desire to visit the Archives.

Yalisa's grin grew. "That sounds like a grand adventure. Very smart to head for an event that only takes place every decade. Eskar has no love of crowds and loud noises, otherwise we might have joined you. But we can take you as far as Melbain City. We were planning that as our first stop." She turned toward Lanar, who had thus far stayed out of the conversation. "And have you decided on a destination, Lanar-deni?"

"I believe I, too, would like to see this Rumpus. Ten years is a long time to wait for another." His voice was somewhat stilted, his tone formal, as if he was not used to speaking often. "Would you mind if we traveled together?"

Zeli looked to Varten, who shrugged. "Not at all. Happy to have you."

Lanar nodded gravely in acknowledgement. He had a very matter-of-fact way about him, which reminded Varten of Papa, though his papa was far more jovial.

"It's always good to help a fellow countryman. We Lagrimari need to stick together," Yalisa said.

Varten shifted on his feet, uncomfortable. He was half-Lagrimari, but would never be considered a countryman. "We can pay our way," he added.

"No need," said Eskar. "You are guests. Beloved ones at that." He beamed at Zeli, still attached to Yalisa's side.

"I, for one, would be interested to hear of how an Elsiran came to speak fluent Lagrimari." Lanar's statement quieted the chatter. To Varten's ears, even the volume of the docks lowered. His heart forgot to beat for a moment. He should have thought this through more.

If he told these people who he was, would they still want to help him? Or would they be afraid of drawing the ire of his sister?

"The king speaks Lagrimari fluently." Everyone stared at him. That was, apparently, the wrong thing to say.

Lanar spoke up. "The king was able to learn Lagrimari because of the spell tied to his blood, which allowed him to awaken the Queen Who Sleeps."

Now everyone stared at Lanar. "I-I didn't know that," Varten stammered.

"Few do. I wonder what is in your blood." Lanar peered at him with eyes that looked older than his face. Though he seemed a no-nonsense sort, the deeply speculative gaze was a little unsettling.

Varten shrugged, hoping they would all just let the matter drop. Yalisa gave him a sympathetic expression. He fidgeted, feeling the scrutiny of the others upon him. When Eskar spoke, he sagged with relief. "Does anyone need anything before we pull anchor?"

"I'm ready to go when you are," Varten said. Zeli and Lanar responded similarly.

"It's two days to Melbain. Welcome aboard." Eskar helped his sister climb onto the deck, and then reached out an arm to assist Zeli.

"What's your ship called?" Varten asked, noticing a patch of fresh paint covering what must have been the former name.

"Haven't named her yet. I wanted Yalisa to do it, but she's been indecisive."

"It's a lot of responsibility," his sister called out. "I'm just taking it seriously."

Eskar smiled and shook his head. Watching the recently reunited siblings caused a pang to ricochet through Varten's chest. He hoped Jasminda did not find out he was gone before he returned. Hoped this trip wouldn't leave him with regrets or any morc scars than the ones he already bore. Varten's last sea voyage hadn't ended well, and he fought off a heavy foreboding.

Instead, he took a look around the ship. The bridge was enclosed in glass. Steps led to a cabin below. There looked to be enough room for the five of them to sit comfortably down there, but the accommodations were sparse. Zeli settled in next to Yalisa, talking and reminiscing happily, while Lanar paced the deck, inspecting the ship with an air of deep suspicion.

Varten stood, determined to offer Eskar his help. He'd learned some about sailing from Ani's brother, Tai, and would rather put that knowledge to good use than worry about what was to come.

In a matter of minutes, they were on their way. Rosira's port shrank in the distance as they raced toward the unknown.

CHAPTER TWENTY-ONE

With even steps and temper
shall we lay our burdens
on the scales.

—THE HARMONY OF BEING

Jasminda arrived at the small, dingy building in the Northside neighborhood in a nondescript vehicle, a jalopy that bore no resemblance to the pristine, shining town cars generally utilized by the palace. A gray overcoat covered her from neck to ankles and a matching floppy rain hat hid her hair and face.

She'd altered the shade of her skin so that anyone getting a glimpse of her beneath the disguise would not be able to identify her as appearing Lagrimari. She wished she'd had time to master the shifting of features that Darvyn could accomplish that could turn her into another person entirely, but it was one of the most complicated uses of Earthsong, and though she now had the power to accomplish it, she still lacked the skill.

However, she was only visible on the street for a few brief moments before being ensconced in the building's darkened entryway. The driver who accompanied her, dressed in a plain workingman's shirt and trousers, opened the interior door and led her into an office full of men and women at desks cluttered with an excess of typewriters and telephones. Even inside there was no indication that this was one of the satellite offices of the nation's Intelligence Service.

Her assistant Camm was already inside, talking with an older woman who sat at a desk with no less than seven telephones. He straightened and strode to her as Jasminda entered and let her meager disguise fall away.

"Your Majesty," he said quietly, "he's on the lower level in the interrogation room."

The new acting director of the Intelligence Service had believed that Zann Biddell would be more malleable to questioning now that he was officially under arrest—albeit for another crime. Of course these were the same agents who hadn't managed to gather enough evidence to arrest him for his actual offenses, so she wasn't hopeful.

Two Intelligence Agents appeared and led her and Camm to a stairwell in the corner. They descended into a dimly lit concrete box leading to an equally dim hallway lined with doors. One of the agents opened a door in the middle of the hall and ushered them through with a short bow.

Inside, a bare bulb in the ceiling created harsh shadows. A small metal table and chair were pushed against a wall directly under a window looking on to another room. With the exception of a few chairs scattered around the space, it was otherwise devoid of furniture.

A secretary sat at the table, headphones affixed to her ears, scribbling on a pad in shorthand as she stared through the window into the other room. Jasminda stepped up behind her, peered through the tinted glass, and froze.

"Is that him?"

Camm came to her side. "Zann Biddell in the flesh."

"And he can't see us?"

"No, this is a transparent mirror, Your Majesty," one of the agents said. "Inside of the interrogation room, it looks like a regular mirror. He can only see himself."

And himself wasn't much to look at. There was nothing visually that marked him as evil. He was small and plain, with a forgettable face. His head was shaved, with nothing of the oddly pale stubble that would mark him as half-foreign. She'd never been face-to-face with Biddell and found him disappointing in person. Wouldn't it be easier if his villainy were painted across his skin or marked with something terrifying like horns or red, blazing eyes?

An interrogator was in the room with him, seated with his back to the mirror. Biddell looked unperturbed, hands bound with metal cuffs and placed on the table in front of him. He had been held already for two days while his paperwork was sorted, but he didn't look worried in the least.

"Is there a way for us to hear what's being said?" Jasminda asked.

The agent nodded and moved to a speaker on the wall she hadn't noticed before. He turned the dial and Biddell's silvery voice filled the room.

"I don't know where you're getting your information from, Agent Verall. But I will repeat it as often as I must until it penetrates. I had nothing to do with the smoke bombing, or any of the other attacks." His gaze was wide open, unblinking. But Jasminda's Song clearly sensed the lie.

Hundreds of years ago, that would have been enough to convict a murderer in the halls of justice. But now, since Earthsong had been absent from Elsira in any real way for generations, she could know the truth and not be able to do anything about it. Not via the legal system at any rate.

"But you admit," the agent was saying, "that you do not find the attacks to be tragedies."

Biddell raised his shackled hands as if to motion with them, forgetting he could not, and sighed. "Whoever is responsible for the unrest is a patriot, I'll grant you. They are doing what must be done to save our land and our way of life."

Jasminda felt like a hot knife was being run underneath her skin, attempting to flay it from her flesh. She fisted her hands and breathed deeply, forcing herself to stay where she was and keep listening.

"I will not apologize for being a separationist. No good can come of trying to blend oil and water together. They will never mix. Elsira is our land, as it should be. Let the *grols* practice their witchcraft somewhere else."

"You realize that statements such as this along with your recent editorials in the same vein are quite damning." Agent Verall's voice was even, conversational. No hint of the anger racing through Jasminda's veins.

"Having an opinion is not a crime in this land. Unless the new queen has managed to change our laws." Biddell shifted in his chair, rattling at the chains on his ankles and wrists. "She is innovative, I'll grant her that, but I am confident that there is no evidence of the crimes you accuse me of."

"I'm sure you've made certain of that," Verall said, wryly. Biddell chuckled and the bastard interrogator laughed with him.

"I've heard enough," Jasminda said, fury heating her. "How do I get in there?"

"Your Majesty?" The agent next to her looked aghast. Camm's lips were pursed; he shook his head silently.

"I would like to question the prisoner." She spoke slowly and clearly.

"I'm—I'm sorry, Your Majesty, that would be highly irregular, it's—"

"Do I need to go above your head for this, Agent?"

The man paled and looked to the transparent mirror and then back to his queen. "Of course not. Please follow me."

Camm trailed her silently as she followed the flustered agent down the hall and around the corner. Two more suited men, pistols holstered at their sides, stood on either side of the door to the room that must hold Biddell. They recognized the queen and straightened, then sketched perfunctory bows. She stood before the door, icily staring until one of them opened it.

Agent Verall looked up, startled, and Jasminda met Zann Biddell's gaze in the mirror. He hid his surprise well with a mask of implacability, but Jasminda felt the truth with her Song. The last person he'd expected was the new queen.

"I'd like to speak with Master Biddell, and then I'd like you to organize his transfer to the palace dungeon." She did not look at Verall directly, but caught him blinking at her as he rose slowly.

When he went to speak, she raised a hand. "Now, please."

The room cleared quickly. She gave a final look to her assistant as the door closed and found him frowning at her.

Shaking off Camm's concern, she paced to the chair Verall had vacated, removing her gloves. This was a dreary room, bare bulb and cinder blocks, gray on gray, lifeless. If there was a psychological advantage they were trying to achieve, she wondered if that might be done better through other means.

She sat and faced the figure who had caused so much destruction. He was feeling smug, though his face was expressionless. The only outward hint he gave of any emotion was a small narrowing of his eyes.

"Your Majesty," he finally said, inclining his head slightly.

"Master Biddell. Honestly, I'd expected more. You are a remarkably average man to have created such terror in our land."

"I'm a simple fisherman. The only ones who should fear me are the fish." He sat back trying to give an air of casual aplomb.

Jasminda clasped her hands before her. "You talk a lot about witchcraft and its dangers. Do you really believe that Earthsong is not real?"

Biddell looked rueful. "Magic exists. I know this. But I also know that with such power comes inevitable tyranny. Hasn't the True Father shown us this? Hasn't the Goddess?"

"What of compassion?" Jasminda tilted her head, diving deep into his emotions, trying to determine if there was any shred of pathos within him. "Many of the Lagrimari who managed to keep their Songs have emptied out hospitals around the country, healing those who allowed it. Boosting the paltry harvest as much as they could. Helping the land. You conveniently forget the benefits of Earthsong."

"I forget nothing. Not the stories of the veterans of the Breach Wars. The terror in their eyes and voices as they recount the horrors of hailstorms and mudslides killing their friends, ripping our country apart." His light-colored eyes held only the merest hint of gold. His gaze was flinty and never left her face.

"You should also recall that an Earthsinger can sense lies. Can feel emotion. So tell me again how you had nothing to do with the smoke attack this week on the apartment building, the temple bombing, the hospital fire last month, or the hotel sabotage? Please, tell me these lies to my face."

His jaw tightened and he looked away for the first time. Not with anything close to guilt but with anger. Scorching flames rose higher within Jasminda, his anger only stoked her own.

"Tell me how you and the Dominionists or the Reapers or whatever you want to call yourselves are not responsible for nearly a hundred dead since the fall of the Mantle. Do you know how many Elsirans are among that number? Do you care?"

His jaw worked from side to side. A hint of something close to remorse was a tiny ember within. "There is always collateral damage in wartime. The veterans I spoke to told me that as well."

"But you yourself have never served. Didn't choose to join the army and help defend the land, did you?"

He looked away, unsettled. Ashamed.

"Oh, forgive me, I forgot. You tried to, didn't you? But were deemed unfit for service. What was the cause again? I reviewed your files but I think it's slipped right out of my head." His anger built, adding more fuel to her own inner fire. He did not answer.

"Seizures, was that it? An affliction you've suffered from since childhood. You know, I read once that Udlanders have unique nutritional requirements due to generations living in such harsh climates in the icy north. Their bodies have adapted amazingly, but when they travel and are denied specific nutrients only found in their land, their bodies have a very severe reaction." She tapped her lips. "A pity your mother never told you that."

And just like that, he snapped. Rage filled his eyes and he stood up sharply, sliding his chair back with the force of his motion. It clattered as it fell. They were about the same height, and she had nothing to fear from him physically even without his shackles. The fact that the mother who had abandoned him as a baby was a foreigner, an Udlander no less, pejoratively called Icemen and thought to be little more than barbarians, was something Biddell kept well-hidden. To the outside world he was an Elsiran patriot, a nationalist, and a leader.

The door to the room opened but she waved off the armed agents. Once it closed again, she clasped her hands on the table calmly. "My mother is a sore spot for me as well. It's unfortunate, is it not, to grow up without one."

He looked like a bull, breathing through his nose, face red, sweat dotting his forehead and upper lip. Slowly, he calmed himself. She sensed him reel in his murderous impulse toward her. She could only imagine the names he was calling her in his mind, the many ways he dreamt of ending her life, but his lips didn't open.

He righted his chair, and pulled it back to the table, then took his seat. His breathing was still somewhat labored but he was once again composed. "The loss of a mother is a tragedy," was all he said.

"Certainly."

"And no, Your Majesty, I never had the privilege to serve my country in the military. I found other ways." His emotions shifted so abruptly that her breath caught. The rage not just muted, but gone, tucked away out of reach and replaced again by insolence. "You know we do have something in common, you and I. We both came from humble beginnings, but whereas I have found my way amongst the common man, you have moved on to much loftier circles. Appointed queen, even before you married the king. Had you not married, would you have ruled together?"

She wasn't sure what he was leading to, and spoke carefully. "Yes. It was an unusual occurrence, but the Goddess had the right to name Her successors. She named us both, independent of our marriage."

"King Jaqros of course comes from the line of rulers. An

Alliaseen has sat upon the throne since the days when the Queen Who Sleeps was originally awake." A strange smile played upon his lips. "But an ul-Sarifor? Am I saying that correctly?" He was not, but she didn't bother to correct him. "What was the precedent? The reasoning?"

She breathed in deeply. "I know you do not follow the Goddess Awoken, but She does everything for a reason."

"I'm sure She does. And the reason to elevate an ignorant child to the highest leadership in our land? An inexperienced, Borderland bumpkin full of witchcraft and foreign blood? It makes me wonder how five hundred years of sleep has affected the poor Goddess's mind. I fear incompetence at best, treachery at worst."

Jasminda's jaw clenched. "Treachery?"

He spread his hands as far apart as he could. "She is the sister of the True Father, is She not? I've heard whisperings. Their shared blood must be tainted, else how could one be so evil and the other retain goodness? No, I think that She awakened and saw a land vastly changed and sought to destroy it. How better to do that than install an unfit, unqualified leader? A reckless, foolish girl with no idea what she's doing who is already leading us into ruin. Drought, embargo, hunger, lawlessness, protests—all under your watch. All of which you have done nothing to help or prevent. Tell me, why do *you* think She made you queen? Because of all of your experience and mastery?" His laugh was cruel, it edged into the doubts within her heart, watering the poisonous seeds almost lovingly. They drank it up.

She lifted her chin. She had often wondered the same thing, asked Oola more than once, but gotten nothing but vague platitudes in response. Yes, she was a child of two lands, and yes, she represented the unification bodily, but was that the reason she was queen? Was that enough?

Some of her feelings must have bled through into her expression, for Zann Biddell was suddenly brimming with smug joy. This made her hands fist. She needed only a trickle of power to keep tabs on Biddell's emotions, but she filled herself with more and more, relishing the feeling of it rushing within her, powering her.

The self-satisfied expression on his face made her ill. *He* made her ill. This murderous xenophobe with the silver tongue who had brought so many over to his cause. He must be stopped and it was clear that even in the face of his lies being exposed, he would not confess.

She suspected he had allies within the Intelligence Service, Elsirans who believed as he did and bowed to her face but worked in secret behind her back. The former director himself had poisoned her, after all. It would be foolish to assume that the man's disappearance had cleared out the supporters of his ideology from the organization.

She pulled Earthsong to her, far more than she needed, but enough to fill her Song. The self-important, smarmy, son of a hog needed to be stopped. His reign of terror, provoking people to violence and hatred and fear, could not continue. Maybe he should feel what real witchcraft could do. Maybe he should feel a bit of what he was inspiring in others.

Oola was able to manipulate the emotions of others, to send Her thoughts to Singers and Silent alike, along with specific desires. Daryvn looked down on the practice, called it unethical puppetry, but Oola didn't seem to care. Jasminda was a bit past caring herself, especially with this cretinous excuse for a human in front of her.

She narrowed her eyes, wondering exactly what it would take to wipe that grin from his lips. She couldn't hurt him with her Song, couldn't open wounds on his skin or steal the breath from his lungs. Life energy didn't work like that. But she could share her own pain.

She thought of life growing up in her valley and pushed away the joy at the memories of her childhood, when her whole family was together, Mama and Papa, the twins always underfoot, Varten peppering them with constant questions about everything under the sun and how it all worked. Roshon quieter, rarely smiling and far more serious, but never far from his brother. She tucked those memories into a corner of her mind and focused on the others.

Traveling to town for supplies. The cutting looks and remarks. She had been just a child when a runaway horse had trampled another girl about her own age. Jasminda had run over to help, healing broken bones and internal injuries, or at least making them better, since her Song had been too weak back then to completely fix someone. The shrieks of the girl's mother shouting about witchcraft echoed in her mind. The hurt and shame as she withstood the tongue lashing before her father rushed over to take her away. These were the feelings she pushed to Zann Biddel.

The ache of loneliness and grief, the deep sadness at watching her brothers make friends easily as long as she stayed away. The sorrow etched into her mother and father as they witnessed injustices they were powerless to stop. Folk crossing the street to avoid her. Leaving a store when she entered. Accusing her of stealing. Cleaning whatever she'd touched. The fear and disgust wafting from them as she tried to live her life.

She magnified the emotions, years and years of abuse in one concentrated burst, and funneled them all to Biddell at once. Her gaze was inward so she didn't witness his lips flatten. Didn't see him shudder at the potent force driving into him.

His body began to shake, but she didn't stop. She was charged full of anger; reliving the old pain broke the callus she'd formed around the feelings. They all poured out. Tears streamed down Zann Biddell's cheeks. He made sounds of distress. His eyes rolled up in his head. He began to seize and shudder. He fell from his chair onto the ground.

Focused as she was on driving hurt after hurt into him, she barely noticed his distress. It was only when the door crashed open that it truly registered. Agents rushed in to tend to the quaking man on the floor, foam and blood frothing around his mouth. Still, her eyes were open but her mind remained elsewhere.

A pinch above her elbow drew her back to the present. She whipped her head around to find Camm standing next to her, face long and grave. "Forgive me, Your Majesty. It appears Master Biddell is experiencing a seizure. We should leave while the physician attends to him."

She blinked her eyes and focused on the room again. A doctor in a white coat kneeled next to the prisoner who had stopped seizing. Jasminda breathed in deeply, releasing her hold on Earthsong. The ocean of energy receded as if it had not been a torrent within her moments earlier.

"Yes, you're right." She stood, grabbing her gloves from the table and placing them on shaking hands. No one was paying attention to her, they all watched the man on the floor. None suspected what she had done, how could they? It wasn't visible and not even most Lagrimari knew what was truly possible with a powerful Song.

Her breathing stuttered as they retreated down the hallway and up the stairs. Agent Verall met them on the main level. "The prisoner will be transported to the dungeon once the physician gives the go-ahead, Your Majesty."

She nodded in agreement, but didn't trust her voice to speak. Her throat was dry and aching and she felt as if she'd run a race. It was the Song she'd expended. She wasn't drained by any means, but she had unwittingly lost control. A glance at Camm showed him staring at her warily. He suspected something, though he wasn't any more well versed in Songs and what they could do than anyone else here.

Outside, he handed her back into the rattletrap auto that had brought her here in secret. No one would know what she did. No one but Zann Biddell. She peered at Camm out the window as the vehicle pulled away. She had asked him to alert her if she went too far, but she didn't really need the warning. She knew today that she had indeed crossed an invisible line.

She just wasn't certain if she regretted it.

CHAPTER TWENTY-TWO

Embody your hopes in your work.
Let your deeds be a home for your
good intentions.

—THE HARMONY OF BEING

Zeli spent the passage to Yaly almost entirely with her jaw hanging open. The as-yet unnamed ship sailed down the coast, passing mountain ranges and forests and other ships of all kinds on the busy waterway. The well-traveled route was far more congested than she ever would have expected the sea to be, though between Rosira and Fremia's capital city of Adara, there were no other ports of note.

Eskar, their captain, was a wealth of information. He explained that though Raun had only embargoed Elsira, the action had caused a disastrous ripple effect to the trade in and out of the country. As such, Adara was far busier than ever.

The ship didn't slow as it passed the Fremian city's metal spires and glass towers. Smoke and noise and congestion wafted from its shore, and Zeli was glad not to be going there. She'd thought Rosira a big city, but it was a Midcountry outpost compared to the megacity that was Adara. The taciturn Lanar made a rare statement advising them that Yaly's cities were even larger. She tried to prepare herself.

The body of water that led to land-locked Yaly was called Dunbay. After her first glance of a true urban labyrinth, the greenery and marshland on the banks of the bay were quite welcome. Eskar pointed out the course they were taking on the maps, and Zeli tried to commit this new, vast world to memory.

"The majority of the bay belongs to Fremia," he explained, "however, it is the only way to access Yaly from the Delaveen Ocean. Fortunately for the Yalyish, Fremia remains neutral in times of conflict."

"But Fremia is so much smaller," she said. "Couldn't Yaly crush them?"

"There is a reason they haven't all these years. Yaly is a large land, but fractured. It would take the movement of mountains to make all the commonwealths come together to work as one. A broken thing is never strong. Fremia is smaller, but cohesive. Unity is part of their culture. Unity and excellence. Their small force can, and has, routed one twenty times as large."

"How do you know all this?" Varten asked in wonder.

Eskar dipped his head. "I worked with the Sisterhood for the past few years. Some of the Sisters were very politically minded. I learned much through listening to their conversations."

Zeli had been happy to spend the majority of the journey

chatting with Yalisa, whom she never thought she'd see again. The former mistress of Zeli's employer had been sent to the camps in Lagrimar, a victim of political scheming. Zeli told her of how the Magister, in whose home they'd both lived, had been nearly killed by his daughter's fiancé, but little Ulani had saved his life. They mused on the man's whereabouts.

"He was likely arrested as one of the True Father's agents," Yalisa said, sadness filling her voice. Though her former lover had been the one responsible for her arrest, Zeli could tell she still had feelings for him. Once Yalisa had held a position she'd envied—but it hadn't lasted.

"You think he will be executed with the others?" Zeli whispered.

Yalisa blinked. "He probably deserves it." She took a breath, shaking off the moment of melancholy. "What do you hope for in Yaly?" she asked with a small smile. "I'm surprised you'd be so interested in such a rowdy-sounding event. Didn't you always like the quiet, simpler things?"

"I did. But . . . this is practically once in a lifetime. I've realized that the way I used to think about things needed to shift. The world is changing, we need to as well."

"Hmm." Yalisa looked thoughtful. "Yes, change is inevitable . . . Eventually. It did take Lagrimar quite a long time."

"What do you hope for?" Zeli whispered.

Yalisa laughed, a sound full of both mirth and uncertainty. "Anything. Everything. Life. I do not think we even know how to live properly. I would like to learn." She tilted her head up to the sky where the midday sun brightened her face. "I want to breathe in life. To have it empty its lungs inside of me, and rise into the air filled with all of the experiences and feelings and joys and fears and everything in between."

She sobered somewhat and turned back to Zeli with a chuckle. "But I don't even know what to hope for, and that is the real tragedy, is it not?"

Zeli nodded, in complete understanding. "But I know you'll find out. I'm so happy for you, and I hope not to lose touch with you."

Yalisa grabbed her hands and squeezed. "Of course, *uli,* we shall not lose one another forever. Maybe I will travel for a few years, or perhaps Eskar and I will settle down somewhere, but either way, I hope you will come and visit wherever I am. You and your . . . friend?" The small smile she gave hinted at more with Varten, but Zeli's cheeks heated and she shook her head at the idea of *more.* Though sometimes it was difficult to remember that wasn't what she wanted.

"I would like very much to visit you, when all this is over." Part of her wanted to forget about the Rumpus and just stay with her now. Yalisa had been a mother figure to a young orphaned servant, one of the only people who had truly cared for her.

They were quiet after that, taking in the sights of the busy bay and Melbain City looming in the distance. Zeli had been to Sayya, Lagrimar's capital city, once as a child; she didn't recall much but noise and stench and fear, but as the bay narrowed and their ship was funneled into a wide river, she realized that even her glimpse of Adara had not prepared her for a true megacity.

Great metal towers rose in the air for what looked like kilometers. Their small ship passed under bridges filled with belching autos—no horses and carts were mixed in with them like on Rosira's streets. Smokestacks poured thick, bilious smog into the air, turning the sky from blue to gray, even though the sun shone.

There was an underlying noise to the city, a buzzing drone that threatened to drown out all thought. The temperature was similar to Rosira and the people she saw hurrying through the streets wore drab, dark coats, heads covered with hats. Her wonderment was mixed with revulsion at the thought of living in such a place.

The river led them past a dozen or more docking areas, packed with crafts of various sizes, but Eskar sailed on. Soon they found a spot in an overcrowded marina. Once they exited the boat, they had to negotiate a narrow, floating walkway until they finally arrived on dry land.

While Eskar went to the marina office, seeking someone who spoke Elsiran, Zeli was faced with saying good-bye to her friend and mentor. "How long will you stay in the city?" she asked.

"Maybe a day or two. Long enough to say we've visited, though I don't know that I'd like to stay here very long." She looked up at the towering structures dubiously.

Zeli was glad that Yalisa had her brother with her. Neither spoke the language, they did not have much money, or even their Songs to rely upon, but they also had no fear. After surviving the True Father, why should they?

Eskar returned and they all said their good-byes. Zeli tried, and failed, not to cry as Yalisa and her brother disappeared into the city to explore a bit. Once they were out of sight and her tears had still not stopped, she ducked her head and fiddled with the strap of the small bag that held what few possessions she had. She did not want to face the others in such a state.

"We should see about transportation to Gilmeria," Lanar announced, startling her with his voice. He'd spoken so rarely on the trip down, fortunately abandoning his questions about how Varten had learned to speak Lagrimari. "It's quite a ways away."

Zeli recalled the map. They would have to travel north again, toward the mountains bordering Lagrimar. Airship or train were the best options to get to Gilmer City quickly. Varten got directions to the air station from an attendant who spoke broken Elsiran and they made their way on foot through the busy streets.

Pedestrians here were even ruder than in Rosira. Zeli was jostled and shaken so much by passing elbows and shoulders that she thought she might turn into a milkshake. After one particular bone-jarring rattle, Varten put a protective arm around her. She sank into his side, avoiding a large handbag headed for her face, though she was careful not to grip him too tightly.

Yalisa's knowing smile haunted her memory—it had been a little too on target—and as soon as they turned onto a quieter street, she pulled away abruptly. She tried to ignore the small expression of hurt that crossed his face when she did so.

The air station was in the center of the city. Airships big and small filled the tarmac. Zeli had only ever seen the king's airship in Elsira, which was tiny compared to the airbuses built to ferry hundreds of people across the continent.

Lanar, who mysteriously knew a few words of Yalyish, went off to investigate schedules and prices. Though he had not shared much about himself, he must have been a prisoner of war like Eskar, stuck in Elsira since the last Breach War. They agreed to meet back at the entrance to the air station. Beside her, Varten was quiet. She hadn't talked to him much on the journey, so absorbed by seeing Yalisa again. Of course, he'd been busy with Eskar, learning the workings of the fishing ship.

People milled about in large groups, but a ripple of disturbance caught Zeli's attention. "What is that?" she gasped as something cut its way through the crowd. Exclamations and curses rang out as people tripped and leapt away.

The gap grew closer, revealing a tiny, mechanical dog scurrying across the floor. Its body was metal, including a very busy, articulated tail. It paused, turning its silver head to look around, then seemed to focus on Zeli. Two shiny, glass marbles served as its eyes, and while she wasn't certain such a thing could even see, the contraption hastened its movements, coming straight for her.

She reached down to stop its forward momentum and picked it up, dodging its still moving feet. The creature was lighter than she'd expected and vibrated, letting out a little "yip" before a warm tongue reached out to lick her. It wasn't wet, rather it was made of some kind of beaten leather, soft and ticklish.

A man's voice called out, and she spied a figure jogging through the wake of confusion the little dog had left. He was portly and grandfatherly—or at least what she imagined a grandfather might be like. Round and gray and balding, with ochre skin and twinkling eyes. He moved with surprising speed until he'd caught up with the mechanical creature.

The dog licked her again and she giggled. The old man worked to catch his breath while the crowd around them went back to normal, as if nothing strange had happened. He smiled and spoke in a fast stream of Yalyish.

"I'm sorry, I don't understand," she said, first in Lagrimari, then in Elsiran.

He stopped and squinted at her, then reached for the side of his head. What was left of his hair frothed out messily around his head, but his motion revealed what looked like a metal ear. He adjusted the contraption, which hissed alarmingly, before quieting.

"Now, what was that?" he asked in Elsiran. "Ah yes, miss, I thank ye for rescuing m'dog." He reached for it, and she handed the still wiggly creature over.

"You are welcome," she said carefully. She turned to a stunned Varten and whispered in Lagrimari, "What do you think that thing on his ear is?"

"Well, missy, lost m'ear in the Tin War of '02. Got this replacement from Fremia. Came upgraded with a language module."

Varten squinted, while Zeli's jaw dropped. "You understand Lagrimari? Is that an amalgam?"

"I thought they weren't making amalgamations any more after the Physicks headquarters was destroyed," Varten said, again in Lagrimari. His voice was unusually cautious.

The man responded in Elsiran. "Oh no, no more of those. All the stores selling out, no more recharges, all useless junk they are now as soon as they run out of power. But this mech is based on a similar idea. Different application. Cutting edge. Me granddaughter is an engineer down in Adara, working on assistive tech. She got me on some list of testers. I can't speak Lagrimari, but I can understand any tongue on Saint Melba's green earth. Comes in handy." He motioned to the dog still wiggling in her arms to be let free. "I thank ye for helping Ziggy here. He tends to run off."

"Is he another of your granddaughter's creations?" Varten asked, wide-eyed.

"He is indeed. Zigs is me best companion. Now, I do some tinkering myself. I reckon that's where me granddaughter got the idea of it, and it's how I got me name. Allow me to introduce meself. I'm the Tinker." He sketched an elegant bow at odds with his more humble appearance.

"Your name is the Tinker?" Zeli asked, agape. She was both astonished that that was a name and at the fact she had understood so much of what he'd said. He spoke both slowly and clearly, but it was more than that and she wondered at what exactly the metal ear did, and how it was accomplished.

"Why yes, that's what they call me." He winked, chuckling.

Lanar returned then with a curious glance at the Tinker. "Passage on an airship will cost us dearly. All the prices have been raised on account of the popularity of the Rumpus."

"Yer all going to the Rumpus?" the Tinker asked, voice swelling. "'Tis highway robbery what they're charging folk for the trip this close to the event. Yer both Lagrimari?" He motioned to Zeli and Lanar.

"Why?" Lanar asked, narrowing his eyes at the same time that Zeli answered, "Yes."

Lanar gave her a speaking glare, effectively communicating that she should be more circumspect around strangers. Then again, he was a stranger, too.

The Tinker hooted and slapped his thigh. Ziggy, now held in one arm, yelped. "I never met a real-life Lagrimari before. Boy have I got some questions for ye. How 'bout this? I haven't been to a Rumpus in an age. I'll give ye all a ride up, free of charge, and ye can tell me all about life under a madman."

Zeli blinked. The offer was unexpected and not entirely welcome. She had no desire to talk about the True Father. Evidently Lanar agreed. "That will not be necessary," he answered coldly.

With a deft movement of his arm, he shepherded both Zeli and Varten away from the grinning man.

"I'll be at platform eighty-nine if ye change yer minds," the Tinker called out amiably. Ziggy punctuated the message with a metallic bark that sounded both cheerful and sad.

"He was quite a character," Varten said, motioning toward the older man's retreating form.

Lanar was able to speak volumes without saying a word. A raised brow and haughty expression left no doubt as to what he thought about the Tinker. "Airship rates are all around ninety Dahlinean shings per person, one way."

"That's a lot?" Zeli asked.

"About one-hundred and fifty Elsiran pieces."

Varten whistled.

"Do you have the funds to cover such?" Lanar asked. "I do not."

But Varten nodded and fished out his wallet. "I can get your ticket. I'll have to visit the bank afterward though."

Zeli looked back and forth between them, a question forming in her mind. Varten caught her eye and lifted a shoulder. "I told him who I really am." Her gaze shifted to Lanar.

"And I promised not to refer to him as *Your Grace* during the journey." The man didn't smile, he never seemed to, but there was humor in his voice at least. "I deeply appreciate this and will pay you back as soon as possible."

Varten brushed this off. "It's not really my money anyway."

She could tell by Varten's expression that he hadn't told Lanar their real reason for going to the Rumpus. They'd promised not to tell anyone.

The inside of the air station was just as congested and noisy as the outside. They pushed their way through the masses to reach the currency exchanger. Varten handed over his stack of crisp bills and received a fistful of strange coins in return.

This Yalyish money wasn't made of any metal she recognized, it was multicolored and shifted shades when the light hit it in certain ways. As they walked away, she gasped in delight while Varten held up a coin and tilted it this way and that, making the colors dance. "Incredible," she said on a breath. This city wasn't all bad.

Lanar, who was studying the airship schedule posted on the

far wall, looked over his shoulder at them and pursed his lips. "Best put that away."

But it was too late.

A hand reached up to grab Varten's arm. Someone shoved Zeli out of the way, while a boy about her age punched Varten in the stomach. Another—or maybe the same one who'd punched him, she couldn't be certain—snatched the coin from his hand.

Enraged, Zeli righted herself and ran forward, landing a fist on the back of one of the attackers. This one pinned Varten in a bear hug, while his companion grabbed the wallet from Varten's pocket as he struggled and cursed.

It all happened so fast. Almost too fast to believe. One minute they were surrounded by thieves, Zeli couldn't even tell how many there were, the next minute it was just the crowd again, everyone rushing to and fro. Passing them by without a second look.

She shook, unable to even gather her breath to shout—though what good would it do now? Varten was doubled over, holding his stomach, and then Lanar was there, scanning the crowd with hard eyes and a grim expression.

"Should we call for a constable?" Zeli wondered.

Lanar clucked his tongue. "We should call for a doctor, though I don't believe there's any medicine for foolishness." His voice was a whip crackling in the air. "Why would you flaunt your money around like that, are you an imbecile?"

His tone made Zeli's bones turn brittle; she froze in surprise at his venom. Varten straightened his back, but there was no righteous anger in him. His hand still covered his stomach but his shoulders were slumped. He looked like a deflated balloon. His head dropped until only his hair was visible. "I've got more in the bank," he mumbled.

She reached out to him then, placing a hand on his arm. "Are you all right? Are you hurt?"

He shook his lowered head. "I'm fine. And I'm sorry, I *was* being stupid."

"It wasn't your fault. *I* was the one who wanted to see the money change colors."

"But you didn't rob us." His voice was low and rough. She'd never heard him sound like this.

"No, and neither did you." She wanted so badly to see his face, to reassure him. "It was a mistake. I-I didn't expect . . ." She looked around again at the endless throngs of people. Any of them could be a criminal. Just because people dressed well and didn't have the air of poverty and desperation she'd grown up wary of didn't mean they were good.

"You're not an imbecile," she whispered, just for him.

He lifted his head then and gave her a rueful look that said he didn't quite believe her. A heavy band squeezed around her chest—that desolate, barren expression was so foreign on him. It was just *wrong*.

Varten was meant to be lightness and smiles and good humor. He was not this gutted thing, so obviously beating himself up.

Lanar sighed. "The banks are closed at this hour. We will not be able to book passage until tomorrow."

The Rumpus started tomorrow and if they didn't arrive until midday, they could well miss their opportunity to access the Archives.

"There's another option," she said, annoyed at Lanar for the way he'd spoken to Varten. Annoyed at the thieves and the crowd and the city. "Platform eighty-nine?" She had no desire to sell her people's pain for transport, but that was the currency they had available.

Lanar's eyes narrowed in distaste and she thought about how little they knew of him. Nothing really, as he wasn't much of a conversationalist. Yalisa and Eskar had seemed to trust him enough to offer passage, but just because he was a countryman that didn't mean he was a friend. His words, quick and hurtful, had added to an already bad situation. She was no longer certain she wanted him around.

She focused instead on Varten, grabbing his arm gently. This was their mission, they'd undertaken it together, and they didn't need anyone else's approval. His expression radiated uncertainty. "The Tinker will help us."

Although she wasn't always sure about trusting her own judgement, she had a good feeling about the Tinker. And at least they had something he wanted, an odd something, but it could be bartered.

However, Varten looked to Lanar for confirmation. It seemed he would not make a decision without it. Growing even more annoyed, she turned to face the man.

After a short lifetime, he nodded. "Very well, *the Tinker* it is."

She bristled at his tone, and almost missed Varten's sigh of relief. She wanted to speak to him privately, reassure him that they could do this on their own, the way they'd planned. She wasn't even certain how much she believed it, but Varten's confidence was part of what had been propelling her forward. This was probably just a temporary setback because of the speed and surprise of the robbery. It would just take him some time to return to normal.

But a tickling in the back of her mind warned caution. As they headed out of the station and back onto the tarmac, she stayed alert, her heart heavy and her guard up now more than ever.

Varten was having difficulty swallowing. Next to him, Zeli's head was on a swivel, hypervigilant to their surroundings to prevent another attack. But all he could do was feel the arms around him, squeezing him like a vise. Pinning him motionless and helpless.

He was back in a cold room, straps holding him down on a hard table. Needles piercing his skin. The liquid injected into him was freezing, it made his veins burn cold. His throat threatened to close up and he tried breathing in slowly through his nose to get some air.

His mind didn't return to the prison very often, though it existed there at the edges, the metal bars and cement floors looming just out of sight whenever he closed his eyes. Moments of powerlessness brought him back. When his body betrayed him and his mind was set adrift, lost in a sea of suffering.

He should have stayed in the palace in Rosira, at least there he couldn't hurt anyone. Get anyone hurt. The thought of something happening to Zeli nearly undid him. He'd never forgive himself. Just like he hadn't forgiven himself for the last time his ineptitude had resulted in harm and pain for people he cared about.

His ears pounded and he stumbled, blind to his surroundings. A smaller hand in his, squeezing tight, brought him back. He blinked, suddenly back in the present, and looked down at Zeli, whose face was creased with concern.

He longed to reassure her, but couldn't say a thing. What was there to be sure of?

His own stupidity had resulted in them being robbed. Life in the country, life in a cell, hadn't prepared him for this city. These people. He'd put the target on his own chest and hadn't used plain common sense. Just another liability.

They approached platform eighty-nine and his spirits fell further. He'd taken an immediate liking to the Tinker with his obvious eccentricities, but the pile of metal sitting on the platform didn't look like it would fly anywhere. It didn't look like any of the other ships they'd passed. Instead of sleek and aerodynamic, it was boxy and blocky. A disparate mass of dull gray parts that seemed more like a scrap heap than a vehicle.

The three of them stopped short, staring at it. Confusion and dismay settled across Varten's shoulders. His vision swam and he thought he might pass out.

The shrill dissonance of a mechanical bark cleared his head. Ziggy ran up, clattering across the blacktop, showing his obvious delight. He sped over to Zeli, who squatted down to pet his metal hide. Lanar took a quick step away from the little dog and eyed the "ship" dubiously.

"Ziggy? Where'd ye get off to now?" the Tinker cried as he came from around the other side of the ship. A broad smile split his face, causing something within Varten to settle. "Ye decided to take me up on me offer then, eh?"

He couldn't bring himself to answer, so Zeli spoke up. "There was a situation," she said. "We were robbed. We won't be able to pay you anything until the banks open in the morning, but I promise we do have funds." She looked at Varten, "I mean, one of us does."

"Aw, *pshaw*," the Tinker said. "I've told ye my price. I'll take ye up for the stories alone."

Lanar stepped forward, arms crossed. "You must understand, talk of life under the True Father is not entertaining. It can be very painful to relay."

The Tinker's face fell as his brows rose. "Oh, no, no, I don't want to hear about the awful things. I wouldn't put you through that. I want to know about normal life there. Breakfast, and how the sun looks when it rises, and what songs you sing when you're working, things like that."

Lanar tilted his head in confusion, but Zeli smiled. For a

moment, Varten was caught in it, in how bright her face looked and how her eyes shone. It almost pierced the carapace of guilt quickly forming over him.

"Why do you want those kinds of stories?" she asked.

The Tinker leaned forward conspiratorially. "A good story is worth its weight in steel. They spark ideas, don't they?" He tapped his head. "Never know where inspiration will strike. Collecting stories, talking to people from interesting places is all a part of creating. All a part of this puzzle called life we're tryin' to piece together." He rubbed his hands together with anticipation. "Come aboard, come aboard. We'd best be leaving if we want to get ye there in time for the Rumpus."

Lanar sniffed, wholly unimpressed. He eyed the oddly shaped ship dubiously. "What type of craft is this?"

"Why it's not a ship, per se. Wait right here, I'll show ye."

He disappeared behind the . . . well, whatever it was and in moments, the metal structure began to creak and groan. Steam billowed from small exhaust pipes along the top of a flat portion, perhaps a roof? And then the whole thing shuddered and began to rise.

And rise.

And rise.

It truly wasn't a ship, it was . . . Well, sort of like a mechanical spider. With five legs, and a body that must house the cockpit. Dark glass panels encircled the half-dome center mass. One of the windows slid open and the Tinker leaned out, waving.

"This is *Leggsy*!" he shouted. "I'll send the lift down for ye."

They all stared up at it, Zeli in awe and Lanar in what looked like dread. A smile pulled at Varten's lips. He didn't want to smile, he wanted to wallow in guilt and shame, but it came all the same. This was far better than an airship or a train.

A mesh basket descended from the underside of the body, held by thin telescoping metal rods. When it touched the ground, a door on it popped open. Ziggy ran over and jumped into the basket with a gleeful bark.

Zeli looked over at Varten with wide eyes, and he shrugged. "Might as well get in," he said, moving closer. He led the way with Zeli right behind him and Lanar bringing up the rear.

A wary hesitance flowed from the man like fog, but what other options did they have now? Once they were all on the platform, the basket's door closed and it began to rise with a subtle shudder. The trip up gave them a terrific view of the air station, the city around them, the river and bay, and beyond. And then they were enclosed in darkness when the platform came to a stop.

Ziggy yipped once, and the lights flickered on. The interior of the . . . contraption was old, worn, and well patched. Varten had always had an interest in mechanical things and this was the most fascinating machine he'd yet encountered.

They exited the basket into a narrow hallway where his head nearly brushed the ceiling. The smell of oil and warm metal comforted the ragged place inside him. Ziggy led them down the corridor and up a set of ladders—their legs bent in unnatural ways, allowing them to negotiate the rungs—and onto the main bridge. There the Tinker sat in a padded captain's chair in front of a glowing console.

Varten had learned about seagoing vessels from Ani's brother, Tai, and of airships from Clove. He recognized some of the controls, though there were many different ones here. Curiosity beat through the haze of guilt. Would the Tinker show him how everything worked?

"Strap in," the Tinker said, motioning to the jump seats behind him. They folded down from the sides and included safety belts.

Varten belted in next to Zeli, with Lanar across from them. "How fast does this thing go?" he asked.

"Ah, well, fast as a train on flat land. Faster uphill," he said with a wink and swiveled around to man the controls.

Leggsy shuddered and then began vibrating. The engine was beneath them, Varten felt it spin up. Zigs settled under the console by the Tinker's feet and appeared to fall asleep, if that was possible for a mechanical dog.

The Tinker spoke into a headset in Yalyish, likely talking to ground control. "We've got the go-ahead," he said over his shoulder. "Hold onto yer teeth!"

Leggsy bounced once and then its long legs began to move. The motion was graceful, the bridge remained surprisingly stable—Varten would love to get a peek at the shock-absorption system. They walked along the city streets, obeying the traffic laws for the most part, even as they towered over all other vehicles.

The roads were clogged at this time of day and it was slow-going, but once they left the busy section of the city behind for a quieter, more residential one, they moved considerably faster.

The Tinker steered *Leggsy* over the other vehicles. It walked over busy intersections, ignoring the electric semaphores that guided the traffic. "The coppers don't like it when I do that," he confided, "but there's no law against it. Laws don't take into account vehicles like this. Special dispensation." He tapped a certificate taped to the wall. Varten couldn't read it, but it looked official.

And then they were out of the city and in the countryside, and this is when the Tinker abandoned the roads completely and picked up more speed, quickly reaching an all-out run, racing over the fields and over hills. Splashing through streams. Outrunning any wheeled vehicle. He could see how this could be as fast as a train, without needing any tracks.

"You don't get into trouble for racing over people's land?" Varten asked.

"For all her weight, *Leggsy*'s light on her feet. Don't leave any damage. Some folk don't like it, but they'd have to catch me to do something about it." His chuckle was unreserved, and Varten actually cracked a smile.

"We'll get there by morning. Ye don't want to miss the opening ceremonies of a Rumpus! No, ye don't want to miss that at all."

CHAPTER TWENTY-THREE

Who suffers if a bird's call goes unheard?
Are they chirping into the emptiness?
Does the Void swallow their voice or
do they sing
because they have a song?

—THE HARMONY OF BEING

The first step in learning to master Nethersong, according to Murmur, was to commune with the Mother. Kyara held herself back from issuing a snide retort when he said this, but still wondered how exactly one went about communing with a mountain. Mooriah was evidently attuned to her mood and shot her a censorious glare. Kyara held her hands up; she hadn't said a thing.

At Murmur's insistence, the Nethersingers would have their lessons in a cave set high in the large chamber of the underground city. Ella and Ulani were able to watch from a ledge a level above, but, according to the ancient man, couldn't be in the same room.

Ella agreed to this, as she still had a line of sight on her daughter. And Kyara silently vowed to protect Tana from any surprises that should crop up along the way. She eyed Murmur warily as he led them to their new classroom.

Inside the small cave, the temperature was almost uncomfortably warm. A fire had been set up in the center of the space and some sort of herb was burning, making the air smell sweet. However, a thick humidity hung around them, so different from the rest of the city.

There was little furniture, just a few woven mats around the fireplace and some chipped pottery. A cistern in the corner collected water from a slow drip down a long, pointed rock formation hanging from the ceiling.

Once she, Mooriah, Tana, and Murmur were seated on the mats around the fire, Murmur instructed them to close their eyes. "Open yourself to the embrace of the Mother," he said in a droning voice. "Quiet your will and she will invite you in."

Kyara had never tried to meditate before. In Lagrimar, the Avinids—a fringe group who worshipped the Void—were proponents of the practice, and that was enough to keep her far away from it. But Mooriah claimed that being embraced by the Mother was as easy for a Nethersinger as connecting to her power.

"It should be like using your other sight," the woman said, which for Kyara was as simple as changing her shoes. Even entering the World Between had not proved truly difficult, now that she knew she could. It required focus, but she found it similar to tying a complicated knot. Listening to the Mother, however, was not so easy.

She tried to relax her body and soften her will, but that just made her feel droopy and boneless. She attempted to empty her mind, but the effort gave her a mild headache. Frustrated, she repositioned herself on the flat mat, which provided no cushioning against the hard stone beneath.

Something in the cave sizzled, and she opened her eyes to find Murmur sprinkling a powder onto the fire that caused the flames to pop and hiss. The thick air grew smoky and the sweet smell intensified.

Kyara's eyelids grew heavy; her body turned weightless, like she was flying. She struggled against the sensation—Murmur was drugging them. Anger fought its way to the surface; she couldn't let herself succumb. Then her limbs were suddenly dense, made of lead, and she was falling.

When she was finally able to open her eyes, the cave was completely dark. "Hello?" she called out, disoriented. When she got her hands on Murmur, she was going to throttle his old jelly neck.

She could actually sense her physical body, still seated on the ground in the cave, but whatever or wherever she was now, was different. Weightless, she had the odd disconnected sensation of both sitting and standing at the same time.

"Kyara?" Tana's voice held fear.

"I'm here." Kyara didn't see anything at first, and then the girl appeared beside her, a slightly ghostly sheen to her the only thing to indicate that she wasn't a physical presence. Mooriah and Murmur became visible a moment later. Murmur wasn't solid like the rest of them. Perhaps since he wasn't a Nethersinger by birth, his form here was far less substantial. Like a replication of a replication, soft and fuzzy. Kyara longed to rail against the ancient man, but didn't want to alarm Tana.

"Where are we?" the girl asked.

"Inside the Mother." Murmur's voice creaked with age.

"Weren't we there before?"

"We were inside her body, now we're inside her heart. You may use your power here. Unleash it and allow it to flow."

"And we won't harm anyone?" Kyara asked.

"No, not here," Mooriah replied. "It's part of the magic of the Mother." Kyara wasn't certain about any of it, not about accessing her power so close to the others or Singing in general.

"You cannot harm a Nethersinger with your power, Kyara." Murmur's voice floated over her.

Hopefully, she could wrangle her Song under control and then, perhaps, get some answers from the old man. She reached for the whirling energy inside her and tapped into it. But whereas it had always been a hurricane before, now it felt docile. A little kitten purring in her palms. Literally.

A soft, glowing light winked into existence, embodying her power as a tiny, feline creature lying asleep in her open hands. She gasped at the sensation of its weight and heft.

"The power of the Mother," Murmur rasped with reverence. "Externalizing your power into an avatar is a gift from her. It will help you separate what you can do from who you are. The Mother is mighty indeed. Death, life, spirit, matter are all hers to control. That is the legacy of the Folk, the one we strove so hard to protect from the Outside. Though in the end, we failed." His sorrow was palpable.

Kyara was so entranced by the soft, gentle thing in her grasp that she barely heard him. "What do I do with this?"

"Nurture and protect it, the way you would a real animal. It is your power and you must bond with it."

"But death is not so quiet and unassuming."

"Death is constant," Mooriah said. "It is endless, why should it need to rage when it can come quietly and destroy even the most powerful with a whisper? Why do you need to run, or struggle, or curse and cry and berate when you can glide, and flow, and be smooth?"

She lifted her hand and a tiny, chirping bird flickered into existence, resting on her outstretched finger. "When I want it to, it can grow," Mooriah said, and in the blink of an eye, the tiny birdling was a massive raptor, with sharp claws and an intimidating beak. And then with a snap of the fingers on her other hand, her power transformed back to its tiny, hatchling form. "It can be whatever you need."

Kyara shook her head, focusing on the kitten in her palm, which was breathing deeply, fast asleep. She sensed the lion lurking within, but that power wasn't needed now and so was not showing itself. She tentatively rubbed a hand over the sleeping creature's head, pushing down the soft, downy fur. "Unbelievable."

"Look at mine!" Tana called out with excitement. A very small lizard was curled in her outstretched hand. Kyara had never seen the girl beam so brightly. "She'll be a dragon when she's big!" Her voice held all the joy of a child opening her birthday gifts.

Her glee was both charming and worrisome. Kyara drew closer, not wanting to douse her delight, but needing her to remain cautious nonetheless. "What you said yesterday, about thinking that I'm some kind of hero. You have to know that I was forced to become the Poison Flame. I don't enjoy killing people. Neither should you, regardless of the power we have."

"I don't want to kill people. I just want to protect myself and my sister." She spoke in a hushed tone, her eyes wide.

"Protect from what?"

Tana blinked and the lizard disappeared from her hand. She lifted one of the long sleeves of her dress. They wore the same clothes inside the Mother as in real life, and Kyara guessed their bodies were the same, too, for Tana's arm was covered in scars. "My father used to say that I killed my mother. I guess it's true, she died giving birth to me. He blamed me. Took it out on me with beatings and whippings." Tana's voice held no emotion but Kyara grew angry on her behalf. If she hadn't already killed the girl's cretin of a father, she would have gladly done so again.

"When he met Ulani's mama, he left off some, but after she had Ulani and ran off, he started back up. Locking me in the closet. Beating me. Ulani had to sneak me food 'cause he'd forget about me for days, and I'd be left in there to starve." She sniffed and a tear crested her cheek. Kyara put an arm around her and held her close. The girl certainly felt like solid flesh, warm and just a touch frail.

"If I'd been powerful, if I'd been like you," Tana continued, "then no one could have hurt me. I could have stopped him. Stopped our stepmother from selling us away. I may never grow up to be tall and strong. If I'm small and weak what chance do I have?"

She spoke a truth of life, one Kyara couldn't refute. But she did have to set her straight on one thing. "Having power doesn't mean you can't get hurt. The ones you love will always be able to cut you deeper than anyone else. But I am starting to believe that we have these strange Songs for a reason. And there's a reason that only a few of us get them. Every Lagrimari is born with Earthsong except for us, we're rare and special. Rarer still to survive having this ability." She rested her head on top of the girl's.

"You are strong and powerful, Tana, and not because of Nethersong, but because of who you are. Please don't think I don't understand. I know what it's like to be beaten down. I have scars, too." She rolled up her sleeve to reveal the results of years of being used as fodder for blood magic. Tana examined the revealed skin, then met Kyara's gaze.

"We'll learn how to do this together," Kyara said. She didn't want to have anyone looking up to her; she didn't feel she was worthy of the distinction and knew it was only a matter of time before Tana realized her awe and hopes had been put in the wrong person. Kyara wasn't Darvyn, she wasn't anyone's savior, she could barely save herself, but at the same time, she felt a kinship with Tana and didn't want to let the girl down.

She still hated Nethersong, even here and now where it was gentle and subdued. However, she would try to change her attitude in the way she hoped Tana would. Try to model what she wanted the girl to see and be—there was no reason Tana couldn't be the strong, powerful hero she thought Kyara was.

And if Kyara had to pretend to be something she wasn't in order to help the girl, then so be it. It certainly wasn't the worst thing she'd ever done.

CHAPTER TWENTY-FOUR

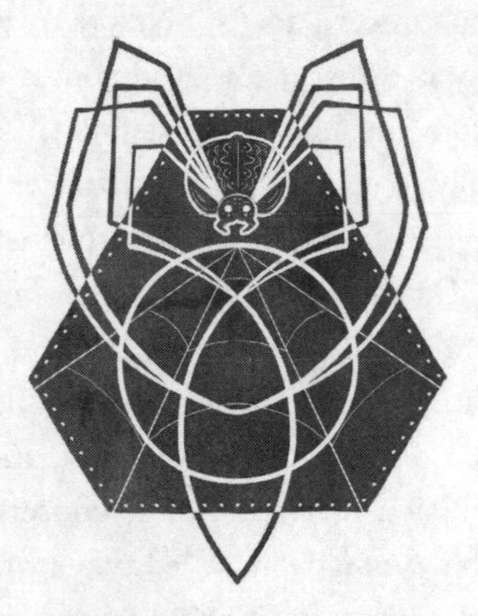

Is gold more precious than
a heart filled to overflowing?
What price can you give to intangible
mysteries of love?
Only thieves assign its value.

—THE HARMONY OF BEING

"That was irresponsible and reckless!" Nikora screams when you awaken from the viewing trance, energy sapped, senses dulled. "Your experiment has done nothing but waste more of Dahlia's precious flesh!" Spit flies from her mouth to hit you, causing you to flinch. You raise a finger to clear it from your brow.

You have no time for her hysterics, but you shake off your exhaustion and focus on her foolishness. "Nikora." Your voice is calm and the pitiless tone you use makes her freeze, mid-diatribe.

"Look at all my experiment has accomplished. We sent a small reconnaissance force that gave us valuable information about our enemy."

"Elsira is of no concern to us." Nikora spat. "They are your enemy. Our enemy is death itself. And your assurances that this trial would yield some benefit have fallen flat."

Breathing deeply so you do not reach for her neck and begin to squeeze, you steeple your fingers on the table before you, ignoring their bluish tinge. The fire in the parlor burns fiercely at your back, but everything here is still far too cold.

"Would you rather lose your own men while learning how to manage the wraiths long enough to get information out of them, or lose foreigners who, as you say, are of no concern? I am interested in efficiency. We have effectively killed two sparrows with one arrow, that is true allyship. I am upholding my end of our bargain, and I consider this trial run a grand success." You offer a smile that once dazzled your followers, but she merely narrows her eyes.

Calling the wraiths again to go to Elsira was a stroke of genius on your part; of course it was pure, unadulterated luck that had the portal from the World After appear in the heart of the palace. Certainly the place had been on your mind, and all magic responds to intention. It had not been conscious choice but a well-timed boon.

The energy you expended on the spell to watch the action play out has your lids feeling heavy. But tiredness is weakness and so you straighten, forcing your body to submit to your will. It helps that through the viewing trance you witnessed the girl queen and your sister battling the wraiths, struggling, and against only three. The revelation helps strengthen you.

"I think he has a point," Cayro, Nikora's second-in-command adds. You all sit at a rough-hewn table that looks just shy of collapse in the corner of Nikora's sitting room. Cayro is farthest from the fireplace and cloaked in shadow. "We do not have the manpower to spare. Let us sacrifice others while we hone our abilities."

She grits her teeth and stares at the man then back at you. "Hear me, Eero, and hear me well. I will not allow you to derail my mission. If you are my ally and are to continue enjoying the benefit of my hospitality, then your aims and mine must be in sync. I know who you are and what you are capable of. You are not fooling me."

She motions sharply to Cayro and they both rise and leave. Once they are gone, you give in to the smirk pulling at your lips. You once met a wild dog like her, deep in the desert. It bared its teeth and growled, believing that it had some sort of power. But its blood soaked the sand just like any other creature that ever crossed you.

Imagining the feel of her neck between your hands is sweet.

For the next few days, you run the words of the incantation used to summon the wraiths over and over in your mind. It is a sloppy and indelicate thing. You had again failed to control the wraiths during that trial run. The creatures had been just as vicious and mindless as ever, their goal only to destroy.

Never mind that these spirits had no quarrel with Elsirans at all—it was the Physicks, after, who were responsible for their deaths with their Nethersong harvesting, you'd discovered—but their vengeance was stronger than their reason and fate had directed that energy toward your old enemy. You sensed, deeper in the portal, spirits who had kept more of their minds, better candidates for Nikora's silly interrogations, but they had not come forward. The ones eager to return to the Living World were full of anger and desire for revenge. Even among the living these types of men could be dominated easily. What you will need if you are to free yourself and regain your rightful place is a way to call upon the wraiths and control them with finesse, the way you do the Wailers.

But that second recitation of the spell triggered something locked deep in your memory, a place you never tread. The past is behind you so why turn around? *Never take a retrograde step,* your father taught you that. But now, for the first time, it has been vitally important to dig around in that vast archive of your life, so full of arcane bits of flotsam and jetsam you have tried to discard.

There is a secret hiding in there somewhere, the key to all this, but for the life of you, you cannot figure it out. After days of struggling you finally admit that you need help remembering.

There is someone who knows. But no, you cannot contact her and she would not tell you anyway, even if you had a way to speak to her. Still, the idea will not leave you. It's been placed by some force you cannot identify, some urge you cannot so easily throw away.

When dawn comes and the servant brings the morning meal—the same bland food you have eaten for days now—you tell the man that you need to speak with Nikora.

The servant doesn't speak, doesn't acknowledge you, but not a half hour later another comes and takes you through the icy passageways and back to the sitting room. Nikora and Cayro are at the rickety table, flipping through loose pages written in a language you cannot read. Curiosity prickles, but you push that weakness away.

"Yes, Eero?" Nikora asks, distracted.

"I believe the key to controlling the wraiths lies in the incantation you use to summon them."

Her eyes narrow, but she does not interrupt.

"Where did you learn it?"

"The Seekers discovered it during their missions across the world. Every part of the spell was carefully considered before it was tried." She speaks to you as one would to a slow child. You grit your teeth in an effort not to show your impatience. Though in your mind, a vision of squeezing her skull between your hands comes unbidden. Imagining its pulpy contents steaming as they're exposed to the cold air calms you. This is the future you work toward.

"And yet," you offer, "the wraiths express undirected violence. The incantation seals the blood spell, it is the only aspect of the spell that is changeable."

"But we are not summoning them at all," she insists. "The spell is just to open the portal to the World After. Those near the portal enter our world."

That is at the root of the problem, but she must be too daft to realize it. Cayro lifts his head, cutting an odd glance at her.

"I am not unfamiliar with the magic of the blood," you say, evenly. "Its mastery is how I was able to hold power for so long. We need to adjust the spell to better accomplish our goals."

"How did you learn it?" she asks.

"Learn what?"

"Blood magic."

The question stymies you. "I cannot recall. I have lived many lifetimes and learned many things."

She snorts, derisive. "What would be helpful is for you to use that knowledge to take the Songs of the Wailers and give them to me." You suppose that would help her, but the current arrangement suits you.

Reasoning with Nikora is proving to be a dead end. This woman is far too stupid to lead for long. Her devotion to the frivolous faith these Physicks hold has blinded her, but your eyes are open.

You scan the room as she prattles on and on about St. Dahlia's mission and how blessed it is and destined for success. How the Physicks will rule once immortality is theirs and they rebuild the Great Machine.

The jar of desiccated flesh is nowhere in sight, thank the seeds, but on the sideboard next to the table lies a small stash of strange objects that were not there before. Several pairs of spectacles, two compasses, pens, loops of metal and stiff rope, boxy devices with wires sticking out of them, mugs and shoes and watches and even a telephone. A handful of small discs are off to one side, they are not unlike the medallion that Nikora wears.

Are these all amalgamations? She must be stockpiling them, hoarding their remaining quintessence. These medallions mimic Songs. With one of those, you can leave this place. Leave this madwoman to her spirits and her lost cause.

As she prattles, you yawn and ask for a drink. She pauses, midsentence, surprised at the interruption, and tracks your walk around the table to the other side, closer to the sideboard with the object and trinkets. You fall into a seat that can barely hold your weight.

She is still gaping like a fish, but Cayro watches you carefully. A flash in his eye makes you linger on his scrutiny, then focus once again on the woman who is ostensibly the leader of the ragtag outfit. Taking over from her will be too easy. That is, if you even want to do such a thing.

"Some refreshment would be much appreciated," you repeat. There is a moment when you are not sure she will listen, then she yells for a servant who peeks his head in and scurries off with instructions.

"Resources are in short supply, here, Eero." Her voice is clipped. The way she says your name sounds dirty. You will teach her manners before this is all said and done.

"Just something for my parched throat. As a close ally, I know you cannot deny me such a basic form of hospitality. So, if the incantation is not the problem, then what do you think it is?"

You tap your fingers on the tabletop, affecting a casual demeanor. Cayro stacks his papers neatly, his fingernails clean, hands appearing soft and callus-free. Not that yours have ever known a day's labor, either.

Cayro takes your measure with obsidian eyes. "We wonder if it is simply the nature of the spirits who are waiting when the portal opens. If we can dispatch them and access others, perhaps those not so eager to leave, we may find more success. It may require retrieving a soul from the Eternal Flame."

Nikora slams her hand down to shut Cayro up. He snaps his mouth shut, but does not appear chastened. Nikora seethes.

"Is taking a soul from the Eternal Flame even possible?" you ask after a beat.

She looks annoyed but nods. "It is theorized, though we have as yet not attempted it. The theory is that the spirits gathered on the outer edges of the World After are the ones who seek revenge. Their souls have yet to be cleansed by the purification of the Eternal Flame, and they effect their petty grievances on us. But older spirits, ones that have known peace and are readying themselves for rebirth, those will be able to pass on the wisdom we seek. It is just a matter of having enough expendable bodies near the portal that the vengeance-seeking wraiths can glut themselves. Then we defeat those and allow time for the spell to draw out the souls from the Flame."

The servant returns with a steaming beverage. It is burning hot and you don't even taste it as it scalds your tongue and throat. Her plan is inane; much better to control the spirits who come out than try to drag one from a power as great as the Flame's.

As the servant leaves, you trip him and the platter clatters to the ground. This distraction is all you need to reach to the sideboard behind you and grab one of the small medallions lying there without disturbing anything else. In a matter of seconds, the servant has righted himself. You pocket the coin in your trousers.

Nikora and Cayro stare angrily at the silent, bald man. Neither has seen what you've done.

Back in your room, you palm the medallion and close your eyes. Immediately, you can tell it is weak. Perhaps that is why it was left out unguarded. You have controlled an amalgam before, using Ydaris's medallion back when she first arrived. You dislike the taste the combined magics leave in your mouth, but now any magic is priceless.

However, there is not enough here for you to effect an escape. Not enough to knock out guards, destroy this infernal castle, fly or travel through space the way you know Physicks can do. The way they spirited you away from your prison cell all those weeks ago. What a waste of resources they'd expended. You cannot even cancel the spell that prevents you from using blood magic they haven't approved.

For that, you will have to kill Nikora. Once she's dead, her spell will fade and you will have access to the resources you need. Then you can reclaim what is rightfully yours. What you struggled and sweat and bled for for hundreds of years.

Still, the medallion is not totally worthless.

It can still help you to reclaim your land and your people from your sister who has no right to them. For it can help you contact her.

Using the power of the medallion might not allow you to travel, but you can send your voice and image. There is power enough for that.

You focus on the intention and picture your twin. Where is she now? When she would visit, she would often smell of honeyberry flowers and freshly cut grass. Perhaps she is even now out walking the grounds of the palace. Luxurious grounds in a temperate climate unlike this frozen wasteland where you currently reside.

In all your years of conquest, you never made it to Rosira, never saw the city of your birth. You never left Lagrimar until the day the Mantle came down, but today is a new day. You successfully destroyed the Mantle and will be truly free soon enough.

For a moment nothing happens, and then her face winks into existence above you, floating in the air. You catch glimpses of her surroundings, she is not outside, but in a modestly decorated room—at least by your standards. If she is surprised to see you she masks it well.

"Sister. Are you not happy to see me?" You spoke these words once not too long ago, before she cruelly betrayed you and stole your Songs.

Now she stares, her face a mask. "Happier than I was to receive the gifts you sent. Those were from you, were they not?"

"Gifts?"

"Three of them. I cannot say they were welcome, however, and I should not like to receive any more."

You chuckle. "I wish I could take the credit, but alas, I am far less free than I would like to be. Unable to give to you what I truly would like to."

"Did you trade one cage for another?" A smile is in her voice. It warms you some. You have missed her.

"A more gilded version and quite a bit cooler."

"I have been looking for you," she says.

"You prefer me in your prison to someone else's."

"I would prefer you free, if you could manage it. I will come and get you; where are you?"

"Honestly, I cannot say. Though I am no maiden in need of rescuing. And you and I have very different ideas about freedom. Besides, I have a plan."

She raises an eyebrow. "And you think I will help?"

"Did you not just offer to help?"

"I offered to retrieve you, that is different."

"Perhaps. But I have a question for you."

"And I for you, brother. What is it, exactly, that you want?" Her voice is low and slow.

"What I always wanted, dear sister. Equality."

A hint of worry flickers across her gaze. "What is it you want to ask?"

"I am having some difficulty recollecting—are you familiar with Yllis's research when he studied the blood magic? I know he showed you his journals." An expression close to heartbreak crosses her face at the mention of her former lover. A pang of regret hits you. You had to kill him after all, but that was war. He would have killed you first.

"What are you asking me?" she rasps.

"Before things between us soured, when he would still share his discoveries, he had mentioned exploring more complex ways of combining blood magic and Earthsong. Did he ever use Nethersong as well? And did he succeed?"

She shakes her head. "What makes you think I would help you in what you seek? Especially when you would only use it against me."

"I have never given you more trouble than you could handle, dear sister. However, some things are inevitable. Things like your love for me." You smile widely and almost feel that it is genuine. Her love is real, as is yours, honestly, but she has always loved you ineffectually. Or perhaps it was because *you* were ineffectual back then. Her love felt more suited for a puppy or some small, soft thing to be petted and cooed at but not respected. In that way she was like Sayya. The girl from so many years ago for whom you named a city. You would have been true to her, but she rejected you. The pain of heartbreak still threatens to tear you apart.

Sayya is long dead. Could you bring her back from the Eternal Flame? Or was she reborn into another life, had other loves? You wrangle your thoughts back from this precipice.

"I will not help you with the dead, brother. I will not help you destroy this place. And nothing that Yllis knew will help you, either, he had no experience with what you are trying to do."

"I'm not so sure you know what Yllis had experience with. And did you not say you wished to see me free?"

"If you could manage it without harming anyone. If you could find the light of goodness within your nature. I believe it is still there. What would you do with your freedom, I wonder?" A shudder rolls through her, and she turns sharply, looking off behind her as if she heard something.

"When will you return?" she asks, turning back.

"When it is time. When I can reclaim what is mine."

"None of this is yours, brother. And no one living will allow you to take it back."

"You might not have as much choice about that as you think."

She sighs deeply. In that motion she reminds you of your mother, a small woman with deep strength. You desperately wish that was enough, but it never has been. "If you were worried for me," you say, "then I hope that your mind has been set at ease."

The energy of the medallion wanes. It is a weak little thing, suitable for children and parlor tricks only.

"Stay safe, brother. Until I see you again."

You chuckle. Her statement is ominous in its own way. "And you as well." And then you allow the connection to wink out.

Her face is still familiar to you. Her voice even more so. You think back to those long days when you were in another cell and she would come to talk to you. Reminisce. Tell stories of days long past and people long dead.

It was nice. It felt a bit like . . .

But you can't allow base sentimentality to step in. You squashed that long ago. Being human and mortal and powerless once again has made you soft. You must regain strength as soon as possible.

You will meditate, run through your memories until you find the thing that has been itching at your mind. The key needed for you to wrest control from the feeble, misguided zealots and return to your twin as promised.

On top.

CHAPTER TWENTY-FIVE

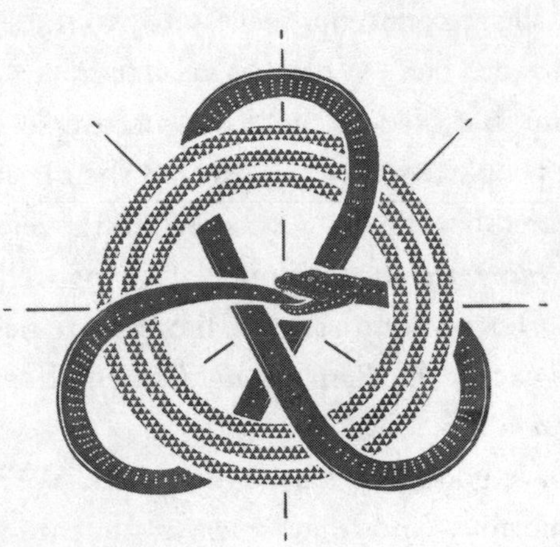

The rich will find the hollow within
and seek to fill it.
The blessed will find the hollow without
and never rest til it is whole.

—THE HARMONY OF BEING

Jasminda took the hidden passages from her office to the Indigo Drawing Room, located in what she called the Blue Wing of the palace as it also housed the Blue Library. She'd cleaned out all the cobwebs and dust with her frequent travel using these narrow, secret corridors. It wouldn't do for anyone to see her enter or exit this particular meeting room.

When she arrived via a concealed door in the paneling, she found Nadette, Ilysara, Camm, and the rest of the small team Nadette had put together, seated at a large, round table, newspapers spread out around them. Everyone looked up when she entered and scrambled to their feet.

"Sit, please," Jasminda said, waving them down. "The vote is in four days," she announced unnecessarily to the somewhat wary faces turned toward her. "Where do we stand?"

Camm rose, but Nadette held out an arm to stop him. She had put these people together and oversaw their tasks. The woman stood and cleared her throat. "As I stated in the report I delivered to you *this morning*, the media strategy is going well. It is meeting expectations. Our pro-unification editorials are being printed in all the papers except the *Rosira Daily Witness*. The editor there is firmly pro-separation.

"But we have good traction in the others. We're holding another poll tomorrow. And I have every confidence that we'll continue seeing the uptick in those citizens who plan to vote for the unification."

Jasminda nodded, not missing the somewhat aggrieved tone in the woman's voice. Zann Biddel and the Reapers had managed to sway public opinion much further in a shorter period of time, but they were preying upon peoples' prejudices and fears. Pleading the case to citizens' better natures, appealing to their honorableness and love of humanity, was somewhat more difficult. The progress was much slower.

She had struggled with the language of the measure, needing it to truly represent the heart of both sides of this mess, even as it hurt her to do so. In just a few days, all Elsirans and Lagrimari in the country would vote on one of two options: grant full citizenship to all refugees from Lagrimar, or create a separate state within Elsira where the refugees would enjoy the full rights of citizenship. Outside of that district, however, they would be subject to the same treatment as any other foreigner—they'd need a visa to travel freely through the land, difficult-to-obtain work papers if they wanted to get a job. It would be a step up from what the settlers had endured for years, but not nearly enough.

She approached the table and bent over to read the fruits of their labor. The team had worked fast, placing editorials in amenable papers. Nadette's morning report had included the fact that other editorial pieces, not originating from their media team, had begun showing up in newspapers as well. Regular folk reaching out in favor of including the refugees—exactly what Jasminda had hoped for.

"Thank you all for all your work," she told the team. "I do appreciate it. And I don't mean to be a bother, it's just that this means everything to me. A vote for separation would tear my family apart. It's very personal and I am, I admit, overly invested."

Nadette sighed deeply. "I can't know how you feel, but I promise you, we are all committed to this cause."

Jasminda met the woman's eye and smiled. "Thank you, I—"

The door to the meeting room opened, cutting her off. Zavros Calladeen, the Minister of Foreign Affairs, stood in the doorway staring down his nose at her.

"Your Majesty, might I have a word?" He sketched an almost infinitesimal bow.

The existence of this group in this meeting room was not common knowledge. The fact that Calladeen knew about it—and her presence here especially—was not good.

"I'm rather busy right now, can this wait, Minister?"

"I'm sorry, Your Majesty. It has to do with an important matter of jaywalking." He fixed her with a blank look, but his words cut through her.

She and Camm shared a glance and she straightened from her position leaning over the table and tried to look as regal as possible. “Certainly, Minister.” Back ramrod straight, she exited into the hallway.

“Perhaps the library is empty at this hour?” he suggested.

She couldn’t tell from his tone whether he knew that’s where she’d just come from, but given how much else he knew, she wouldn’t bet against it.

Once in the library, she spun around to face him as he shut the door. She opened her connection to Earthsong and found him simmering with indignation and . . . disappointment? That was unexpected. There was also a sheen of fatigue around him.

“Your Majesty,” he said, appearing somewhat weary. “How long are you planning to hold Zann Biddel in custody?”

Jasminda pursed her lips, deciding how much to reveal. “His arrest was perfectly legal and aboveboard. And how do you know anything about it?” Biddell had been moved to a private part of the dungeon and was not with the general population, but she’d long suspected Calladeen had his own network of eyes and ears.

His jaw was tight as he spoke. “His arrest is public record, and while it was legal, his continuing incarceration is, shall we say, a gray area.”

Jasminda breathed deeply, trying to control the temper that rose whenever Biddell was mentioned. “He is being held in the interest of national security. Why, may I ask, is this local matter of interest to the Minister of Foreign Affairs?”

“I am sworn in my duty to protect Elsira and her people.” He spread his arms apart. She raised her brows.

Calladeen sighed and surveyed the room. “Would you like to sit, Your Majesty?”

“I would not.” The man was nearly swaying on his feet, but she had no intention of making things easy for him and protocol dictated no one could sit in the presence of a monarch without permission.

He straightened his tall form. "As an advisor to the crown, it is my duty to warn you that you must tread carefully here. Zann Biddell is very powerful. Holding him in this manner may cause problems down the road."

"Do you deny that he is a criminal?"

"Criminals are brought to trial and evidence is presented. What exactly are you doing with him?"

She rolled her eyes. "He's not being tortured, for Sovereign's sake. He's being questioned. He's done untold damage to this nation and needs to be held accountable for it. Someone sworn to protect Elsira should understand that. Is the court system willing to do anything about him? They've certainly had enough time. How long should we wait while the attacks on our people continue?"

Calladeen shook his head slowly. "You are on shaky ground, Your Majesty. Which I think you understand." Dark eyes pinned her in place. "What does His Majesty say?"

Jasminda glared, crossing her arms. Calladeen's brows rose. "Ah, King Jaqros does not know. And I take it he does not know about your little public information committee over there?"

"If you are pro-separation, that is you prerogative, Minister. But my concern is unifying this nation, not dividing it. I will take the steps necessary to protect it and hold it together."

"On the contrary, I am not pro-separation." His intense gaze shifted and Jasminda frowned. "I think it is a waste of resources and ultimately a stupid idea. Those behind it want to place all the Lagrimari on a plot of land in the north of Elsira. Well, there are landowners there who would need to be appeased. A costly and shortsighted proposition."

She blinked. "I-I did not realize you felt that way."

"You have never asked me, Your Majesty." His voice held mild censure.

Jasminda refused to be chastened by this. She avoided this man like the plague and with good reason.

"And what of Raun?" he asked.

"What about Raun?"

"I had thought you were to make an entreaty to King Pia regarding the embargo. My office was told by King Jaqros that you would be spearheading all future contact with the Raunians. We are unable to move forward without you."

Jasminda shook her head, still reeling from his admission. "I'm working on Raun."

"So you will be attending the foreign relations subcommittee meeting which begins in ten minutes?"

She glared at him.

"Or were you planning to remain here overseeing your secret, pet project?"

Heat began coming off her in waves. "Pet project? You just said you support unification. That team in there is vital to the vote going our way. The future of Elsira is at stake!"

His face gentled, something she never recalled witnessing before. "I'll grant you that unification is important, but it's not the *most* important thing. There are other vital issues requiring your attention as well. This embargo is crippling us. Regardless of how the vote goes, if we have no food to feed our people, if our economy collapses, then it will make little difference. With your brother marrying the king's daughter, you are in the best position to come to some agreement with Raun."

She heaved in a breath. She could not admit that she had no idea how to negotiate with Raun. Where to begin? What to say?

She didn't even know why their king had started the embargo in the first place. No one did.

"King Pia will not speak to me," she said through clenched teeth. "The negotiations regarding the wedding soured and since then communication between us has been scarce. I need to focus on the issue that is threatening to destroy the land."

He shook his head. "Our supply shortage and economic stagnation will destroy us first, Your Majesty. Rioting in the streets would be just the beginning if things get as bad as the reports project."

There was truth in his words, but she couldn't admit it—at least not to him. Too much history lay between them, too much mistrust and subterfuge. "I will deal with Raun in due time, Minister."

The door opened and her assistant Ilysara ran in, looking harried. "There you are, Your Majesty," she exclaimed. She looked suspiciously at Calladeen, then switched to Lagrimari. "I've been looking all over for you."

"What is it?"

"We've had a communication from King Pia of Raun."

Jasminda shot a glance at Calladeen, who appeared annoyed at the interruption.

Ilysara continued breathlessly, "She's on her way. Here. The king. Now. She sent no warning, apparently wanting to take us by surprise. But she's on a ship, which will be docking in Portside in a matter of *hours*."

Jasminda straightened and a knot tightened inside her. "Hours? What—? How—?" She took a breath as thoughts jumbled in her head. "How did this message arrive?"

"Dolphin? At least that's what I was told by the ambassador." Her assistant looked perplexed by this, but Ani and the twins had told Jasminda of the Raunians' use of dolphin messengers.

She turned on Calladeen. "Did you know about this? Is that why you came to see me?"

"Know about what?"

She'd forgotten they'd been speaking in Lagrimari. "King Pia is on a ship that will arrive in Rosira in a matter of hours."

The man blanched. "I did not know this. I promise you I had no idea. I have never heard of such before—to give no warning for a state visit."

Much as she didn't want to, she believed him, and Earthsong backed up her gut feeling. She sighed and dropped her head, coming to terms with this new reality. When did the weight of the world come to rest on her slight shoulders? Why *had* Oola put it there?

She took another moment to feel all the self-pity that rushed at her, unbidden.

And then she brushed it aside. Opened her eyes. Squared her shoulders.

"All right. She'll be here soon. We'd best prepare."

CHAPTER TWENTY-SIX

The wise will hear the melody and sing along.
The blessed will teach the tune to all they encounter.

—THE HARMONY OF BEING

Kyara's Nethersong avatar had grown into a growling, vicious-looking wildcat. Its hackles were raised as its ghostly form prowled in front of her, pacing back and forth, gaze locked on the target Murmur had provided. A row of improbably lush, leafy trees stood at the far end of the cavern, spaced evenly apart. Her task was to specifically aim for the center tree and destroy it, leaving the rest untouched.

She sucked in a breath, feeling the cat's skin ripple in response. They were viscerally connected, she and this imaginary creature that embodied her Song. She sensed its moods and reactions and knew that it sensed hers. Since she'd discovered her deadly power, she'd felt as if it was always barely leashed. Never quite under her control. Now that it had manifested itself in a visible way, a leash wasn't needed. Whatever magic was held in the walls of this mountain allowed this being to work as an extension of herself.

She focused on the center tree and released the massive feline. Its body dissolved into a blur of motion; it was gone and back again before Kyara had finished blinking. However, while she had directed her Song's actions, she'd done so with no precision. Every single tree was blackened. The two on the ends crumpled and fell into a heap of ashes, fully decayed in an instant.

Behind her, Murmur sighed deeply. "Your heart still is not in this." He stepped up beside her and waved an arm. The trees were once again whole, standing in a perfect line.

"Nethersong requires intention just as all magic does," Murmur continued, "and if your intention is weak or unfocused, then so is the expression of your power. Look at how well the young one is progressing."

Tana had taken to the training like a scalpel to viscera. On the other side of the cavern, her lizard, now a fierce dragon, let loose a fiery breath, which only affected the specific tree she'd targeted. Kyara sighed wistfully.

This was nothing like how her own brutal training had progressed at the hands of the Cantor. Of course she was glad that Tana was not being broken down to bloody bits and then rebuilt the way Kyara had been, but it was still bittersweet. Perhaps the gentle touch would not have worked for Kyara. Maybe she needed brutality in order to gain control.

"You must embrace your Light—your power," Mooriah said,

stepping up to her other side. It was like being in the middle of a disappointment sandwich. "You're still trying to keep it at arm's length when instead you must *open* your arms to it. Your progress is too slow. The wraiths will destroy the entire land before you are able to become remotely competent." The woman glared then turned away, muttering a curse before disappearing altogether, leaving the heart of the Mother.

"Was she always such a ball of sunshine?" Kyara grumbled.

"Once, she was indeed lighter and happier," Murmur said. "She was our shaman, responsible for the spiritual and often physical well-being of the clan. Her husband was our chief and they were good leaders. Together, they united the clans and helped us keep our way of life even as so many left the mountain for the Outside. But death was not the respite it should have been for her."

Kyara swallowed at Murmur's mournful tone. She'd never spoken to Mooriah of her life or afterlife much. Annoyed as she was by the woman's imperious manner and amoral methods, such things had not come up.

"I'm not sure how to erase ten years of conditioning and hatred of my Song," she admitted. "I don't know what to do differently."

Murmur peered at her with his colorless eyes, though here, in this strange, magic-made place, his irises and lids were indistinct enough not to be as uncanny as they were in real life. He finally looked off but she couldn't read his expression. But he appeared to come to a decision.

"You must meet the Breath Father. It is usually a rite of passage after certain milestones have been reached in your training, but I think you should do it now. Perhaps the meeting would help to unlock your block and accelerate your development."

"Is he . . . sentient?" She'd always assumed the Breath Father was like the Mountain Mother, part of Cavefolk myth and not an entity that could be met with. According to legend, the two deities had created the Folk from stone and water or some such.

"You will not believe my words, child. Best meet him for yourself and decide." Murmur looked like he wanted to say more, but held back.

"What is it? Is there more I need to know?"

He took a deep breath. By now she was used to focusing on his face and not the expansion of muscle below. "Remember to breathe, dear. As deeply as you can. And bring the caldera with you—the one you call the death stone."

Kyara stiffened, she hadn't told anyone that she'd brought the strange rock along. "How did you know I brought it with me?"

He simply smiled cryptically and then turned to call Tana back from where she was playing with her lizard avatar. They all left the heart of the Mother to return to their physical forms.

Even wrapped tight in its bundling fabric and stowed in the pocket of her trousers, the death stone felt like it was going to burn a hole through her thigh. The heat wasn't physical, the bundle actually felt quite cold, instead, the all-consuming weight of heavy foreboding was trying to eat through her clothes and right into the skin.

She followed Murmur down sloping tunnels she'd never been in before. The path was well-worn and lit with the strange glowing rocks that offered a muted shine, just enough so the journey wasn't claustrophobic.

They traveled a long way, and she wasn't sure she'd be able to find her way back again. Nerves ate at her, and Murmur didn't seem inclined to puncture the silence with conversation. Finally, they emerged in a huge cavern filled with water. Except that when she looked up, a filtered blue sky was visible above them. This place was actually outside of the mountain with some kind of covering protecting them from the overhead sun. The surface of the water glowed softly from the dampened light.

"This is the original caldera," Murmur said with reverence. "We call it the Origin. Created by an ancient volcano, this crater was filled in over time with water and power and is the holiest place in the Mother."

"What's up there?" She pointed to the thing protecting them from the sky. The covering was filmy and made the sunlight refract into waves of rainbow colors shining down.

"It protects us from the Outside. It's constructed from a sheet of fluorite so those of us too old to withstand the sun's rays can still come here." He gazed at the quiet lake reverently, but a growing sense of unease crawled over Kyara. The place was beautiful indeed with its colorful glow, but something about it tickled her senses in an uncomfortable way.

"So what happens now?" she asked, still staring up. When Murmur didn't answer, she turned around to discover he'd disappeared. She didn't understand how, he was standing next to her and then as soon as she turned her head, his body was just . . . gone. Into thin air. He certainly couldn't have moved that quickly.

She swallowed and considered retreating the way they'd come, but the path had disappeared, too. The only dry land was under her feet; she now stood on a tiny island in the midst of the crater's lake.

She must have entered some kind of vision. It hadn't required meditation or drugs, she was just instantly inside it. Her wariness multiplied.

Steam poured off the placid surface of the lake and it began to bubble. She trembled, not wanting to fall off the sliver of land beneath her, which was barely bigger than her footprints. Not wanting to know what was in the water to make it churn and roil like that.

Would Tana eventually have to undergo this as well? The girl would be frightened out of her mind—Kyara was nearly so. She sank into her other sight, hoping it would provide some comfort, some level of control, or even some answers. There shone the light of death, the darkness of life, and the staticky Void, all here in the lake, swirling around one another but separate, like water and oil stirred but always pulling apart.

Out of the mess, something new began to coalesce. It was the variegated energy of the Void, neither light nor dark, but present always between them. Somehow, the Void was solidifying, if that was even possible, and converging into a human-like form.

She opened her eyes to witness this shape rise from the water and float upward. The figure was difficult to make out, appearing to her eyes to be made of air and wind and steam more than solid flesh, but a face resolved into a bearded form—a man, with long coiled locks flowing down his back.

Kyara stared as he drifted closer, a man of air—of Void?—but visible nonetheless, and the power coming off him . . . Her knees began to shake as the presence approached. Standing before the Goddess Awoken had been awe-inspiring; this was bone crushing.

"Kyara," the figure whispered in a voice that was both many and one. These were the whispers she'd heard in the desert, leading her to the crystal city and through the tunnels. She'd thought it was the Cavefolk speaking to her, but if so, they'd used the voice of this . . . whoever this was. The name *Breath Father* stroked her mind and she shivered.

"Why have you come to me?" The voice was timeless and, this close, pierced her marrow.

"M-Murmur said it was a rite of passage." She shivered and thought she might vomit. "That you could help me control my power."

The figure flickered, sometimes more visible, sometimes less, but the sensation of its presence never let up. "Your power is vast. And yet your training is stagnant. Why is that?"

She clenched her jaw to stall its shaking before being able to speak. "I don't know. I don't want this power." Her voice was tight and small.

"Then why come at all?"

"For the girl."

The figure drew even closer, nearly nose to nose, and Kyara looked up into ancient eyes—the only solid-looking thing on him. Just as colorless as the rest of his form, but somehow substantial. "No. You came because you require balance."

She wanted to draw back, but remained motionless, conscious of the still-bubbling lake. "What do you mean?"

"What do you know of the power you wield?"

"What I was taught. To kill, harm, control. To manipulate the energy of death." His face shifted and changed too much to hold a single expression, yet she sensed disappointment from him.

"And what of life?"

She shook her head. "I have no provenance there."

"Do you not?" he asked archly.

"I—I don't understand."

"That is because your people have lost the way. The universe exists because of balance, tip the scales too far outside of equilibrium and a restoration is required. Life, death, Void—it must all equal out."

"So we've gotten out of balance?"

"Oh, certainly. The coming war is a way of righting the scales.

You are a way of righting the scales, and your part is to ensure that life, death, and that which lies between exist harmoniously."

"Me?" She could barely even respond to that.

"There should be more, but there are not. So it falls to you."

"But I don't . . . I can't . . ."

"There have always been sentinels," he continued as if she hadn't spoken. "Those who monitor the three worlds. Mooriah was one. But now those places have been left without their guardians. This is part of what must be corrected."

She was still confused, but didn't say anything as he floated around her, inspecting her from all sides.

"The stone you bear, the trapped Song of the Nethersinger. Why are you afraid of it?"

She fingered the outside of the pocket where the death stone lay, nestled against her thigh. "It's nothing but more death. I had no choice in what kind of Song I was born with. Had no choice about the lives I've taken. This caldera . . . I don't know what it does and I don't really want to. I just don't know what to do with it."

He stopped his perusal and settled before her once again, his form flickering and changing slightly with each breath. "You have been done a disservice." He lifted a ghostly arm and a wall of water rose to the side of them. Kyara gasped and tried not to lose her footing. Rainbow-colored light danced in the waterfall that flew up from the lake and then arced back to crash down again. The light formed an image with a multicolored tinge to it. As it solidified, her stomach lurched. She closed her eyes.

"I don't want to see that."

"Open your eyes, my child," the Breath Father said. "Bear witness."

She took a deep breath and then did as he commanded. She was seeing herself at eleven, running around the courtyard of the harem she had grown up in. "Ahlini," she whispered. Her only childhood friend, alive and well, eyes shining, braids flying out behind her as she pumped her arms and raced around a corner.

Little Kyara was laughing, too. Until she followed around the corner and was stopped by a frowning woman in uniform, one of the *ul-nedrim* guards. Kyara wasn't allowed to play with the harem girls. But the guard looked around slyly and inclined her head slightly. Kyara grinned and took off running again.

Adult Kyara had no recollection of that. This memory, if it was one, had been lost to the ravages of time. "This is real? Not just another vision?"

"It is real," the ghostly man intoned.

The images continued: Ahlini teaching Kyara to read from her own slates, sneaking food from her plate to supplement the meager rations servants received. Kindness. And not just from her friend. Kyara also did not recall the small things that the adult *ul-nedrim,* the other rare daughters sired by the king, had done for her. Not being boys and ineligible for whatever dubious benefits harem women had, they were second-class citizens. Destined only for guard duty or drudgery. But the *ulla*—the woman in charge—had looked out for Kyara, unbeknownst to her child self. She'd been given extra clothes, extra rations, lighter duties than others in her position in different cabals of the vast harem. Kyara's eyes misted to watch the things she never knew had been happening.

And then that fateful day. Kyara was playing shelter-and-search with Ahlini. Her friend went off to hide and not long after the screaming began. Kyara followed her friend's shouts to find the girl in a storage room being choked by a bedraggled man in tattered clothing. A man who had somehow gotten into the harem.

Ahlini's untrained Song had lit every lamp and then sparked flames on the shelving as she'd tried to protect herself. Kyara had beaten at the man uselessly and smashed a jar over his head, but he was locked in madness. He reached out an arm and smacked her. She flew across the room and crashed into the wall.

Kyara had blacked out, never knowing how she'd killed the man and Ahlini, but in the vision, she saw the tiny kitten avatar leap from her prone body, transforming midair into the ferocious wildcat. It had entered the man's body, instantly exploding the Nethersong within him and killing him.

The cat did not target Ahlini, but they were so close, only a hairsbreadth away from one another that the poison of Nether was absorbed by her as well. The avatar seemed to know what it had done and regret it immediately. It shrank back into its kitten form and retreated sadly into Kyara's body.

The image changed to the infirmary. A guard cradled Kyara against her chest and lay her on the cot. The *ulla* arrived, out of breath.

"What's happened?" she cried.

The guards shook their heads. "It looks like plague," one said. "But it makes no sense."

"It is not plague." The old woman stroked a hand over Kyara's forehead. "I had a dream about this child before she was born, a message gifted to me by my ancestors. In our branch of the House of Eagles, there is a tale that has been passed down for generations. It tells of an oncoming storm, one that will upset the three worlds and pit the living against the dead. When it comes, it will be silent like a viper approaching unseen through the brush. I sense within this child the oncoming clouds."

The guards seemed perplexed, but hung on her words.

"She is special, she is a scorpion and we must protect her from the True Father."

Kyara startled, recalling the little book she had found, *The Book of Unveiling.* It had been written by Mooriah's descendants and told a cryptic tale of her story, calling her the Scorpion. She'd lost the book somewhere, in one prison or another. Had the *ulla* been one of Mooriah's line?

In the vision, the guards nodded, more loyal to the woman who led them than the despotic king. But in the end, the Cantor herself had come for Kyara, accompanied by a contingent of Golden Flames. They had overpowered the *ul-nedrim* guards, cutting them down mercilessly, and dragged Kyara off to the dungeon. The *ulla* was executed for hiding such a valuable resource.

The colors of the image faded and then the waters fell down to the frothing lake. Tears streamed down Kyara's face. She scrubbed at them violently. "Why did you show me this?"

The Breath Father did not emote, but the constant shifting of his form slowed sympathetically. "You were cared for, Kyara, always. You were loved and protected."

"Those women died trying to help me."

"Yes. They gave their lives because of their faith, their knowledge that you were special. They didn't know how special, but the wheel of fate was rolling across your life even then." The death stone in her pocket pulsed suddenly, as if it had woken up and wanted to be used. A burst of frigid air blast down her thigh and she shuddered.

"Our lives are not always what we think they are," the Breath Father continued. "Our histories are oft tainted by memory."

"So what am I supposed to do?" she breathed.

"If you cannot have faith in yourself, have faith in those who believe in you. The *ulla*, Mooriah, Murmur. They understand something about your potential and the need you must fulfill."

"And if I disappoint them?"

"You disappoint them if you fail to try. That is what they are asking of you."

She fished the stone from her pocket, still pulsing icily inside its wrappings. "And this? What does it do?"

"The Song of an ancient Nethersinger—it is mighty indeed. Its creator, a man named Yllis, poured a desperate intention into it—love and fear and strong desire—all of which increased its potency beyond the original Songbearer's ability. And over the centuries, fed by death and time, that power has grown beyond anyone's imagining. Once you unleash what it holds, there is no going back. You have only to touch it to release its fearsome force into this world and become a goddess of death."

"I don't want to be a goddess of death." Dread welled within her at the thought.

The Breath Father nodded sagely. "Then you are wise not to use it. In the hands of the careless, the unworthy, or the reticent, the death stone is more dangerous than even an army of wraiths."

Relief warred with disappointment. Part of her had hoped . . . What? That the stone would allow her to be the hero instead of the villain for once? She tried to shake off the dismay. But who could gainsay the Breath Father? He'd called her wise to avoid the death stone's power.

Slowly, his figure retreated back toward the far edge of the lake. "Your path is your own, Kyara, but remember what I have said. Balance is the key to the universe. It is all we truly need, and you must find it or create it both within and without in order to succeed. The scales require a sacrifice. They are waiting."

The steam began to retreat, reversing its course as if it was being sucked back into the water. The man of air and mist joined with it to sink down beneath the surface of the once-again tranquil lake.

The intense sense of power retreated with him until she no longer felt it constricting her. She turned to find that she was no longer on an island in the middle of the lake but once again at the entrance to the Origin caldera. She retreated on shaky legs, hoping she could find her way back, but for the moment, not caring if she did.

CHAPTER TWENTY-SEVEN

Dance with unhalting steps to share
your joy.
Offer it to the ground.
Stamp the soil down.
And let it echo across the land.

—THE HARMONY OF BEING

True to her word, Zeli told stories while they traveled across the country in the great mechanical walker. Stories of the land of Varten's father, a place he'd never seen and hadn't really thought much about before. But he hung on her every word.

She painted a picture of a childhood that was so different from Varten's as to be unrecognizable. She did not speak of her parents or of losing her Song—except for a brief mention that it had happened when she was just six years old.

Mostly she spun tales of walking barefoot around a picturesque lake near her home, enjoying the quiet moments of sunlight on her face in between chores, the taste of kinnifruit juice dribbling down her chin or the pies and tarts the staff would share after some big celebration or other, when food was unusually plentiful.

He wondered at the spaces between her stories, the things she left out. There was no talk of school, though she'd learned to read and write in order to better serve her mistress, a girl of the same age who sounded as selfish and spoiled as any Elsiran aristocrat. (And people thought their two races were so different.) She did not speak of having friends or time to wander and play and cultivate her own interests. She talked around so many topics that Zeli's Lagrimar was a tapestry full of holes.

The Tinker was largely quiet as he operated the vehicle, shining a sweeping light out before them to illuminate the countryside at night. Varten had a thousand questions he kept inside, not wanting to interrupt or bring up things that may be painful. He was happy to listen and imagine what it must have been like, growing up the way she did.

She talked until her voice grew raspy, and then she fell asleep. At some point during the night, her head slipped onto his shoulder. He was wide awake, holding himself very still, eyes closed, not wanting to jostle or move her. Enjoying the weight of her against him, but knowing he did not deserve the simple act of trust.

He must have also fallen asleep at some point because when he next opened his eyes, sunlight streamed in through the tinted glass and Gilmer City rose up before them.

The city was at the edge of a large lake, partially bordered by mountains. *Leggsy* rounded the far side of the lake, traveling between its sparkling green-blue waters and a busy roadway. The metropolis they approached was much larger than Rosira, but unlike in Melbain City, giant buildings didn't poke out across the skyline.

This place was constructed differently. Spread out across the north of the lake, the structures were lower, six to ten stories for most, with many shorter than that. Snowcapped mountains loomed up behind it to the north and even the air inside of *Leggsy* had cooled considerably during the trek.

Though they hadn't used roads for most of the trip, as the vehicle approached the city, the Tinker was obliged to merge onto the highway. The streets were clogged with people evidently headed into Gilmer City and toward the Rumpus. They traveled at a snail's pace, along with everyone else, but soon enough the highway turned into a wide avenue bordered by brightly colored boxy buildings painted in vibrant blues and yellows and reds. Some were brick, some stone, and others of a material Varten had never seen before, solid, yet porous with odd striations in it.

"Ye'll want to get to the city center," the Tinker said, eyes alight. "That's where everything happens. I've a spot to set old *Leggsy* down that isn't too far away."

His "spot" was actually the flat roof of a wide building, painted a shade of green that did not occur in nature. *Leggsy* climbed the structure easily and then hunkered down into its resting state, where its legs were jumbled and looked like nothing more than a junk heap.

This time, they climbed out the top hatch of the contraption and then down a ladder bolted to the side. Once they were all firmly settled, the Tinker got his bearings.

"City center is down there, just past that domed building. I'm going to head over to my favorite pub, out of the madness and whatnot. All that's for young people." He grinned and Varten wished they didn't have to part. There was something so warm and calming about his manner, his strange accent, even his metal ear.

"We can't thank you enough," Zeli said. She knelt to where Ziggy stood at her feet, wagging his articulated tail. "And I will miss you, too." He yipped, and ran up to give her face another licking for good measure.

"Thank you," Varten said, holding out his hand. The Tinker enclosed it in a warm grip and shook.

"I hope ye find what yer looking for," he said, eyes twinkling. "If it's anywhere, it'll be in the Rumpus."

A wooden staircase led from the roof to the ground, five stories below. They climbed down with Lanar bringing up the rear. He had been quiet for the entire trip, barely saying a word, to the point that Varten had nearly forgotten the man was there. Now his expression was so occluded Varten wasn't sure if he was still angry or completely indifferent.

The feeling of deep shame returned as they stood on the corner, saying their good-byes and then watching the Tinker's retreating form. Zeli peered up at Varten, her concern more evident than ever. He dug up a smile for her and then turned in the direction they were supposed to go. "We'd better get started."

Lanar's silent presence was starting to become oppressive, now that the Tinker's kindly energy was no longer a distraction. The man followed slightly behind them, arms folded behind his back, and every time Varten turned to glance at him, he wore a dark expression—somewhere between ponderous and irritated.

He'd come for the Rumpus, same as they had, and he didn't owe them any explanations. But Varten wondered all the same what his goals were and why his censure had hurt so very much the day before.

Zeli was unusually chipper as they crossed the street, moving in the direction of the thickening crowd. Though she'd spent hours talking the evening before, she remarked on the city, the buildings, the weather, and the vehicles as they drew nearer their destination.

A great horn sounded and the excitement around them grew palpable. People picked up the pace and soon they were surging forward like a wave on the sea, carried along by the rest.

The horn blew again and the chatter rose to a deafening level. Zeli looked at him and something inside him awoke with excitement. It sounded like the Rumpus was about to begin.

Varten had expected decorations—streamers or balloons or flags flying for the celebration. But the large square at the heart of Gilmer City, packed to the stuffings with people, wasn't adorned in any way. The staccato blasts of moments ago were now quiet and the gathered celebrants contracted, moving closer and closer together, shifting with anticipation. Soon a pregnant hush dropped over them.

Varten wasn't sure which way to look. Zeli was on his left, her hand clutching his shirt so they wouldn't be separated. She was at least two heads shorter than him and definitely couldn't see anything all the way down there. Even at his height, he could barely tell what, if anything, was going on, but he noticed some people riding on the shoulders of others for a better view.

"Get on my shoulders," he said, "maybe you can see what's happening."

She looked shocked at first and then peered down to her dress, but finally nodded. Varten knelt and helped situate her. Her skirt was wide enough to accommodate the position without being immodest. When he rose, now supporting her slight weight, she towered over the crowd.

"There's a platform, down at the end," she said. "And people are gathering. They're wearing . . . masks and costumes. I think they're dressed as animals."

Varten looked around him; others in the crowd were straining to see. Many smarter people had entered the buildings surrounding the square and were hanging out of windows or on rooftops. All appeared to be dressed normally, there weren't any strange costumes on display in the audience at least.

"They're doing some kind of pantomime," Zeli continued. "Some are dressed as hunters with bows and arrows. And then there's . . . Well, I'm not sure. A woman dressed in gold . . ." She trailed off.

Shouts and laughter rang out. People had climbed on top of trash cans and scaled lighting poles to see the antics on the stage. Those with a good view of the proceedings cheered and applauded. On the top of a nearby roof, Varten's roaming gaze was caught by a still figure among all the motion. A young boy of Zeli's complexion with a cloud of unruly hair stood there. Instead of facing the stage, he was looking down at the audience. From this distance, Varten couldn't tell what the child was staring at so intently.

Zeli wobbled and he held her legs tighter. "Sorry," she said, laughing. "The bear has caught the woman in gold and now one of the hunters looks like he's trying to negotiate with it. They're doing a sort of dance, he keeps tripping and falling."

The crowd erupted in laughter again. When Varten looked up, the boy on the roof was gone.

The play lasted a few more minutes. The woman in gold turned out to be a bride who married one of the hunters. The animals removed their masks and revealed themselves to be kings or gods or something, Zeli wasn't sure, but the others knelt before them. When it was over, the horn sounded again, and a man began speaking through an intercom system blasting over the square.

They could not understand him as he spoke in Yalyish, but the excitement of the crowd grew and grew. Soon everyone was cheering and shouting and they were pushed forward again, moving to some unknown destination.

Varten helped Zeli back to the ground and held her hand as the packed people surged. "Let's try and get off to the side," he shouted. She nodded and they pushed their way to the sidewalk to pause in front of a row of buildings. They'd lost Lanar in the press at some point.

"I think that must have been the opening ceremony for the celebration," she said, breathless after the exertion of negotiating the mob.

Music began and the celebrants started dancing. People, who before had been dressed in trousers and shirts or simple dresses, produced multicolored scarves and capes and wrapped themselves in them, transforming the already rowdy crowd into a writhing riot of colors. Varten and Zeli pressed themselves into the doorway of a bright blue building, watching the audience turn into a party.

"Which one are you here for: the Bride Hunt, the Game Hunt, or the Quest?" a voice said from behind them in Elsiran.

They spun around to find the building's door open, and standing inside was the boy Varten had noticed on the roof. He was all of eleven and wore a heavy woolen sweater and thick trousers a few sizes too big. He was a little disheveled, but in the way of children who aren't fussed over too much.

"I-I don't think we know what those are," Varten answered.

The boy stepped forward, looking eager to explain things. "The Rumpus has three kinds of participants—four if you count the spectators, but I don't. Some are here to find a husband or wife. They wear yellow or gold *hunas* and join the Bride Hunt."

Zeli leaned forward. "*Huna,* I do not know this word."

He grinned and made a flipping motion with his hand. "Those are the scarves and capes—they're made specially for the Rumpus and each color has a meaning."

Varten looked back at the passing crowd. There was quite a lot of yellow and gold on display.

"The Game Hunt started as a true hunt for boar and wolves and bears in the countryside," the boy continued, "but the Rumpus grew too big, and the animals too few, so now it's a scavenger hunt."

At Zeli's confused expression, Varten translated. The boy watched them carefully, tilting his head at the sound of Lagrimari. He held himself very still. Varten was used to seeing children always in motion—but maybe this stillness was a result of city life.

"What about the Quest?" Zeli asked.

"A hunt for knowledge." The boy's eyes grew big and somewhat wistful. "Scholars and seekers from all over the world—all trying to get into our Archives. But it doesn't let just anyone in." Pride laced his voice.

Zeli and Varten shared a look. Varten hoped he was keeping

the eagerness from his expression. "How do we join the Quest?" he asked.

"Are you sure you wouldn't rather head to the Bride Hunt? I think you'd both do well." The boy grinned again, an action that crinkled the corners of his eyes but did not brighten them. It was a strange smile indeed, full of a weariness odd in one so young. Coupled with the stillness, it reminded Varten of something.

But Zeli had gone stiff beside him, drawing his attention. She was . . . shivering. Varten placed a hand on her back, drawing her closer and recognizing fear in her expression. She wasn't afraid of the young lad, but her gaze was troubled and haunted as she stared off at the wall, unseeing. A memory maybe. One of the holes in her tapestry. Something to do with the Bride Hunt?

She blinked and shook off whatever had gripped her. "Thank you for your help," she said slowly. "I suppose you all grow up here knowing everything about the Rumpus."

"It's all anyone ever talks about, nine years out of ten." The child shrugged.

"What's your name?"

"I'm called Remi," he said, sticking his hand out. They all shook and made their introductions.

"And where are your parents, Remi?" Zeli asked. "You aren't lost are you?"

Instead of answering, he tilted his head to the side again. "You are Lagrimari?"

Her back straightened and she paused before answering. "Yes."

But Remi just nodded. Then his gaze shifted to somewhere over her shoulder. Varten turned to find Lanar standing a few paces away, staring. He'd found them—for this Varten was grateful. A familiar face, even one so recently familiar and so aloof, was welcome. True to form, the Lagrimari man stayed a ways off and did not approach. Zeli eyed him warily, evidently not as pleased at his return as Varten was. Remi watched him, too, the way you might watch a stray dog that has wandered into view.

"How do we enter the Quest?" Zeli asked.

"You already have." Remi tore his gaze away from Lanar. "Follow those in the blue *hunas* to the Archives. That's where the challenge is given."

"You don't happen to know what the challenge might be, do you?" Her voice shook a little—nerves, maybe. She stood close to Varten, not leaning into his hand, which was still on her back, but not pushing him away, either. He found himself unwilling to move, with her so warm beneath his palm.

"To hunt you must seek, to seek you must find," Remi answered with a shrug. Then he gave a quick wave and sprinted around them, disappearing into the crowd.

"What a strange child," Zeli murmured, turning to look after him.

"Well, he was helpful. Sort of."

"I guess we do know more than when we started." She shifted back, pushing against his hand, then froze and stepped away, looking suddenly embarrassed. Varten's palm was unreasonably cold. He shook off the unfamiliar sensation that had invaded—his hand felt numb and tingly—and then began looking for the celebrants in blue.

There were far fewer of them than the marriage seekers, or the red-clad game hunters—he still didn't know what any of the other colors were for. But he finally spotted a tight cluster of blue scarves up ahead, moving toward a side street.

"I see them. Over there." He pointed then held out his free hand for her as they pushed their way through the congestion of bodies again. She paused before taking it and hurt strummed through him. But he held on, using his body to cut through the others. His size and height allowed him an advantage and people tended to get out of his way when he nudged, gentle as he could, keeping a firm grip on Zeli. He looked back over his shoulder every now and then to see Lanar following. Had the man mentioned seeking the Archives as well? Neither he nor Zeli had ever mentioned it, on purpose. Maybe Lanar was just trying to keep his eye on them, on him, since Varten had already proven himself untrustworthy.

Zeli grunted, and he looked down to see her rubbing a shoulder. "You all right?"

"Fine, I just really hate being jostled."

He pulled her closer, releasing her hand to circle an arm around her shoulders. She was very close now, the smell of the oil she used to moisturize her hair filling his nostrils with a light sweetness.

As they walked, avoiding stray elbows or the whirl of a spontaneous dancer, Varten began to feel lighter. Though he did not enjoy the swarm of bodies, the excitement they exuded was infectious. The music was fast and loud and made him want to spin around himself. And having Zeli tucked under his arm did something strange to his brain.

She had one arm around him as well, the other placed against his stomach, probably for balance since the street was unevenly paved and the jam of people made her stumble occasionally. When he shifted suddenly to avoid a laughing, twirling woman who'd crossed his path, Zeli pressed against him harder. He was still tender from yesterday's punch, but that wasn't what knocked the air from his lungs.

He focused on keeping his feet under him when a smiling man

carrying a tray of wooden cups stopped before him and offered him one. Surprised, Varten reached for it, sniffing a delicious, candied aroma. He took a sip and groaned; whatever this was tasted like melted gold drizzled in honey. He offered it to Zeli, who frowned.

"What is that?"

He shrugged. "They're passing them around."

She looked around, somewhat worried. "We don't know what's in this or where it came from." But she reached for it anyway, removing her hand from his belly, and took a measured sip. Then she smiled.

"This *is* good." She drained the rest of the cup. There was no bite of alcohol in the drink but he felt a little slower and looser all the same.

Someone speaking in Elsiran caught his attention. A young man dressed all in white stood on a platform off to the side of the street. They'd passed others like him shouting, though none in a language they could understand.

"Visitors, friends—the Rumpus is a time to lay our burdens down!" the man shouted. "As an acolyte of Saint Gilmer, I have dedicated my life to carrying out his mission. During the Rumpus, we celebrate him and all he has provided to strengthen the ties that bind us together."

They stopped to listen, though most of the crowd continued walking. Zeli looked up wide-eyed, tilting her head and trying to understand the words.

"Over the course of a decade of toil and travail, our links weaken," the acolyte continued, clasping his hands together, then breaking them apart. "But never forget, to celebrate is to live, to love, and to be merry. Rest your weary shoulders and take part, and you will feel the benefit. You will feel the blessing of Saint Gilmer the Searcher. The pursued and pursuer. Whether you seek entertainment, a partner to walk this life with you, or the knowledge to create both, you may find it here. Lay your burdens down, seek and find and rejoice."

He held his hands above his head, palms up, then clapped them together and brought them to his lips. He closed his eyes and bowed. When he opened them again, he looked at Varten and smiled.

Then he looked away and began speaking in another language. Perhaps the same speech repeated? Varten recognized only the words *Gilmer* and *Rumpus*.

"People from around the world come," Zeli said. "They must translate some things into various languages."

Varten nodded and caught sight of a stream of blue-clad people turning up ahead. "Come on!"

This new side street was narrower and less crowded. As they headed away from the music in the square, a new set of musicians began playing nearby and the dancing changed. Around them, people started singing a Yalyish song. It was bright and folksy, very catchy even though he couldn't sing along.

But Zeli was laughing as an older man beside her did a series of spins. He turned to her and motioned for her to spin as well. At first Varten thought she'd be too shy, but then she relented and turned around on her toes once. The man clapped and did another turn, so Zeli did, too.

Not to be outdone, and caught up in the joy and exuberance and warmth running through his veins, Varten started spinning as well. Zeli's laugh was even more infectious than the music. He reached out for her, took her hand, and they spun together.

The entire crowd danced as they moved toward their destination. It was a mobile party parade in the middle of the street. Now dizzy, Varten did not stop dancing. He let his arms and legs glide and move along with the melody of the guitar, drums, and horns he still couldn't see.

Beside him, Zeli moved freely as well, graceful and rhythmic and easy. She stumbled on a crack in the street and ended up crashing into him. Instinctively, he tightened his arms around her to keep her from falling. Laughing, her eyes met his. She seemed closer, standing on her toes.

He couldn't help himself from leaning forward. When their lips touched it was as if a blanket fell over the world. The music faded, the revelers quieted. Everything stopped, even his heartbeat. Her arms moved around him, bringing him closer. He lifted her to bring her even nearer. Holding her there, something new and indefinable moved through him. Something like music or electricity made his very bones begin to sing.

When their tongues touched, Zeli startled. He opened his eyes to find her staring at him, breathing heavily. The crowd moved around them, water around a boulder. They gaped at each other for a moment before he put her down.

She touched her lips, appearing stunned, but didn't say anything. He held his breath.

The invisible musicians were closer now, drowning out anything she might have wanted to say. She blinked as if waking from a dream, and looked around. Then she turned and started walking again. Slowly, not leaving him behind, but not touching him anymore.

The crowd had thinned somewhat. There was enough space for them to walk unmolested, so he didn't reach for her again. Though his hand itched and felt empty.

Every now and again she would look over at him furtively, as if trying to solve a riddle he'd presented. He supposed he *was* the riddle, for he barely knew himself.

For a brief moment, he'd been just as unencumbered and free as the acolyte had advised. Caught up in a moment of singular joy. But a person can't just set down their burdens, not when they're tethered to you. Dragging themselves behind you.

Not when the weight of them pulls against you with every step. Even the wonder and merriment of the Rumpus couldn't change everything.

CHAPTER TWENTY-EIGHT

When you play, do it not with
people's minds or hearts or feelings.
Play to win, or play the drum,
the horn, the keys.
Play rousing, soothing, raucous, lilting melodies.

—THE HARMONY OF BEING

Jasminda sat stiffly on the ungenerously cushioned chair. She supposed she should call it a throne, but shouldn't it be more comfortable to achieve such a lofty title? Next to her, Jack's seat was conspicuously empty.

She'd spent the past two hours calming the staff to the best of her ability and giving out a dozen reassurances to various supervisors that they would be able to successfully handle an impromptu state visit by one of the most notoriously unpleasant leaders of the continent. That they could do in hours what was usually accomplished in weeks.

Too bad there was no one to reassure her.

Guardsmen lined the throne room, standing at attention. The entire Council was here, as well as various aides and a handful of aristocrats. This room seemed like the best place to entertain a royal visitor, though as the bottoms of her thighs lost feeling, she began to rethink the notion. Perhaps something less formal, to create a feeling of congeniality and make King Pia lower her guard somewhat. Then again, such informality may be taken as an insult. Best to lean on decorum and the established protocol for these types of events.

Jack would know. Calladeen likely would, too, but she was firm in her decision not to enlist his assistance. Who knew what he'd want in return for helping her? And she couldn't risk looking weak before him.

A page ran into view from the back of the room. "She's on her way, Your Majesty," the young man said, out of breath.

Jasminda nodded and he dashed away again. No more time for second-guessing, she would just have to do the best she could. She straightened and lifted her chin, affecting her most regal expression. Usher had told her that it made her look quite formidable—she wasn't sure if he was just being kind, but she took the words to heart.

The double doors of the throne room opened, revealing a group of Guardsmen who marched down the center. Behind them came the Raunian entourage.

The long, narrow space did not allow for a clear view of King Pia for some time. She was shorter than expected, shorter, it appeared, than Ani and probably only rose to the height of Jasminda's shoulders. Her hair was a cap of pure white, cropped very short without any of the blue or green dye her people were known for. She wore a robe of sapphire and gold with bell sleeves.

On her face lay an intricate web of tattoos. Ani had explained the meanings of her own markings, rank and taxes and shipping rights and family ties and significant accomplishments. From the amount of ink scored onto her cheeks, forehead, and chin, it was clear that King Pia was quite a force to be reckoned with, even if you didn't know her title.

But even more shocking was the retinue she'd brought. At least fifty men and women entered solemnly behind her. As they filtered in, Camm whispered from in back of the throne.

"She brought a total of one hundred people, Your Majesty."

Jasminda kept her shock from her face, but just barely. Quite a large retinue for an impromptu foreign visit from such a small country. The island nation had less than half of Elsira's population. Jack had only brought a half-dozen to Fremia, including his guards. What was the purpose of this? The throne room had never been quite so full.

Her staff's concerns echoed in her mind. Could they accommodate so large a group within the palace?

"Make sure Usher knows and alerts the staff," she said, trying not to move her mouth.

"I'm on it." Camm's soft footsteps retreated, and Jasminda swallowed.

Though petite in size, King Pia had an energy about her that put Jasminda in mind of a thundercloud. Earthsong revealed that the woman exuded confidence, she was calm, and a bit smug. Jasminda bet Pia knew that she'd caught Elsira off-guard and was happy about that.

Two familiar faces were a part of her entourage: Pia's son and Ani's brother, Tai Summerhawk, along with Lizvette Nirall, the current ambassador to Raun. Lizvette's gaze was contrite and her emotions apologetic and worried, as they should be. She should have given some warning about this visit. Jasminda would be having words with her about this.

Finally, the king completed her long, slow trek down the center of the room to stand before the dais holding the two thrones. Jasminda inclined her head slightly. "King Pia, we are honored to receive you. We trust that your journey here was safe?"

"Quite safe, Your Majesty, thank you." Her voice was velvet and silver. Like the final chime of a bell before time runs out. Time for what, Jasminda did not know, but she felt the ticking down of the clock anyway.

"And let me congratulate you on both your precipitous rise to power and the return of your lost family members. I know my daughter was greatly gratified by the latter." Pia's dark eyes reminded Jasminda of onyx chips, fathomless but with a bright reflection. "Speaking of which, where is my daughter?"

"Please accept my apology, Your Majesty," Jasminda said. "Had we more notice of your arrival, I'm certain my brother and your daughter would have been here to greet you. They departed yesterday on her ship, the *Rapskala*. However, I've sent a speedboat after them to request that they return."

Some of the smugness faded from Pia's expression. "Ah, you must forgive me for the unannounced visit. We intended to undergo a sailing tour of only the surrounding territory of our island, a trip of two days. Then, on a whim, I decided we might as well head east so that you and I could discuss things in person. Ambassador Nirall was quite shocked and implored me to send advanced word, so please don't blame her."

Jasminda's gaze shot to Lizvette, who looked on stoically, but surprise at Pia's announcement rang through the Earthsong connection.

Pia continued, looking at Lizvette with kindness. "She fervently appealed for me to evaluate Elsira's new leadership with fresh eyes, and I found her arguments convincing. The rest of my staff"—she waved at the retainers surrounding her—"are well aware of my eccentricities."

That a two-day tour could turn into a nearly two-week journey across the ocean was more than eccentric, but Jasminda merely nodded. She didn't know what game Pia was playing, but the woman had calculating eyes—the eyes of someone not only older and wiser, but tougher and shrewder than Jasminda could ever hope to be.

"Well," she said, rising, and deciding to take another tack. "Let's not stand on ceremony. You and I have much to discuss regarding the relations that have soured between our two peoples. Let us do so woman to woman, queen to . . . king."

Pia smiled and inclined her head in response. Jasminda descended from the dais and approached the other ruler, holding out her hands in greeting. Pia looked at her outstretched hands and raised a brow. Too late, Jasminda realized she'd given the Elsiran greeting. She had no idea how Raunians greeted one another.

Pia did not raise her hands to meet Jasminda's outstretched palms, leaving her standing there, greeting given but not reciprocated. Jack's advice to learn more about Raunian culture came back to her along with Calladeen's exhortations. But she had been focused on other areas, domestic rather than foreign.

Now she stood in her own throne room, embarrassed and shamed. In her peripheral vision, the Council bristled. She could not identify Calladeen and refused to turn her head, but could imagine his expression.

Slowly, Jasminda lowered her arms, not breaking eye contact with Pia. She clasped her hands in front of her, mimicking the other woman's stance.

The grim line of Pia's mouth curved ever so slightly. "Woman to woman. It *is* about time this country got some feminine energy in its leadership," she said. There was no need to give voice to the slight she had effected. Everyone present had seen it.

Jasminda's nostrils flared. She couldn't lift her chin any more and still be able to see, couldn't mask her expression any more than she already was, but rage and humiliation were an inferno within her. Via Earthsong, she felt the other woman's satisfaction at landing such a blow.

Very well then, Jasminda thought. *If that's how you want this to go.* She produced a voluminous smile and led the way.

CHAPTER TWENTY-NINE

If you believe,
convinced,
convicted,
holding fast to your vast flaws,
no court may pardon you.

—THE HARMONY OF BEING

Zeli's heart thundered inside her chest, its pace rapid and concerning. Every few steps she'd think she'd caught her breath and then the memory of the kiss would wash over her, pushing out everything else. The people, the noise, the music and laughter and dancing all disappeared and she would be back in that moment again, holding on for dear life. Unable to get her bearings.

Even now, with the crowd thinner, down to a normally busy day in Rosira, she would accidentally brush against Varten, jostled by something, and gasp. She nearly tripped three times and he steadied her, but she couldn't bear to be touched by him because it always ended. And then she'd do nothing but want it again.

She pushed down the feelings that had so quickly taken over. Where had they come from? She didn't want to be kissed. Didn't think she'd even like it after her first time had been so terrifying. But Varten was nothing like that. Nothing like *him*. And her heart simply refused to obey common sense and get back under control.

Fortunately, their destination loomed up ahead. A cluster of people with blue *hunas* gathered at the base of a huge building in the shape of a pyramid. The building looked like it had been built in layers by different builders with different materials. The bottom was limestone, on top of that gray rock, above that was glass—thick and warped. More layers rose from there, the higher glass layers looking shinier and smoother, and at the peak sat a brilliant, pointed red crystal, reflecting the late afternoon sun.

A clock chimed somewhere four times. They'd spent the day in the street walking and laughing and dancing. She didn't feel as if she'd been on her feet all day; she suspected she'd feel it later.

The pyramid had a pair of enormous double doors at least two stories high, gilded with golden carvings. She couldn't make out the detail at this distance, but they looked grand. The group gathered here was far smaller than she'd thought it might be. Then again, there were many, many more yellow, gold, and red *hunas* in the city center—the search for knowledge was just not as popular as the other options. Hopefully that would work to their advantage.

Anticipation hummed inside her, making her feel nearly as light-headed as the drink had. As the kiss had. She shook her head to clear it—they'd made it this far. They were actually at the Rumpus, about to face the challenge. When they started, she wasn't certain she'd even believed they'd get here.

She turned to Varten and her excitement cooled. He was uncharacteristically quiet, face drawn and pensive. Did he regret the kiss?

Lanar stood on his other side, though she thought they'd lost him in the celebration. A strange, cloudy haze seemed to follow the man around. He was obviously not enjoying the festivities. Whereas Zeli and Varten had lost themselves in the dancing and merriment, Lanar showed no signs of falling victim to that sort of levity.

So she stayed quiet, clasping her hands in front of her and wondering at Varten's sudden change of mood. He must regret it. He was a prince, after all, and she was . . . nobody. Not a Sister, not even a novice anymore now that she'd abandoned her duties.

He was probably right to have second thoughts, it had definitely been a mistake. What was in that golden honey drink anyway?

"Want a chocolate stick?"

She turned to find Remi next to her, face plastered with the remnants of the chocolate confection in question. It must have been one of the candies being sold by vendors set up along the streets.

"Do you have another one?" she asked, noticing his empty hands.

"I ate mine, but I can get you one if you like."

"No, thank you." She had no money at all and Varten had still not been to the bank.

At the pyramid's base, a group of acolytes in long white robes with funny round white caps on their heads had gathered. One of them lifted a small cone to his lips, which amplified his voice loud enough that the entire audience could hear.

His voice was rich and resonant and he spoke slowly enough that if he'd been speaking in Elsiran, she might have understood. "What's he saying?" she asked Remi.

He motioned her down, so she knelt beside him. "To get

inside, you need to . . ." Remi kept his voice low and closed his eyes in thought. "Find a way in. That's the challenge. Gain entry to the Archives before sunset and you may possess as many of its secrets as you can gather in twenty-four hours."

The crowd chittered with excitement but Zeli's heart sank. The challenge to getting into the Archives was getting into the Archives? The man up front kept talking, but Remi frowned. "He's just repeating it again with longer words and more sermonizing about how great Saint Gilmer is."

Zeli stood, looking at the massive building with new eyes. Some folk had evidently been ready for this possibility, though as she understood it the challenge was different each year. About a dozen large men near the front were assembling a battering ram from a bunch of smaller pieces. All too soon they had it put together and surged forward to pound at the giant doors.

Others moved out of their way swiftly, and groups began clustering together all around the base, inspecting what they could see and reach of the building. Zeli didn't even know where to begin.

"The glass layer starts at about twenty paces up," she murmured. "They don't look like windows that can open, but they might be. Maybe with a ladder . . ."

Instead of watching the building, Varten peered at the area around the pyramid. They stood on the south side, a plaza paved with a concrete slab extending about one hundred and fifty paces to the street. On the east side lay a grassy park surrounded by a low fence. A street bordered the west side, with only the width of the sidewalk to separate it.

"Let's get a look at the back," Varten said, already moving. Lanar stayed where he was, a statue sprouting from the concrete, but Zeli and Remi went along. A handful of others had the same idea and toured the perimeter of the building.

In the back was a narrow alley that dead-ended at the park, and no doors were visible along any of the exterior walls. The front doors were the only obvious way inside.

Back on the plaza, the battering ram did not seem to be making any inroads in breaking down the decorated double doors.

"How long has this building been here?" Varten wondered.

"Hundreds of years," Remi said, now eating a handful of hard candies he'd produced from a pocket. He crunched through them, heedless of any potential damage to his teeth.

"The building must need supplies of some kind, where are they delivered?" Varten mused. "What's the purpose of the alley if not to facilitate deliveries?"

"Well, if it's really only open one day every ten years, maybe not many supplies are needed," Zeli said.

"The acolytes don't have access the rest of the time?"

Remi continued his crunching, speaking while chewing. "No, but they've collected a bunch of Gilmer's other writings in another building."

Varten tapped a finger against his lips. His mind seemed to be churning and he had a light in his eyes she'd observed when he was thinking through something. She'd seen it when they'd studied the journal, and when Eskar was showing him how the boat operated. He may say he wasn't a good student and didn't like school, but he certainly liked to learn and think. And she suspected he was good at it.

"No electric or plumbing conversions then," he mumbled, eyes glazed over. "And if it's full of ancient books, it must have been constructed to deal with humidity properly. Some kind of natural temperature control . . ."

Zeli had no idea what he was talking about, but didn't interrupt his process. He turned away from the building to the street, then toward the park. While he pondered, several other groups attempted to scale the pyramid in different ways. One team created a human ladder, with smaller and smaller people climbing on top of one another. The woman at the top had a sledgehammer that she was taking to the glass.

"Are they allowed to destroy it?" she asked. Remi shrugged.

While Varten continued to mutter to himself, Lanar appeared captivated by the red stone at the top of the building. His gaze didn't waver from it; he looked almost in a trance.

Without any warning, Varten marched off around the plaza, walking in a random pattern, zigging this way and that. Remi and Zeli shared a bemused look before following. They meandered through those observing the battering ram and various wall-scalers. Varten seemed to be searching for something on the ground. Then he abruptly turned toward the grassy park and leapt over the short, metal fencing.

"What is it?" Zeli asked, racing after him.

"Not sure, I just . . ." Varten turned around and walked back to the fence, then began counting off steps as he crossed the grass again. He stared at the ground for a long moment until Zeli stepped into his line of sight. Then he looked up, sheepish.

"Sorry, I was just thinking about how the Archives must have been here before the city, or built around the time of its founding, but it's pretty far from the lake. Cities usually begin close to bodies of water, especially fresh, drinkable water. So they placed this building here, while the city grew from way down there." He motioned south, back toward the lake. "And Gilmer City has been modernized with electricity and plumbing. There's a whole world below our feet, pipes and tunnels for bringing water in and out." He spread his hand around to the other buildings.

"So, what are you saying?"

"What if we can get in from below?" He stomped his foot and a metallic thud rang out. He bent to clear away a tuft of unruly grass, revealing a round metal disc in the ground.

They kneeled down to inspect it. While Varten tapped at it, Zeli looked up and noticed that Lanar had finally torn his attention away from the pyramid's peak and was walking over to join them.

"We may be able to access the building from below," she told him, motioning to the disc in the ground.

"Hmm," Lanar said, squinting doubtfully. "It is unlikely this building was ever plumbed."

Varten stopped inspecting the round plate and sat back on his haunches, shoulders sinking.

"It's an interesting thought," Lanar continued, "but rather improbable." Without another word he turned and ambled back to the plaza.

The dejection on Varten's face made Zeli's blood boil. "I don't care what he says, it's a good idea. Look, they've been at that battering ram for ages and the door hasn't budged, neither has the window they're banging on. No one else has any better ideas, least of all him."

But Varten was shaking his head and rising. "No, Lanar's probably right. I don't really know anything about architecture or anything at all. And even if there were pipes, they'd be too small and filthy to get through." The cast of his eyes and jaw were dejected.

"I still think we should try—at least look around down there. It's worth a shot. We've come all this way."

Varten stared, unseeing toward the pyramid. It's like he wasn't even there anymore, all his excitement and thoughtfulness wiped out by Lanar's careless words. "It's too heavy to lift anyway." He toed at the disc with his boot before sighing and turning away.

"Varten, wait!" But he moved off slowly, shuffling back toward the plaza.

Zeli let out a groan of frustration. Why would he just give up like that? What was wrong with him? She stomped her foot once, then again just because it felt good. Next to her, Remi watched his retreating figure with solemn eyes. She sighed and crossed her arms.

"Are you giving up, too?" Remi asked.

She turned sharply to him. "If he couldn't lift it, I certainly can't."

Remi shrugged and fished more candy from his pocket, which appeared to have an endless supply.

The battering ram thudded like a pendulum. One of the human ladders wobbled and then rippled, thankfully able to catch the woman at the top with the mallet when she lost her footing.

The sun was lowering and the temperature getting colder by the minute. All the warmth and joy of earlier had faded away.

Zeli shook her head. She wasn't giving up. They'd come this far, hadn't they?

She dropped to her knees stuck her fingers in the small holes drilled into the metal plate. The disc was thick and didn't budge a bit. If those two ridiculous men hadn't left, maybe they all could have tried together. She strained again, then sat back, out of breath.

"I can help," Remi offered, looking solemn, but comical with remnants of chocolate mixed with the cherry candies he'd been eating coating his lips and cheeks.

"I think we need chains and an ox to move this thing."

"Let's just try, eh?" He crouched down and stuck tiny fingers in the holes. Zeli shook her head and moved back into position for another attempt. She was humoring Remi—children always thought they were invincible, and she certainly wasn't going to be the one to kill his little spirit.

They pulled and tugged, straining with the effort, but nothing happened.

Zeli lay back in the grass, all at once tired and hungry and sweaty. At least the temperature wasn't bothering her anymore. "This isn't working," she said.

"One more time," Remi said.

"We could hurt ourselves if we're not careful." Her arms already felt noodley.

"Just once more?" He blinked innocently, and she chuckled. Adorably strange child.

"All right. Once more." They pulled and heaved and grunted and the disc actually slid a fraction.

Zeli blinked, unsure if she'd imagined it or not. Remi gave her a huge, red-tinted smile. She took a few breaths before nodding for them to try again. With that slight movement, they were able to gain additional leverage, enough to slide the disc completely out of the way.

It was impossible—but true. The hole below was dark, and cool air wafted up. She didn't like the idea of low, dark places. It reminded her too much of being kidnapped, being sold. Waiting with the cries of others amidst the stench of a hole in the ground.

But this was different, she reminded herself. There was some chance, small or not, that whatever she faced would be worth it. Besides, could whatever was down there be worse than what she'd already faced and lived through?

Probably not.

She swallowed and looked up, searching for Varten in the crowd. He stood out, a head above most, but too far away to hear her if she called out. Too dejected, too fragile maybe. She wasn't sure. She didn't want to do this alone, but she could.

"Here," Remi said, producing a box of matches from his pocket.

"Thank you. Stay up here, just in case it's dangerous." She thought he might protest, more little boy pride, but he merely nodded.

Zeli lit a match and stuck her hand into the hole, revealing the metal ladder leading down. She looked around until the match burned down and blew it out before it singed her fingertips.

With a deep breath, she nodded to herself, and descended into the darkness.

CHAPTER THIRTY

Who's to say
one day
we will not recall
the future
as well as the past.

—THE HARMONY OF BEING

You pace your room restlessly, heedless for once of the intense cold flooding your bones. Where is the servant to stoke the fire? But the thought flits away as soon as it comes and in a moment you've already forgotten.

What you need hovers just out of reach, locked in the fortress of your ancient mind. The spell used to summon the spirits is familiar, but not. You are on the verge of a great discovery but it keeps eluding you.

It makes you want to smash something.

The door to the chamber bursts open, stopping you midpace. You are about to rail at the servant for such an indecorous entrance—but it is not one of the silent guards, it is Cayro, sour expression marring his pallid face.

"How can I help you?" you ask with a slightly mocking bow.

He narrows his eyes and settles unbidden into a seat by the fire. "I want to know what you are planning."

You perch on the threadbare seat across from him, affecting an innocent expression. "Planning?"

"I've been to Lagrimar, you know. I was a Seeker in my youth."

"Is that so? How did you find my land?"

"Hot. Disgusting. Full of starving people embittered by hatred for you, their so-called leader."

You lean back and steeple your fingers, waiting for him to continue speaking. He is not flustered by the silence; it seems that once again he is taking your measure.

"I think it is a mistake for you to be here," he finally says.

"Then I take it you were overruled?" You smile as he clenches his jaw. "Does Nikora not respect your advice and counsel? Pity."

His eyes bore holes into you. But hc is hundreds of years younger and isn't adept. Your skin might as well be made of diamonds for all the effect his glare has.

"Was there a reason for this visit or did you just want to rehash old times?"

He blows out a breath and looks off into the fire. "I know a way out of here. A path to freedom for you, and I would see you use it."

You sit rigidly, not betraying any emotion.

"There is a tunnel through the mountain that leads down to its base," he says. "A city lies not twenty kilometers from there. I will show you how to get out if you agree to leave." His gaze spears you again, intense and calculating.

He seems serious, though this could still be a test. "And who will control the Wailers? Who will provide the Earthsong you need?"

Cayro shakes his head. "This plan of Nikora's is absurd. We should not waste what's left of Dahlia's flesh on this mission. What's more, we should not sacrifice our people's lives for this. Better to regroup and rebuild our strength. Find another way to restore our magic. Locate our scattered brethren and reform ourselves. This quest is folly."

"Then why do you follow her?"

His chin juts up. "I am a believer."

You try to keep the smirk from your lips. "What, pray tell, do you believe in?"

"In Saint Dahlia, her goodness, her power." His shoulders straighten with earnest emotion. "To use her to summon spirits is heresy. It is not what she would have wanted."

You cross your legs, affecting a pose of ease. "Perhaps you're right. And I agree, Nikora's plan is madness. But will you really help me go free? Why not just kill me?"

Cayro tenses his jaw and looks away. "Your debt to the Physicks could be useful. I would expect a favor in return at some point."

Ah, the real reason for his visit. "So you let me go, off to my own devices, and then what, I offer you a boon in the future?"

"I'm certain you will discover another way to regain your power and take over the Elsiran land. It may be a good place for my people once we regroup."

"A safe haven for the Physicks?"

"Indeed."

You stroke your chin and think it over. This ally may be useful to have, when you need him. And easy to crush when you do not. "Very well. When would this escape take place?"

"I have loyal men among the guards. When it is time to move, I will arrange to have my people on guard duty. Wait for my signal, and we will make it happen."

Cayro rises and takes his leave quickly, believing that he has forged a useful alliance. Dissension among the ranks of the Physicks can only help your cause. Eyes turned toward fighting one another will not be looking in your direction. And if something untoward were to happen to Nikora, then her blood spell would be null and void.

It is one path forward, a window opening while the door remains barred. You ponder in front of the fire for a long while.

The answer you've been seeking comes to you in a dream. It hits like a bolt of lightning, like the strikes of Nethersong used to obliterate the spirits and banish them from the bodies of their hosts.

A memory from centuries earlier, long repressed, returns. It is from when you were a power-starved lad with a taste for Earthsong and your sister staunchly refused to give you more. You knew of blood magic, knew that Cantors like Yllis studied and innovated it. That the Cavefolk in the eastern mountains practiced it and used it to accomplish things that Earthsingers could only imagine.

Those of the Folk who left the safety and cloistering of their caves had emerged and shared secrets—your mother having been one of them—but the true masters of blood magic were the shamans who never left the mountain. With them lay its most powerful secrets.

And so you went to them.

You traveled to the east of what was then the whole of your land. There you met those who were leaving, the pale-eyed Folk unused to light and fresh air who were tired of life underground. They had been leaving in droves since your grandparents first arrived in this land from some dying world. Your father, aunts, and uncles had found spouses among these former Cavefolk.

After leaving the protection of the Mountain Mother, the Folk became known as the Silent. They had no inborn Songs, though their children who had been conceived with Earthsingers might.

Your mother had taught you some simple blood spells remembered from her childhood, and you longed for more. Blood magic was power in its own right. And there were whispers that it rivaled Earthsong.

So you sought it out. Made the journey with nothing but faith to guide you, that and the lessons of your mother. *Never take that which the mountain does not want to give. Always treat the Mother with respect.*

At the mouth of a cave, high in the mountain you met a man. He was old then, his skin translucent in the flickering light of your lantern. "Why have you come here?" he asked, blocking your way.

"I came to visit my mother's people."

"You are not one of us."

"Can I not be?"

He'd grunted and turned and you'd followed him deep into the cave city. In a little-used, out of the way chamber, he fed you and bid you to leave.

"Teach me," you begged. Back when you would stoop to such a thing. But he did not budge. "Teach me, for one day soon there will be no one left to teach."

The truth of your statement shone in his eyes. Though the city still lived, it was already beginning to die as more and more chose to leave. In two, maybe three generations, if the current exodus continued, it would be a town of ghosts.

"What is it you wish to learn?" the old man said after a while.

"Everything."

From the shaman, you learned how to remove a Song from a Singer, how to fashion calderas from blood and words and intent. You absorbed blood magic's possibilities, its drawbacks and limitations.

Clarity greets you now when you awaken from this memory-dream. You have not thought of that old man in centuries. You have forgotten the source of your education, the reason you were able to take power. So odd. But even now as the knowledge afforded by the memory swells in your mind, trepidation fills at skirting so close to the past.

Never take a retrograde step.

Only the future is real. What does it matter when and where you learned this? Why it was taught to you? It was better to have forgotten.

When you left that place, all those years ago, you asked why he deigned to teach so much.

"Many years ago, I had a vision," he said, "a prophecy of a war that cannot be avoided. And shortly before you arrived, I had another one." Pale eyes pierced him with blades of scrutiny. "'The one who walks in the Dark will embrace the Light.'"

You'd grown indignant. "Is that supposed to be me? Walking through these dark caves? I don't believe in prophecies."

"Darkness surrounds you, but a turning point lies ahead. The tools I have provided, they can save us all . . . or doom us," he murmured. "It is the only gamble I have to play."

You shake off the words from long ago and recall instead the spell to open the portal. You can now picture its shape and architecture, the way it was put together.

You can see the flaws.

Blood magic is different than inborn Songs. It requires intention and material. Not just blood, but something to hold it. Something around which to create the caldera—the container for the magic.

If a spell went awry, it was usually either the material or the intent behind the incantation that was wrong. Different words, synonyms with different emphasis behind them, could lead to many different results.

Inspiration strikes. You rush out to find the guards at your doors. "Take me to Nikora's study. I need writing materials."

They look at one another and at first you are not sure they will comply, but then they lead you with maddeningly plodding steps through the castle.

You burst into the study, surprising Cayro and Nikora. "Paper, pen! I think I know what's wrong with the spell."

"There's nothing wrong with the spell," Nikora cries and you shoot her an icy glare. She goes silent, pushing her nose into the air before waving at the sideboard, where a box of paper is stored next to the dwindling pile of amalgamations.

You began to write furiously, pouring out the memories that have returned. Synonyms of terms, other ways of constructing the spells, the knowledge of a people lost to time. Lost to their own traditions. Swallowed up by a new people who replaced them.

You may be the last connection to them. This may be their last work.

You ignore all else as you write, certain that you have found your way back to power.

You would thank the old man if you could, if he was somehow still alive, but though your memory of him has returned, you cannot remember his name.

CHAPTER THIRTY-ONE

Become your own master.
Bow not to another.
You are a proficient bearer of
your own destiny.

—THE HARMONY OF BEING

Murmur's voice droned in Kyara's head as he gave instructions on ways to tweak her performance. She was having a hard time focusing, since the Breath Father's words from the day before were still reverberating inside her skull. The vision he'd showed her replayed in her mind over and over again, destroying her ability to concentrate.

Ahlini's smiling face, the *ulla*'s stricken one, the kindness of the guard. Why hadn't she remembered any of that before? Why were only the worst things etched forever in her memory—the pain and trauma, the abuse, the killing?

She made a promise to herself to hold close the positive experiences she'd had and try and use them to overwhelm all of the suffering. An intense longing for Darvyn swelled and she had that to wade through as well in order to get back to the present moment.

Tana's squeal of delight brought her back. Kyara blinked the haze away from her eyes to witness the girl's triumph. She had moved on from attacking static trees to hitting moving targets. Smoky creatures, similar to the wraith spirits, flew in swirls and spirals at the other end of the cavern. Tana's dragon avatar breathed purple fire into the mass of writhing forms, singeing them into nonexistence.

When all her targets were gone, the dragon retreated and the girl clapped her hands. True joy shone on her face and it nearly brought a tear to Kyara's eye. Tana deserved her happiness, and her growing skill was impressive.

Every evening, they would return aboveground to Darvyn's camp where he would be helping Ulani master her Song. The little puppy Fenix had manifested from pure Earthsong was still there. Ulani had named him Raven. The girls would chatter and play while the adults looked on. Watching the children both warmed Kyara's heart and saddened her.

There would be no children in her and Darvyn's future—at least not ones with his smile. All of the *ul-nedrim* and *ol-nedrim*, the harem-born children of the True Father, were sterile. She'd never thought much about it before gaining her freedom, and tried not to focus on it now as there was nothing she could do. Part of her was glad that the True Father's vile seed could not be spread any further. And though the moniker the king had appropriated belied it, Kyara never had a father, had never really missed one. That Darvyn may not get the chance to be one was the most distressing.

Still, there were plenty of orphans like Ulani and Tana who needed loving homes. And maybe that was the better choice anyway, to offer a home to a child already alive as opposed to bringing a new one into the cruel world.

Her mind was wandering again, flitting back and forth between these thoughts of a future that might never be and a past that she was only now beginning to truly understand. Of course, if she couldn't get any further in her training, then the future would be short indeed. Much better to stay focused on the present. And in the present, she was trailing far behind Tana.

In fact, she was on the remedial track, still working on targeting the center tree and leaving the rest untouched. She breathed deeply and her avatar kitten appeared, then morphed into its powerful wildcat form. The leonine figure paced in front of her before she directed it outward. It shot forward and was back in a fraction of a second. This time the center three trees were blackened and crumbling, but the two on the end were intact.

"Better," Murmur said coming up beside her.

"But still slow and inaccurate," Mooriah added. "You must try harder."

Kyara grit her teeth. "I *am* trying."

"*Harder* is what I said."

Kyara bit back her retort and calmed herself. The targets were reset and she did the drill again. And again. With each attempt, she made incremental progress that buoyed her with hope. But Mooriah was strung tight as a bow and ready to snap.

Finally, after what seemed like hours, Kyara was able to target only the center tree. A smile graced her face though she did truly feel like celebrating. "I don't understand why this is so difficult. I've been able to control my aim before."

"With the use of external sources of Nethersong or in emergency situations when you weren't thinking about it so hard," Murmur said. "You must be able to do it on your own and your mind is what is currently getting in the way."

"Her stubbornness, more like," Mooriah grumbled.

The thin strand of control that Kyara had kept over her temper around the woman so far snapped and she whirled to face her. "What exactly is your problem? I just completed the test."

"And you want some sort of award for taking two days to do what that child did in an hour? This isn't a leisurely vacation we're on. You've already wasted enough time staring at the ocean when you could have been training."

Kyara took a step closer, seething. "So I was supposed to trust a five-hundred year old woman who wanted to drag me back to the place where they tried to kill the man I love? I'm here now, and I'm doing my best."

"You're here and if this is your best then we're all doomed." Mooriah's face was blank as slate and Kyara wanted to smack her. She nearly did but Murmur placed a hand on her shoulder and squeezed gently. His touch was barely substantial but did its job in staying her hand. However, anger still bubbled inside her.

"I. Am. Trying."

Mooriah leaned in until they were nearly nose to nose. "Try. Harder." She took a step back and spread her arms out. "We must defeat the True Father, the three of us. A dead woman, a child, and the Poison Flame. We must be at full capacity or he will win."

A hint of vulnerability cracked her stony exterior. That was what cooled the rage beneath Kyara's skin. "What did he take from *you*? I thought you grew up here, protected from him?"

Mooriah's shoulders sank, causing her to deflate a bit. "He killed my father. My mother, too, I suppose you could say. Made me an orphan."

Kyara swallowed. "I didn't realize." She dropped her head. "I'm ashamed to share his blood. So please trust that I will work as hard as I can to see him defeated."

"Share his blood?" Mooriah frowned.

"I was born in the harem. He sires sons almost exclusively, but there are a few of us daughters around."

The woman shook her head. "You are not his daughter."

Kyara froze. "What makes you say that?"

She snorted. "Because I have kept track of my descendants. My children lived in the mountain for a time, several generations in fact. But I'd always wanted them to live outside. Eventually, they left the Mother for life in Lagrimar. They adopted my father's house, that of the Mistress of Eagles, and became Sarifors.

"The True Father is not your father, Kyara. Your mother fell in love with a soldier who died before you were born. When she was taken to the harems, she was already pregnant with you. You are one of mine. You were never his."

Kyara stumbled backward. The shock was so great that it tore her away from the spirit realm of the heart of the Mother back into her body seated in front of the fire in the small cave. The bodies of Tana, Mooriah, and Murmur were around her, still in their trances.

Kyara stood on wobbly legs and left the cave. Across the chasm,

Ella was cooking something over a fire. She looked up when Kyara emerged, but if she said something, Kyara couldn't hear her for the rushing in her ears.

Her whole life—she had to reimagine the way she looked at her whole life. Everything she'd ever thought about herself was different now. She wasn't *ul-nedrim* at all, she was of the House of Eagles. The Mistress of Eagles with her prophetic knowledge and perceptiveness was her lineage. She was actually related to Mooriah. The thought made a shiver go down her spine.

She leaned back against a wall and closed her eyes, trying to picture herself amidst this new reality. She felt Mooriah's presence, but the woman stood next to her quietly.

"Why didn't you tell me before?" Kyara breathed.

Mooriah sighed. "I honestly did not think that you would want to know. From the moment I arrived you have been . . . prickly."

"I'm an orphan. Family is . . . a dream come true." She opened her eyes to find Mooriah sorrowful, gaze heavy.

"Then I apologize. It was wrong of me not to tell you."

They stood together in silence for a while as Kyara got used to the feel of the new ground beneath her feet.

Finally, she sucked in a breath and pushed off the wall. "All right, I'm ready to go back. I have a lot of work to do. But later . . . I have questions."

Mooriah smiled sadly. "Of course. I'll do my best to answer them."

"Thank you."

"And Kyara?"

She turned, brows raised.

"I am proud that you're mine. I am hard on you, which is my way, but know this, if we must be only three, and I could have chosen who to stand with, I would have chosen you."

A lump formed in Kyara's throat. She stared at Mooriah, mouth agape, before retreating into the steamy heat of the cave. She sat before the fire, covering her face, trying in vain to hold back the tears.

CHAPTER THIRTY-TWO

The earth underfoot is priceless,
valued by all.
Who owns the air or ocean or mountain?
Who taxes our breath, our joy, our dance
in currency other than Harmony?

—THE HARMONY OF BEING

"That woman is impossible." Jasminda groaned once King Pia and her Cabinet ministers had left the meeting room. This was the third day of talks to end the trade embargo and the leaders had done nothing but go around in circles. "What does she even want?" She dropped her head into her hands and sighed.

The *thunk* that sounded on the table in front of her startled her. A crystal glass half-full of brown liquor had been placed there. Jasminda looked up to find Minister Calladeen seated beside her, holding his own glass. He and some of his top staff had been present for the past two days of meetings. As Minister of Foreign Affairs, and, according to Jack, an intelligent, talented diplomat in spite of his many other flaws, she had to admit he'd been helpful.

He'd kept the meetings on track, offered numerous suggestions for compromise, and had not reacted to Pia's cutting remarks or thinly veiled insults. Plus, he'd been extremely deferential and respectful to Jasminda. *At least he knows how to behave in front of guests*, she thought.

Now she studied the glass he'd set before her. She wasn't much of a drinker, and part of her wondered if he'd poisoned it. But death at this point might be welcome; at least she wouldn't have to deal with that impossible Raunian harpy anymore.

"Thank you," she said, lifting the glass gingerly to her lips. The liquor burned as it went down, but she relished it. The sensation jump-started her body, making her muscles and bones feel something other than pure exhaustion.

She exhaled slowly as her insides warmed. "I cannot believe that we are on the verge of economic collapse from an embargo that *she* started because Prince Alariq offended her by questioning the quality of the Raunian ships we'd purchased."

Calladeen tapped the table with his own glass before draining its contents in one swallow. "Alariq was always careful. He accused Raun of selling us substandard ships very purposefully. He must have been enacting a longer-range plan, one that he was, sadly, unable to see out before being murdered."

Her veins began to heat as the alcohol took hold. Was this extra potent or was she just a lightweight? She should probably stop now, but she took one more sip. "Do you know what Alariq's plan was?"

Calladeen frowned and shook his head. "I know that he was

seeking to use some kind of leverage against Pia. Playing the Raunian shipbuilders off of those in the south, but beyond that, no. We were meant to have a meeting on the matter the day after he was killed."

"He left no notes or anything?"

He snorted. "Alariq left a great many notes. King Jaqros has been through them, however, to my knowledge he never found anything detailing his brother's plans for Raun. That kind of thing Alariq kept in his head."

Jasminda sat up straighter and pushed the glass away. She was outmatched against Pia, everyone could see that. "What do you think we should do, Minister?" She turned toward him.

Calladeen stared forward, unseeing. "We need to understand the game she's playing. What does she want? What does she need?"

"Her ego stroked," Jasminda said, and Calladeen actually laughed. This shocked her into silence. It appeared to shock him as well.

"I sense that her relationship with her daughter is . . . tense," he said, after recovering. "I wonder if that played some part in her decision to visit in person."

Jasminda sighed. "I'd wondered that as well. She must have known that Ani was planning on leaving—she and her crew have been here for weeks and that can't be good for business. I know they've been antsy. And given the lack of progress on where the wedding should be held . . ." She shook her head.

Ani and Roshon should be back in Elsira by tomorrow evening. Perhaps her daughter's presence and finally meeting her future son-in-law would soften the woman, but Jasminda doubted it.

Jasminda's attention was also split by the impending vote on separation. Nadette's latest report on the work of the secret public relations campaign they were waging was disappointing. Their progress was achingly slow. The Dominionist/Reaper rhetoric had caught fire as if it had been doused with gasoline, but their more logical and humanitarian arguments were still slower in spreading.

Jasminda trusted Nadette, but she still wanted to be involved in how the messages were being shaped. Perhaps the tone they were using was not impassioned enough. The uncertainty was maddening.

She hoped at least that Papa and Varten were having a smooth time of it up north with the refugees. Someone should be. She made a mental note to call her father and check in.

In the meeting room, Calladeen drummed long fingers on the table. "I sense that King Pia is stalling these talks for some reason. She's notoriously difficult, but her tactic of changing the subject, especially when we come close to finding common ground . . . Something else may be going on. Perhaps this afternoon's meeting will shed some light."

Pia had requested their next session that day be down on the docks, so she could inspect Elsira's trading center in person. Jasminda had been so frustrated, she'd agreed immediately. Being outside and out of the stuffy room would at least make things more tenable.

"Maybe you're right," she said, truly hoping he was.

But her tiny spark of optimism was doused several hours later as she and Pia walked along the cobblestones of the port side by side. They were followed by Royal Guardsmen, Elsiran Councillors and staff, along with the Raunian entourage—Jasminda could never tell who among them were bureaucrats and diplomats and who were guards, or maybe all were both? Raunian men tended to be large, their women small, but she wouldn't make the mistake of underestimating any of them.

The docks were sparsely populated an hour from sunset, with

the bulk of the work down here beginning at sunrise. A few sailors saw to the maintenance needs of their vessels. A handful of ships were loading or unloading goods, but traffic was light.

A colony of seagulls had spread themselves out over several empty piers, chattering to one another and defecating on the splintering wood. Pia noted the birds with distaste, making Jasminda wondered how they dealt with the pests in Raun.

They walked on in a silence that soon became discouraging. There truly wasn't much to see here, which underscored the grievous state of Elsira's economy.

"What is it you really want?" Jasminda finally asked. "I know this all started with an insult by Alariq, but he is dead. I'm sorry he can't issue an apology from the grave, but we don't yet know how to do that in Elsira."

Pia's lips turned down. "His insult was the catalyst that started me looking in on the trade practices here, and I did not like what I saw. We don't generally involve ourselves in the internal affairs of other states, but the situation in Elsira is quite remarkable. Your policies have been exclusionary for so long. You want the goods from other countries but share so little. Many of the workers in your docks are barred from citizenship. They're prevented from holding the basic rights that all humans should share."

Jasminda blinked at the passion in her voice. "I-I agree. Many Elsiran policies are archaic and need to change. As I'm sure you can see, they are a detriment to me personally, as well. I have felt the force of Elsiran intolerance my whole life.

"But my husband and I are making changes, trying to steer this ship. However, it's enormous. And there's so much to do. It would be infinitely easier if jobs weren't drying up, if food stores weren't nearly empty. These piers should be packed." She waved an arm, indicating all the empty space around them. "The fact that they're not, and all of the effects that ripple out from that, are crippling us."

Pia's expression remained dour as she observed what little activity there was on the docks. She looked up at Jasminda, eyes narrowed against the glare of the setting sun, her skin bronze in its full glow. "This action was not undertaken lightly, I assure you," she said. "And it is not just me who has concerns. For years, I have heard from international trading partners who take issue with Elsiran policy, but were making too much money to risk speaking up. I am not afraid of risk."

Jasminda swallowed at the harshness of her tone.

"You and your husband are both young, untested leaders. We need a good-faith example of change in this land in order to trust you."

Inwardly, Jasminda groaned. Pia held up a hand to stop her when she began to speak. "I like what I'm hearing about this curfew. That shows real backbone." A hint of a smile broke through the coldness of her gaze.

"I'm paying for that in the press," Jasminda muttered. Though by now, she was used to being savaged by the news media.

The other woman smiled viciously. "Yes, it cannot be helped. You must learn to read between the lines in the newspapers. It will make your spine stronger."

Jasminda considered what this meant, unsure how to respond, when a horrible clanging noise rang out and the sky, painted in the oranges, pinks, and purples of the setting sun, darkened ominously. Clouds formed out of nowhere, a black, billowing, stormy shroud churning overhead.

Around them, people began to shout. Jasminda gathered Earthsong to her as the sky tore apart. A plume of black smoke detached itself from the swirling mass in the sky and shot like a projectile toward the ground. Then another and another did the same, falling out of sight, somewhere in the city. Jasminda's heart seized at the number of spirits pouring from the portal—this one so much larger and more furious-looking than the one in the Council Room. That had been exactly a week ago—it seemed that the True Father had used that time effectively.

A spirit dropped down and entered a dockworker one hundred paces from Jasminda. The burly dark-haired man shook and twisted and then transformed. His body morphed, changing size and color until he was a taller, thinner, younger man with wispy blond hair and a hooklike nose.

Next to her, Pia let out what sounded like a Raunian curse. "What dark magic is this?"

Jasminda tried in vain to arrest the progress of the spirits emerging from the portal. Oola had said She'd trapped them in a cage of pure life energy, but they were moving so fast and Jasminda didn't even manage to catch one.

Shaking off their shock, her Guardsmen tightened around her. But there was nothing the men could do to protect her. They were all just potential victims.

"We need to get you back to the vehicles," Captain Bareen, her lead Guardsman, said.

Pia's people formed a knot around her to protect their king. But as they all hurried down the cobblestones, one of Jasminda's Guardsmen was speared by a column of black smoke and transformed into a large woman with strange markings on her neck.

The woman didn't speak, she didn't attack. She merely stopped walking and stood there, staring into space. The wraith inhabiting the body of the dockworker was the same. They stood locked in place as if waiting for something.

Guardsmen pulled Jasminda away and back toward the street.

But Captain Bareen paused; his reluctance to leave one of his men behind flowed to her via Earthsong.

"Captain!" she cried. He shook off his reticence and returned to her side.

"If they can be saved, we will do so," she said, as they hustled up the ramp leading to the street.

As people screamed and ran for safety, those who had been transformed were rigid as statues. If they were indeed awaiting orders, she certainly did not want to be here when they came through.

Finally, the bombinating swarm in the sky cleared. How many spirits had come down to overtake people and find hosts? A hundred, perhaps more? Jasminda and her entourage were almost to the line of vehicles waiting on the main street when a loud screech rang out, vibrating her bones.

The conspicuously motionless people within her field of view had apparently received their instructions. As one they started moving. Fast.

The woman who'd entered the Guardsman's body raced up the ramp at superhuman speed and grabbed a retreating soldier. She easily picked up the man off his feet—he must have been double her weight—and tossed him away like a sack of trash.

Jasminda's other Guards and Pia's people grabbed their weapons. A Raunian woman gripped a pistol and let loose the first shots that ripped through the spirit woman's body, but the bullets did not slow her one whit. Captain Bareen cursed.

Jasminda shook off the Guardsman who clutched her arm and steadied herself, focusing her power. She pushed a blast of wind at the wraith to knock her off her feet. When the woman got up again, Jasminda hardened the air around her, locking the creature in place.

Her attention turned to others around her, fighting off attacking spirits, and to screams in the distance from people she could not see. But the wraith woman struggled against the invisible bands holding her in place and broke through. Jasminda spun around just in time to catch her as she targeted another guard. An Earthsong fireball didn't stop the creature, who showed no sign of damage from the flames. Jasminda used wind to pick her up and toss her away, but the wraith scrambled onto her feet again and charged.

Finally, Jasminda opened up a hole beneath the creature's feet, causing her to fall in. Then she quickly refilled it with dirt. She could sense the wraith clawing through the dirt, making her way back to the surface, and dug the hole even deeper, sinking her farther.

Across the street, a sandy-haired teenage boy was smashing the window of a butcher shop with unnatural strength. Its frightened owner stood inside, two long knives in his grip. Jasminda tried to hold the boy in place as she had the woman, but he fought the invisible bonds. She tightened them, pressing the air around him tightly until they finally held.

Down the street, bullets rang out ineffectually as a constable tried to defend himself against an attacker. The wraith didn't appear to feel them, perhaps because he was already dead. But it was the fate of the ones whose bodies had been overtaken that Jasminda worried about.

One thing at a time though. She worked to disable and trap all those who'd overtaken bodies within her field of vision, but it was too few, as she well knew. Fighting each one was a strain on her Song.

Screams sounded to her right and she turned, scared that King Pia would be overrun and she would have an international assassination on her hands. The king's people had pulled her farther away; Jasminda was shocked to find Pia holding her own against the wraiths. A group of five had converged on the Raunian entourage, who were successfully fighting them.

Raunian weapons were just as ineffectual as Elsiran guns, but the men and women themselves were able to take on the superstrong wraiths hand to hand. Pia got in a good punch on a man easily twice her size, who went down hard. Within moments, only the Raunians were left standing with an assortment of unconscious wraiths at their feet.

The Guardsmen hustled an amazed Jasminda into her vehicle and Pia and her crew fell into theirs. Captain Bareen slid into the passenger seat. "We'll get you back to the palace as quickly as possible, Your Majesty."

"No, we need to drive through the streets. I can help." The look on his face was troubled. "I'll be safer in the car than out there, but I can't hide away. Not when no one can defend themselves." No one except the Raunians, apparently.

He shook his head and let out a breath, but commanded the driver to take them down Bishop Street. A voice on the radio announced the rest of their party was headed back to the palace, and Jasminda was grateful, hopeful they'd make it there safely.

The first street was quiet, but when they turned the corner, a melee was in progress. With her Song, the wraiths felt different, she couldn't sense them as she could normal people. They were quieter somehow. No emotion came from them, not even rage. However, they did have a spark of life energy left, possibly from the host, and she used that to distinguish who was alive and who was a wraith.

She restrained the spirits she encountered as best she could, holding them in place or burying them under layers of dirt, cobblestone, or cement—she could think of no other way to stop them. But soon, the weight of all the spells began to wear on her. The strength of her targets beat against her strength and she wished she was better at wielding the power Oola had given her.

Darvyn's lessons came to mind and she struggled to manage and distribute her power in so many places the way he'd taught her. Though she was tiring, she wanted to do more, but if she was incapacitated, all her spells would fail and the wraiths she held under her power would be free to continue wreaking havoc.

The intersection up ahead was blocked by a crash, and fires had sprung up on several blocks. Everywhere she looked there were injured people, those she could not spare much energy to heal as well as keep the wraiths in place.

"It looks like the attack is centered in Portside, Your Majesty," Bareen said, tapping the radio. "There were minimal sightings of those . . . things, east of Earl Place."

She sagged against the town car's seat, fearing her Song was nearly tapped out. She'd tried her best, but could do no more. Then the wraiths she held immobile with spells began to shudder and convulse.

"Stop the car!"

The driver complied and she focused within. She could *feel* the wraiths under her power tearing themselves away from their hosts. The amount of Earthsong within the people rose dramatically and that feeling of distance and wrongness faded.

"They're leaving!" Bareen shouted. Dozens of pillars of black smoke were retreating into the sky, forming a writhing mass there. The churning, dark cloud hovered until all the spirits had joined, and then it was gone, winked out like a dying star.

She took a few deep breaths and opened the door of the vehicle, standing on wobbly legs. Guardsmen were at her side in seconds.

She closed her eyes and unburied all of the people who were now suffocating underground. They would all need healing and she had precious little Song left with which to do it.

The streets were suddenly quiet, except for moans of pain. The wonder and apprehension of the men surrounding her pulsed through her.

"We'll need to triage the victims," she said to Bareen. "Round up any Earthsinger with a Song left. Get a message on the radio, gather the Lagrimari translators. Those in the city with Songs will likely be Keepers and children."

The captain began issuing instructions. Jasminda tilted her head up toward the sky, once again beautifully painted with the sun's dying light.

A dark figure in silhouette up above made her tense, then she recognized Oola. Thank the Sovereign. The Goddess swooped down from the sky and descended a few blocks away. There would be many to heal and Her help would be vital.

The day they'd been fearing had come at last, and one thing was clear—they were severely outmatched.

CHAPTER THIRTY-THREE

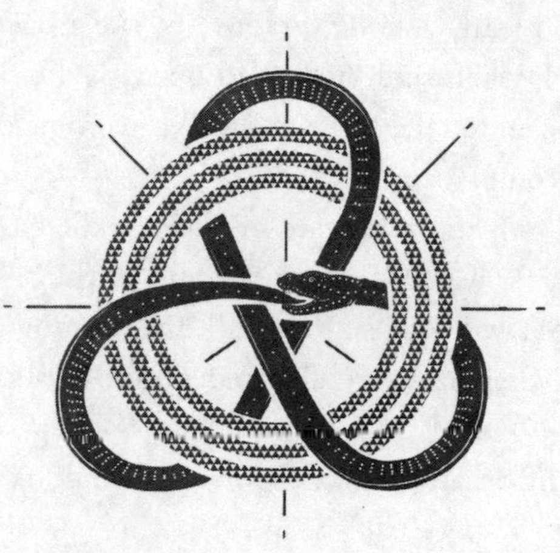

A bridle may restrain
and shackles may retain
but the freedom patience provides
cannot be trained.

—THE HARMONY OF BEING

Zeli stood in the darkness, waiting for her eyes to adjust. Cool damp air chafed her skin and she shivered. Overhead, the sky was visible in a perfect circle. Remi's head popped into view, but he was backlit, so she couldn't see his face. She waved, hoping his childish curiosity wouldn't impel him to try to follow.

The sound of trickling water echoed softly, and she could make out a tunnel of stone, which curved subtly outward. The space down here was larger than she'd imagined, about twenty paces wide, and tall enough for two of her, if she could stand on her own shoulders. A trench ran down the center of the tunnel. She couldn't get a feel for how deep it was in the gloom, though the odor wafting up made her crinkle her nose. The smell wasn't as putrid as she'd feared, though. Honestly, she'd been subjected to far worse back when she was locked up with dozens of children and only a bucket to relieve themselves. The aroma down here was delightful in comparison.

She could only move forward or back on the narrow walkway, and the Archives was in front of her and to the right, about two hundred paces away. Zeli started walking, lighting a match to get her bearings. Stepping carefully and afraid of slipping into the foul water, she grazed the wall with her fingertips, shuddering in revulsion at the occasional slick spots. She couldn't focus on what that might be.

The match burned out and her footsteps echoed eerily through the space. She steeled her nerves, reminding herself of her purpose even as the creepy atmosphere made her a bit dizzy. Thankfully, it wasn't long before the darkness was splintered by flickering light up ahead. Her pace quickened. Torches were lit down a corridor to the right. This was about where she thought she should turn to get to the pyramid.

Her steps grew more cautious as she peered into the opening in the tunnel. This new passage was narrow. The trench disappeared and the rough stone of the ground and walls was replaced by smoothly honed limestone, the same material as the bottom layer of the Archives' exterior. Only fifty paces ahead, an iron gate blocked the way; metal between its unadorned bars obstructed the view to the other side. The metal wasn't rusted or corroded from being down here in all this dampness; by all appearances it could have been brand-new.

Where the latch should be there was a knob that looked like it was made of dark glass. Multifaceted and irregular, though generally spherical. She reached for it, but paused. Though it wasn't bloodred in color, it reminded her of a caldera.

The only calderas she was familiar with were the king stone—the heavy, oblong thing that now stored all the Songs stolen from the True Father, and the death stone—a smaller caldera that had been retrieved from deep in the ocean by Queen Jasminda's family several years ago. Zeli had given the death stone to the Poison Flame on the Goddess's instruction. And the king stone had been stored in the vault in the Elsiran palace, under lock and key since the True Father's capture. At least that's where it was supposed to be.

She'd been advised by the Goddess to never touch the death stone—it gave Singers, and perhaps even former Singers like her, horrible visions. However, Zeli had been given no such warnings about the king stone. The Goddess had told her that each caldera had a purpose, certain requirements for its use. Some, like the death stone, could affect a whole swath of people, and others would do nothing at all unless touched by the person it was meant for.

If this knob was a caldera, then it was likely part of the challenge. She held her breath and grabbed hold of it.

Nothing happened at first. Her vision didn't black out, she didn't see anything strange, but a low hum began in her ears.

"What kind of hunter are you?" a voice whispered *inside* her head.

"I . . . ah." She cleared her throat. "I seek knowledge."

"And who will this knowledge benefit?" It was more like the suggestion of words than an actual sound in her mind, but it made her shiver.

"My people, the Lagrimari. And others, too. If we can stop what is coming—the wraiths and the True Father—then everyone will benefit." Silence reigned around her. She kept hold of the knob, waiting for the next question.

Finally, a cold air blew around her, making the torches on the wall flicker.

"You may pass." This time, the sensation was just an echo, fading away inside her head. Under her palm, the knob turned and the gate swung open on silent hinges.

She stepped through, and into a room of blinding white. After the tunnel, her eyes took a moment to adjust. There was light everywhere, but no lanterns in view—the walls just glowed. She couldn't even identify the material they were made from, something smooth and featureless so that she couldn't determine where the floor ended and the walls began. A raised platform of the same material in the center of the room was barely visible. The space might be rectangular, or possibly oval-shaped. She'd never seen anything like it.

One moment, she was looking around, contemplating what to do now, and in the next she spotted a staircase that she could swear hadn't been there seconds earlier. It was directly across from her and painfully obvious. She shook herself. "Focus, Zeli," she whispered.

The stairwell was a good deal darker than the strange, white room, and made of marble. She went up several flights with no outlet until it finally ended and she emerged in an enormously wide room.

She turned around in a circle, her jaw falling open. This was the inside of the pyramid. Sloping walls went up and up, the glass layers letting in the only light. The battering ram thumped away on the other side of the metal doors, but in here the sound was muffled, just a dull thud. Those wielding it were gaining no headway, but Zeli was actually *inside.*

Then her surroundings really hit her. She stood at the edge of a very large, very empty room. There were no books, no shelves, no other floors, no furniture, not even so much as a chair. The only thing breaking up the space was the rectangular, ruby-colored column in the very center. The red pinnacle visible at the top from outside was really the tip of an obelisk, like a tent pole holding up the building. Aside from that, this was just a giant, bare pyramid that was supposed to hold the archive of the knowledge of a god.

She grabbed her stomach as it hollowed out. Was this all a trick?

"Not what you expected?" a voice said from behind her.

She spun around to find Remi leaning against the wall, arms crossed, sadness weighing down his gaze.

"How did you get here so quickly?" She was certain he hadn't followed her, she would have heard his footsteps echoing on the stone.

He pushed off the wall and stepped toward her. "You are the only one to make it inside this year. Sometimes there are two or three. Sometimes no one does."

"But the last time the Archives was open was before you were born. Is it common knowledge how many people get in?" Her confusion mingled with her disappointment and the vacuum inside her belly grew.

The boy just stared at her, assessing, until she began to feel uncomfortable.

"Remi?" Her voice broke on his name.

"Actually, my name isn't Remi." His eyes, too old for such a young face, sharpened and a glow rose from his dark skin. Light in a blend of colors, like a liquid rainbow, swirled around him, obscuring the child from view. When it faded, the child was no more. In his place stood an adult—what the boy may have looked like in twenty years. Instead of the ill-fitting trousers and shirt, he now wore a long white caftan with blue embroidery. It grazed his ankles, ending just above his bare feet.

"My name is Gilmer. Welcome to my Archives."

Zeli stumbled back several steps, shaking her head and trying to make sense of what she'd just seen. "Y-You're Gilmer? *The* Gilmer? T-This is your Archives?"

He nodded sadly. "Yes, I'm *the* Gilmer and *this* isn't my Archives." He spread his arms open. "The Archives is me."

CHAPTER THIRTY-FOUR

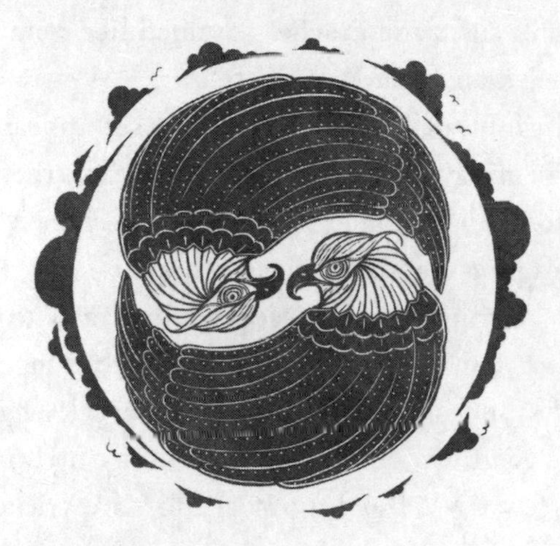

No matter how far the path
or how long you trod
there is rest at the end
and along the way
if you are vigilant.

—THE HARMONY OF BEING

Zeli sat before the god known as Gilmer on cushions that he had spirited into existence. He looked like a normal man, then again, at a glance, the Goddess Awoken looked like a normal woman. Only being around Her for any length of time had corrected that misapprehension.

"You have questions, I'm sure," he said, his voice a sonorous tenor.

Zeli swallowed, her mouth having gone dry. "I don't even know where to begin. What-What should I address you as?"

"Gilmer is fine," he said with a chuckle. "No honorifics are necessary." He took a deep breath. "Would you like some tea? You must be famished."

Zeli blinked, surprised at what sounded like genuine concern in his tone. "I—thank you. Yes, please."

A simple, slightly chipped ceramic tea set appeared between them, steam venting from the pot. She startled, then tentatively reached out for it, but Gilmer beat her to the punch and poured two cups of fragrant tea, which tickled her nose.

"Where to begin?" he said, tapping his lip with a long finger. "Well, first, I should apologize for the subterfuge. I do enjoy watching the Rumpus. I'm only awake for a week every ten years, you see, and I've grown quite addicted to soaking up experiences during these few days. But I am sorry to have tricked you. The disguise is simply useful."

Zeli gripped her mug tighter. "Are you cursed?" she whispered.

"What? No." He laughed, throwing his head back. "Oh no, my dear. It is a choice. Living for as long as I do is a bore. Centuries ago, I decided to space things out a bit. The world was changing so quickly, I wanted to experience more of it. Invention, industry, technology. It's all so fascinating. I thought I might appreciate it more if I didn't consume quite so much." He leaned forward, as if imparting a secret. "You see, I have somewhat of an addictive personality."

Her brows rose, but she hadn't heard of anything like that before, so she remained quiet.

"And I am not actually immortal, so extending my life with these long rests was the best way I could think of to prolong things, without going mad. To experience life as a child again . . . well, the world would be quite a different place if all could do so."

He took a slow sip from his teacup and gazed at her over the rim. Now his eyes made more sense in his grown-up face.

"You, I believe, are acquainted with the Queen Who Sleeps?" he asked.

Though the hot liquid had warmed her, cold swept over her skin at the question. "She is the Goddess Awoken, now. But yes."

Gilmer nodded. "Ah, of course. Well, my sleep is somewhat like Hers. Though mine is, of course, voluntary. And I awake when I choose. It's a different sort of spell. My followers created the Rumpus for the week in which I am awake to celebrate my return and to recommit themselves to me." He sighed and stared off to the side. "They insist on continuing to worship me. An absent god is better than none at all, I suppose."

Zeli frowned. "Do you have the power to stop them? From worshipping you? If—if that's what you want?"

He considered for a moment and shrugged. "I suppose I could forbid it. Attach heavy punishments for their prayers and supplications, but people are people. Some would still gather in secret, convinced this was just a test of faith. The hearts of men are stubborn in that way."

She swirled her cup a moment, watching the movement of the liquid. "What if you did something really terrible?" Chancing a glance up at him, she found him stroking his chin.

"Well, I suppose that public opinion would sway in that case. But there would, no doubt, be those who thought that because *I* did it, it must be right. Belief is irrational—loving and hating are two sides of the same coin. So maybe you are right, maybe changing one into another would not be as difficult as I think. It could be I am just too vain to try it." He chuckled and drained his cup.

Then he turned sharply toward the door. The battering ram

had paused. "Thank the matriarchs," he muttered. "Shall we let your friends in?"

"Can we?" she asked, brightening.

"Yes, of course. You may do what you like. You have access to the Archives and may share it with whomever you choose." He smiled graciously and a bit of lingering fear from the shock of his appearance and transformation faded.

"Please then, let them in."

Gilmer smiled and inclined his head. He did not move, but closed his eyes. "Followers, friends. The Archives have been entered."

He spoke at a normal volume, but the words entered not only her ears but her mind and her consciousness. He truly sounded like a god, voice resonant and filling every inch of space inside her, until it vibrated within.

"This year only one contender managed to gain entry to the Archives. Best of luck next time, now please, go and enjoy the Rumpus." Zeli blinked in awe at the display of power.

His voice—the audible one—quieted to a whisper. "Adia, will you please gather the tall, young Elsiran and his Lagrimari companion and escort them to the main doors?" Then he opened his eyes suddenly and smiled at her. She ducked her gaze, embarrassed at being caught staring.

In moments, the double doors rattled. They did not appear to be barred or latched. There weren't even any door handles on this side, just smooth metal. Under their own power, or more likely Gilmer's, the doors opened outward. Gasps sounded from those gathered on the other side.

Through the doorway, the setting sun bathed what she could see of the remaining crowd in oranges and reds. Right outside, white-clad acolytes kneeled with their heads bent. Gilmer sighed and rose, then paced over to the entry. He stood there, arms crossed, before the prostrate acolytes.

A minute later, a raven-haired female acolyte appeared before him with Varten and Lanar in tow. Gilmer bowed in thanks to her and the woman flushed scarlet. Then the god led Zeli's companions inside and the two enormous doors closed again.

Varten stood in the entry looking up and around, jaw open, while Lanar merely glared at Gilmer. For his part, the god smiled at the Lagrimari man. "Good to see you again, old friend," he said extending his hand for a shake.

Zeli flinched, frozen for a moment. "Old friend?" She looked from one man to the other, taking in Lanar's pinched expression.

"Why yes," Gilmer replied, "I am not the only one with a secret identity. Am I, Yllis?"

Lanar or Yllis or whoever he was blew out a breath and crossed his arms defensively.

Gilmer tilted his head. "Why the pseudonym? There are very few alive who would have recognized your name."

Yllis's gaze slid to Zeli and then Varten, who had come to stand next to her. "True, but these two have been reading my journal. And I wasn't certain how they would react if they knew who I was."

Zeli took a step back; Varten tensed beside her. "*You* wrote the journal?" He looked to Zeli, who shook her head, completely dumbfounded.

Gilmer clasped his hands behind him and rocked on his heels. "I think this conversation calls for more tea."

Gilmer had produced more cushions and tea from wherever it was he got these things. Varten came to sit beside her, while Gilmer and Lanar—or rather, Yllis—stood in hushed conversation by the doors.

She studiously ignored Varten, still angry with him from earlier. Instead, she straightened the teacups and poured more for the newcomers, feeling his eyes on her.

Finally, she sat back, staring straight ahead. "What?" she said through clenched teeth.

"I'm sorry," he whispered. She turned, and was arrested by the misery evident on his face. "I should have been there to help you. That's why we came, and I just got caught up in . . ." He trailed off and she waited for him to finish the sentence, but he just stared at his hands.

"In what?" she prompted.

He shrugged. "I'm not really reliable. I mean, I shouldn't be in charge . . . of making decisions or anything. I just screw things up."

She blinked rapidly. "But you were right. Remi and I managed to pry open that sewer cover and that's how I got in here. I think it was the only way inside."

Varten's shoulders were still slumped and Zeli reached for him, intending to offer a comforting hand, then withdrew. She wasn't sure she should touch him, wasn't sure he wanted her to.

"You missed quite a lot," she said, grabbing a cup instead. She didn't really want any more tea, she just needed something to do with her hands.

"I see."

"No, you didn't. Remi turned into Gilmer."

"What?" His jaw hung open comically.

"Remi is Gilmer and Gilmer is the Archives." She motioned to the empty space surrounding them.

Gilmer and Yllis approached and sat on the remaining cushions. "Yllis refuses to tell me how he managed to come back from the dead," Gilmer said, sounding annoyed. "I do it every ten years, but then again, I never go all the way to the World After. But I know that you must have. I saw what was left of that city after your battle with the True Father."

Yllis shook his head. "My tale is for another time. Since we have limited access to the *Archives,*" he looked pointedly at said Archives, "I would not wish to waste it."

Gilmer sniffed. These two did not behave like friends.

"How did you know we'd read your journal?" Zeli asked. She wasn't sure he would answer, the pause was so long, but finally he sighed.

"I remained, out of sight, after I left the journal for Oola." His face softened for the first time. "I was not ready to face Her, not yet. But I saw the two of you take it. I'd intended for Her to . . ." He looked off. "It does not matter. When it was clear She had other priorities, I decided to come here for myself. It seemed convenient to travel together.

"When we first met"—he turned to Gilmer—"you tried to teach me a way to win the war. Eero had trapped himself on the other side of the Mantle with the Singers, I was stuck in the west with the Silent, until I found a way through my spell for the Mantle. I knew Eero was draining Songs, stealing them for his own purposes, and I spent years searching for a way to stop him and reverse it. When you arrived, I thought it was the answer to my prayers."

Gilmer looked down. "I did my best to teach you," he said quietly.

"Your method for restoring Songs did not work once you left." Yllis spat the words.

"Because you did not do it properly. I can only teach a willing student." Gilmer's dark eyes turned to Zeli. "Perhaps she will be more amenable."

The scrutiny of both these ancient men made Zeli want to squirm. She lowered her gaze, but turned toward Yllis. "Why didn't his method for restoring Songs work anymore?"

"Ask him." Yllis threw up his hands. "He must have left something out. I tried for years more, without success."

Gilmer's jaw tightened. "I left nothing out. I saw your plight, felt the pain of the separation of your people and the suffering caused by your . . . former friend."

Zeli's eyes widened. "Are you talking about the True Father? You were friends with him?"

Yllis nodded, features downturned. "Aye. We were friends. I loved his sister more than myself. To me he was a brother. Once."

"'A gift from the heart to my beloved,'" she whispered, remembering the inscription of the journal. "Signed only 'O.' That's for Oola, the Goddess Awoken."

Yllis's eyes brimmed with tears. "I filled many notebooks while seeking new discoveries. She gave me most of them." His longing was palpable.

Was this why the Goddess had been so bothered by the sudden appearance of the journal? It reminded Her of a love long lost.

"Why didn't you show yourself to Her?"

Yllis straightened and sobered, shedding the melancholy like a cloak. "There will be time for that. For now, danger is at our doorstep. Eero has already attacked Elsira twice."

"Twice?" Varten was appalled. "Already? What happened in the last attack?"

"Nothing you can change, boy," Yllis said coldly. Zeli wanted to smack him.

Gilmer lay a hand on Varten's arm. "Your family are all fine. But Eero is already planning his next strike."

Varten was vibrating with tension, and Zeli saw the moment it seemed to slip away from him. She glared at Gilmer, who put up his hands. "I just calmed him down a little. I did not hurt him."

"We don't have time for this," Yllis spat.

Zeli whirled on him. "You are here because I invited you inside. I'm the one who gained access to the Archives, not you. So if you can't be civil, I will invite you to leave."

The man's brows climbed up his forehead. Zeli felt a little light-headed at the uncharacteristic display of force. Gilmer, however, grinned.

"I knew I liked her. Tell me, child, what do you know of blood magic?" he asked.

She shook her head. "Nothing. I've heard of it, but that's about all. It was forbidden in Lagrimar."

"Yes, well, I'm sure that Eero forbade things that could have harmed him. Blood magic is the most ancient of powers native to this world. The Founders of Elsira and Lagrimar, much like the matriarchs of my siblings and me—those who birthed us—were from elsewhere. But that world crumbled and died, destroyed from within and all were forced to flee.

"Your Founders and our matriarchs were of the original line. Their children, me, my siblings, your Goddess, we all have a similar lineage. We are not as powerful as our parents, but strong enough to be considered deities here."

"You are Seconds," Yllis said.

"Yes, if the original line from that destroyed world are the Firsts, then we are the Seconds," Gilmer said. "Though we did not count ancestors the way that you all did in the north."

He clasped his hands together and sighed. "My siblings and I arrived in this land to find the people at war. We tried to bring peace." He shook his head. "At any rate. The blood magic practiced in the mountains separating Elsira and Lagrimar and found elsewhere on this continent was potent stuff. Very powerful and easily abused. The clever discovered it could be combined with Earthsong to create new things."

Gilmer turned to Zeli. "Did you bring it with you?"

"Bring what?" Varten asked, but Zeli knew. She felt the truth of what he was really asking, but was ashamed to say. She shouldn't have brought it, hadn't told Varten that she was doing so. It was dangerous, but when she'd left the palace, leaving it within the reach of the Goddess had felt just as wrong.

She twisted the sack in which she carried her meager belongings and reached inside to pull out an object as long as her forearm and covered in brown fabric. She unwrapped it carefully to reveal the king stone. "When Queen Jasminda and the Goddess defeated the True Father, they trapped all of the Songs he stole within this caldera." Inside the red encasement was a dagger, blood still dark on its blade. The caldera was warm in her hand, as if it generated its own heat.

"You stole it?" Varten's voice was awed with a hint of reproach.

"I didn't want to leave it with Her. I don't trust Her." The fire of betrayal still burned hot within Zeli when she thought of the Goddess. Yllis remained silent, gazing icily at the caldera.

Gilmer was quiet for a moment, his mind far away before he focused back on her. "These calderas are powerful objects, used for centuries to change the course of Earthsong. Their creation requires a sacrifice, and another sacrifice is needed to use them. Sometimes small, sometimes large."

"Blood, right?" Zeli asked.

Yllis spoke up. "Major calderas, such as the one you hold, require a death in order to become active. Long ago I created one. Its purpose was to hold my Song after my death and give it to Oola so that She might finally end the war with her brother." His dark eyes never left the king stone, and Zeli wanted to hide it from him. As if he felt her discomfort, he looked away, toward the red obelisk in the center of the space. "In order to release the stolen Songs within that stone, Eero must die. His life must be sacrificed."

Gilmer reached forward, a question in his gaze. Zeli nodded and allowed him to take the king stone from her gently. "My old friend is right in one regard, death is one form of sacrifice. But it is not the only way."

Yllis frowned. "It is the only way the Cantors discovered, and we spent centuries researching blood magic and calderas."

"And you don't listen." Gilmer's voice was even. "You did not then and you are not now. The problem with scholars is that you so often seek knowledge for its own sake. You understand what you choose to, filtering your discoveries through your own perceptions. There are many forms of sacrifice in this world. Think of the meaning of the word." He focused on Zeli. "What does it mean to you?"

She thought for a moment. "To give something up."

"Anything?"

"Something important to you," she said.

"Something of great value," Varten offered. "Something precious."

Gilmer nodded. "If you want to release what's inside this caldera, Tarazeli ul-Matigor, House of Bobcats, what are you willing to give up?" His soft smile was almost fatherly.

What was she willing to give up? She'd risked much to get this far—her safety, her future, but she already knew that wasn't the type of sacrifice he meant.

"I can show you how to restore Songs, starting with your own," Gilmer said.

Her breath caught at his words. “You can bring my Song back? Can you just bring everyone’s back?”

Gilmer shook his head. “That is not for me to do, and furthermore, I cannot from here. Some level of proximity is needed.”

She exhaled, trying not to show her disappointment. “But mine?”

He held the king stone like an offering and held her gaze. “You have to choose what you will give up.”

“What sort of thing should it be?”

Yllis snorted. “This doesn’t make any sense. It’s blood magic, it needs blood and death. Maybe the girl should open an artery.”

Zeli swallowed, and Varten shot him an angry glare, but Gilmer remained just as calm as before. “This magic is created with blood, true. But the spell to unlock it needs only a surrender. A yielding. What do you hold dear? What makes you who you are? What is as easy as breathing to you? What is holding you back?”

His last question gripped her hard. She stared at the encased dagger, an idea forming in her mind. But that didn’t make sense, did it?

Gilmer continued, “There is a debt that is owed this spell. Blood flows through our veins, brings us life, and its spilling is the loss of the precious. But there are other things that sustain us. Other valuable commodities that fuel our tanks, if you will. What brought you here today?”

She struggled to find the right word. “Duty.”

Gilmer tilted his head. “Just duty?”

Her mouth trembled. “No.” She blinked slowly, turning to Varten, who looked encouragingly at her.

What she’d overheard in the Goddess’s office had set her on this path. She’d been filled with a feeling that caused her to rush out and find Varten, to seek comfort from him.

She straightened, recognizing what it had been. "Fear," she whispered, sotto voce.

"What?"

"Fear," she repeated, louder this time. "I was afraid. Afraid of what the Goddess was planning, of Her inaction. Of what Her brother is capable of. Fear that my people will have nothing, that *I* . . . will have nothing." She shook her head. "I have nothing. I never have," she muttered.

"And have you had this fear for a long time?" Gilmer asked.

She met his gaze. "My entire life."

The door of her home kicked down, her parents brought out screaming, branded traitors for being members of the Keepers of the Promise. Their execution. Zeli sold into servitude.

The darkened wagon that transported her to the capital where the True Father drained her Song. A sack over her head. Being tossed in a pit. A pair of lips pressed against her rigid ones. Fear, fear, and more fear had lived within her. Dogged her steps. It's what had made her join the Sisterhood.

Hope had lived alongside it, kept her going through many difficult times, but the fear of starving, fear of being alone, that had motivated her even more.

Varten's presence beside her was impossible to ignore. She was afraid of him, too—not of him exactly, but of what it would mean if she gave in to the feelings she had for him. What would happen when it had gone as far as it could, and then ended.

Fear was her fuel, Gilmer was right.

"But how can giving up fear be a sacrifice?" she asked.

"Because it is precious to you."

"But I'm not afraid on purpose. It just . . . is."

He sat back on his cushion. "Do you breathe on purpose? Do

you manually pump the blood through your veins? How is a sacrifice of blood or life any different?"

She shook her head, still perplexed.

"Does your fear make your life better and happier?" Gilmer asked.

She looked down to her lap.

"No?" he continued. "Then why have you not given it up before? Why have you allowed it to push your steps for eighteen years?"

"But I'm not in control of it," she pleaded.

"Aren't you?" Gilmer raised a brow. Beside him, Yllis frowned.

Zeli's mind raced as she tried to wrap it around what Gilmer was saying. "But how do I get rid of it? How can I sacrifice my fear?"

"You let it go." He held his hands up, wiggling his fingers slightly.

She pressed her lips together in frustration. "That's—it doesn't work like that."

"Doesn't it?"

The man was maddening. "You yourself said that human hearts are stubborn."

"Yes, I did." Gilmer's eyes glittered as he leaned forward. "That is precisely why it's a sacrifice. Because it is hard to do. Wouldn't slicing your palm be easier? We believe our fears keep us safe—and it's true they can warn us of danger, help us avoid an imminent attack. But you are not under attack every moment of every day.

"Your fear is not what gives you courage, your bravery exists outside of it. Certainly, you were brave to come here and seek aid for your people. But you did this in *spite* of your fear, not because of it. Imagine what you could do if you let it go. You would be unleashed."

His voice held the promise of a wonderful world just on the edge of her grasp. It was one she wanted so desperately to reach.

Lay down your burdens, the acolyte standing on the corner had said. *Rest your weary shoulders.* She was tired of being constantly afraid. She wanted something else for herself.

Something within her shifted. She felt it loosen and break free just as the backs of her eyes began to sting. "I want that. I want to let it go."

Gilmer smiled and it was full of warmth and love. In that moment, she completely understood why he would be worshipped. "Good. Then I have much to teach you."

CHAPTER THIRTY-FIVE

Go
forward
beyond
above.
If motivation grips you, keep moving.
Never stop.

—THE HARMONY OF BEING

Kyara had stayed behind in the training space long after the others left. She was enjoying finally being able to wield her power with some dexterity. The wraith-like apparitions seemed to dissolve under the force of her wildcat avatar's jaws.

Whatever spell Murmur had created for these training exercises increased in difficulty. The wraiths became multicolored and her task was to only destroy the orange ones, while leaving the other colors alone. A deep sense of satisfaction went through her after she'd completed all the levels of the exercise for the tenth time.

Once she had returned, fresh off the knowledge of Mooriah's revelation, she had progressed rapidly. It was like a cork had been unstoppered inside her. Precision and mastery of her Song seemed second nature and she reveled in it.

Time might as well not exist in this spirit realm, but her body needed food. She quieted her Song and exited the vision, then stood and stretched her aching muscles, which had been seated in the same position for days. She could not wait to tell the others about her progress—but no one was around.

She didn't sense Murmur or the other Cavefolk, with whom she'd had virtually no contact since arriving. Shrugging, she decided to just go out and meet Darvyn. Mooriah would probably be out there with Tana.

However, when she reached Darvyn's campsite, no Earthsong-created fire hovered over the ground. There was no sign of Darvyn or anyone else.

Fear vibrated through her with the force of an avalanche, but she forced a measure of calm and focused on her inner sight. She couldn't find Darvyn that way, but she should be able to spot the others. If they were nearby, that is.

She slumped with relief when a handful of glowing figures revealed themselves. Only they appeared to be inside the mountain? They certainly hadn't been in the tunnel, which was the only entrance to this isolated ledge.

Confused, she paced around the campsite until she noticed a small cleft in the rock where a handful of tough grass clung. Several stalks were snapped, hanging lazily. She grabbed hold of the edge of the crack and levered herself up. A path came into view, out of sight from ground level. It was just a short climb up the crack to reach it and jump down.

She followed the path around a curve and discovered another plateau, larger than the ledge and without any protection from the steep drop down. However, here is where Fenix had apparently made his camp. She hadn't seen him for days but now Darvyn, Mooriah, Ella, and the girls were all with him—and all wore stricken expressions. Ulani crouched on the ground, clutching her puppy, Raven, to her.

"What's happened?" Kyara asked, stumbling upon their party. Darvyn rushed over to her and wrapped an arm around her. She didn't realize how truly exhausted she was until she leaned against him and had him bear some of her weight.

"The True Father has attacked again. This time he released wraiths on the city." It took a moment for her mind to register his words.

Stunned faces, some tear-streaked, looked back at her. Fenix's expression was solemn. "He has found a manner of controlling the dead that the Physicks have not," Fenix said. "They have returned and now do his bidding."

He waved a hand in the air and a shimmering portal opened before him. This one reflected an image, like a looking glass, of the city of Rosira. In the strange apparition, columns of black smoke poured from a hole in the sky. Spirits dove into the bodies of the living and transformed them, these hosts then attacked other citizens.

Kyara moved forward, toward the portal, awestruck by both the violence and the magic by which she was seeing it. She reached toward the golden ripple, but Darvyn held her back.

"You cannot touch this," Fenix said. "It would kill you."

Kyara swallowed as the horror played out in the image. "Is this happening now?"

"It is over. The wraiths retreated. This looks like yet another test."

"We're too late," Mooriah said. She stood off to the side with her arms crossed, eyes vacant. Fenix crossed to her as if to comfort her, but she shook her head and stepped away.

His head dropped and he appeared dejected. "Your uncle certainly has not changed in all these years."

Kyara was certain she felt a shift in the very fabric of reality. "The True Father is your uncle? That means your mother is . . ."

Mooriah looked over at her sadly. "My mother is the Goddess Awoken, yes. I was cut from Her womb while She slept. Not quite dead, but not alive, either. I never met Her, but that is why I have this power." She fisted her hand and lashed out, hitting a nearby scrubby bush with enough Nethersong to erase it from existence completely. Outside of the heart of the Mother, the avatars were not visible, but the effects of the power were. Only a small pile of char remained.

Fenix raised a hand and the air around Mooriah began to shimmer with a gold tinge. "You don't need to throw a shield around me," she seethed. "I am not out of control."

"What do you mean that is why you have this power?" Kyara asked.

"When a mother dies in childbirth, the child's Song may turn. Being born of death creates a powerful connection." Mooriah's eyes were stormy. "Mine was not dead, but neither was she alive."

Cold took over Kyara's limbs. "I didn't know that."

"We should be there now. We should have been there to help them fight."

"The attack has ended," Fenix said. "You will be there the next time."

Darvyn peered in the portal, watching the images unfold. "Jasminda and Oola were able to fight off some of it and then the wraiths just . . . left. The damage looks intense, but at least it's done for now."

Mooriah shook her head. "We must stop him before the dead take over the country and then this world."

Kyara shivered. "And how, exactly, do we accomplish that? The simulations we've been training with are all well and good, but I've seen those things in action. They're powerful, fast, ridiculously strong. How do we defeat them?"

"With Nethersong, we can banish the spirits from the bodies they take, freeing the hosts." Mooriah leveled her gaze on Kyara.

"I don't know how to do that."

A flash of annoyance crossed the woman's face. "Well, you must practice."

"How?"

"Try it on me."

Kyara blinked, surprised.

"Use your other sight. A wraith will have the Nether of the dead. Focus on it, but don't draw it into yourself, push it away from the host. Go on, try."

Frowning, Kyara sank into her other sight. Mooriah's Nether shone bright as the sun. The reminder that she had invaded someone's body, some unsuspecting person, rubbed Kyara wrong. Using her Song, she reached for the death energy in the woman and latched onto it. A sense of invigoration filled her, the temptation to draw the energy toward herself was great. But instead she pushed, and found it easy to do. The Nethersong did not belong in the body it was occupying and so forcing it out was almost trivial.

She opened her eyes to the Living World and gasped to see a body crumpled on the ground and a thick column of black smoke hovering in the air. Ella had her children in a death grip. Raven stood before the girls, hackles up and growling low, in protective mode. Mooriah's spirit could enter any of them now.

But Fenix was whispering urgently to Darvyn. He led him over to Ulani and motioned for Darvyn to take hold of her shoulder. Ulani listened closely as Fenix kept talking in a low voice. Kyara's gaze went back to the figure on the ground. While Mooriah still hovered menacingly, Kyara knelt and turned the body over.

Soft, rasping breaths inflated the chest of the old woman. Stringy, thin hair covered her face. When Kyara brushed it aside, her jaw dropped.

"Ydaris?" This was the former Cantor of Lagrimar, the True Father's second-in-command. Kyara's former mistress who had both raised her and terrorized her for half her life. She stood and backed away on shaking legs just before Mooriah re-took the woman's body.

The transformation from withered, old hag to the healthy, more youthful form of Mooriah was swift. The two women stood staring at each other for a long time.

"You said she terrorized your descendants," Kyara said, finally.

Mooriah nodded then turned toward Tana. "It is your turn now. Banish me from this body; practice so you will know what to do during the next attack."

"And once she's done that," Fenix added, "try taking over Ella instead."

Kyara's head whipped around. He held up a hand to still her protest. "Earthsingers connected to the source energy cannot be taken and transformed. I have shown Darvyn and Ulani how to extend this shield to others."

Darvyn nodded in confirmation, but Kyara's heart raced. She wanted to trust Fenix. He had been a prisoner for longer than she could fathom, and he had saved all of them.

"Go on," Kyara said to Tana. "Mooriah will not hurt your mother."

The girl still looked worried, but closed her eyes. In moments, Mooriah's spirit shot once again from the body of the old woman. Darvyn and Ulani had linked their hands, while Ella still held on to her youngest daughter. The column of smoke twirled and darted for Ella, but bounced back, striking an invisible barrier. It darted again, targeting Darvyn, but was repelled. Finally, it returned to Ydaris's form and transformed again.

Ella was shaken, but holding her composure. "That woman you . . . are using. Is she harmed?"

"Her body will reflect any damage inflicted upon me. But the process of taking the host is not inherently harmful for short periods."

"And for long periods?"

"Eventually, the host will die if possessed for long enough. Then I will have to find a new body." Mooriah's tone was matter of fact, but Ella shivered at the grisly revelation.

"This woman is not one to be concerned with. She is a murderer of thousands and caused untold suffering." If she was trying to reassure Ella, it wasn't working. Kyara made a note to tell the woman more about the Cantor and her crimes, but ultimately suspected Ella was thinking of all the others who would be affected by the wraiths.

"We should head back to Rosira now," Darvyn said. "It will take some time to get down the mountain and find transportation."

"I can get you all down the mountain in a moment," Fenix said.

"Your power will work on Nethersingers?" Kyara asked.

He nodded.

"Will we . . . go through one of those?" She pointed to the magical mirror still showing scenes from Rosira.

"No, none alive without a direct connection to the Eternal Flame could survive travel via portal." His gaze shot to Darvyn for a moment, then flitted away.

"But you can't take us the whole way?" Mooriah asked.

"I cannot come with you to the city. Bringing you down the mountain will tap my energy."

Mooriah began to protest, but he held up a hand. "Two centuries of captivity weakened me more than I can say. I must return every few days to my world to regain my strength. The power of your Flame is not enough. However, now that war has arrived, I will again appeal to the others to come and help. I must be able to convince someone." His expression was not as hopeful as his words.

"There's one thing I don't understand," Tana said. Everyone turned to look at her. She wilted a little under the scrutiny, but continued bravely. "We can banish the spirits, but then they can just take over other bodies. How do we get rid of them completely?"

"What did you do to them in Yaly?" Kyara asked Fenix. After the Machine had been stopped and the portal closed, he'd done something to remove all the spirits from all the bodies, almost at once. They'd simply disappeared.

He shook his head, frowning. "It is not something I can teach—not even to an Earthsinger." He looked again at Darvyn and squinted. "Not even to you, I am sorry."

Darvyn looked uncomfortable at Fenix's scrutiny, but Kyara couldn't tell if he was disappointed or not. She glanced at Mooriah. "There must be some other way. We'll have to find it." Mooriah nodded, albeit uneasily. Was there really a way for them to win or had this all just been for naught?

CHAPTER THIRTY-SIX

Is night a consequence of day
or a companion?
The search for meaning can be fraught.
Take care to see only what appears.

—THE HARMONY OF BEING

A hush had fallen over the ballroom. Jasminda stood before a squadron of journalists who wielded notebooks like swords. A half-dozen microphones jutted up before her at odd angles, attached to the podium at which she stood. The devices had just transported her voice to audiences around the land listening on their radiophonics.

The foreign press was here as well. Tales of the mysterious wraiths attacking Elsira had spread far and many were curious, fearful, or both.

Well, now they all knew. Quiet reigned for the seconds it took for her words to settle in. She had given a brief, but thorough, recounting of the events as they'd happened. The True Father had escaped with the aid of foreign mages and now had the means by which to open portals to the World After. The wraiths were under his control and he meant to use them to attack and conquer Elsira.

It was not conjecture or presumption, the former king had sent a message—a very clear one that appeared in Jasminda's office in the middle of the night. A letter, hovering in midair—a messy scribble on rough paper, but legible enough. She had been there working late, trying to piece together a means by which they could face this new opponent, but the missive was not entirely unexpected.

Eero was vain and petty. He would not do something and not take credit for it. He wanted them to know in no uncertain terms that he was coming for what he thought was his. And that the damage would be less intense if both she and Jack stepped down and handed the country over to him.

She did not mention the letter to the press, there was enough discord and uncertainty already without adding to it. But the unequivocal confirmation that the True Father once again had access to magic, that he could likely steal Songs again and was even now plotting the downfall of her nation, was enough to keep her from sleep for the rest of the night.

The faces staring up at her were raw with shock and just beginning to stir from the staggering blow she'd been forced to deal them.

And then, like a pack of wild dogs, they attacked.

"Your Majesty, will you lift the curfew after this latest attack or will you double down?"

"Are you certain it's the True Father and not the Lagrimari refugees behind this magical warfare?"

"Who has the True Father allied himself with and why? Are they enemies of Elsira?"

Faces blurred before her and voices mingled unintelligibly as they shouted over one another in effort to get their questions answered. She tried to separate each query in her head so that she could think through them and answer reasonably, but it was overwhelming. Volleys of words were thrown at her like mortar shells. She struggled to keep her composure.

In what space she could find between their shouting, she spoke as carefully as she could, giving what answers she could. And then moved on to the next. To the side of the stage, her assistants Camm and Ilysara stood observing, ready to step in and rescue her when needed.

"Hazelle Harimel, *Rosira Daily Witness*."

Jasminda held back a flinch. The woman's screeds against the curfew in general and Jasminda in particular had only grown in recent days. The chatter hushed as the other reporters quieted to give the woman her turn. A courtesy they'd barely extended to other, younger journalists. Harimel had indeed earned some level of respect.

"Your Majesty," she said, gray curls crisp and bouncy. "How can you reassure the people that the crown has this situation under control?"

Jasminda wanted to laugh. *Under control?* How could that remotely be possible? But no one wanted to hear her frustration, exhaustion, or grief—they didn't want the truth, they wanted reassurance that the queen could do the impossible and keep them safe.

She cleared her throat. "I have put together an advisory council and we are doing everything possible to safeguard our citizens and our land from the violence we expect. We have never faced quite such a situation before. We will need the assistance of the people. All of the people, staying alert and helping one another. We're all facing this threat together."

Others shouted for her attention, but Hazelle Harimel wasn't done. "Isn't it true that the Goddess Awoken installed you as queen, abdicating Her throne to you, independently of your marriage to King Jaqros?"

Jasminda narrowed her eyes. "Yes, that is not new information."

"Why was that, Your Majesty?" The woman tilted her head to the side.

"I fail to see why that is relevant."

From the corner of her eye, Jasminda saw Camm step forward. Below the podium, out of sight of the crowd, she raised a hand to halt him.

"It's relevant," Harimel said, smiling cruelly, "because with this revelation that the Goddess knew about the True Father's escape and kept it from us, many will question Her loyalty and legitimacy. And if you rule only by Her word, then your legitimacy would logically come into question as well."

A blanket of silence fell across the room. Jasminda could barely hear her own breaths, though her heart drummed ferociously in her chest. She'd practiced answering hostile questions that morning with her assistants and thought she was at least partially prepared. But this avenue of logic took her quite by surprise.

She cursed her lack of imagination.

The silence dragged on as she could not come up with a single thing to say. Perhaps she should have taken the out that Camm had offered, and now she was stuck.

A low thumping began, vibrating the floor. The doors flew open and half a dozen Royal Guardsmen marched in. Every pair of eyes—except those of Hazelle Harimel's—moved to the doorway. The canny reporter held Jasminda's gaze for a long moment before looking away.

For her part, Jasminda turned slowly, feeling as if she were almost not in control of her own body. And then, the tension broke.

"King Jaqros!" The murmur went up and was repeated by a dozen mouths. He stood there, amidst the Guardsmen, looking weary and beautiful. Heavy circles ringed his eyes and while the military uniform he wore was sharp, his hair was a fright. It was as if he'd spent his entire trip running his hands through it.

Jasminda raced off the stage and ran to him, throwing herself into his arms, heedless of the others watching. His embrace was tight and she sank into it for long moments. His coat and skin still bore the chill of the early winter day, but she barely felt it.

He pulled back and looked into her eyes, regret and grief pouring from him. She squeezed his hand and wordlessly they turned to walk back to the podium, to face the microphones and the salivating pack together.

"Good morning everyone," he said, dredging up a remarkably sincere smile from somewhere. "I'm very sorry to interrupt, but I couldn't stomach not seeing my wife the instant I returned from abroad."

Several female reporters beamed, and Jasminda's own heart melted a bit.

"King Jaqros, has the Prime Minister of Fremia promised aid?" someone shouted.

"Are they responsible for this latest attack?"

"Do you think that the monarch of Raun should have such steady access to the palace?"

Jack held up his hands, chuckling. "My trip was lovely, thank you for asking." He gripped Jasminda's shaking hand again and sobered. "I did not come to steal my wife's thunder, I know she has things well in hand. I was briefed on the attack on my journey home and came merely to lend my support to her actions and decisions. Hard days are ahead for Elsira, but we will band together to rise above it as we always have."

Though Jasminda stared at Jack, in her periphery she saw Hazelle Harimel fight her way back to the front of the group. "You support *all* of your wife's decisions, Your Majesty?"

Jack stiffened and nodded. "As I said."

"What about the continued incarceration of Zann Biddel on trumped-up charges? Inquiries into his case keep getting handed off with some nonsense about paperwork."

Dread filled Jasminda's belly. She squeezed Jack's hand, hard, as beside her he slowly turned to stone. She had intended to tell him about Biddel, it's just that communication had been infrequent between them the past few days, what with King Pia's arrival and the whims of the Fremian leader.

But in truth she hadn't wanted Jack to know. Hadn't even had time to consider what to tell him when he returned, busy as she was handling one crisis after the next. To his credit, his outward appearance didn't change.

"I will repeat it once more in case anyone did not hear me clearly. I support the queen's decisions." He took a step away from the microphone, releasing her hand.

Jasminda nodded to Camm, who rushed to the front of the stage. "The king and queen have much to discuss. Thank you all for attending, please direct any further questions to the press office."

Reporters grumbled and complained, but all the noise was just the roar of the ocean in her ears as the Royal Guardsmen hustled her and Jack out of the ballroom and down the wide palace hallways.

They walked quickly, not speaking. Jasminda glanced at Jack, whose face was impassive. But Earthsong revealed the hurt roiling within. Shame made her face grow hot.

Once they were alone in Jack's office, she sat on the couch while he paced and removed his coat. He tossed it onto a chair and stopped moving long enough to ruffle his hair again.

"It was a legitimate arrest," she said.

"What was his crime?" Jack spoke to the floor.

She paused. "Jaywalking."

A heavy sigh escaped from him. "And he has been in custody for how long?"

"Five days."

Jack looked at her then, expression bewildered. "Jasminda!"

She clenched her hands together. "It's all aboveboard. He's being treated as well as every other prisoner. Better even. There's no cause for complaint."

"Jasminda." His voice was scarily quiet. Jack did not yell often—not at her at any rate—but she'd never felt such frustration and disappointment from him, either.

He sank into the seat beside her. "You know this isn't right."

"He's a terrorist. A murderer. Leader of a dangerous group trying to tear our country apart."

He shook his head slowly. "Until we have evidence of that we cannot keep him on such a flimsy excuse. Even if the jaywalking had made it to a judge and he'd been convicted, he would have served less time. You have to release him."

She slid away, guilt beating at her. The man was off the streets and in isolation, unable to contact his network and incite more violence. Between that and the curfew, no one else had died from terrorism.

She tapped her finger against her thigh as her own anger grew. "No," she whispered.

Jack's head jerked back.

"What you said to that reporter, was that a lie?" she asked.

"What?"

"When you said you support my decisions? That was all for show? You only support me when I agree with you?"

"I do support you, but I would expect you to tell me when I've made a mistake. And this is a mistake."

She shook her head. "No. It isn't. There have been no attacks from his group since Biddel's been in custody. It was the right thing to do."

"Jas—"

She stood sharply. "You cannot make me see your side of things just by repeating my name over and over again. Our streets and our people are safer with him locked away. I may not be a perfect queen, and I may not even be a legitimate one," her voice broke, "but I'm holding firm on this."

He stared up at her, blinking. She fisted her hands, staring back. The two of them had endured tests together, and had tested one another. Jack had always tried to protect her, and furthermore he had always respected her. Would that change?

He ran his hands across his face then blew out a breath and stood facing her. She let go of Earthsong and focused just on his eyes, his golden eyes, the ones she'd fallen in love with.

"All right," he said finally. "All right. I still think this is a mistake, but I . . . I trust you."

The pain and stress of the past week broke and she collapsed against him. He caught her, as he always did, and she shuddered against him, just shy of sobbing. Jack held her, the way he always had, the way she hoped he always would.

CHAPTER THIRTY-SEVEN

A tune may be sung with just one note
but add to that a panoply
and get lost in their melody.
For many voices lift and raise a
solo into Harmony.

—THE HARMONY OF BEING

Kyara was used to being feared. Much of the time, she was afraid of herself. She had been born with the power to kill, after all, and it came as easily to her as breathing. Easier now that she could wield it more effectively and precisely than ever before. Even in just the past few days of training, she'd gained a mastery over her Song she'd never before thought possible. So when most of the nearly four dozen people seated before her began to scream, she was not concerned in the least. Nor was she surprised.

The day before, Fenix had spirited them into the foothills of Elsira with a magic that left Kyara tingling and tense. After he'd disappeared back through a golden portal, the rest of them had quickly been picked up by an army transport and returned to the base, where Darvyn had made a phone call and organized their return to Rosira via a military vehicle.

They'd been taken directly to the palace, flanked by Guardsmen and led to a place called the Ivory Drawing Room. The translation into Lagrimari had made her expect to find walls covered in stuffed warthog heads, where aristocrats would go to sketch pictures of the tusks surrounding them. Elsiran culture was so mystifying that such a thing would not have astonished her, though she was relieved to find merely opalescent wallpaper and a cream-colored carpet and heavily brocaded armchairs surrounding small tables.

Mooriah, Ella, Tana, and Ulani had all stood a bit agape at the finery. Darvyn was used to it and Kyara was focused more on the nerves rising in her belly. The king and queen had requested they attend a strategy meeting on the topic of the "wraith problem," and Kyara was meant to speak to a small crowd of officials.

Ella's shout had her gathering her Song to her, defensively. A tall, sturdy-looking Elsiran man had entered the room. Ella and the girls squealed as they raced to him, vying for first position in his arms. Her husband then; Kyara relaxed a fraction. Somehow he managed to hug them all at the same time, then scooped both daughters into his arms while Ella wrapped herself around his middle.

Kyara had never seen Tana smile quite so brightly before. It's like the girl was lit from within. Even mastery of her Song had not pleased her so much. A lump formed in Kyara's throat and she looked away. Darvyn curled an arm around her. But before she could get too emotional, the king and queen arrived.

There was little ceremony with their appearance, no servant announced them, they just stepped into the room side by side and took in those gathered. Quite different from the formality the True Father had insisted upon when going anywhere within the glass castle.

Darvyn greeted the monarchs heartily, and Benn brought his family over and made introductions. Kyara stood slightly apart, feeling disconnected. She did not know the king and queen as well as Darvyn did and was not comfortable around them.

Then a friendly face breached the entry. Roshon stepped into the room, along with his fiancée, Ani. Kyara went over to greet them.

"We've just arrived. We were on our way south when we received the summons," Roshon explained. "Ani had half a mind to ignore it, but then we heard of the attack and raced back."

"Where's Varten?" Kyara asked, expecting to see his twin beside him like he usually was.

"He went north with Papa."

"What's that now?" a new voice said from behind them. Dansig ol-Sarifor stood there, looking a bit world-weary. He hugged his son and Ani, and then opened his arms for Kyara. She swallowed and stepped forward, accepting the embrace and trying to hide what the gesture meant to her.

Yes, they'd spent months in side-by-side cells and Dansig's kindness and fatherly care had helped keep her sane. But it was still odd to be treated with such gentleness. She squeezed him before retreating.

"What's that about your brother?" Dansig said.

"He didn't go with you up north?" Roshon's brows were raised.

Dansig frowned and shook his head. "He said he was staying here in the palace."

Ani and Roshon looked at each other. "Jasminda said he was with you."

Just then a contingent of over half a dozen Raunians appeared, led by the small, white-haired woman who was their king. Ani's mouth firmed until two more figures stepped in behind them: a blue-haired man and a willowy Elsiran woman.

"Tai! Lizvette!" Ani waved them over. Her mother, King Pia, looked over sharply at the sound of Ani's voice, but remained ensconced amidst her entourage. Tai and Lizvette peeled away to come over. The siblings embraced heartily and Ani actually shed a few tears.

"They haven't seen each other in over two years," Roshon explained. Introductions were made, though Kyara had met the two briefly the day of her thwarted execution. Ani and Lizvette sized one another up, Lizvette with curiosity and Ani with something closer to suspicion. Kyara supposed if she'd had a brother she'd have been equally wary of meeting his chosen partner.

Next to enter the drawing room were close to twenty grim-faced Elsiran men in dark suits ambling in like an undisciplined platoon. They glowered at the Raunians, then at the Lagrimari present, and cast dubious glances at Ella, who was also foreign-born.

The noise in the room continued to rise, along with Kyara's anxiety. When the elders of the Keepers of the Promise showed up, she nearly threw up her hands. Aggar and Talida came in first, scanning the room with barely concealed hostility, but their gazes stuttered at the sight of Kyara.

She crossed her arms, straightening her spine while they stared. Darvyn was at her side in an instant, his glare just as harsh, and the two turned away. A woman with jagged claw marks on her face was the only one to approach and greet Darvyn.

"This is Rozyl," he said, introducing them. Kyara nodded, familiar with the woman and the fact that though she was a friend of Darvyn's, she, too, had called for and sanctioned Kyara's execution. Kyara did not hold it against her, but it was unlikely they would ever be close.

Finally, it appeared that everyone who was supposed to be here, had arrived. The room was packed and servants brought in additional seating until there was one for everyone. However, all stood until all the royals present had taken their seats. King Jaqros and Queen Jasminda sat at a small table in the front of the room, waiting for everyone else to settle. Darvyn, Kyara, and Mooriah walked along the edge of the room to position themselves against the wall next to the head table.

"Thank you for coming so quickly," the king began. He had a nice voice, authoritative without being condescending. She was glad he and Darvyn were friends. "The situation we face is urgent. The True Father could attack again at any time. Many of you will know Darvyn ol-Tahlyro, also known as the Shadowfox." He swept an arm toward Darvyn. "He was a rebel leader in Lagrimar fighting against the True Father."

The king paused, waiting for the queen to translate his words into Elsiran. "I'm certain that Kyara ul-Lagrimar is not unknown to most of you, either. If you are not aware, she saved the life of my wife, who was poisoned by terrorists. The method by which she was able to save Queen Jasminda is of particular interest to us, and is part of the reason for this meeting.

"And this is Mooriah ul-Sarifor. She is a . . . relative of the Goddess Awoken." He sounded unsure and Kyara wasn't certain exactly how much of Mooriah's heritage Darvyn had shared. Whispers went up throughout the audience as others questioned the presence of these three Lagrimari.

"Kyara?" Queen Jasminda turned to her. "The floor is yours."

Kyara swallowed and stepped forward, wiping her palms on her trousers. She'd never been called to speak in public before. Didn't like all the attention on her, especially from so many people who had so recently wanted her dead. She cleared her throat.

"What happened here yesterday, the wraiths . . ." She looked to Darvyn for reassurance. His expression was grave, but he nodded. "We have faced them before. Darvyn, Roshon, and I were there when they were first unleashed. You have already discovered that they are very difficult to defeat. Nearly impossible, in fact.

"The only way to banish them," Kyara continued, "is using Nethersong."

"Nethersong?" one of the black-suited Elsirans asked. "What in Sovereign's name is that?"

"Just as Earthsong is life energy, Nethersong is death energy. There are very few people alive who can wield it. Only three." She shot a glance at Mooriah. "Well, two and a half," she muttered under her breath.

The Elsirans whispered among themselves for a moment. A long-limbed man, younger than the others, with a dark red goatee spoke up. "So you are saying that three Nethersingers are all that stand between the wraiths and us? What can you even do against them with this death energy?" Queen Jasminda's translation did a good job of mimicking his derisive tone.

"Allow us to demonstrate," Kyara replied.

"Wouldn't you need a spirit in order to do that?" Roshon asked.

"Yes." She held his gaze. His brow descended in worry. "Everyone, please remain calm."

She took a deep breath and turned to Mooriah, who stood placidly as if she hadn't a care in the world. Kyara closed her eyes and drew on the knowledge she'd discovered on that mountain plateau. Sinking into her other sight, she reached for the Nethersong filling Mooriah's body. Here she was able to distinguish it from the Nether of the host's body—of Ydaris. Diving even further, she sensed the snarl of energies from the amalgamation magic that had been used to bring the spirits into the Living World. Mooriah had snuck in somehow on the residue of this magic and it clung to her.

There was something like a thread that would untangle the mess and release the spirit. She did as she'd practiced, pulling on this thread of Nethersong that bound Mooriah's spirit until it came loose easily.

She returned to her normal sight in time to witness Ydaris's form crumple to the floor as the inky, diaphanous substance of Mooriah's spirit floated to hover near the ceiling.

Screams filled the room. Some folk dived under the tables and covered their eyes. Kyara had anticipated the response but still it rankled. She knew the fear wasn't of her precisely—this time Mooriah was to blame, but she was still tired of it. Frightened people screaming at her was the soundtrack of her life.

Queen Jasminda threw up her hands and darkness filled the room. The yelling faded away. "Please control yourselves," she said slowly. "We would not have brought you here to harm you."

When the light returned, the Elsirans who had taken cover—notably not the relatively youngish man who'd questioned her—took their seats again. Soon, everyone's gaze was locked on Mooriah's spirit form, still suspended over Kyara's head.

On the ground Ydaris moaned. Kyara's other sight revealed

that Void energy was quickly filling her. She was still alive, after several weeks' possession, but without an infusion of Earthsong she would not be so for long.

Queen Jasminda called out to the guards at the door. "Have them bring in the prisoner." Moments later, a shackled Elsiran woman was brought in. She was older and gray-haired, save for hints of red still staining her temples. Her posture was erect, proud, heedless of the chains on her wrists and ankles. Ella gasped, apparently recognizing the woman.

The prisoner stood, surveying the people staring at her and then Mooriah plunged into her. In seconds, the body transformed, shrinking down and darkening until Mooriah once again stood before them, nearly swimming in the taller woman's dress—standard-issue prison garb.

After the uproar of the first demonstration, the response this time was slightly more subdued. People wheezed and sputtered. Many of the Elsirans slapped their palms to their chests and tapped three times, some sort of sign to ward off evil, no doubt.

Mooriah shook off her handcuffs and kicked away the leg irons as if they were nothing. She surreptitiously wiped away a bead of blood on her finger on the skirt of her dress. Darvyn kneeled beside Ydaris's body, infusing her with Earthsong. Kyara nearly told him not to bother, but that wasn't exactly in line with her new vow not to kill. The old crone was breathing heavily, but had not been harmed.

The little Raunian king pinned Kyara with a shrewd, intelligent gaze. "Expel her spirit again, but this time, have her try to enter me."

Her advisors protested, some loudly, but the king silenced them with a raised hand. Kyara looked to Queen Jasminda. Elsira already had enough problems with Raun without adding spirit possession of their king to it, but the queen nodded.

Mooriah just shrugged and so Kyara sank into her other sight and banished the spirit once again from the prisoner's body. However, this time, when the black column lunged for King Pia, it stopped a breath from her skin as if it had hit an invisible wall. Mooriah tried again and again, but could not penetrate the small woman. She returned to the body she had just abandoned and transformed into herself again.

"Hmm," was all King Pia said. But a rotund Elsiran man stood, huffing with anger.

"Raunians must be involved in this dark magic. Why else would it not affect them?"

Lizvette turned to face the man, obviously affronted. "Don't be ridiculous, Minister. In Yaly, I learned that amalgamations cannot affect those who have had contact with selakki oil, something quite common in Raun. Those creatures were brought here with amalgam magic, that's why the Raunians are immune."

"It's true," Tai said. "Amalgamations have never worked for me, and I was able to disable or mute the effect of any device I came in contact with."

Pia considered her son's words. "That would explain how me and my security forces were able to fight the wraiths. Our guns had no effect, but our fists certainly did." She turned to the assistant sitting next to her. "Have every available shipment of selakki oil diverted here as quickly as possible. As much as can be spared." The young woman nodded and began scribbling onto her pad.

Pia held Jasminda's gaze. "Your Majesty, my staff and our resources are at your disposal."

"Thank you, Your Majesty," Queen Jasminda said, inclining her head.

"So a Nethersinger can eject the spirits," Rozyl asked from her place standing against the wall, "but they can just enter a new body almost immediately?"

Kyara nodded. "But this is only the first step of a larger plan." If Fenix could have taught Earthsingers to banish spirits back to the World After the way he could, they would stand a chance. But as it stood, they needed a different method of defense.

"We do have a step two," Darvyn added, rising. "There is a way to keep the spirits from entering new hosts." He looked pointedly at the Elsirans in the room. "But you aren't going to like it."

"I don't even like step one," Aggar said aggressively. "To entrust our safety to an assassin is ludicrous. She's spent a decade cutting down the lives of Lagrimari while in service to the True Father."

Kyara was geared for a scathing response, but Queen Jasminda beat her to the punch. "And now she stands with us, against the True Father. Which would you prefer?" Aggar wisely shut his mouth, but discontent rolled off him in waves.

"What is the method to prevent the spirits from overtaking new hosts?" Roshon asked.

Darvyn sighed. "Earthsingers, those who are actively connected to the source energy, cannot be overtaken. We can also extend that protection to those who we are in physical contact with. Those who want to be safeguarded will need to gather close to willing Singers and create a chain. The length of the chain of protection will depend on the strength of the Singer."

All was quiet for a moment and then the room burst into an explosion of sound. The Elsiran officials jabbered and bickered. No one was translating their words, but Kyara could imagine the arguments against allying with people they still considered to be witches and relying on magic to save them from more magic.

Finally, the din quieted to a dull roar. "I'd like a demonstration," the tall Elsiran man announced.

"Certainly, Minister Calladeen," Darvyn said in a tone of voice indicating he didn't like the man much. "Would you like to volunteer to be a part of the chain?"

The man's nostrils flared and he crossed his arms, not moving from his seat. None of the suited Elsirans would consent to take part, either, however, King Jaqros stood and came to Darvyn's side. Roshon, Lizvette, and Ella's husband, Benn, also joined the chain. They stood, hand in hand, while Kyara expelled Mooriah and her spirit tried and failed to enter each of them.

More arguing ensued after the demonstration was complete. Kyara was already sick of hearing the voices circling each other uselessly.

"Are there even enough Lagrimari with their Songs to make this a real possibility?" one of the Elsirans asked.

Darvyn looked to Rozyl, who sighed. "The Keepers have retained some Singers. There are more children than anyone else . . ." She trailed off, thinking. "But I'm not certain if we can protect the entire city."

"What if there were more Singers?" a female voice asked from the doorway. A short Lagrimari teen stood there with Varten next to her. Behind them stood a Lagrimari man with silver hair.

"Zeli-yul!" Ulani shouted, grinning.

The young woman, Zeli, smiled at the girl before facing the others. Her eyes glinted with lionhearted authority and she walked forward, not appearing agitated by the dozens of eyes now on her.

"More Singers would certainly help," Darvyn said. "But where would we find them?"

"They are already here. Every Lagrimari in this land was born with a Song and far too many were stolen. What we need to do is bring them all back."

Unlike with the other revelations, this time no one present said a word.

CHAPTER THIRTY-EIGHT

Neither conceal your light nor
hide your darkness.
Do not avoid allowing what's true of you
to shine through.
Would you be vacuous—an empty shell?
A secret not worth keeping.
A story not worth repeating.

—THE HARMONY OF BEING

Ensconced in the plush armchair near the fireplace in her office, Jasminda regarded her brothers, seated side by side on the couch—both were tense. Zeli, next to Varten, was perfectly at ease, and Yllis, who stood near the fireplace, was an emotional lockbox. Her Song could not penetrate him at all.

While Jack was off dealing with other parts of the strategy

to battle the True Father, Jasminda had needed to speak to both of her brothers. Apparently, Zeli and Yllis came along as a package deal.

"So you weren't with Papa at all, instead you snuck off to Yaly without telling anyone?" Jasminda didn't bother trying to mask the hurt in her tone. Varten flinched at the accusation.

"I convinced him to keep it a secret," Zeli said apologetically, meeting her eyes. The girl, who had been a bundle of nerves the last time they'd met, was much altered. She pointed at the morning's paper on the coffee table between them. The headline read, THE GODDESS'S STUNNING SECRET! BUT CAN SHE BE TRUSTED? EXCLUSIVE BY HAZELLE HARIMEL. "That is why we left."

"Did you know? About the True Father's escape?" Jasminda gripped the arms of her chair.

Zeli slowly nodded, her composure crumbling. "I knew the day it happened. The Goddess swore me to secrecy, and I didn't know what to do besides obey Her."

Jasminda's heart tore into pieces at the grief and shame in the young woman's expression. She slid forward, wanting to reach for her and comfort her, but was too far away. "You believed in Her. We all did. She . . ." Jasminda shook her head. What had Oola been thinking? What was Her plan? Did She even have one? "She has an agenda of Her own and we are not always privy to it. I'm so sorry She put you in that position. I truly am."

Zeli took a deep breath. "I wasn't sure what She would do to anyone who tried to cross Her—even you. We decided secrecy was best."

She and Varten then took turns explaining how they'd read Yllis's journal and traveled to Yaly to search Saint Gilmer's Archives, where they'd met yet another ancient Earthsinger who by rights should be dead. There were a lot of those around these days.

"Gilmer gave me my Song back," Zeli said, voice thick.

"But how?" Confusion, wonder, and hope warred within Jasminda.

"With this." She reached into the ragged pouch slung around her shoulder and retrieved a bundled package. When she unwrapped it, Jasminda's heart nearly stopped. "I've been calling it the king stone."

The dagger that Jasminda had plunged into the True Father's back the day the Mantle fell lay in the young woman's hand. Encased in a spell made of blood and magic, it looked dull in the light.

"How were you able to use that to restore your Song?"

"You and the Goddess trapped all of the Songs the True Father stole in here when you disabled him that day," Zeli began. "If this caldera can be unlocked, those Songs will go back to their rightful owners. Gilmer couldn't free them from such a great distance, he was only able to extract mine."

She looked down at the object she held. "He taught me the spell he used—the blood magic words at least. He also taught me the idea of it, the intention, but we do not have all we need in order to truly release the Songs. The spell requires more."

"Is it blood?" Roshon asked, leaning forward intently.

Zeli shook her head. "A sacrifice. More than blood."

Jasminda recalled the price of a powerful caldera. Death. Her limbs lost all feeling. "I would think dying would erase the need for a Song."

"Not death, either. Not necessarily."

Jasminda shook her head, impatience taking over. "What did you sacrifice then?" she snapped.

Varten jerked, glaring at her fiercely. Jasminda held up a hand and breathed deeply. "I'm sorry. But what was it?"

Zeli sat straighter, in an instant she looked older and somehow . . . mightier. “I sacrificed my fear.” Silence followed the bold statement.

“I don’t understand,” Jasminda finally said.

“Something precious. Something that’s a part of you, that’s difficult to relinquish. *That* is a sacrifice.”

Jasminda blinked. “Fear . . .” she whispered.

“In order to restore their Songs, the Lagrimari people will require a sacrifice. Not of the vein, but of the heart.”

Zeli’s words reverberated inside Jasminda’s head. “If it’s truly possible to give everyone their Song back, then we might stand a chance against the True Father.” She looked up, excitement sweeping through her. “There would be enough Singers to protect the non-Singers from the wraiths. Without bodies to possess, Kyara and the other Nethersingers might be able to find a way to banish them for good.

“There’s another problem though. Even if every Singer is willing to protect the ungrateful Elsirans, the wraiths move so quickly. By the time the portal appears, there’s no chance for folks to find a Singer to help them. Logistically, it’s a nightmare.”

“I may be able to help in that regard.” Everyone turned to Yllis, who’d remained quiet so far.

“After I was killed by Eero, I went to the World After, as all do. But I was determined to find my way to the World Between, back to Oola. I had studied magic for so many years and felt certain there was a passageway between the worlds. I searched for it for . . . well, I don’t know how long. There is no time there. But eventually I found what I was looking for. The passageways were not what I expected, however, and I became stuck in the Void.”

Jasminda was only glancingly familiar with the Void. She’d heard Darvyn discuss it before, but as a concept it was new to her.

"The Void is something like the space between worlds," Yllis said, answering an unasked question. "A glue of sorts that holds things together—when the worlds are in balance, that is. When they're not in balance, like when the Physicks rent the barrier in order to let the spirits flow into the Living World, the Void goes a bit . . . haywire. I felt when that happened and recognized that the old Cavefolk prophecy of a war between the worlds was coming to pass. And so I found my way out of the Void and came here."

Jasminda opened herself to Earthsong and examined him again. He had very little life energy and a great preponderance of something she almost couldn't identify. Something hazy and staticky, which put her in mind of the burn of cola against your nostrils when you first take a sip. Was this the Void?

"So what are you saying, Yllis? *Why* did you come back?" she asked.

He moved languidly away from the fireplace to settle in the other armchair opposite her. "After so long spent investigating the passageways and locked within the Void, I became sensitive to its energy. I can sense the disturbance in the Void when a portal opens, and I believe I can give some kind of warning. I was able to feel the opening of the last attack, even thousands of kilometers away. I've felt each of the other trials that Eero has done."

He steepled his fingers together, balancing elbows on knees. "You need a way to give an alert and gather people together so that Singers can help non-Singers. It will only be a few minutes, but I can give you notice of an impending attack."

Varten's leg began to bounce. "Perhaps we can create shelters, places where people can go when the warning comes in. They'd be manned by the Singers willing to help and non-Singers can go there to be protected from the wraiths."

"The city already has emergency shelters," Jasminda said. "For hurricanes that hit the coast during the rainy season. We can direct people there."

"Some could be manned by Raunians as well," Roshon added. "King Pia says the vats of selakki oil will be arriving tomorrow. She diverted a shipment that had been headed south."

Gratitude filled her. "Well, this may work," she said, cautious. Variables and question marks still riddled the plan, but it was solidly possible. "Zeli, what else do you need to restore the Songs? We could use as many Singers as we can get."

Zeli twisted her mouth in a grimace. "Two things. One, a willing sacrifice from every Lagrimari wanting their Song back. Gilmer said it must be consciously and sincerely given. That, I expect, will not be easy."

That was putting it lightly. "And what's the second thing?"

"I need to find the Rosiran obelisk."

Jasminda looked questioningly to Yllis, who frowned. "When I was a Cantor, we used the obelisks to focus and extend our power. There was one in each city and every Singer could connect to it. They allowed us to link without touching, to combine and magnify Earthsong."

"Gilmer had one in his Archives," Zeli said. "I'll need to be at the obelisk in order to restore the Songs."

"Well, where was the Rosiran obelisk?" Jasminda asked.

Yllis spread his arms. "Here, in the palace. But it's gone."

"What do you mean it's gone?"

He pursed his lips. "This place has grown and changed much in the centuries since I was last here. I do not recognize the layout any longer. But the obelisk was large, with a great chamber built around it. I cannot fathom why it's now hidden."

"It must have been in the older section," Varten said, knee jumping as he thought.

"Would Oola know?" Jasminda asked. Yllis froze, tension visible. "Have you talked to Her since you've been back?"

He looked away.

"Have you talked with Mooriah?" she asked softly. Chaos had reigned after the strategy meeting had broken up and she hadn't noticed where Mooriah had disappeared to. Yllis refused to answer. It looked like a family reunion was on its way; Jasminda wondered if it would be a joyous one.

In the meantime, they had quite a list of impossible things to do in order to prepare for the next attack.

CHAPTER THIRTY-NINE

The table legs must each bear their weight
evenly.
Their sturdy feet well-grounded,
flat and strong.
Like roots, they plant themselves and face the
consequence
of being what keeps its restless form
held down.

—THE HARMONY OF BEING

Darvyn stared out of the window of the town car up at the majestic house they'd pulled in front of. Heavy clouds had gathered overhead promising rain. The temperature was cold enough that it might even be snow.

"Are you certain this is the place?" he asked his driver, Erryl.

"Yes." The man punctuated the statement with a big nod. "Got the info off a new palace maid whose brother is a Keeper. The Keepers have taken over this house all right, unlikely as it seems."

While apparently in Elsira this was just a mere house, to Darvyn it was a mansion. Pale stucco the color of sandstone was topped with a dark, clay-tiled roof. The home had no front yard to speak of, just a strip of grass with large, verdant shrubbery separating the building from the iron fence protecting it from the street.

With his Song, he sensed the property's inhabitants. Nearly two dozen were inside the house, along with a handful of guards hidden along the perimeter. He wiped a hand down his face and turned to Zeli. "Are you ready?"

She nodded resolutely. The girl had changed from the frightened mouse he'd first met weeks ago, bathing in the pride of serving Oola. Now she was stoic as a hardened soldier. Serious and driven, but without losing the innocence of youth or the spark of optimism that had also marked her.

Darvyn could not imagine what it must be like to lose your Song, and then to have it restored again . . . He deeply admired the young woman's strength and fortitude. They exited the vehicle and stood on the narrow walkway.

"What did it feel like?" he asked. She turned to him, expression open and questioning. "Giving up your fear."

She appeared pensive as she searched for the right words. "Like setting down a satchel filled with rocks that I'd carried my whole life. It's not permanent, Gilmer said it will come back, but now I will know how to deal with it better."

Darvyn nodded, envying her suddenly. "All right, you asked for help in using your Song. Tell me, how many people do you sense inside the building?"

She closed her eyes, concentrating. "Twenty, I think."

"Twenty-two," he said. "There are two elderly people on the main level. Their Earthsong is reduced due to their age."

She scrunched her eyes shut and nodded. "Yes, I can feel that."

"The ability to know what you're facing is important. But don't rely only on Earthsong. Use it in combination with your other senses." He took a deep breath and exited the vehicle, waiting for her.

Rozyl had requested Darvyn come to speak to the Keepers. At first he'd balked. Given his history with the group, he wasn't certain he was the right person. But Rozyl had said that she was having a tough time persuading them to help convince their Singers to man the emergency shelters. Most Keepers still held the Shadowfox in high esteem and his word would go far. They also did not believe that Songs could be restored, and Zeli had volunteered to accompany him and prove it.

"Do you know how to open locks?" he asked, trying to extend the teachable moment as well as offset his own discomfort. Zeli shook her head, but appeared eager.

"Heat can melt the lock. That's the method I prefer. Though you can also manipulate the air to turn the latch, depending on the type of locking mechanism. I suppose you could freeze the metal and break it off, too. There are options." He shrugged.

"Or you could just ring the bell," a voice said from the other side of the fence, its owner hidden by a prickly bush.

Turwig appeared, his grandfatherly quality making Darvyn homesick for a moment. Though he'd grown up on the run and never had a permanent place to call home, the old man was the closest thing he had to a father.

"Darvyn," Turwig said, inclining his head.

"This is Zeli," Darvyn said, motioning to the young woman beside him. The old man's eyes brightened, but Darvyn noted he hadn't yet opened the gate. "I'm here to speak with you and the other elders about our strategy for the next attack."

Turwig nodded and stepped backward. Darvyn used Earthsong to push open the gate, a waste of power really, but he rationalized that it would be instructive for Zeli.

They followed Turwig into the house, where the front door was opened by a waiting guard. Security here was high, but with such tension against Lagrimari among the Elsiran populace, that was understandable.

"How did you all acquire this house?" Darvyn asked as they stepped into a large foyer.

"It was vacant. The former owner passed away during the summer. We are technically squatting here. Does the queen wish to remove us?" Turwig raised a brow.

Darvyn rolled his eyes. They walked across the tiled floor, passing rooms furnished in what he recognized as an old-fashioned Elsiran style replete with dark wood and lush, thick fabrics. A group of young men and women in a sitting room looked up, shock and awe rippling from them through his Song.

The Shadowfox's appearance here was unexpected. His split with the Keepers was not widely known, but rumors had filtered down to him, questions about his low profile in recent weeks while the rest of the group had been so visible and vocal. A frisson of guilt speared him—he could be doing a lot of good here, if only he could still trust them.

Zeli followed silently behind him, even her footsteps were quiet on the ornate tile. Turwig led them to a bright room in the back of the house, an entire wall of windows displaying an overgrown garden, graying and shriveled in preparation for the cold season.

Overstuffed couches and armchairs were grouped into clusters around the large space. Most of the leadership of the Keepers were gathered. Rozyl looked up at Darvyn's entrance, a sense of relief from her hitting his Song. Aggar and Talida stared coldly from the corner. Four men he didn't recognize sat with Hanko and Lyngar, speaking earnestly around a low table.

A graying woman shot from her seat to approach. "Tarazeli?" she called out, eyes wide.

"Gladda!" Zeli exclaimed, rushing over to be enveloped in the woman's embrace.

"I'm so glad to see you doing well, child. What brings you here, and with the Shadowfox, no less?" The woman beamed over at him.

Darvyn recalled meeting her many years ago and was glad for the reminder of her name. He cleared his throat to address the suddenly quiet room. "I've been charged to relay a message from Queen Jasminda. She humbly requests the assistance of the Keepers in protecting the populace."

The gazes of the others unnerved him somewhat, public speaking had not often been required of him, but he pressed on. "The True Father will attack again. He could strike at any moment—all of you either witnessed the wraiths or saw the aftermath of their assault. This plan that the queen and king are putting forth requires the assistance of every Singer we can get."

"You expect us to believe that this child's Song was restored?" Aggar scoffed, shifting his bulk in his seat.

"I'm not a child." Zeli spoke gently but firmly. "And if I had no Song, how could I do this?" The wide armchair in which Aggar sat rose into the air. The man gripped the armrests and sputtered, kicking his legs out in panic. Darvyn couldn't hide his smirk, though he managed not to laugh as the man and the chair lowered gently back to the floor.

"How do we even know your Song was taken, girl?" Lyngar grumbled, his well-lined face sagging further.

"I was there when she was sent to Sayya," Gladda said. "I've know her since she was a child. Her parents were Keepers and friends of mine. She was shipped off for tribute far too young, and I comforted her when she returned, empty and broken." She looked at Zeli with great fondness. "This is truly a miracle."

Zeli shook her head. "Not a miracle. All who have lost their Songs can have them restored. Not just me."

A chorus of disbelief rose as people broke into side conversations. There were questions, many questions, about the manner in which the Songs had been restored and what type of sacrifice would be necessary to ensure all Lagrimari would be affected. Few could wrap their minds around the idea of giving up fear.

Darvyn marveled at how calm Zeli remained, barraged by the group, and not everyone polite. She explained the concepts over and over again with a gentle patience Darvyn could never hope to master.

"We don't know exactly what the sacrifice should be or if it is individual or collective," she was saying, perhaps for the third time. "Should everyone make the same sacrifice or can they be different? None of us know yet. It is something we need to find out."

"Why don't we know?" someone asked.

Zeli pursed her lips. "When the Godd—when *Oola* and Queen Jasminda created the caldera, the king stone, they did not do so with any intent for the Songs to be released. In the heat of the moment, with the True Father ready to steal Oola's Song again, they acted only to remove the stolen Songs from him and render him powerless. Usually, calderas are created with a method for unlocking them. As this one was not, the task is harder. But the presence of my Song restored is proof that it is not impossible. We need your help to spread the word. The more who know about the sacrifice, the better it will be when I find the obelisk. Then I'll be able to do the spell, but it will only be successful with the aid and cooperation of the people."

Darvyn nodded. "And we will also need your help with the existing Singers, convincing them to go to the storm shelters around the city and help the non-Singers and the Elsirans during the next attack."

Mutters of discontent were a soft roar around the room.

"Our Singers are happy to help those who have lost their Songs," Talida said, "but why should any of us give aid to the Elsirans?"

"And who says the Elsirans even want the help?" Lyngar snarled.

"There will be those who won't accept our offer," Darvyn admitted. "But protecting them is good for us all. If there are fewer wraiths attacking, then all of us are safer."

Reluctant noises of agreement sounded. Darvyn slowly met the gazes of everyone present. "We've been fighting the True Father for hundreds of years. This could well be the final battle. We have tools and the beginning of a plan, but we need your assistance to put it all into practice."

A lump rose in his throat as quiet descended. He and Zeli had made their case, now it was up to the Keepers. One of the few men unfamiliar to Darvyn stood, drawing his attention. He, like the three others with him, looked to be in his early thirties and was unshaven with unruly hair. "I have no qualms protecting Lagrimari from the True Father and his unholy army. But I'll not waste my Song on any Elsiran pigs."

Darvyn's jaw clenched. "And who are you?"

The man narrowed his eyes. Aggar rushed to stand. "It doesn't matter. Our Singers will decide if they want to help or not. We will not make them if they choose no."

"Many of our Singers are children," Darvyn said. "They'll need guidance on what to do. They look up to the Keepers, the ones who have been instrumental in feeding and clothing and educating them both here and in Lagrimar. You all can make a strong case if you choose to. The people will listen."

Aggar crossed his arms combatively and Talida turned away, dismissing him. Darvyn's blood began to steam and he tried to take solace from Zeli's calm energy.

"We will discuss this further," Turwig said, coming up behind Darvyn with Rozyl on his heels.

With a motion of his head, Darvyn pulled them both aside. "Who are they?" he asked, jerking his head toward the four rough-looking men he couldn't recall ever meeting before.

Rozyl gritted her teeth. "Let's go outside." The four of them stepped into the weedy garden, and Rozyl waited until the glass door was completely shut before answering.

"Those four are emissaries of the Sons of Lagrimar."

Darvyn reared back as if struck. "The terrorists? What? Why?"

"They used to be Keepers in the eastern mountains helping the miners. We'd lost track of them," Turwig said ruefully. "It's been over a year since any have checked in. We thought they might have been discovered working against the True Father and killed, but then after the Mantle fell they reappeared. And as you know, they were not pleased by our reception in Elsira."

He took a deep breath. "They came to us a few days ago, requesting a meeting. The elders voted to grant it to them."

Darvyn shook his head and Rozyl shrugged. "There's . . . guilt among the Keepers," she said, "where they're concerned. Someone should have been sent after them to check on them. No one ever was."

Turwig's gaze went to the ground. "Things sometimes slipped through the cracks," he said softly.

"Do the elders approve of their tactics? The attacks against Elsirans aren't ingratiating us here," Darvyn said.

Rozyl raised a brow. "Neither did being good, polite little refugees."

Darvyn stared at her incredulously. She raised a hand. "I don't approve of their tactics, either, but don't act like they turned a receptive country against us. At a certain point, we do have to defend ourselves."

"They used to be one of us. So did you." While Turwig's gaze couldn't be considered accusatory, it was piercing nonetheless.

"Yes, and there's many reasons I'm not anymore," Darvyn said. "This type of thing is one of them. The very act of hearing them out is a betrayal."

"There are some who would say that suggesting we put ourselves at risk to help Elsirans is one as well," Rozyl hissed. "We're in uncharted territory and we need to consider every option. We're desperate. You know how that feels."

Zeli shifted, catching his eye with her steady gaze. It was almost as if she'd used Earthsong on him, the building rage that felt like a brewing storm inside him subsided. He took a deep breath. "What do they want?"

"A seat at the table," Turwig said. "They feel they've proven their loyalty to our people with their attacks. They want a voice in leadership."

Darvyn ran his hands through his hair and looked at the gray sky, muttering a string of curses.

Rozyl sighed heavily. "There are many sympathetic ears among the elders. We think we'll be outvoted and they'll be given what they want." She and Turwig shared a significant glance.

Through the glass wall, the others in the sitting room were engaged in vigorous debate. Darvyn wished he'd never come. Should he tell Jasminda and Jack of this new development? Did they need one more thing to worry about on top of everything else?

He blew out a breath.

"They'll be gone by the time you get back to the palace," Rozyl said. "I thought about telling her, too, but . . ."

"But what?"

"But after the vote tomorrow, we might not even be under her rule anymore."

Darvyn shook his head. "You think the referendum will pass? You really think the Elsirans will eject us from the country?"

Rozyl's dark gaze bored into him. "It's not just the Elsirans who are voting for separation."

The first drops of rain fell then, splashing onto Darvyn's face—tears from the sky in place of his own.

CHAPTER FORTY

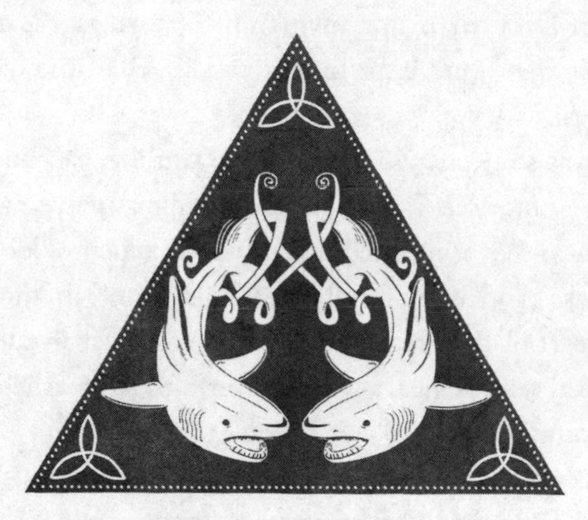

Teach children how to build a wall
to keep their legacies secure
let brick and mortar join to form protection.
Then enemies and friends and foes and
family with ceaseless woes can
battle the ensuing isolation.

—THE HARMONY OF BEING

Zeli returned to the palace from the trip to the Keepers' new headquarters feeling like a tick ready to burst. Darvyn had asked her to let him inform the king and queen about the presence of the Sons of Lagrimar and she'd readily agreed. She certainly didn't want to bring news like that to the monarchs. Darvyn was actually friends with them, let him handle that conversation.

He'd been especially tight-lipped on the drive back, obviously struggling with the revelation. What must it be like to be the Shadowfox, to have worked so hard for the liberation of his people only to be stabbed in the back by those he trusted? Varten had told her some of Darvyn's history, which he in turn had learned from Kyara while they were imprisoned, passing the time with stories of their lives.

Kyara was someone Zeli wished she could get to know better. Tales of the notorious Poison Flame had been passed around for so long that discovering the woman wasn't much older than Zeli was a shock. And now learning that the same infamous figure held the heart of the greatest Earthsinger to ever live left Zeli in awe. The ways of the heart were mysterious; she wished someone could explain them to her.

When she entered the Blue Library, her own heart stammered at finding Varten there, his ginger head bent over a scroll of some kind. She'd been hoping to see him—since their return to Rosira, there had been little time for them to talk and she missed him. She wasn't certain where they stood with one another and memories of dancing in the streets of Gilmer City—and all that had happened during the Rumpus—were a constant photoplay in her mind.

Varten was concentrating on what looked like architectural drawings when she approached. "Are you searching for the obelisk?"

He jumped, startled. A wave of something warm and intoxicating hit her as he turned. "You shouldn't go around sneaking up on people," he said with mock affront.

"I didn't sneak up on you. I walked normally across the room, you just didn't notice."

He narrowed his eyes playfully then looked back to the drawings. "These aren't much help. The only blueprints on file are of the additions made to the palace over the past hundred years. They don't show the older parts of the building, see how all of this is shaded in gray?" He pointed to large sections of the plans with no detail in them whatsoever. "I've spoken to the palace steward and he said this is all they have." Zeli sat next to him, leaning over to study the rendering.

"Has Yllis said anything more about the obelisk?" he asked.

"No, just that it had been in a chamber in the heart of the palace. But there have been so many additions and renovations, he hasn't been able to get his bearings." She traced her finger across the page. The Elsiran writing was printed in neat blocks, but she saw nothing here that could help them.

"Can he sense the obelisk with Earthsong?" Varten's voice was very close to her ear. She realized that she'd leaned far into his personal space and froze. Their arms were touching and she hesitated to lose the contact.

"He doesn't have his Song, he gave it to Oola to awaken Her, remember? And no one else would even know what to look for." From the corner of her eye she registered his surprise. She really should sit back, but didn't dare move.

"Oh, I didn't realize," Varten said, apparently unaffected by the small point of contact. "So if—when you restore everyone's Song, he won't get his back?"

She struggled to follow his logic and with great effort pulled away to sit all the way back in the chair. "No, Yllis won't get his Song back unless Oola does something—shares with him maybe. I don't know exactly how it would work since he's technically a wraith."

He twisted to face her. "Mooriah still has her Nethersong—oh, but she never gave it away." He shrugged and they settled into silence.

His fingers drummed on the surface of the table as he stared into the distance. She wanted to reach for him and hold his hand, but wasn't sure if she had the right. Or if he would welcome the contact.

"Is something . . . wrong?" She winced. "I mean, something new?"

His fingers stopped their movement and his posture stiffened. "It's the vote tomorrow. If the referendum passes, what does that mean for . . . the people I care about? Will Papa have to leave?" He paused, then looked at her from the corner of his eye. "Will you?"

She did grab his hand then and squeezed it with both of hers. "I don't know what will happen. Would you be willing to live in a land full of Lagrimari?" Her voice was light, but her heart was heavy.

He squeezed her back. "If you were there, yes."

She swallowed and smiled, looking down. He slid his fingers down her wrist, pressing gently as if feeling her pulse. Her heart was racing a bit.

Varten cleared his throat. "Um, have you talked to the Goddess? She must know where the obelisk is."

"She's still missing. Nobody has seen Her in days."

"Maybe She's trying to find Her brother."

"I hope so," Zeli said, unable to hide her doubt. "But there's no way to know. We might just be on our own."

"Again," he whispered. "Maybe we should try to create our own drawings of the old section of the palace. We can go from room to room and measure and recreate all the missing parts of the plans. The obelisk could have been walled up during one of the renovations by people who didn't understand what it was."

Zeli beamed at him, a slow smile spreading across her face. "That's a good idea."

He shrugged and tapped his lips with the fingers of his free hand. She tightened her grip on him. "You have good ideas, Varten, it's okay to trust them." He ducked his head, for some reason unable to accept the praise.

"Want to start now?" she asked, letting him off the hook. He smiled gratefully.

Within minutes, he had found a sketchpad and acquired measuring tape from the palace steward. He and Zeli started where the detailed blueprints ended, evaluating the rooms in the original section of the building, making measurements, taking notes, sketching walls and doors. They worked for hours, Zeli testing her new lock-picking skills to enter unused rooms full of dusty, covered furniture.

As Varten continued to add to his sketchpad, he frowned. "Something is strange here."

"What is it?" Zeli let the measuring tape slide back into its case with a snap.

"There's a gap." He led them from a room bearing only a long dining table covered in a white cloth back into the hallway. They were in the same corridor where their secret parlor was located.

"This hallway is two hundred and fifty paces long. But the rooms inside only add up to two hundred and eighteen paces. And that's accounting for the width of the walls."

They stepped back into what might have long ago been a small dining room. The narrow chamber featured a marble floor and walls with no windows. But none of the rooms in this section had any windows.

"So there are thirty-two paces missing," she mused. "That's too big for a closet."

"Big enough for an obelisk?"

They stared at each other for a long beat before rushing back into the hallway. The next twenty minutes were spent remeasuring and checking the sketches until they'd located the missing space.

A wall stretched between two doors, papered in a faded damask pattern that looked gray but could have been red many years ago. Zeli ran her hand across it feeling the smooth, even surface.

"If there's a room behind here, there must have been a door at some point," she said.

Varten drummed his fingers against his thigh, scanning where the floor met the wall and doing the same for the ceiling. He ran a finger under a curling strip of paper that had lifted away from the molding along the floor. After he gave a tug, it ripped from the wall, revealing cracked plaster.

Zeli stayed watchful; though they hadn't yet encountered another soul in this corridor, she didn't imagine the palace staff would take too kindly to this sort of defacement. Varten continued peeling away strips of paper, which came away easily. Beneath the wallpaper, water damage from an old leak had left a brown stain. Other than that, the plaster revealed nothing—no obvious doorways that had been covered over.

"We'll need a hammer," Varten said, wiping dusty hands on his trousers.

"Wait, let me try." Zeli closed her eyes and drew in Earthsong to fill her Song. She couldn't help but smile at the sensation of life energy flooding her. On a deep breath, she focused a concentrated blast of air and pummeled it into the plaster. The wall cracked and then shattered, raining bits and pieces of gypsum all over them. Too late she realized that she could have directed it away from their bodies with a blast of air.

Her chest felt heavy from the exertion and the feeling of euphoria faded away. Her Song was already drained, just from that simple action. She wasn't a strong Singer, and still very far from proficient after so many years without her Song, but she was still proud of herself.

Her blast had also cracked the old and rotting wooden lath strips, which lay horizontally behind the plaster. And behind that was a wall of stone.

She helped Varten clear away the wood, creating a large pile of rubbish from the castoffs. They moved faster once the rounded corner of a stone archway came into view. Soon an entire bricked-up stone entryway was visible. Carved into the top stone of the arch was an inscription written in a script similar to that of Yllis's journal, but Zeli couldn't read it.

"This is more like modern Elsiran," Varten murmured. "Must be from when the languages started to diverge."

"What does it say?"

"'Keep the secrets. Spread the lies. Remember the truths.'"

Zeli frowned. "Strange. I wonder what that means."

"And who put it here?" Varten shook his head as they considered both their progress and this new impediment. The bricks had obviously been added many years after the original stone entry had been constructed.

They'd need a chisel to get through it and maybe a few strong workers. Or Earthsong. Zeli's power was depleted, likely for the rest of the day, but there were others who could help.

"Do you think the obelisk is behind here?" Varten whispered.

"It must be," Zeli replied, allowing herself to hope.

CHAPTER FORTY-ONE

Hidden places still need light.
Make sure your secrets get the
brightness of the
sun
to occasionally
subdue the melancholy.

—THE HARMONY OF BEING

Ella Farmafield kept a tight hold of her daughter Ulani's hand as they wound their way through the stalls of the night market. The little puppy, Raven, trotted along at their heels, tongue hanging out. Benn wasn't too far behind with Tana; they had stopped at a trinket stand, where the girl was picking out another sparkly bracelet that Benn would no doubt buy her. He couldn't deny either of the girls anything—case in point, the puppy of mysterious origin that now lived in their home. Luckily, the creature had been created already housebroken and was not prone to chewing. And he was fiercely protective of the girls, which Benn appreciated.

Ella found her husband's indulgence of the children sweet, but was wary of the nightmare of raising children spoiled rotten by their father. Though that seemed an unlikely outcome—neither child asked for very much, and the likelihood of them truly becoming spoiled was slim. If her eldest daughter wanted a case full of inexpensive costume jewelry, it would probably do little harm.

Ulani tugged at her hand and Ella realized she hadn't been paying attention and had inadvertently led them toward a street corner where three Elsiran women held a silent protest. No, it was actually two women and one mannequin clad in Sisterhood robes with scraps of cloth tied over its eyes and mouth.

The Sisterhood had been in upheaval since the revelation that the Goddess had hidden the True Father's escape. It hadn't even been common knowledge that the two were related, much less siblings, much less twins. Many didn't believe it, calling the reports lies, but there were plenty who did and were disgusted by the news. Temple attendance had plummeted and more and more Sisters were taking part in these silent protests.

One of their vows upon joining the order included a prohibition on speaking against the group, and so they made their displeasure known silently. Just that morning, Ella had read in the newspaper that the High Priestess was still urging patience, stating that the Goddess would return and explain Her actions and in the meantime, all believers needed to band together in prayer during this time of need. But how long were they expected to wait?

Ulani was particularly sensitive to criticism of the Goddess, and so Ella veered them away, crossing the street, closed to traffic for the market, to avoid the women. Except on this corner a small group of young men had gathered, and silence was in no way required of them.

"Free Zann Biddel! Free Zann Biddel!" The shouts were largely drowned out by the noise of the crowds doing their shopping. But it wasn't their words so much as the props they held that made Ella grow tense.

Instead of picket signs with slogans painted on them, these men carried the symbols of Elsira—carved wooden fishes as long as their forearms and tree branches representing the tree and the fish of the nation's seal. And if those branches and heavy wooden carvings looked an awful lot like weapons, well . . . she wasn't the only one who'd noticed.

Most shoppers gave both groups of protesters a wide berth, which made the already crowded streets even more so. And this was the last night market of the year—the temperature had dropped over the past few days—winter was here.

Raven yipped, feeling either Ulani's tension or her own and Ella turned away.

"Miss Ella!" a voice called out. She grinned to find one of her customers hurrying toward her.

"Berta!" she exclaimed, wrapping the woman in a hug when she reached her. "How are you? How's the baby?"

"Wearing me out, as usual. A bit colicky, I'm sad to say, but it's to be expected. The others all were, too." The round-faced woman was several years older than Ella and had recently had her third child. "And who is this?" she asked, beaming down at Ulani.

"Benn and I have adopted, this is Ulani and her sister there is Tana."

Berta smiled. "So precious, and quite a change for you, isn't it?"

"You have no idea." Ella knew that becoming a mother would bring trials and tribulations, but living in an underground cave for a week while an ancient shaman taught her daughter to use her death magic had not once figured into her plans. Of course, she didn't mention any of that to Berta.

"And this vote, how will it affect your family?" Berta's question had been heavy on Ella's mind ever since the vote was announced.

"I wish I knew. I can't even vote, not until my citizenship comes through, but Benn cast his today—for unification, of course."

Berta nodded. "It won't affect us too much as foreigners, but I do hope the thing passes. Every day going back home to Fremia looks more and more appealing." She shook her head.

Ella understood. She hadn't thought of returning to her native country of Yaly as a real possibility, but Benn had brought it up the night before. If the vote passed and life for their blended family became difficult in Elsira, they had to keep all options on the table.

"Well, the polls just closed a few minutes ago," she said. "We'll get the results by morning and will be able to figure things out then."

"Mama, can I have a candy?" Ulani asked, tugging at the hand she held.

"I'd better get on," Berta said. "Best of luck to you and your family."

"You as well," Ella said and the woman rushed away. "Now, what kind of candy has caught your eye, little one?"

Ulani grinned and pointed to where a group of children had gathered next to a stall selling an assortment of treats. The girls' friend Iddo was there with two handfuls of candy that he was trying not to let fall, and that she was almost entirely certain he hadn't paid for. Ella rushed forward, either to scold or assist him, she hadn't decided yet, when a high-pitched wail penetrated the noise of the crowd.

Almost as if they'd rehearsed it, everyone in the market froze. And then the already busy streets turned to chaos.

A loudspeaker bolted atop a streetlight crackled to life. "This is not a drill. Head quickly and calmly to the nearest emergency shelter. I repeat, this is not a drill. Head quickly and calmly to the nearest emergency shelter."

The message repeated itself and people around her took off at a run. One of the children asked around a mouthful of candy, "What's happening?"

"It's the attack alarm!" Ella shouted over the din. "Follow me!"

Iddo grabbed a younger boy's hand and the group of kids followed Ella and Ulani down the street, struggling not to be trampled upon. Raven managed to keep up, moving at a quick trot; at first they lost Benn and Tana in the press—but then they were there, Benn holding his older daughter in his arms as he fought his way through panicking people.

The neighborhood shelter was in the basement of a local theater. Ella picked up Ulani and quickened her pace, mindful of the others behind her. They reached the theater's side door, which stood ajar. Ella wrenched it all the way open and started down the steps. Children filed in beside her and she set Ulani down. She didn't see Benn or Tana and realized they were still outside on the sidewalk.

"Stay here," she told Ulani, whose wide eyes were fearful. Ella raced up the steps.

"I can't go down there," Tana was saying. "I need to help." Benn pursed his lips.

"There are only three of us," Tana continued. "I can't hide down there, I need to fight the wraiths."

The war on Benn's face was heart-wrenching. He was a soldier, he'd signed up to put himself in danger and was in a unique position to understand Tana's plight. But just the thought of their eleven-year-old daughter in a battle of any kind still made Ella weak.

"They can't harm her," she whispered.

"And even if they could, I—" Tana's voice wavered. She held her father's hand. "I control death."

All around them people ran for cover, terrified of the imminent attack. A few came to the shelter, mostly non-Elsirans though. Ella noted them as they hurried down the steps to the promised safety.

Benn still hadn't spoken, he and Tana were locked in a silent argument. Ella placed her hand on his broad back. She was worried, too, but she'd seen what Nethersong could do. Benn hadn't.

"I'll come with you," he said, finally.

Tana shook her head. "Please stay here so I don't have to worry about you," she pleaded. "Ulani will protect everyone down there."

Benn's face was set, and Ella was afraid that he wasn't going to be reasonable about this. Then again, was it reasonable to let a child face down an army of angry spirits led by a five-hundred-year-old king?

"I've got her," a voice called out, running up to them. Kyara was there, breathless. "I promise, nothing will happen to her."

She spoke in Lagrimari and Ella translated. Benn's brow was still furrowed, but at the sight of Kyara he finally nodded. "All right. All right."

Tana wrapped him in a fierce hug, which he returned. The girl pulled away and hugged Ella, whispering in Lagrimari, "Make sure he's okay."

Ella stepped back and nodded, not even feeling the pang that usually hit her when Tana's preference for Benn over her became clear. The two had shared a bond from the beginning that went both ways.

"We have to go," Kyara said, taking Tana's hand. The Nethersingers raced off into the rapidly emptying street together. Ella tried to guide her husband down the stairs. But he refused to move until Tana had disappeared around a corner.

Tears streamed down his face as she was finally able to lead him into the shelter—one that should have been much more full of people. "She will be all right," Ella whispered.

They shut the doors behind them and linked hands, with Ulani at the head of the chain, using her power to protect the rest. Screams and crashes sounded outside and Ella shook, praying to all the saints for strength and protection. And that her daughter was right and death couldn't touch her.

Wraiths poured from the opening in the sky. Though it was nighttime, their inky darkness was even blacker than the night. Kyara and Tana had stopped in a tiny patch of grass located at the intersections of two wide streets, just a couple of blocks from the rapidly emptying market.

Kyara dropped into her other sight and instructed Tana to do the same. They stood hand in hand as the darkness above them became flooded with the fluid forms of wraiths. The portal they emerged from shone bright with Nethersong; it led to the World After and an infinite number of spirits waiting there. A shiver rippled through Kyara as she considered the potential of the threat they faced.

In her pocket, the death stone's icy fire practically burned through the fabric of her trousers. Though the Breath Father's words had hit hard and she never intended to use it, she still kept it on her person at all times, knowing she needed to ensure the powerful caldera did not fall into the wrong hands. The current crisis was more than enough to handle without adding to it with a disaster of that magnitude.

"All right," she said, trying to keep her voice steady for Tana's sake. "This is as good a place as any to make a stand. Stay in your other sight, we should have enough range to handle a large section of Portside from here."

Splitting up may have been wiser, but she couldn't very well leave the girl on her own. The spirits raining down seemed to be focused on this neighborhood, so this is where they'd work to defend and she had no idea where Mooriah was. Tana squeezed Kyara's hand in response.

Spirits weren't stymied by walls or any material barriers; they shot through buildings with ease and some even went underground, seeking out the folks hiding in basements. Tana's family, huddled in one of the emergency shelters, came to mind. The Singers who'd agreed to help had been told to stay close to their assigned locations—hopefully they were doing their jobs, she and Tana must do theirs as well.

Trying to be as methodical as possible, Kyara searched the area around her in sections, ejecting the spirits from the hosts they'd taken over. One after another she forced them out, the knowledge that they would just seek out another living body scraping at her.

Many of the wraiths seemed to be converging in one location. "Do you see that, there?" she asked Tana. "About ten blocks down."

"Yes, why are so many of them focused on that building? What is it?"

"I don't know. But we should go see."

They raced down the now-empty street as rumbles and crashes of devastation clamored around them. The wraiths appeared to be focused on causing as much destruction as possible. They were using their superior strength to punch holes in walls, shatter glass, and overturn vehicles. But as Kyara and Tana ran, the wraiths they encountered and dispelled were focused on the power lines.

The two Nethersingers drew closer to the building that so many of the dead had congregated around. She couldn't read the Elsiran words written in bold, block letters, but the logo on the sign displayed a pipe and a drop of water. This must be some sort of water facility. She settled back into her other sight and got to work expelling spirits from bodies.

The Elsiran capital was completely wired for electricity and every place she'd been in the country had running water. It looked like the True Father was targeting his army's attack on the utilities. Elsirans long used to the luxuries would find life difficult indeed if he succeeded.

Though she and Tana were doing their best, they were only making a dent in the number of wraiths running up to the building and tearing it apart with their bare hands. The heavy doors leading inside had not yet been breached, but it was only a matter of minutes.

More than one spirit tried to target them, but the Nethersingers were easily able to deflect the shades with their power. Tana was beginning to wobble on her feet though, the exertion getting to her. Kyara shot out a hand to steady her as more wraiths flowed from the portal. Unsure how much longer Tana could keep this up, Kyara began to get worried.

The sound of a vehicle roared behind them. She chanced a glance backward to find a large truck pull to a stop. A dozen Raunian men and women piled out armed with batons. Each also bore large packs on their backs. They leaped into the battle, knocking out wraiths with the batons—nonlethal weapons, Kyara noted, though the hosts would feel the effects of the blows when and if they returned.

Roshon's fiancée, Ani, was among them. The young woman gleefully rained pain down upon the heads of the wraiths—even one-handed she was fearsome. She yelled a string of words at Kyara, who shook her head, not understanding.

Then Ani pulled out something from her pack. It was a square of dark fabric, cut in a long rectangle as tall as she was, and made of something like mud cloth or waxed canvas. Ani yelled again and Tana translated. "The wraiths can't get through the cloth. Force the spirits out and her people will cover the bodies."

The fabric must be coated in whatever that substance was that gave the Raunians their immunity. In Kyara's other sight, the sheets of fabric were invisible—pockets of emptiness amidst so much death energy.

"All right," she responded. "Why don't I push the spirits out and you tell the Raunians which bodies to cover?"

Tana nodded her agreement and began speaking in halting Elsiran to Ani. The next few minutes blurred as Kyara drove out the spirits, while the Raunians continued fighting hand-to-hand as well as gathering spirit-free bodies together to cover and protect. An Earthsinger would be needed to revive them and heal their injuries. She caught glimpses of bloodied hands and some limbs twisted into painful positions before the dark cloth covered them from sight.

Even with the aid of the Raunians, the wraiths had breached the outer door and walls of the station and were rushing in, no doubt causing all manner of destruction.

Streetlights and the lights inside of nearby buildings winked out—either the power lines or the electricity generator must have also been damaged. The strategy was a good one and would leave the city paralyzed for days or weeks to come.

Tana was holding up, but just barely, looking drunk on her feet as she pointed out body after body to the Raunians, and continued to expel some spirits. Kyara felt little better. She'd never thought her Song could be drained like an Earthsinger's could be, though every minute she felt on the edge of burnout. Depletion wasn't a real risk as there was plenty of death energy around in a city—and sadly, some of the former wraith hosts were among that number. Many had already died, and an Earthsinger would be needed sooner rather than later before the others succumbed to their wounds.

Once she realized that the freed hosts were still at risk of death, Kyara began to pull Nether from them. This boosted her Song, but did not help her flailing energy. Her focus was fractured between jettisoning spirits from bodies and pulling Nethersong from the dying to keep them on the cusp of life until help could come. She was afraid she was going to unravel if this lasted much longer.

Pulled taut, nerves frayed, and senses bleary, gasps from those around her dragged her attention away from the carnage. She shuttered her other sight and followed the gazes of the others, tilting her head back to watch the night sky—now illuminated by a figure practically glowing from within.

Her first thought was that Fenix had returned, but then her gaze focused and she made out Oola, hovering not far from the portal. The flow of wraiths had stopped, thank the seeds, and the Goddess Awoken peered into the tear in their world.

From this distance, Kyara couldn't make out the woman's expression, but She tilted Her head back and forth as if examining the portal. Then, as if responding to a silent signal, the spirits began to flee their hosts on their own, racing back to the portal, passing Oola in a whoosh of thick, black smoke.

Still staring up, Kyara felt the energy drain from her. Her Nethersong was not depleted, but her human body was. She collapsed in a heap, and the last thing she remembered was the glowing woman lit against a dark sky.

CHAPTER FORTY-TWO

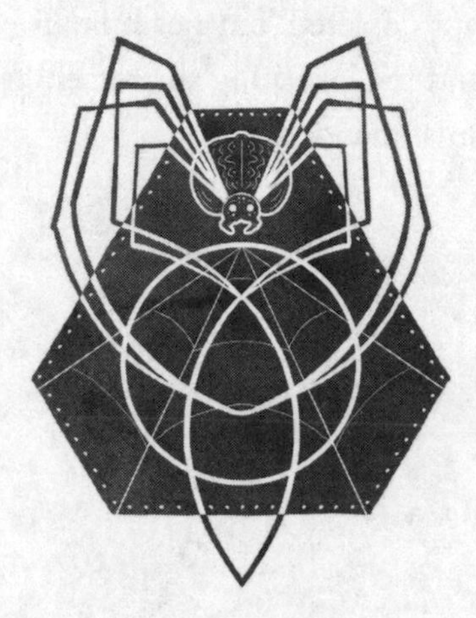

Charity given for personal gain is a
nightmare striking in the middle of the day.
A waking horror best left to be met
again in sleep.

—THE HARMONY OF BEING

Your body deflates as you close the viewing portal showing the streets of Rosira. Behind you, Nikora and Cayro breathe loudly, panting like possums, leaving hot breath on your neck. You have half a mind to silence them forever. Daydreams of tearing the life away from their flaccid bags of flesh bring a smile to your face. After the triumph witnessed through the portal, you fear your face may split.

"Why did you stop the attack?" Nikora demands.

You turn toward her. Having her at your back in the first place was foolish. "Strategy."

She narrows her eyes and grins slyly. "Are you certain you were not stymied by the arrival of your sister?"

Your lips snap shut, annoyance clawing at you. She is just grasping at straws, she has no idea of what she speaks. "My sister is of no concern. It is better to leave them fumbling and badly damaged. I have proven that a larger attack will yield consequences. Our final strike will give us what we want."

"Don't you mean give *you* what you want? While these blitzes are entertaining, you promised me that your use of Dahlia's precious flesh would be for more than pursuing a petty grievance."

You flinch at the use of the term "petty." There is nothing petty about your need for revenge and supremacy, but listing several lifetimes' worth of injustice perpetrated by the Elsirans is not a productive use of time.

"I shall not allow this to continue," Nikora says. "You've proven control of the wraiths, and I have lost no further men. But how has this brought me closer to *my* goal? I have given—" A commotion at the door interrupts her diatribe.

A servant enters with one of the Wailers behind him, the man's blank face slack and addlepated. His hands clutch a length of chain. Two silent, vacant-eyed wraiths shuffle behind him, hands and feet shackled by the chain. They are meek as babes, which is exactly how you've instructed them to be. Nikora's eyes widen.

"So you see," you say proudly. "I have provided you with not one but two docile spirits to question. Ask them whatever you wish, if you think they will answer." You mumble the last under your breath.

Cayro's lips curl in disgust, but Nikora's eyes shine with glee.

That should keep the both of them busy for at least a little while. "I will begin questioning them immediately," she says.

They leave to do exactly that, while you reflect on the battle. The presence of the Nethersingers was certainly unexpected. As was the resistance from the Raunian brutes. But neither group truly worries you. There are far more dead than living, after all.

After these exercises—proofs of concept really—you have finally mastered complete control over the spirits. The meager preparations and attempts at defense by the Elsirans and their allies might as well be a shield made of smoke. The sharp spear you wield will have no trouble slicing through such an insubstantial obstacle.

You will not be stopped. You hold the advantage over your sister, her people, and your so-called captors. Only one last piece to the puzzle is needed—Nikora's spell still binds you, and your manipulation of her can only go so far. She must be taken care of before you can enact your final plan.

Then you will return to your rightful home and deal with your wayward remaining family. You imagine the look on her face when she is forced to submit to your conquest. Your cheeks will soon hurt from smiling so hard.

Oola's face haunted Mooriah. She had never met her mother in person. She'd been cut from Her womb after the woman's spirit was already gone, trapped in the World Between after Eero's betrayal.

Her father, Yllis, had been solely focused on finding a way to bring Oola back. When he realized his daughter was a Nethersinger, he'd sent the baby off to live among the Cavefolk, where she couldn't accidentally murder anyone, and where both she and those around her were protected.

He'd come to visit, infrequently, and she'd gotten to know him after a fashion, but they had never been close. And then he'd gone off to fight her uncle Eero and never returned.

She hadn't known what to expect, seeing him again for the first time in five hundred years. That first glimpse she'd gotten in the meeting room when he'd arrived at the strategy meeting had been a shock. She'd been so agitated, she left quickly and had been avoiding him ever since, trying not to be in the places she thought he might be. As far as she knew, he hadn't sought her out, either, which assuaged any guilt she might have had about her actions. So the reunion, when it took place, occurred by chance.

She happened upon him in a palace corridor, she at one end, he at the other. Across the distance he looked the same—still almost a stranger, a man whose love she'd never been sure she had. A man who'd always seen her mother when he looked upon her.

His silver hair was unchanged, the thick coils gathered neatly at his nape and stretching down his back. The hair of an old man on an unlined face—ageless and as unemotional as ever, she'd wager. A wave of sadness and love swept her, freezing her in place. But just as quickly and volatilely came the anger. The abandonment. The betrayal.

He was a wraith, as she was, and a sliver of strange magic inside her recognized him as such. Muscles tense, pulse racing, caught in the red haze of rage, Mooriah lashed out. He'd always called her temper fiery, usually with an air of chastisement in his voice. She'd show him fiery.

A pulse of Nether blasted from within her, severing her father's connection to the body he inhabited. It crumpled to the floor, the Void taking over, while his spirit form hovered in the air above it.

Her fury now satiated, remorse crept in. Yllis's spirit circled the body once, then twice, as if waiting for something, then dove back in. She didn't even get a good look at the poor man acting as the unwitting host.

But a realization struck her that her Song, eager as it had been to cause mischief, had not been the source of the outburst. Wraith magic had expelled her father. Wraiths—even if they weren't Nethersingers—could force out other wraiths. She had not realized that before and tucked it away for the future.

The still body transformed, taking on her father's face and form before rising. She was too far away to see his expression. She considered turning around, escaping down the hall in the opposite direction, but she was no coward. Her emotions were quiet now, and she supposed she owed him an apology for her outburst. Still, she remained motionless until he took a step toward her. Then they both moved forward, stopping an arm's length apart.

"Father." She cleared her throat. "I apologize. That was not well done of me."

He grunted. She supposed that was all the acknowledgement she would get. "Why did you not go into the Flame, my daughter?" His voice was both familiar and strange.

She swallowed, tucking away her disappointment. This was the first thing he wanted to know? "I had no desire to have my soul stripped clean, to be recycled into some other life. I had a reason to retain my memories. The prophecy—Murmur never came out and told me that I should avoid the Flame, but he'd hinted that I would be needed again. And he was right."

In the World After, spirits were meant to join the Eternal Flame. They could stay out of it for a time, getting glimpses into the Living World and saying their silent good-byes to their loved ones and the lives they'd once had, but the Flame was a constant lure.

Resisting it had been difficult, often painful, but she'd had a purpose. And she'd carried it out.

Yllis sighed deeply. "I suppose it only makes sense that our family be here to see this through, we did start it after all."

Mooriah didn't start anything—she had not asked to be born a Nethersinger—but she kept that thought to herself. Instead she said, "Have you seen Her?"

A well of pain opened inside his eyes. "No," he whispered.

"She must know we're both here."

"She knows. She has Her own reasons for ignoring us."

After all the time her father had spent searching for her mother, now they were finally in the same place and it was Oola who'd disappeared. "You must have some idea where She is."

He blinked slowly before meeting her gaze. He did not voice his agreement, but she saw the truth there.

"So you are avoiding Her, too?" Mooriah shook her head. "It's time. I need to meet Her."

She thought he might deny her, but instead, he surprised her by reaching for her hand. He had never been demonstrative, never been the type of father who hugged or kissed. The rough feel of his palm was novel, callused and scarred from many blood spells. Hers were the same.

Hand in hand, father and daughter left the building. There might have been a hundred eyes on them but Mooriah didn't notice. They crossed a garden, the dying grass crisp beneath their feet. Behind the palace rose a rocky ridge, the peak of the ancient volcano on which Rosira had been built.

"How do you know where She is?" she asked.

"I can feel Her. I've always been able to, we are connected."

Her shoulders sank. She'd never had reason to hate her Nethersong the way others had, but there were times like these when she wondered what Earthsong would be like.

Yllis squeezed her hand. "It isn't Earthsong that binds us, it is something deeper. If you search yourself, you'll realize that you can feel Her, too. She's inside of us."

Mooriah wasn't convinced. They climbed the rocks, which only rose a short distance above their heads. There was no true path, but she did sense something familiar in the route they took. The sensation pulsed within, though she'd never been here before.

They turned a corner and could go no farther. Before them, seated upon a boulder, looking out toward the sea, was her mother, the Goddess Awoken.

Oola rose slowly, so slowly, and turned to face them. Her face was expressionless. Dark eyes glimmered and Her white dress fluttered in a gust of wind. The shapes of their faces were similar. Mooriah saw pieces of herself in her mother, but the woman was a stranger.

No one spoke for a long time. Mooriah could not think of what to say, she just stared at this cold woman before her. Oola's gaze went from Mooriah to Yllis, back and forth until, finally, tears spilled down Her cheeks. The sudden and unexpected display of emotion caused the dam inside of Mooriah to crack. Her feelings broke through the protective barrier she'd had in place for so long and her body doubled over on a sob.

She tried in vain to hold it back, shaking and heaving, clutching her arms around her. Her father's hand rubbed her back for a moment and then she was wrapped in warmth. Strong arms squeezed her and the scent of jasmine and electricity enveloped her.

"Don't cry, my daughter," her mother whispered. "There will be time for crying later."

Mooriah wasn't sure that was true. Her heart was so full and so empty at the same time. She couldn't put into words what she was feeling. Duty and love and pain and abandonment warred inside of her.

Her mother pulled back and cupped Mooriah's cheeks in Her palms. Her father's steady hand still ran slow circles on her back.

"Mama," Mooriah whispered. And then her mother smiled.

CHAPTER FORTY-THREE

We are not as predictable as leaves, falling from
trees in seasons prescribed by the spinning of
orbs that chase the sun.
We revolve around timelines individual
made original
and unimaginable. For they cannot be foretold,
only forewarned.

—THE HARMONY OF BEING

"Order a recount."

Jack closed his eyes slowly as his wife's voice grew more frantic. He couldn't stand to see the disappointment and sorrow on her face. The only thing he could give her was bad news and he hated to be the one to do so.

"Sixty-seven percent," he stated simply. "A recount will not change those numbers. Sixty-seven percent of the Lagrimari voted for separation." He heard a thump and opened his eyes to find that she'd fallen into the armchair in front of the fireplace.

"More Lagrimari voted for separation than Elsirans," she whispered into the flames.

"A good deal more." He set the vote results down on the desk and stalked toward her. Only 56 percent of Elsirans had favored separation.

"You and Nadette and your team, you all made a big difference."

"If only we would have known that the Elsirans weren't the biggest problem," she said wryly, slumping farther into the seat. "I just don't understand." She looked up at him with an expression of pure confusion and sorrow.

Jack wiped a hand down his face. "I wish I could say something that would make it clear, but I don't understand myself."

He braced his hands on the mantel and breathed deeply. There would be no unification. The people had spoken. Now they just had to figure out how to handle things going forward.

"We will still offer a path to citizenship for the Lagrimari, just like we do for people from other countries," he offered. It was currently a long and expensive one, but they had been working on easing the process. This was just more incentive to do so. "With such a high percentage of Elsirans voting against the separation, we may be able to get the Council to approve some kind of measure granting rights for any Lagrimari who want to stay."

It was sure to be an uphill battle for their insular nation though. Jack thought of his father-in-law, Dansig, of Benn and his daughters, of others who had adopted Lagrimari orphans and whose families were now in a strange sort of limbo. How many would even want to stay here? Jasminda's expression hadn't changed and Jack's heart cracked at not being able to offer anything more.

A knock at the door sounded. It had been like this for the past twelve hours—ever since the attack. Messengers from around the city delivering updates on everything from the vote to the casualties to the damage incurred. The polls had closed before the attack and it was luck—or maybe a lack of luck—that none of the counting stations had been targeted by the True Father.

No, the worst of the damage had been to the utilities, running water and electricity were now in short supply across the city. Repair crews were hard at work, but it would be quite some time before things were back to normal.

Jack opened the door and accepted a stack of reports from the teenage page. The young man bowed before turning and running off.

"What now?" Jasminda asked when Jack returned to his desk.

He set down the mass of papers and began sifting through them. "Engineering reports. Initial repair estimates. Minister Stevenot wants a meeting at the top of the hour to share what the Department of the Interior has so far."

She was silent for a while as he flipped through the rest of the pages, making quick assessments about what needed immediate attention and what could wait.

Finally, her voice broke through the silence. "Why do you think he stopped, last night? The True Father."

Jack dropped the report in his hand and faced her. "Kyara said the attack ended just after Oola appeared. Maybe She did something to stop it?"

Jasminda's brow furrowed. "You don't think . . . Oola couldn't be working with him, could She?"

Jack shook his head. "To what end? I know She's often had a blind spot when it comes to Her twin, but he's working to destroy us. She always has Her own agenda, but I don't believe it's our destruction."

Jasminda pursed her lips.

"I don't know if I'll ever forgive Her for letting you die in order to test Kyara," he added, "but this army? This destruction? What does She gain from it?"

Jasminda shook her head and crossed her arms, shivering. "Where has She been and where did She go after the attack? I wish She was here if only to answer some questions." With a heavy sigh, she pushed up from the chair to approach the desk. "Do you have the report about the shelter usage?"

"Somewhere in this stack," he muttered, flipping through folders until he found it and handed it over. Hopefully, all the work ahead would take the sting off of the referendum results, but Jack wasn't optimistic.

She settled into the chair, scanning the pages of the report. "Shelters were, on average, at less than thirty percent capacity. So sixty-four percent of Elsirans want to have Lagrimari around, but not too close, I guess. And they don't want to trust Earthsingers with their safety."

"To be fair, we didn't have a lot of time to deliver the message about the shelters," Jack said.

"Now that the power is off in most of the city the radio is out, and the newspapers can't be printed." She tossed the papers down.

"What do you want to do?"

"I don't know." She shook her head. "I really don't know. I think—"

She looked down and then took another deep breath, as if

coming to a decision. "I think we need to do something drastic." Jack sat next to her, giving her all of his attention.

"Half the citizens want to burn the Goddess in effigy for hiding the True Father's escape. They don't trust us either and it's not only to their own detriment, but everyone else's. The more people the spirits overtake, the worse the attacks will be."

Jack nodded, urging her on. "You were right." She blew out a breath. "I was . . . I was blinded by my anger. My rage. Our voices aren't going to carry right now, but I know someone's who will."

Realization dawned, but he wasn't certain. "Who?"

Her teeth clenched. "Zann Biddell." It was obvious that she hated the conclusion she'd come to. "I'm wondering if he would be amenable to making a few announcements."

Jack spoke carefully. The issue of Biddell had already been a minefield between them. "You want him to convince people to go to the shelters?"

"Getting their attention will be hard, but he could do it."

"Do you think the Lagrimari will protest?"

She spread her arms. "We have no idea how the True Father is staging these attacks, no idea how many more there will be, or how much power he has left. He could have found a whole new energy source to fuel the amalgamations for all we know. Until we can find a way to stop him permanently, we need to limit his strength in some way and right now, reducing the number of potential hosts for his army is key. Our differences don't matter anymore, not in this situation."

Jack's fingers moved rapidly against his thighs as he thought. "Do you think Biddell will cooperate?"

"I don't know. Maybe we can appeal to his patriotism? It's in his best interest just like everyone else's to be protected from the spirits."

He leaned forward. “Do you want me to talk to him?”

She gave a barely there smile. “I made this mess. It should be me.”

“And what will you offer him? Freedom?”

The hint of a smile bled from her face. “If that’s what it takes. Unless we find a way to stop the True Father, nothing else really matters, does it?”

He reached for her hand and she met him halfway, gripping his fingers in hers. “We’re going to find a way,” he said. “We’re going to beat him once and for all and make a place that’s safe—a home—for everyone who wants one. If I do one thing with the life I have left, it will be that.”

She squeezed his hand harder and he repeated the vow to himself. It was almost like a prayer, though he had no deity left to pray to. Only his hope. Only his love.

CHAPTER FORTY-FOUR

Are destiny's ties binding or elastic?
Iron or plastic?
Will you run screaming from its bruising grip
or embrace its hold, enthusiastic?

—THE HARMONY OF BEING

Jasminda's feet, which were supposed to be taking her toward the dungeon, instead veered off. She found herself standing in front of Camm's and Ilysara's desks with no real recollection of how she'd gotten there. She blinked rapidly and avoided both of her assistants' curious gazes before ducking into her office.

Then she peeked her head back out. "I'd like to not be disturbed." Camm, seated closest to her, nodded, bemused.

Certainly she could spare a few minutes to gather her thoughts before heading down to the dungeon. She dreaded seeing Biddell's smug face, dreaded asking anything of him, but it was the right choice. He had proved his superior skill in wrangling the people and affecting their opinions. He would no doubt be able to do it again—that is, if he agreed.

She fell into her favorite armchair near the fireplace, the fire's crackling light bringing warmth to the drafty room. The consequences of her actions were coming back upon her. She still had no regrets about incarcerating Biddell, but there was a heavy price inherent in being a ruler. Give and take, and compromises, and pounds of flesh to be collected.

Before her on the coffee table, someone had spread out the day's newspapers. The headlines had not grown more complimentary, at least not where she was concerned. The vote results were emblazoned upon every front page. Her failure in large black print for the world to see. She sat back heavily in the chair and closed her eyes, breathing deeply.

The office door opened. She sighed dramatically, knowing that neither Camm nor Ilysara would have interrupted her had it not been extremely important. But the heft of the new presence began to weigh upon her. She opened her eyes to find Oola, Yllis, and Mooriah walking in together.

She sat up straight, blinking in surprise. They looked like a family, the resemblance clear now that they stood side by side before her. Loomed was more like it. Part of her wanted to stand and assert her meager authority, but what really was the point amongst these ancient people?

"To what do I owe this visit?"

"May we sit?" Yllis asked.

"I'm quite sure you may do what you like, but please." Jasminda motioned to the couch. Oola and Yllis sat together, while Mooriah chose to hike a hip onto the arm and perch herself there.

"Would you like some refreshment?" Jasminda's voice held humor if only to diffuse the tension building in the air.

Though the reunion appeared to have gone well, Jasminda had experienced some of Oola's memories, knew of Her love for the man beside Her. Knew also of the pain between them from long ago as the war with Her brother and their mutual guilt for their part in Eero's downfall had slowly driven a wedge between them. Whether the old wounds had faded with time or a reckoning was still on its way, she did not know. But it was obvious they had something important to share with her.

"Has something new happened?" Apprehension rose as three grim faces regarded her.

"No." Oola's voice was resonant as ever, and Jasminda released a relieved breath.

"My mother has something she wishes to tell you." Mooriah's matter-of-fact way of expressing herself further put Jasminda at ease. The woman looked at her mother expectantly.

Oola's chin tilted up. "You have often wondered why I made you queen."

Jasminda stiffened. "Yes."

"You doubt your ability. Your right to rule." Dark eyes bored into her like a drill.

"Yes, I have."

"Do you doubt Jaqros's?"

The question caught her off-guard. "An Alliaseen has been the ruler of Elsira ever since you left. He was raised to rule."

"Yes." Yllis nudged Her and She glared at him. But the corners of his lips cracked a fraction. Such strange relationships these people had. So much said without uttering a word. Jasminda wished she could interpret it.

"Yllis installed an Alliaseen as regent of the land to act in my stead. But their blood is no more royal than my own. Than ours." Oola took Yllis's hand in Hers and returned Her intense gaze to Jasminda. "If it is destiny for a descendant of royalty to rule, then it is your destiny as well."

Jasminda swallowed. She did not speak, waiting for Oola to continue. But it was Mooriah who spoke.

"Six generations ago, my great-great-great-grandchildren left the caves and found their way into Lagrimar. They took the name of my father. The House of Eagles—Sarifor. They kept the secrets, spread the lies, and remembered the truths, just as I'd instructed. Two branches of that tree remain: your father and his children, and Kyara. If my mother was queen, if our line is royal, then so are you."

Oola smiled slightly. "You have long suspected as much, I believe."

Jasminda couldn't deny it, though Oola had never explicitly stated it before and it was too much to hope for. Too much to believe. "And you never told me because you thought it would do me no good to know?"

Oola pursed Her lips and looked away, sighing. "Indeed. But my . . . family have convinced me that my logic in that regard has some detriments." Yllis snorted and Mooriah rolled her eyes.

Oola's expression turned apologetic. "You are unique, Jasminda. You empathize with the lost and abandoned. You have felt the wrath and the pain of isolation and separation. You grew up weak and so use your new strength with care. You are generous and kind, steely and determined, stubborn and purposeful. You are much like me, flaws and all."

The goddess looked uncomfortable. "If I could remove your bitterness, I would," she said. "For it is corrosive. It was the people who insisted I become queen—you know it was nothing I wanted. Perhaps it was not right of me to accept. Or perhaps the time for kings and queens is coming to an end." She stared at the newspaper on the table in front of Her. "The people speak in ways that we often do not understand. But you should know why you have the position that you do. It was my legacy, my burden. I felt strongly that my time to bear that particular weight had passed. You will be a better queen than I was—you already are."

Warmth bloomed inside Jasminda's belly. It filled a hole she hadn't even been conscious of before. The doubts and fears were still there, but they were cocooned inside this knowledge. The vague sense of betrayal she felt over Oola's omissions battled with the comfort of a lineage now known. Of a family discovered.

Oola was flawed, as was Jasminda. But they could both acknowledge their imperfections and work to improve them. She wasn't sure if Oola had any intention or desire to be better, but Jasminda certainly did.

"Thank you for telling me," she said, rising. "It is something that I needed to know. Will you find my father? Make your peace with him?"

The Goddess nodded solemnly.

"Good. If you'll excuse me, I have somewhere I should be."

The dungeon wasn't Jasminda's favorite place. She supposed every sane person would say the same, but she had spent a nervous few hours here several months ago and hadn't ever planned to return. Now each step she took brought her closer to a meeting she still didn't want, but that the country sorely needed. She could never forgive Zann Biddell, but she could work with an enemy toward a common good. She hoped.

Each footfall on the stone floor was like an echo of the screams of some victim of his malice. She girded herself, strengthening her resolve and building her outer shell before she faced him again. The last time they'd met, she'd lost control. She could not afford such a display today.

The cell that Biddell had been given in the solitary confinement wing of the dungeon was large and held more amenities than most. As she approached, he sat on a wooden chair reading a book. More were stacked beside him on the ground. His feet rested on the narrow cot and a wooden table against the wall held the remnants of his lunch.

He turned at the sound of her footsteps and paled when she stepped up to the bars. The book cracked shut, held between his palms like a prayer.

"Master Biddell." Jasminda stood straight, her face wiped clean of emotion.

"Your Majesty," he said warily, rising to his feet. He did not bow, and she was almost grateful for the lack of hypocrisy. But just as he would not show her the respect of her position, she would not apologize for her actions the last time she'd seen him. Now was not the time for insincerity.

"You consider yourself a patriot, do you not?"

He kept a safe distance from the bars, eyeing her cautiously. "Yes, I love Elsira." His voice was low, but threaded with music and energy. "Everything I have ever done has been for her."

Jasminda's brow rose. "You murder Elsirans and destabilize the country, yet tout your love for it."

"You must prune the thorns to love the rose." His head lowered somewhat, but he maintained the courage of his convictions, such as they were.

She needed to get this over with. "I have a proposal for you. I'm certain you're acquainted with the latest news. If you are, as you say, a patriot, then you do not want the land to fall into the True Father's hands. He is close to getting what he's wanted for five hundred years, control of this land. What would a patriot be willing to do to stop him?"

"What are you suggesting, Your Majesty?" The honorific was stated simply, without any snideness this time.

"Almost every living person in this country is a potential soldier in the True Father's army." She held his gaze steadily, even as inwardly she cringed to look at the man. "We need to reduce the number of that army. We *need* the people to go to the shelters and accept help from the Earthsingers so that they cannot be made into wraiths and fight for our enemy. The people are not listening to our pleas, but they may listen to you."

Biddell frowned and began to pace his cell. Jasminda gave him a moment to think. "And if I don't help you?"

She shrugged. "Then you stay here. The wraiths can get to you here, walls don't stop them. When the palace becomes a target, as it will, you will become one of them and your patriotism will turn against your people the same way you will."

His pacing stopped. He stared at her, face blank, but a tic in his jaw gave a hint to the dread the idea spawned within. "And if I *do* help?"

"You will be released. Of course, you'll be monitored, but you may go free and use your organization and connections to convince as many people as possible that their safety is part of our best defense against the True Father. The choice is yours."

Biddell stroked his chin, eyes calculating. "Perhaps it's better if he wins. Maybe this land needs to be purged."

Jasminda shrugged again. "Maybe so." She looked away down the darkened hallway. "Maybe this is a country full of small-minded people full of hatred and bigotry and it would be better if nothing of them survived. Maybe they deserve to have the brutality of the True Father's regime imposed upon them. You make a good point and I find your patriotism impressive. However, I do believe there are good people here. Compassionate citizens with love in their hearts, open to those who are different. More curious about the unfamiliar than they are afraid of it. I have to believe that and remind myself of it every morning, or else I could not rise from my bed."

The weight of the past weeks settled into her bones, making them feel as though they were filled with lead. She faced him again, not bothering to hide her exhaustion. "I could threaten you. Offer to reveal your heritage publicly. Expose you as a public fraud. Have you photographed with that ghostly pale stubble atop your head, which reveals you cannot possibly be as Elsiran as you claim."

His smugness dropped away like a discarded mask and he touched his head self-consciously, a week's worth of hair growth visible.

"But I honestly don't care what people know about you. You are not all that important any longer and I have many more things to worry about than where your mother was born. If you don't agree to help, we will move on to our next plan. You will stay here and maybe the True Father will find you more useful than I have." She turned to leave. "If you change your mind, this offer is open until I am out of earshot."

Her steps began to echo in the silence as she walked away. She would not beg. Especially not him.

She was halfway down the hall when his voice called out.

CHAPTER FORTY-FIVE

The endless, infinite melody,
which makes concordant euphony
cannot be muted by a dampening blow.
Harmony must grow.

—THE HARMONY OF BEING

The rumbling of stone awakens you from a dream-filled slumber. You groan, reaching for the vision of the throne—your throne—sitting atop the steps of the Elsiran palace, a sea of heads both dark and ginger bowing down before you. The future.

However, in the present, a frigid awareness claws at you. A foreboding warning of danger. The deep groan sounds again, and the walls begin to shake.

In the distance, a violent *boom* rings out; dust and rubble fall from the ceiling. Is that cannon fire?

You rise and dress quickly in your stinking furs. The fireplace is cold, the room is icy, and, if you are not mistaken, this castle is currently under attack.

Explosions echo and what sounds like an avalanche roars as the ground beneath you thunders like the head of a pounding drum. You hurry into the hall to find it empty. No guards at your door—if this is an attack, then there are no men to spare. This is the chance you have been waiting for.

Though you carry no lantern, the orange glow of a fire burning outside the walls slips through the cracks in the stone and the holes in the ceiling. You make it to the precarious staircase leading up to where the Wailers are kept. It is likely unguarded as well, but their Earthsong will not overcome Nikora's blood spell carved into your arm. You cannot harm her until it is gone and unless she releases it willingly, only her death will end the blasted thing.

You take the staircase to the lower level as great blasts assault what's left of this decrepit fortress. You make it to the bottom just as another wall drops away. Dodging falling stone, you pause in an archway and catch sight of the fight. A small group of mages surround a rusted, antiquated cannon, though it appears to be firing on its own and must be some kind of amalgam.

Nikora's Physicks have banded together, less than two dozen men and women retaliating with magical attacks against the newcomers' offensive. You spot Cayro in their midst, hands up, gathering magic to himself. Then he turns on his own men and begins taking them down. Chaos ensues and a group of the raiders backs him up. Soon all of Nikora's Physicks are down.

The newcomers are covered in dark furs, and one removes her hood revealing a young woman with a dark complexion. "Are there more?" she shouts over the roar of the wind, racing into the rubble. Voices carry across the echoing stone.

"No, Nikora sent her whole force here," Cayro answers. "She's trying to flee through the catacombs with Dahlia's flesh."

"Should we go after her?"

Cayro peers in the direction of the central hall toward a staircase leading down. "It's a maze down there. I don't want anyone else harmed, and she has neither her medallion nor a compass, so she can't go far. Let's set the explosives and bring this castle down. It will either flush her out or destroy her."

You smile. Cayro has been plotting to remove Nikora all this time? Your estimation of the man climbs a notch—if he kills her, that will solve a number of problems for you.

"And Asenath, thank you for coming," Cayro says, grabbing the girl's arm. "And for trusting me with this mission."

The one called Asenath nods. "You did well. But how close has she gotten? Did the wraiths tell her anything?"

Cayro snorts. "I doubt there is anything to tell."

"Hmm." She puts a finger to her lips and scans the area. You crouch down farther in your hiding spot. "And where is *he*? We cannot allow him to run free."

"I've sent guards to retrieve him, as well as the prisoners. But he's prohibited from causing harm by a blood spell."

You wonder at Cayro's offer of escape, would he truly have helped free you or was that just another deception? Regardless, his insurrection has been expedient.

You skirt the damage, careful and silent, keeping well away from the others, and head down to the catacombs to find Nikora. You need her dead, but you also need that jar if you are to retake Elsira with an army of wraiths. Finding her before Cayro's people set their explosions is imperative.

The bowels of the castle are even colder than the upper levels. No torches are lit, but light from the cracks in the walls above filters down, muddy and dull. You can barely make out your own feet as they trip down the stone steps.

You stop on a landing and close your eyes, listening. All is quiet, whatever creatures call this place their home have likely burrowed away due to the noise of the attack. But just there—the padding of feet, shuffling quickly.

The passageways truly are maze-like, but the main halls are wide and laid out in a grid. So long as you recall how to get back to one, you feel certain you can get out of here again. Making it out before the blasts go off will be the challenge.

You hurry your steps, pausing every few paces to pick up the sound of scurrying feet. You're getting closer.

Candlelight flickers ahead. You enter a chamber honeycombed with cubbies meant to hold bodies. Many are empty but some contain shrouded remains. This is where the maze intensifies into an arcane nest of passageways. You make a mental map of the turns you take, rushing to beat the invisible clock ticking away what could be the last moments of your life. But the risk is worth it.

The ground slopes downward and the next doorway leads to a natural cave barely illuminated by a winking glow. You step through to find Nikora standing in profile, the jar cradled to her chest in one arm, a candle burned down to a nub in the other hand. She stands a dozen paces away; just behind her the ground drops off. The sound of a stream trickles, but you can't tell from your position just how far down it is.

The only exit to this cave is behind you, leading back to the catacombs. You spread your arms apart, affecting a harmless demeanor. "Please tell me you know a way out of here."

She spins around, eyes dancing madly. "This is an attack. The rebels within the Physicks destroyed the Great Machine and now they would destroy Saint Dahlia's ancestral home." She spits out the words. A sheen of sweat coats her skin.

You approach slowly. "Will you not fight? Protect your people?"

She laughs, eyes wide and unstable. "This is the only thing that matters." She squeezes the jar to her more tightly. "Dahlia's flesh must be protected at all costs."

"Let me help you protect the flesh," you say, stepping closer.

"Stay back!" Her body begins to vibrate with madness or fear—you're not sure and don't care.

"We are allies," you coo. "The flesh is just as important to me as it is to you."

She backs closer to the ledge, her grasp on the jar never loosening. "You are a trickster. You think I do not know what you are, that I can't see the truth in your cold, dead eyes. *True Father.*" She laughs. "True Deceiver is more like it."

You take another step. She retreats to the very edge of the ledge. Now you see that the drop is significant. A glint from the stream shows it must be fifty paces down. Far enough to kill? The blood spell prevents you from harming her directly.

"Give me the jar. I will protect Dahlia's flesh—I vow it." You place a hand over your heart, gird yourself for the pain, and reach for the jar.

She does what you expect. Leaps away, dropping the candle to embrace the jar with both hands. Her feet slide right off the stone and there is a long moment where she struggles for footing. And then she falls.

A splash sounds when her body hits the stream, followed by silence.

The wound on your arm begins to knit itself.

You hope the jar has not broken. It will be incredibly disgusting to have to touch the flesh of the dead goddess with your bare hands. You will need to use some of Nikora's clothing to bundle it up.

You kneel in the darkness and feel for the sharp stone corner of the ledge. Running the back of your hand across it opens up a gash. Blood wells on your skin. You swipe your index finger through it and touch it to your tongue.

The taste of copper and power fills you.

Your laughter echoes across the cavern even as explosions start to sound above.

CHAPTER FORTY-SIX

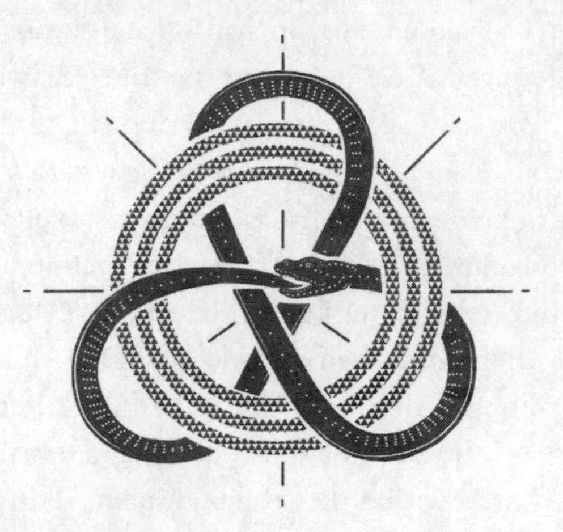

Pride bolsters the spine and shreds the mind,
restoring dignity,
erasing community.
If not in service to unity
it does not serve at all.

—THE HARMONY OF BEING

The room in which Zeli stood was wide enough for the base of the obelisk, but not much wider. The pillar itself looked much like the one in the center of Gilmer's Archives, but instead of a rich bloodred, this one was a pale rose quartz. As if the color had faded in the many years since it had last been seen.

She also had no sense of its relative size. She hadn't been this close to Gilmer's monolith, and the tiny, truncated room here meant she couldn't back up to get a good look at the thing. Up close, the four sides of the stone were perfectly smooth. Lanterns did nothing to penetrate the opaque surface but if it was truly a caldera, something must be trapped inside.

Whoever had closed this up had obviously not intended to leave space for even three people to stand here gawking up at it the way she, Varten, and Darvyn now were. All of them were exhausted, having been up all night due to the wraith attack.

She didn't know where Darvyn had been stationed during the assault—Zeli had been in one of the palace ballrooms, protecting as many of the gathered staff and residents as she could with her Song. In the aftermath, when she'd located Darvyn and asked for his help, his Song hadn't been drained and the Shadowfox had been able to easily break through the bricks and reveal the treasure held within. But now that they'd found it, she didn't know what to do with it.

"Do you feel that?" Darvyn asked. Grit and sweat clung to him. He must be exhausted.

Zeli could feel something, though she suspected it was quite a bit less than what Darvyn sensed. "There's a pulse . . . like if Earthsong is an ocean, this is a puddle."

He nodded, still peering at it with awe.

"Why couldn't you sense it before if it's been here this whole time?" she asked.

"It's weak," a new voice said from the open doorway behind them. Zeli spun around to find Yllis and Oola there, staring at the massive caldera.

"I'd forgotten how beautiful they were," Oola said. She approached and ran Her hand along the smooth surface. "Breathtaking." Zeli had been afraid to touch it, but Oola didn't appear to suffer any ill effects.

"You likely could not sense it before because it hasn't been used in so long," Yllis said. "It was designed to link hundreds of Singers together. Without any in this land, it went dormant."

"Gilmer's still worked, and he's only around every ten years," Varten said. He was pressed into the corner to allow space for the others.

Zeli's Song was just now starting to return after she'd drained it during the wraith attack. But even without using it, she sensed something off with Varten. He'd been distant ever since this room had been revealed.

"Gilmer's Song is powerful. This obelisk will awaken eventually," Oola said, drawing Her hand away with an expression of regret.

"We can awaken it now." Everyone's gaze shot to Yllis. "Well, you can." He motioned to Oola and Darvyn. "Go ahead, touch it."

Zeli shifted out of the way to allow space for the other two Singers to get close to the obelisk. She squeezed next to Varten who stiffened. His action shot a dagger into her heart, which she tried to ignore.

"What now?" Darvyn asked, hand pressed flat to the pale surface.

Yllis looked thoughtful. "Draw Earthsong into you and allow the obelisk to sense it."

It made little sense to Zeli, but she watched carefully, though there was nothing to see. Only, just there—did the stone grow a touch brighter, the pink deepening just the slightest bit?

"Oh," Varten said, leaning forward. Their arms were pressed against each other's and there was nowhere for her to go.

The obelisk was darkening, faster now to a richer color, though still not the deep red of the king stone. Oola and Darvyn both released their holds at the same time. The pond that Zeli had sensed earlier grew into a vast sea. The transformation was amazing.

Her chest grew tight. As the obelisk awakened, the weight of expectation on her shoulders pressed down. Even without her old fear beating against her confidence, she was not sure that she was the one who should be entrusted with restoring the lost Songs.

"One of you should do Gilmer's spell," she announced to Yllis and Oola.

"I don't have my Song any longer," Yllis reminded her. "I cannot."

She turned to Oola. "You can, can't you?"

"Is that what you want?" Oola's gaze on her was heavy as ever and Zeli struggled not to flinch.

"I'm not sure if I can do it on my own. I know the mechanics, but I still don't know how it will work. What the sacrifice will be or how to get the people to offer it."

Oola clasped Her hands and lowered Her head. "And I am not certain that I am the one to do it, either."

Zeli's jaw dropped. "Didn't you start all of this? Shouldn't you end it? You let the True Father escape. Someone could have gone after him, tried to find him. We could have prepared in some way for his return. But you did nothing."

"I searched for him." Her voice was low and uncharacteristically solemn. "Every night, all night. And every moment of the past days. I flew hundreds of kilometers, seeking some sign of him. Trying to feel for him, or for those who took him. But I could not."

Zeli's jaw set and she stared at the floor, unwilling to meet the woman's eyes. But a finger grazed her chin, lifting her head. "I did not do nothing," Oola said. "I did what was in my power to do, though it was not enough. Nothing anyone else would have done could have been enough. If I couldn't find him, no one could. And yet . . ." She dropped Her finger and sighed. "I do owe you an apology."

Zeli leaned back, shock surging through her. The Goddess had never apologized before.

"I was arrogant and prideful," She continued. "And my brother is one half of my heart, no matter the evil that he has done. I have failed him and my people over and over again. But that burden did not need to be placed on your shoulders. You did not deserve the weight, and I am sorry."

Zeli's mouth hung open; she stared into the woman's eyes. "Why did you do it?"

Oola still looked regal and formidable, but also . . . tired. "I do not belong here. Not anymore. I will see this through but then . . . There is no place for me here. Not in the temples, not in the land."

It was just like Her to not answer the question. "What about the faithful?" Zeli whispered instead of pressing the issue.

"Are there any of those left?" She chuckled. "It is time for them to have faith in something else. I think perhaps they should have more faith in themselves. Not in me. It should never have been placed in me. And for the part I played in stoking that particular fire, I am also sorry."

Zeli's head spun trying to process this. Darvyn appeared to be having a similar reaction, while Yllis looked on sadly. "You said you want to finish this. Will you help unlock the Songs?" Zeli asked.

"I do not know any more than you do." Oola spread Her hands. "I don't even know the spell."

This new humility of Hers was more galling than the arrogance. "I can teach it to you," Zeli said.

Oola held up a hand. "Gilmer did not come to me or contact me. He could have. He did not teach it to Yllis or gift him a Song, which he also could have done. He entrusted the spell to you. It is for you to do."

Tears formed in Zeli's eyes as frustration wanted to pour out. "But I'm not strong. I'm not anything."

"You are something, Tarazeli. You have already learned so much. You have sacrificed as well. Now you just must learn to have faith in yourself. You know it, you must feel it. And then you will find what you need."

"But how do you know?" she pleaded as tears spilled over.

"Because *I* have more faith in you than I do in me." Oola's face, which Zeli had only ever seen placid and calm, was now wracked with sadness.

Yllis took Oola's hand, his expression similarly downcast. Darvyn stared at them, his disbelief evident.

Zeli began shivering, tears flowing freely now as the two ancients turned and left. She wanted to cry out, to beg and plead, but she couldn't find the words. Gilmer hadn't said that only she could restore the Songs, but he could have made so many other choices and he hadn't. His knowledge rivaled that of Yllis and Oola and still he'd taught Zeli the spell. What did that mean?

She turned to Varten, still wedged in the corner. His eyes were wide and full of fear. "What is it?" she asked.

He shook his head. "I—I should go. Let you work on this."

"Wait, what? No. Where are you going?"

He swallowed, clearly shaken.

"Please stay," she said, reaching for him.

He avoided her, heading for the door. "She's right. You *can* do this, Zeli. I believe in you. I just—" He shook his head again. "I need to go." And then he was gone.

Zeli swallowed as the empty doorway tempted her. She turned to Darvyn, whose expression was pitying. "You can teach me the spell. If I can help . . ."

"We still need the sacrifice. It won't even matter without that."

He nodded. "You're not alone, Zeli."

She appreciated his offer, but he was wrong. She was on her own again, just as much as she'd always been. If the Goddess was right then she would have to figure this out, somehow.

She wiped her cheeks and squared her shoulders.

Faith in herself. That was all she needed. And she would have to find it fast.

CHAPTER FORTY-SEVEN

Our heritage we can recite until our breath
runs low and tongues go dry.
The ancestors are not deaf to our plight.
But we must craft a legacy worthy of
their scrutiny.

—THE HARMONY OF BEING

The rumbling of the vehicle's wheels over the pockmarked street jarred Varten's bones. His father sat across from him on a bench, Elsiran Royal Guardsmen boxing him in on either side. The auto, a wagon-like contraption, seated eight and drove down the steep inclines from the palace to the city's center.

After he'd fled from Zeli and the obelisk, Varten moped for a day until Papa had finally insisted he do something useful. Accompanying his father in his post-attack clean-up efforts seemed like a better idea than sitting in their apartment all day trying not to remember the look on Zeli's face when he ran away.

The truck rumbled to a stop across from a grassy square bordered by benches. In the city, things were slowly getting back to normal. People were out walking, shops were open, autocars peppered the street along with carts and horses. This section hadn't been hit as hard as the Portside neighborhood. But on the corner, the windows of a bank were boarded up, showing it hadn't been spared, either. Was that damage from the wraiths or from looters? There had been reports of thievery during the panic of the attack and its aftermath.

Now, Papa and other Earthsinger volunteers were already planning for the True Father's next blitz. As Varten climbed out of the wagon, a flatbed truck came around the corner with several young men standing up in back.

"Be a helper, get to shelter! We can win if you go in! Be a helper, get to shelter!" The lads shouted in unison, holding painted signs echoing the message. One rang a handbell, punctuating their words.

With the electricity in most of the city still out, newspapers and radio broadcasts remained unavailable, so the message was being spread the old-fashioned way.

"Those are Zann Biddel's men?" Varten asked as the truck passed by.

"It seems so," his father said.

"He's holding up his end, then."

"Hmm," was Papa's only reply. He stood pensive until the truck disappeared from view, then shook himself and turned toward the building they stood in front of. The massive, three-story structure took up the whole block, a sign reading OLIVESSE's written in decorative script over the wide entry.

"What are we doing here?" Varten asked.

"They've applied to be an emergency shelter. Some of the existing ones in this area were damaged yesterday. Apparently, this department store has a large basement space and the owner is willing to accommodate people. I've been asked to review the location and meet some new volunteers, Earthsingers willing to protect non-Singers."

Varten had never been inside such a large store, he hadn't had to do much shopping since arriving in Rosira—clothes seemed to appear in his closet as if by magic. Though logic told him that Usher, the valet, and his staff must have been responsible. The store was closed for lack of power, but a uniformed guard at the door let them in without a word. A harried-looking woman rushed over to them.

"Master ol-Sarifor? You're the Singer they sent, right? Oh dear, do you speak Elsiran?" She turned to Varten and raised her voice, slowing her speech. "Does he understand me?"

Papa and Varten shared a look. "I speak Elsiran," Papa replied.

"Oh, thank the Sovereign." She placed a hand on her chest, her relief almost comical. "Our owner is eager to join the safety effort. He especially wants to meet you Master ol-Sarifor." Papa's brows rose.

They followed the woman who carried an electric flashlight to light the way through the darkened store. She never bothered to introduce herself and led them down row after row of clothes on racks and then past a wall displaying kitchen appliances, the purpose of most of which Varten couldn't begin to imagine. Finally they went down an aisle that led to a hallway, impenetrable by the light's weak beam.

"Sir?" the woman called out into the darkness.

"Thank you, that will be all," a deep voice replied. A buzzing sound preceded a bright flash of light that illuminated the space. A work light on a stand was attached to a battery pack of some kind. It took a moment for Varten's eyes to adjust, but the woman's footsteps were already heading away.

Standing before them was a tall Elsiran man, quite a bit older than Papa. Varten had never seen him before, but he seemed somehow familiar.

"Do you know who I am?" the man intoned.

Varten shook his head; Papa didn't respond at all.

"My name is Marvus Zinadeel." He peered down his nose at them, obviously expecting a reaction.

Varten swallowed and nearly took a step back. But he stood his ground next to his father as his grandfather scrutinized them, the man's expression appraising.

"What do you want?" Papa asked slowly.

Zinadeel took a step forward, but Papa raised a hand, holding him off. The older man chuckled and halted. A swarm of banked fury rushed through Varten's veins. This was the man who had abandoned his mother, ignored his sister when she was left alone to fend for herself. Tried to steal their home out from under her. Varten fisted his hands to stop their shaking.

His grandfather peered at them carefully in turn before rocking back on his heels. "I find it fascinating what a crisis will do to men. Times like these, times of trial tend to put certain things into perspective." He crossed his arms and tapped fingers against his biceps. Varten recognized the mannerism as one he did all the time. He vowed then and there to never do it again.

"I have made . . . mistakes," Zinadeel continued. "I can admit to that. I had two beautiful daughters and wanted only the best for them. As any father would."

Papa's nostrils flared and he snorted, but didn't speak.

"Eminette was such a bright light. I had high hopes for her life."

Varten couldn't hold himself back. "She had a good life," he said. "She was happy and she loved us and she should have had better parents."

Zinadeel raised a brow. "Maybe you're right, child. Which one are you?"

"Varten," he said through clenched teeth.

His grandfather's gaze skated over him. "Well, Varten, this store represents just a fraction of my life's work. I have built a small empire. I intended to give it to my children and for them to give it to theirs. Sadly, it appears there will be no more grandchildren. Vanesse does not seem inclined. So I have only you."

He looked meaningfully at Varten, who shook his head. "What are you saying?"

"You are my heir, child. You and your brother. I have amassed wealth, businesses, investments, properties. I need someone to leave them to. Your sister wants me to have no contact with you, but you are my flesh and blood."

"You talked to Jasminda?"

"I'm not surprised she didn't tell you. But you are a grown man now, Varten. You don't need protecting, do you? You're old enough to make your own decisions."

Next to him, Papa had turned to stone. Zinadeel seemed content to ignore him. So much for being eager to meet him, as his employee had stated.

"And I should accept this, this *generosity* of yours?" An inappropriate chuckle bubbled up from within him. "These *mistakes* you've made, the ones you haven't even bothered to apologize for? You expect me to just forget about them? Pretend they never happened?"

Zinadeel sighed as if the questions were greatly disappointing to him. "I did the best I knew how to do at the time. I could not have known how the outcome would . . . feel."

Varten shook his head in disbelief.

"What I'm offering you," the older man continued, "is freedom. Financial freedom and power and independence."

"I'm a prince of Elsira, haven't you heard?" Varten replied wryly.

"Purpose then. You're a prince in name only, but every man needs a purpose, do they not?"

That stopped him short. He felt like he'd been slapped in the face, like somehow his grandfather had seen into his heart and noticed the splinter wedged inside it.

"You could learn to run the business—any of them. All of them. Do with them as you see fit. Is that something that would appeal to you?"

A traitorous part of his heart was tempted. Something of his own, a way to have an impact. He didn't have magic or wisdom or any particular skill set that was useful, but he could learn, couldn't he?

Then the reality of what that would truly mean hit. He'd be responsible for countless others, for employees and merchandise and cashflow—people's livelihoods—all dependent upon him. His shoulders sagged.

Papa placed a hand on his arm and spoke to him in Lagrimari. "You know that I would never keep you from your mother's family if that is what you want."

"No, it isn't what I want. I wouldn't betray you and Jasminda like that."

His father's large hand squeezed him gently. "It isn't betrayal you're feeling. It isn't even anger at him for what he's done." He narrowed his eyes. "Tell me what's wrong, son."

"All of that is in there. Somewhere. But he's only offering this because I'm not a Singer. Because I don't look like you."

"Yes, but that's not why you want to tell him no." His father's ability to read emotions had always been alternately a comfort and a curse. He couldn't decide which one it was at this moment.

"If it weren't because you thought it would disappoint us, would you say yes?" Papa asked.

Varten's jaw trembled. "I don't think so," he whispered. "It's too much responsibility. I can't . . . I wouldn't . . ." He shook his head. "I wouldn't want to fail all those people."

"Why do you think you would fail?"

"Because it's what I do."

Papa's brows descended and he leaned in closer. "What are you talking about? You haven't ever truly failed at something you've set your mind to."

Feelings he'd pushed back for a long time were very close to the surface. Zeli's face, hurt and disappointed, flashed through his mind. "Yes, I have."

"No, son. I don't know what you think—"

"It was my fault!" The words burst out of him. "I wandered away on the mountain the day we were captured. They lured me first. If I hadn't gone off . . ." He struggled to get the words out. "Neither you nor Roshon would have fallen for the trap. It was my fault. We were kidnapped and then ended up in a Yalyish prison. How can I think about taking responsibility for strangers, how can I truly accomplish anything, when I failed my own family so badly?" His throat ached from saying the words. His stomach clenched painfully.

Papa closed his eyes on a long blink. When he opened them, he grabbed Varten's other arm and held him in place. "It was *not* your fault. It was no one's fault but those who took us. Blame them. Blame the Goddess for Her interference. Blame me for being in the Goddess's debt in the first place. You can go on up the chain, trying to find those to hold accountable."

Varten shook his head and tried to look away, but his father forced him to hold his gaze with gentle pressure on his chin. "You chose to try to help when you heard a voice calling in distress. You didn't know it was a trap."

"I should have," Varten spat.

Papa breathed deeply. "Guilt and shame are like cancers. They multiply and destroy everything in their path. Anger, too. Resentment. That's why I would not blame you if you wanted to take your grandfather up on his offer. Regardless of all he's done. Apology or not, when you do a wrong you should try to make it right if you can. If you can't, you pay it forward. That is what I believe and how I've tried to live my life."

His father's steadying hands and calm voice made it easier for Varten to breathe deeply. He tried to ingest his words. "We all make mistakes," Papa continued. "That's part of being human. But letting the cancer of the past eat away at you hurts *you* the most." He tapped a finger on Varten's chest, over his heart. "Right here."

Varten nodded, feeling the ache in that organ more acutely now.

"You know what will help?"

"What?"

"Forgiveness. I can sense a man's heart and his intentions. And the most powerful act that someone can take is to forgive."

Varten sniffed. "Is that why you didn't punch my grandfather on sight?"

Papa snorted. "I don't want Jasminda to have to grant me a royal pardon." He smiled sadly. "Do you think you can forgive yourself? Because I never blamed you. Roshon never blamed you.

It was just you holding on to this sickness, which has only done you harm."

His limbs felt heavy. He was cognizant of his grandfather just a few paces away, unable to understand their words, but listening with growing impatience. He put the man from his mind again. "How do I forgive myself?"

"You let it go." Papa raised his hands, fingers spread wide and waggling.

Varten froze. "Let it go," he whispered. "Lay down your burdens." It was what Gilmer had told Zeli about sacrificing her fear.

Papa nodded. "Yes, your guilt is a burden. You need to release it."

Zinadeel cleared his throat. "You realize I'm a very busy man."

Varten held up a hand absently to stop him.

"Now see here, you—" His voice cut off with a strangle. When Varten looked up, his grandfather was gripping his throat, moving his mouth without anything coming out.

Papa looked smug. "Forgiveness doesn't have to be immediate, and I don't think we need to hear any more from him do we?"

"No," Varten said. "I don't think we do." His mind was racing, making connections that he wasn't fully conscious of yet, but something was forming—an idea. Gilmer's words, Zeli's face, his own guilt. It all meshed together in a swirl in his head, but was formulating into something more solid.

"I need to go back to the palace."

"All right," Papa said. "Do you want me to go with you?"

"No, stay and do what you came for. I think . . . I think I have an idea."

He turned to Zinadeel, whose face was turning purple with frustration at not being able to speak. Whatever Papa had done to silence him was obviously enraging the man. Varten spoke to his grandfather in Elsiran.

"I think one day I will try to forgive you. I don't know if you'll deserve it or not. But *I* do. My sister and my father and my brother deserve to be free of the weight you left us with. I think Mama would want that, too—for us to forgive you. One day."

He stepped closer to the man. "If you need to leave your wealth and businesses to someone, leave it to the poor. Leave it to people who need it. I don't want it. My brother doesn't, either. We don't want anything to do with you." His chest was heaving and he felt like he'd just run up a hundred flights of stairs.

"Eminette deserved better," Papa said quietly. "I did my best to give her everything, so she wouldn't feel like she was missing out, choosing us over you. Choosing *me* over you. And I have no doubt that I would do it again."

With a final nod, Varten turned to leave with Papa right behind him. As they reached the front doors of the store, they heard Zinadeel's voice bellowing, Papa's spell now lifted. Varten didn't catch the words, but it didn't matter. He never needed to hear his grandfather's voice again.

Outside, the street seemed quieter than it had been a half hour before. He needed to get back to the palace, back to Zeli, where he should have been all along. He was just figuring out how to do that when the emergency alarm began to blare.

CHAPTER FORTY-EIGHT

Apply yourself with grace to all you do.
For it will serve as sword and shield
when winds of dissonance blow steadily near
and you find yourself with nothing else to cling to.

—THE HARMONY OF BEING

Sirens echo, ringing in Ulani's ears as she rushes down the street toward the theater's basement again. Raven scurries along on his little puppy legs behind her, not wanting to be left behind. The last time the wraiths came, she didn't get a chance to see any of them. Tana told her how scary they were, but she would still rather see for herself. She's seen Mooriah, but knows that somehow these spirits are going to be different. All she wants is a peek, but Mama's got a tight hold on one hand, and with Papa on her other side, hurrying along, there's no way she'll get a chance.

Tana has already gone off to fight with the Poison Flame. Ulani wishes she could fight, too, but she has an important job to do. Papa told her that sometimes you need a sword and sometimes you need a shield—Ulani is the shield.

They arrive at the theater to find the basement doors wide open. Down the creaking steps and then they're in a space that feels much smaller than it did a few days ago. There are so many more people here.

"It worked," Mama says, surprised.

Lots of people Ulani doesn't know stand alongside familiar faces from around the neighborhood. She opens her Song and fills herself up with Earthsong. It feels bubbly and tickles just a little bit. Excitement sparkles in her belly.

But fear pushes against her Song, thick and dark like molasses. Mama is a little bit relieved and a little bit something else—it's a feeling Ulani doesn't have a word for, sort of like waiting for something good to happen, but also thinking it may really turn out bad.

Papa towers over her like a tree giving shade. She presses into his leg to keep from being shuffled around as more and more people run down the steps. Raven steps on her feet, never far away. Outside, the alarm still screams.

"Who's the Earthsinger?" someone yells.

"Who's going to protect us?"

Mama starts shouting orders, telling everyone to line up and hold hands. Ulani won't have to touch any strangers, Mama and Papa will be on either side of her, and everyone else will link hands with them.

"We're supposed to rely on that little girl?" an old man says. Ulani doesn't know him, but his hair looks like broom bristles and a sludge of panic clings to him.

"She's a very strong Singer," Mama says. "If you don't trust her to help, then you're welcome to take your chances out there." She points to the staircase and the man steps back.

Outside, the sirens stop. Ulani takes her parents' hands, closes her eyes, and focuses on her Song. Holding in the Earthsong is like holding in a sneeze that never comes out. She does as Fenix taught her and creates a kind of bubble to protect them. Only it's not a bubble, and she can only pass it through people who are connected to her. It would be better to go around, but that's not how it works.

But something is wrong. The bubble isn't spreading out the way it's supposed to. "Someone isn't holding hands," she whispers.

Mama jerks, probably looking around. Ulani's eyes are still closed. She's trying to force the spell through the barrier it's hit. It's kind of like pouring water through a series of funnels connected to each other, except that one of the funnels doesn't have an opening on the end. She can't reach the one below it.

The room is getting hot with all these people here. Sweat pools on her back and beads her forehead. Raven sitting on her toes makes her shoes feel like an oven; she struggles not to lose her concentration.

Then Papa yells like he's surprised and his hand rips away from hers. Raven barks and Mama wrenches away, too, and the top funnel is completely blocked. She opens her eyes.

It takes a second to understand that both of her parents are fighting people. Papa with his fists and Mama with the little wooden club she keeps in her bag, the one she told Ulani and Tana never to touch. The man Papa keeps punching is Elsiran, kind of skinny, but with a mean face. Mama swings her club at the older man attacking her and a loud crunch sounds as his arm breaks.

Raven growls, standing right in front of her and pushing her backward.

People are screaming but everything is too loud to understand what they're saying. She knows the fighting men are angry, angry at her.

"The True Father wants the Lagrimari," another man screams from the middle of the confused jumble of people. He races toward Ulani, his feelings sharper than a thornbush. She shrinks back as Raven snarls, but the puppy is too little to do much damage and both Papa and Mama are fighting new Elsiran men—the first two are already on the ground, one moaning in pain, the other still as a stone.

She's frozen with fear, not sure what to do, when an older Lagrimari man she's seen at the market lunges for the man coming toward her. He tackles the Elsiran and sits on his chest. Two Elsiran women help to hold the attacker's arms and legs as he flails, shouting, "We're safer without the *grols*! Let the True Father have them!"

The man fighting Papa falls, and Papa swings around, grabbing Ulani and lifting her up. Two more angry red-haired men begin to shout about *grols,* but they can't push their way through the tight mass of people.

Mama knocks another angry man in the head with her club and stands there panting, looking around, madder than a homeless hornet.

Ulani closes her eyes, Papa's arms are tight bands of safety encircling her. "There's two more angry men here," she whispers. "But they're waiting."

He repeats this to Mama who begins speaking in Lagrimari to someone. Ulani senses two men being pulled from the crowd and brought forward. Their energy feels like a deep, dark hole, sad and bitter and endless. Someone shouts that they've found some rope in the corner and all the men who wanted to fight are quickly tied up.

"Zann Biddel planted his people in the shelters," Mama says into Papa's ear.

"What did he think he was doing?" Papa asks.

"I don't know. Sacrifice the Lagrimari to the True Father, barter for peace that way? Only one of them is talking, the rest are staying silent. Loyal to their leader to the end."

A shiver races down Ulani's spine and she opens her eyes to look up toward the door. "Link hands!" she yells.

A dark column of smoke emerges through the wood of the closed doors. It hovers over the stairs and the people rush and leap, falling over themselves to join up.

Ulani is still in Papa's arms with Mama pressed in close. Hands shoot out to grab any part of their neighbor they can, arms, shoulders, heads, feet. She pours the spell through funnel after funnel, protecting everyone who's touching, hoping she can reach them all in time.

But something startles her and the trickle of protection wobbles, though it still flows through the funnels. A lady is staring at her from across the room. She's really a girl, a skinny teenager with long, red braids. Her eyes are hot coals, and Ulani missed her anger because it wasn't thick and slimy like the men's. It's lighter, like a cloud of poison.

The dark spirit hovers above them all, looking for someone to attack. But even the men tied up on the floor are in the funnel, they're being pressed down with feet on their chests.

The angry girl is linked to those on either side of her, but continues to stare daggers at Ulani. The funnel holds and everyone here is part of it, until the girl releases both her hands, pulling herself out of the chain. Her neighbors are safe because the funnel is a circle, the person on their other side keeps them a part of it, but the girl with the braids is at risk. No one dares move out of the chain to grab her, just about everyone else is focused on the spirit floating overhead.

The angry girl grips something in her hand that Ulani can't see. Hatred pours from her like smoke from a chimney. Meanwhile, the spirit swoops down, angling for the one unprotected person. With one hand around Papa's neck, Ulani reaches toward the girl, who's racing forward, lifting her arm.

Raven lunges forward directly into the girl's path, but she kicks him viciously. Tears form in Ulani's eyes as he rolls away, whimpering. The thing in the girl's hand is a rock. She's still too far away for Ulani to reach, too far away to protect. The spirit arrows toward her, a breath away from her skin as she lunges forward.

Papa twists, turning Ulani away from the blow, putting himself in its path. The fist with the rock hits Papa's head just as the spirit starts to breach the girl's body. But the girl joins the funnel when she touches Papa. The spirit can't penetrate and bounces off.

Papa stumbles and begins to fall. Ulani feels his pain as if it's her own.

Mama grabs his arm on his way down, and the man next to him lunges for his leg. They're all still connected, though Ulani lays in a heap on top of him. The girl howls as feet from all around press her body into the cold ground.

Ulani has to focus on the funnels. The spirit arcs and dives overhead, still threatening. Other spirits slide through the walls, seeking hosts to infect. The room is soon darkened by their presence.

Papa's head is bleeding. She wishes she could fix it, but she's not sure if she can split her focus. She doesn't want to risk it, but he's sleeping a kind of sleep that isn't really sleep and it's giving her a bad feeling. Raven limps over and licks Ulani's cheeks, tasting her tears.

She's sorry she wanted to see a spirit so badly—she takes it back. She wants them to go away so she can heal her father. They have to go away soon so she can make sure he wakes up.

CHAPTER FORTY-NINE

Let unseen evidence guide us toward
the mysteries of being.
Pay close attention to
the eyes unseeing.

—THE HARMONY OF BEING

Varten had a tight grip on his father's shoulder as the two of them raced down the street. He hadn't been here for the other two wraith attacks, but he could already sense that this one was going to be worse. The portal was somewhere out of his line of sight, but the sky darkened ominously, filling quickly with writhing spirits ready to find hosts.

"There's a shelter down that street," Papa said, pointing.

"No, I have to get back to Zeli. I have an idea about how to restore the Songs. I think they'll be needed sooner rather than later."

Papa looked around wildly before leading them into an alleyway. It would provide no protection from the spirits, but got them out of the frantic flow of pedestrians scurrying down the sidewalks.

A dark smoke-like column sprinted overhead, swooping down. Varten had a hand on his father, he was protected, but still flinched at the proximity. He felt nothing when the apparition bounced off him and redirected to find another victim.

Crashes sounded as windows broke nearby. Metal crunched and tires squealed. Screams rang out and hysterical people shouted, cried, and streamed past.

"I'm not sure we can make it back to the palace," Papa said.

Varten peered out at the chaos around them, agreeing. "What if this is it? The Songs might be our last chance."

"You really think you know how?"

Doubt clouded his mind, but he pushed through. "I think I might."

"All right, then we'll need a vehicle."

Hand in hand, they ventured out into the street. Two middle-aged Elsiran women were hurrying past. The taller one stopped and did a double take at Papa.

"Earthsinger?" she asked, looking at their joined hands.

Papa nodded and extended his free hand to her and she grabbed on, holding onto the other woman. At the corner, someone had abandoned an older-model roadster. It sat, idling, driver's door open.

"There!" Varten yelled, pointing.

"Does anyone know how to drive?" Papa asked. The two women shook their heads.

Varten had never driven an auto before, but he'd observed each time he'd been a passenger and had been shown the fundamentals of operating one by some of the drivers at the palace. "I think I can figure it out." To the women, he said, "We need to get to the palace. You all are welcome to come, but this is an emergency."

The shorter one looked to the taller one, who shrugged. "I don't care where we go as long as those things don't get us."

They hustled over to the car and piled in awkwardly, a jumble of moving arms and legs trying not to break the chain of protection with Papa. Once settled, Varten reviewed what he recalled of the instructions and placed the car in gear. He tapped the accelerator and they moved forward.

Papa was in the seat next to him, one arm gently grasping his shoulder. Varten looked over and smiled when something thumped against the front of the vehicle. A woman stood there, eyes shining with malice. Her two fists had dented the hood.

Varten rushed to put the car into reverse and back up. The woman charged, but then froze and slid to the side before crashing into the front of a building.

"Drive. Now," Papa said tightly. Sweat beaded on his forehead. He must having been using Earthsong on the wraith.

"Are you all right?"

"I can't hold her," he groaned. Varten shifted again and accelerated forward. The streets were in chaos; people ran from spirits and from each other as wraiths wreaked havoc on the city.

Traffic semaphores were working, but no one seemed to be following them. He was forced to slam to a stop when a runaway horse pulling an empty carriage galloped past. When they reached the first of the steep hills they had to climb, nerves buzzed inside him. The engine revved loudly as he pushed the gas while shifting.

"Don't stall out," the taller woman called from the backseat, just before the engine cut out.

Varten gritted his teeth. "Thanks."

He felt the scrutiny on the back of his neck, but focused on restarting the car. This time, he took off successfully. All around them people were trying to run to safety, while more and more were being transformed.

They drove by a wraith lifting the front end of a parked car and tossing it into a house. Varten turned down a side street to avoid a cluster of wraiths up ahead who appeared to be tunneling through the pavement with their bare hands. The creatures tore down power lines, picked apart buildings, and were generally causing as much mayhem and destruction as possible.

"Does the True Father want anything left of the city?" he murmured.

"He doesn't care about things like that," Papa responded. "He'll build a new city if he has to on the ashes of this one."

When they finally reached the palace gates, Varten was certain he'd shaved several years off his life. Security was nonexistent—even the Royal Guard must have fled to the shelters set up to protect the palace workers.

"Where to?" Papa asked as they ran through the main entrance, hand in hand. Even here, dark shapes arced and dove through the air, searching for hosts to take over.

"This way." Varten led them through the empty hallways, no other living being in sight, just spirits tracking them, waiting for a break in the chain of protection that Papa offered.

They were racing down a hallway in the newer part of the building when the electricity flickered and died, leaving them in darkness. One of the women gave a cry of surprise, and Varten was forced to stop. There were no windows in this corridor and it was impossible to see. But a flicker of fire rose in the air in front of them.

"How's your Song?" Varten asked, as his father's grip weakened slightly.

"All right for now."

Varten quickened his pace, relying on the others to keep up. They wound through the passageways until they reached the obelisk room. The door was open, the rubescent glow of the monolith lit the small room. Zeli sat in front of the column but popped up at their arrival. Her jaw hung open in shock as she took them in.

"What are you doing here?" she asked, breathless.

In response, he just reached for her hand. She hesitated for a moment that seemed to last forever. In that brief time, his heart flooded with sorrow. But she stretched out her arm and took his hand. Varten released hold of his father.

"Go to the shelter in the Summer Ballroom," he said to Papa. "See if there are others you can help or relieve."

"Be careful, son," Papa murmured. And then he and the women were gone.

Varten and Zeli stood in the doorway, fingers intertwined. "You came back," she whispered, eyes wet with unshed tears.

"I'm sorry. I—" He shook his head. "I owe you an apology for a lot of things, but I had an idea."

"An idea? About this?" Hope laced her voice.

"Do you think you can do that thing that Gilmer did to talk to his acolytes? Except for the whole city?"

Her brow furrowed as she thought. Then she nodded. "I think so. I should be able to do it with the obelisk, but why?"

"Because I think I know what the sacrifice needs to be."

CHAPTER FIFTY

The Voice you hear inside
is mine
is ours.
It belongs to all and none at all.
It whispers louder than a scream and if
ignored it still continues
speaking.

—THE HARMONY OF BEING

Taking care not to touch it, Zeli unwrapped the king stone with her free hand. While all her old fears were excised when her Song had been restored, it was still possible for new ones to intrude. But after having felt the amazing freedom of fearlessness, she wasn't eager to take on more anytime soon.

It had been difficult as the doubts intruded. Then the bitter sense of abandonment when Varten had fled. She'd struggled not to let the panic into its former place. She was still struggling as she placed her hand around the caldera, holding the Songs of her people.

Nothing happened when she touched it—it had not been created to respond to touch the way the one Yllis had made was. It was just a heavy, warm presence in her grip.

"I need to touch the obelisk," she told Varten. "Hold onto my shoulder." He complied, his fingertips grazing her collarbone. She shivered at the touch. He squeezed her lightly and she took a deep breath before placing her other hand on the obelisk.

Oola and Darvyn, the most powerful Singers alive, had re-awakened this ancient caldera, though she could sense it only held a tiny fraction of its potential. Still, this was ancient magic and should be enough to do what she needed.

She concentrated on the Song within her, eager and thirsty and ready to be used. Connecting to Earthsong was second nature, even after mere days since her Song's restoration. And as it turned out, using the obelisk was not all that difficult. Normally, she would pour Earthsong into her own Song the way you'd pour water from a pitcher into a glass. The obelisk vastly expanded the size of her glass. She felt as though she was linking with both Oola and Darvyn, wrangling their massive power under her control. The obelisk filtered and refined the power until she could wield it with pinpoint accuracy.

Words and spells recalled from Yllis's journal came to mind. They hadn't made much sense before, but now she understood. So much knowledge had been lost to time, so much had been impossible with so few able to retain their Songs and pass on the knowing. All she had to do to bring her voice to the ears of the people all around the city was to open her mouth and speak.

Her voice was carried on streams of invisible energy pulsing through across the distance. She spoke as Oola did to other Singers, not as sound on the eardrum, but as words in their mind. But not just those with Songs could hear her, everyone stopped to listen when the solitude of their inner thoughts was pierced with a foreign voice.

Even the wraiths paused their destruction, the human part of them thrown into shock at this mental intrusion. In basements and closets and rooms fortified with cement and iron, they all heard. And what's more, due to the unusual way that she spoke to them, they did more than hear, they listened.

And this is what she said:

People of Elsira. People of Lagrimar. The True Father started a war five hundred years ago that divided us. It tore us apart and turned brother against sister, father against mother. Singer against Silent. He separated families and friends with the Mantle so that he could steal our magic for himself and subdue us. Right now, his army of the dead is tearing apart the land that we all originated from. He's trying, once again, to take our home.

But we don't have to let him. We can get our Songs back.

It may sound impossible, but a few moments ago, wouldn't you have found my voice in your head impossible? You don't know me, you have no reason to trust me, but please listen.

The True Father wants us divided. Now maybe the days of Singer and Silent living together side by side are over, and maybe they're not, but today each of us has a choice. We can be transformed into armies for him, armies for hate and destruction and death, or we can form a new army. One working against him.

If you want to survive today and into the future, you have to sacrifice. We all do.

Magic requires a sacrifice. Earthsong, blood magic, all of it. Only this time, the sacrifice will have to come not from the magic users, but from you. From all of you.

What can you give up to save us?

All of you holding hands, seeking protection from the wraiths, look to the person next to you. Are they someone who you wouldn't bother to speak to on the street? Someone who's treated you badly, called you names, shut doors in your face? Someone you fear, who speaks a different language and has different customs and abilities?

Can you admit that the person you're holding hands with right now might not be like you, but their presence in the chain is helping to keep you safe and alive? If you're in a chain then you have an Earthsinger to thank. If you're in a chain and the spirits are passing you by and not invading you, then don't you owe it to yourself and those you care about to let go of your resentment, hatred, and bitterness?

Are you willing to release it in order to save your life? To save all of our lives?

In shelters in the city, Lagrimari refugees hold hands with Elsiran citizens. It is something neither of them would have chosen, had the world not been ending. But as it stands, with the deadly forms of enemy spirits filling the small, dark space, they dare not let go.

The girl's voice begins speaking inside their heads, for a moment jarring those within the chain of protection enough that they almost let go. But one hand tightens on another, and the links in the chain remain intact.

The words spoken directly to their consciousnesses are accompanied by feelings, as if each of them are privy to all this mysterious girl's hope and earnestness. A sense of freedom rushes through them that they haven't felt since childhood. It's exhilarating and a little frightening, if only because it will certainly go away, and they will long for it again.

An impression of peace—the kind of peace that seems unattainable once one is weaned off a mother's teat—brushes over their senses and takes root in their hearts. This sensation is so different than anything they can recall feeling, that it has never occurred to them it could exist.

It draws a stark contrast to the bitterness and disappointment, the blame and jealousy which usually fill them. Which usually are directed against the person they're holding hands with. They've grown up with hate, hearing all the usual complaints against the other person: they're lazy or spoiled, untrustworthy or cruel, boorish or snobbish—the words have left stains that have seeped deep inside them. So deep they can never be cleaned . . . or can they?

For the words in their heads and the sensations brushing their souls reveal another way. Reveal that these long-held feelings and ideas are warped, that they are something separate from reality. A belief about a person is not that person. It is not the belief-holder, either.

These beliefs and these warped feelings can be let go.

Like a heavy burden set down.

Tears form in their eyes as this realization arises. They wonder how they can do what the voice asks of them, how can they let go of this weight they've carried since their memories began?

Their cheeks become wet with tears as this desire intensifies. Yes, they will give it up. Yes, they want this peace that is hinted at, even for a short time. Even if it will doubtless retreat back into the place where it hides.

They do not know that blood spells require intent, but it does not matter. Their tears leave their cheeks and lift into the air. The droplets hover over them, impervious to the hungry, diving spirits, careless of gravity and natural forces. The tears rise and hover, their clear translucence deepening and tinting to red.

They have never heard the word "caldera" before, they would not know what it means, and this, too, does not matter. Because they have chosen to listen, they have chosen to feel, and they have chosen to give up something that has been deeply embedded within them. Something they held precious, even if they didn't know it.

And so, this sacrifice hovers before them, coalescing. Tears from all who gave them up, regardless of race or magical propensity, draw together, reddening and brightening into something that the spirits shy away from.

As more and more give in to the message and the desire to be free from the cancer that has marred their souls, they release the hate and mistrust, and with their release, their tears join together. The floating red masses grow, fed by the tears of the penitent.

Half a kilometer away, in a palace built at the base of a dormant volcano, the king stone accepts the sacrifice and shatters.

Zeli stood just as Gilmer taught her, with one hand on the obelisk, the other holding the dagger that was once the king stone.

No spirits penetrated the obelisk room, even with the doorway smashed open in invitation. All the same, Varten never once let go. His hands kept a firm but gentle grip on her waist. He'd moved to brace her this way when she began shaking. She hadn't thought it would take great effort to whisper the words of the blood spell over and over, pouring her heart and soul and Song into its execution, but it had. Varten's touch might be all that was keeping her upright.

Her Song was full—and while blood spells didn't require Songs, the magical workings necessary to undo what had been done by the True Father was something more than blood magic. Not quite the amalgam magic Gilmer had spoken of, but similar in its way.

"My sister Dahlia first discovered how to combine the magics in this way," Gilmer had told her back in his Archives, as he stood just like this while Zeli watched and listened and learned.

"In the north, they were also putting together this knowledge, so I suppose we'll never know who was really first, but Dahlia had followers, acolytes of her own whom she taught. We, her sisters and brothers, warned her against it but she did it anyway. She was the healer and wanted her followers to be safe and healthy."

As he spoke, the red of the obelisk appeared to deepen, and the caldera itself—the solid, gem-like substance—shifted like liquid beneath the surface. Gilmer repeated the words of the spell slowly, over and over, for what seemed like hours until she could repeat them, too. Until her tone and intonation were perfect though she didn't understand the language she spoke. The demonstration, the transfer of knowledge had gone on for a long time, during which, she'd focused on her fear. Imagined it leaving her body, freeing her.

Gilmer told her that the sacrifice would take on an avatar or embodiment. Something to represent the loss in the material world, for that was the way of this type of magic. For Zeli, the form of that avatar was breath.

As her lungs worked, mouthing the words of the spell and pulling in the needed oxygen, the air expelled from her lips hardened before her. It solidified into a small, round object, colorless but still visible hovering before her. She longed to reach out and touch it, but didn't dare.

Gilmer's words grew stronger and louder. They vibrated her bones, making her shake and shake, and as he spoke, the colorless, floating ball turned as red as the obelisk.

Zeli's heart was beating so fast, it made her chest hurt. She gulped for air as her skeleton rattled inside her. Then the embodiment of her sacrifice shattered into a million pieces, which all dissolved back into air.

She wobbled on her feet. Then fell to her knees. And just like that, it was back.

Her Song.

It snapped back into her body like a magnet drawn to iron, and filled up all the empty spaces in her soul. She reached for it tentatively, not quite believing that she was whole again. Earthsong was there, its infinite sea swelling and rocking, waiting for her, it seemed. So she sucked the energy into her Song, filling herself to the brim, testing her limits the way she used to do as a child.

The air against her skin felt different. Its moisture invisible but tangible. Heartbeats thundered in her ear: Gilmer's, Varten's, and Yllis's—or at least the body he wore.

Pushing out further, she sensed the acolytes still hovering outside the Archives' door. In the streets beyond, the Rumpus's revelers' joy and merriment and frustration and doubt and hope and fear swirled in an endless dance.

It was like she could touch the birds overhead, the nocturnal ones hunting for their evening's meal. The prey scuttling across the earth. Creatures she hadn't thought of for so long were now imprinting themselves on her senses. The world was so loud.

The life and vitality of every living thing that existed was energy that mingled to form Earthsong. Zeli had risen then, eyes closed, once again connected to life itself. And it had felt glorious.

In the obelisk room, in Varten's arms, she began to weep as Song after Song snapped back into place in Lagrimari people all across the city. All across the country, reaching into Lagrimar and all of the citizens still residing there. Connected as she was to Earthsong via the obelisk, using its enormous, magnifying power, the indescribable joy of every man and woman and child who received their Song back was palpable for her.

She became one with their wonder. She sank into their delight as the broken were healed. Her people were whole once more.

In her hand, the dagger became too heavy to hold and she dropped it to the ground, where it clattered. It was a simple thing, not ornate or gilded. Something innocuous that a soldier might carry.

Not a single Song was left inside.

She thought of Yalisa and Eskar so far away, even now receiving their magic again. Gilmer had said that proximity was needed, but as Song after Song was returned, the obelisk grew in strength and reach, now able to send Songs back to Lagrimari wherever they might be. They would not know how or why, but what had been stolen was now returned to all.

Zeli released her hold on the obelisk next. She tore herself away from the power, and fought to stay on her feet. Varten's hands tightened around her waist, a band of safety keeping her up, and then easing her down to sit resting against him.

Now, her own Song was spent. Varten was vulnerable to the

spirits without her protection. She opened her mouth to say as much, but couldn't get a word out. Exhaustion overcame her.

"It's okay," he said, whispering. "Just rest. I've got you. I won't ever let go."

She couldn't physically move her body to protest or pull away. And so she decided to believe him.

CHAPTER FIFTY-ONE

What's broken can be mended.
A shattered spirit's remedy requires
close attention and undivided time.

—THE HARMONY OF BEING

Tai and Ani walked at the head of a group of twelve Raunians, a truck piled high with selakki oil–doused blankets trailing them. They had developed this strategy during the last fight—split all the Raunians into units assigned to quadrants around the city. Each unit was further split into an offensive team armed with cudgels to fend off the wraiths, and a defensive team, watching their backs and covering the downed bodies with blankets or oil so the spirits could not retake them.

While the wraiths had a speed advantage, their superior strength was nullified when fighting a Raunian. Tai slapped his club against his palm, remaining vigilant. Ani marched beside him, swinging her club and whistling a sea shanty. She'd donned a prosthetic that looked like a claw and used both to disable the wraiths while her crewmember, Ena, followed with the blanket. Flanking them were their respective second mates, Mik and Leo.

With a screech, a wraith darted from an alley. Tai kicked a leg out, tripping the man, then thwacked him with the club. Mik and Leo were taking on three more and soon had them down. The wraiths were quickly dragged together and a blanket thrown over them.

It was slow work, moving across the city, section by section, taking on those who attacked them. Rosira was a city of hills, unlike flat Raun, and Tai's unit was mostly quiet as they climbed and descended going from block to block. Everyone was focused and watchful, some more eager for the fight than others.

Ani cackled with glee when two wraiths raced toward her. Tai groaned, moving to her side so that she wouldn't be outmatched. They took them down handily. Each Raunian also carried a container of oil on them—there were only so many blankets, after all. Since the defensive team was all busy, Tai poured oil over the downed wraiths and kept moving.

A commotion behind him had him turning, club raised. A small figure with a crown of white hair moved toward them swiftly. Tai nudged his sister who spun around to see.

"What is she doing here?" Ani hissed.

"Did you expect her to sit this one out?"

Ani huffed in annoyance as their mother approached. Only two of the king's guard were with Pia, the rest must be with other units working to protect the city.

Pia held a staff that was taller than her. She wielded it with the expert hands of someone advanced in the martial art of daipuna, twirling it menacingly as she stalked forward.

"We don't need your help," Ani called out over her shoulder as she searched the dark shadows between buildings for wraiths.

"I'm the king, I can do what I want," Pia spat. "I see you're speaking to me now?"

Ani crossed her arms defiantly. They turned a corner to find a dozen wraiths spread out across the street tearing up cobblestones and pulling out chunks of stucco from a nearby house. All three members of the Summerhawk family raced forward to deal with this scourge.

Clubs and staff flying, they delivered beatings to the creatures. Tai felt some remorse about the bones he was breaking, knowing that they would be felt by the innocent if and when they woke up. But there would be no waking if they couldn't get a handle on the stream of spirits.

Across the street, a group of Lagrimari emerged from what looked like a basement. Leaving his mother and sister to deal with the few remaining wraiths, he approached. The two women and one man were shouting excitedly in their language, but Tai couldn't understand. He shook his head, pointing to his ear.

The man held out his hand, palm up and a flicker of flame appeared over it. Tai's brows rose.

"You have your Song?"

The women chattered excitedly as a strong breeze rose and blew out the flame. They were all smiling joyously. Tai motioned for them to come and join the unit. They had come across a few Elsirans who hadn't made it to shelters. If they found some more, it looked like these folks could help protect them from being possessed.

"We're out of blankets," someone shouted from the truck.

Pia and Ani returned to his side. "Who are they?" his mother asked.

"They've got their Songs back, looks like."

She grinned and turned to one of her guards. "Get them on the truck. Any new wraiths we defeat should be loaded up and the Singers can keep them down." The man ran off to follow her orders.

"Will that work? Singers aren't immune from wraith strength like we are," Tai said.

"No, but your young friend back at the palace said they can put people to sleep and keep them like that. We just need the wraiths disabled."

Tai nodded. That must have been Darvyn. He had many tricks up his sleeve, Tai just hoped these Singers could manage it.

As they continued their patrol, more Lagrimari joined them, emerging from their hiding places and looking for ways to help.

"Why are you out here, Mother? This isn't your fight." Tai looked to his mother's tattooed face. Her dark eyes glittered with the thrill of battle.

"And it's yours?"

"Ani and I are both to marry Elsirans."

"Ah, you and the ambassador are getting married, are you? And no one thought to mention that to me." Her voice was imperious even as she spun the staff and smashed it onto the head of the wraith racing toward her.

"I mean, we will. At some point. I haven't asked her yet—"

"Why not?" Ani said, running up and striking at the legs of the opponent her mother fought.

"It's only been a couple of months. I haven't—"

"You need to lock that down as soon as possible," Ani advised. "Behind you."

Tai swung around and kicked out at the teenage boy who had tried to sneak up on him.

"She's right," Pia said, grunting as she swung at a large woman with vacant eyes. "Lizvette is far too good for you. You'll want to make her yours before she wises up and realizes she can do better."

Tai grit his teeth and took the boy down with a crack to the skull, then poured his remaining oil on the body. "So you two are ganging up on me now?"

"We're just giving advice," the two women said at the same time. Ani scowled and Pia raised a brow.

"And you," Pia said, turning to her daughter, who was wiping blood off her club. "This wedding of yours has caused quite enough commotion. Since we're all here now, you might as well have it in Rosira when this is all over."

Ani blinked rapidly, her mouth open. "We . . . I mean . . . Well, yes, that would be lovely. I'm sure Roshon would agree."

Four more of the True Father's army raced down the street toward them. Ani seemed somewhat distracted as she fought, and Tai had to save her from a blow to the head. Pia's solution had been a good one. He wasn't sure why his mother was being so pleasant all of a sudden. He didn't trust it.

He hoisted a body onto the truck where the Lagrimari sat hand in hand, eyes closed. He hoped whatever they were doing was working, or they'd have to fight off the bodies piling up in the truck bed.

When he returned to his sister's side, she was looking suspiciously at their mother. Tai understood the feeling. This was the same woman who'd sentenced him to two years of hard labor for defying her.

"Since you're in such an amiable mood," he said, "how about ending the embargo?" Lizvette was a brand-new ambassador and if the embargo issue could be settled on her watch, Tai knew it would make her happy. He hadn't ever broached politics with his mother before, but now seemed like as good a time as any.

Pia's brows rose. "On one condition."

The wails of attacking wraiths interrupted them, but others had them handled for now. He narrowed his eyes. "What?"

"You both come home for my birthday."

He turned to Ani, who looked as perplexed as he felt. "When is your birthday?" both siblings said in unison.

Pia rolled her eyes. "The third day of harvest season."

Ani shrugged, wide-eyed. While he and his sister were close, the Summerhawks had never before celebrated anything as a family.

"I'm getting older, you know," Pia said. "I want my family with me in my dotage." She spun around with incredible speed and smacked a sprinting wraith across the chest, sending him flying into an iron fence.

"I can make that work," Ani said, eyeing her mother cautiously.

"As can I," Tai said. He scanned the street before him. Fighting those possessed with spirits of the dead was no longer the strangest thing that had occurred this week.

"Use the obelisk!" Yllis shouted as he, Jasminda, Darvyn, and Oola raced toward the docks, where a large part of the True Father's force was amassing. "Now that it's awake, you will be able to feel it. Reach for it—allow it to focus and magnify your power. It's feeding from all of the awakened Songs and will offer you more longevity and finer-grained control."

The energy of the ancient caldera hummed just at the edge of Jasminda's awareness, roused and restless after a centuries-long nap. Her Song glanced across its edges, still uncertain of how to best utilize this new tool.

All around her, the city was falling apart under the attentions of wraiths bent on destruction. Yllis's voice strained to be heard amidst the noise of the chaos. "Focus the energy. They are beings of death, target them with life. Strike at them with Earthsong itself!"

The normal methods of attack using Earthsong—manipulating the elements of wind, earthquake, mudslide, ice, and more—were of little use against the incredibly powerful spirits. But Yllis had advised them of methods and techniques that had been lost for hundreds of years. Even Oola had needed to be reminded. They could conjure focused bolts of life energy that manifested as bloodred darts of lightning. Doing so was not easy; creating each one was cumbersome and unnatural, and they were unwieldy to handle. Without the aid of the obelisk, she did not think she could have accomplished it.

Jasminda concentrated and brought a crackling, red stream of energy into existence and flung it at a trio of wraiths ravaging a warehouse. Her blast found its target and she exhaled in relief. The wraiths staggered and fell. According to Yllis, the blasts shocked their systems, severing their connection to Nethersong long enough to interrupt the spirit possession. The physical features of the three men blurred and shifted, transforming back to the original hosts as the spirits inside struggled to maintain their hold.

Earthsingers couldn't eject the spirits, but in this state the creatures were powerless and the Void took over, keeping the bodies immobile and slowly allowing the hosts' natural life energy to bring them back under control. The spirits were still there, but dormant—for the moment.

One of the Raunian women working with them broke off to douse the prone bodies with selakki oil. Dozens more bodies, hovering somewhere between alive and possessed, lay stretched across the pavement behind the Singers as they pressed forward.

As a wraith himself, Yllis was able to expel spirits from the possessed; he fought alongside them, pressing forward as a flood of wraiths converged ahead. Yllis was nowhere near as powerful as a Nethersinger though, but Kyara and the others had been deployed elsewhere in the city.

Early reports stated that the dead had been digging through the streets, trying to access the mostly underground emergency shelters. Overhead, the portal to the World After was still open, spirits pouring through, searching for hosts. The fact that the sky was dark and filled with the frustrated dead was the only bright spot. It underscored the truth that so many of the populace had heeded the call to go to the shelters and be protected. And with every willing Singer manning full shelters, the streets were mostly clear. The number of new wraiths being created was trickling to a halt as available hosts dwindled.

And so the True Father's army that had already been created had turned from their human destruction to laying waste to as much of the city as they could. While spirits swirled aimlessly overhead, the wraiths that Jasminda and the others faced were intent upon destroying the docks. The buildings across from the line of silent boats had already been devastated. The structures were old, built of stone to withstand the raging storms of the rainy season, but now had been transformed into broken-down husks. Torn apart by the bare hands of the incredibly powerful army of the dead.

Jasminda laboriously readied another bolt of Earthsong. Fortunately, each one could take down multiple wraiths. The obelisk pulsed at the back of her senses, reinvigorating her with each beat, like a magical drum.

A wily wraith broke free of the pack of her brethren and came at Jasminda from the side, her movements almost too fast to see. Jasminda had no time to react before she was tackled to the ground, where her bones crunched against the pavement.

Pain bloomed through her arm and she knew it had broken. She whipped the wraith away from her with a blast of air, but its speed was on full display as it raced toward her again.

A dart of crimson energy sizzled into her and the wraith was down. Jasminda looked up gratefully to find Oola standing over her. The woman barely glanced her way before returning to the battle. Jasminda rose, healing her arm with a thought and faced the enemy again, more mindful of her periphery.

A chunk of cement, bigger than she was, flew through the air at her. It had been torn directly from the street. She batted it away with a focused wind and the chunk flew to her left, all the way into the ocean.

Breathing heavily, even with the obelisk's aid, she began the strenuous task of spinning up another bolt.

"Let's try doing it together," Darvyn said. Oola glanced at him and nodded. As one, they faced the opposing force and shot Earthsong energy into the entire crowd. Every wraith within their vision fell, twitching and changing, their features in flux for long moments until they settled back to that of their original host.

Jasminda's breath heaved, though she felt oddly invigorated. The carnage all around them was devastating, but a smile fought its way to her face. She turned to Oola, wanting to share in the sense of amazement, but terror quickly took its place.

Walking toward them across a rubble-filled lot where a warehouse once stood was a figure oddly clad in animal furs. The

Elsiran man had his russet hair pulled back in a short queue. He was thin and of average height, but Jasminda's heart froze.

"Sister," the man said to Oola, who turned to face him. "It is good to see you again."

Jasminda and Darvyn were locked in a state of shock, while Yllis stood to the side. All of them staring in silence at the True Father.

The portable radio at Darvyn's belt crackled and a voice called out, speaking in Lagrimari. "Hello? If anyone can hear me, stay away from the cemeteries." It was Kyara and she sounded breathless, exhausted, and terrified. "We assumed the spirits could only take over living bodies. We were wrong."

A slow smile spread over the True Father's face and he began to laugh.

CHAPTER FIFTY-TWO

It was once called Sacred Death.
Consecrated, set apart from that which lives.
We've forgotten the gift it gives.
For what is Sacred Life without its
antithesis?

—THE HARMONY OF BEING

Kyara and Tana stood, hand in hand, on the edge of the cemetery on the northwest corner of the city. The sight before her was like rain falling, except the dark forms of the spirits were the precipitation, diving like missiles into the ground.

Elsirans did not burn their dead as the Lagrimari did. They buried them and marked the grave with a mirror, embedded near where the head of the deceased would be. Across the field before her, tarnished, cracked, and broken mirrors were dotted through with newer ones of the recently dead. All so that the loved one could look through and view the Living World before they joined the Eternal Flame.

Some of the older mirrors were well-maintained, polished regularly by family members. Others were abandoned to the ravaging of time, in the hopes that the person had crossed over. But now they were all being desecrated. Cracked, broken, and destroyed as bodies clawed their way from the ground.

Instead of corpses, these bodies were whole and healthy, already transformed. The wraiths used their superior strength to break through the caskets and dig their way up through the earth.

Behind her, one of the Raunians who'd been fighting with them gasped. It took a lot to shake one of the stalwart sea-faring people, but this was surely enough to do so.

Tana squeezed Kyara's hand. Both of them were exhausted. Their physical bodies on the edge of collapse, even if their Songs were still going strong—buoyed by the portal overhead and the death all around them.

Again, Kyara sank into her other sight, as she'd been doing during the fighting. Her wildcat avatar wasn't tired, and this fact kept her hope high. The creature eagerly leapt in the direction of the wraiths. Tana's dragon and Mooriah's raptor swooped in as well, tearing spirits from bodies and gorging on death energy.

Normally the presence of so much Nethersong would energize Kyara, but all of the benefits she would have otherwise experienced were funneled to her avatar, which grew stronger and stronger the longer it fought. Kyara wished she could say the same. But she only had to last long enough to control the thing.

Strong and fast as it was, the wildcat could only dispel one spirit at a time—and though it took less than the blink of an eye to do so, as the forces arrayed against them grew and grew, as the rain of spirits picked up and multiplied, Kyara knew they would be overwhelmed.

The elaborate, mirror-encrusted crypts of the wealthy shattered. Stone and glass sprayed everywhere as wraith after wraith climbed free of the weak encumbrances. Unlike around the rest of the city, however, these stood still, as if awaiting instruction. Kyara had the heavy foreboding that the True Father was nearby and once he gave the command, his army would attack.

With a hand gripping Tana's, she grabbed for the radio Darvyn had insisted she carry. She wasn't certain that they would survive this, but the others needed to know what was happening. Even if they couldn't stop it.

You stare at your sister from across a stretch of cracked and broken pavement. She gazes at you as if she no longer knows you. Ha! The secret is she never truly did.

Yllis is here, too, something that strikes you as odd, but then everything about this place is a bit odd.

Elsira. You breathe in its rarified air. It has taken you lifetimes to reach this land again. To stand by this ocean in which you played and swam in your youth. But this city is unrecognizable to you now. So different. So crowded and dirty. Perhaps that is why you instructed your wraiths to tear it down. Brick by brick if needed. In preparation for you to replace it with something new.

You carry the jar—the empty jar now. The final spell used up the last of Dahlia's flesh, leaving the jar full of naught but ashes. Oola stares at it, grasped in your embrace like a lover, and you toss it aside, shattering it against the cobblestone walkway behind you.

The Songs you liberated from the Wailers before they died have been drained nearly to empty husks inside you. That's the problem with taking Songs, they run out so quickly. Inside a born Singer they would rejuvenate, but within you, they stagnate.

You will need more. Luckily, there are more to be had here. Hunger strikes a deep chord within you.

Oola's Song is bright and blooming. It would definitely satiate you. And the girl standing next to her—the new queen—along with the boy calling himself the Shadowfox . . . What a meal you shall have. The strongest Songs in the land all together, ripe for the plucking.

The radio crackles again, the words on it too inconsequential for you to listen to again, but the boy's face ripples with anguish.

"Go to her," the girl-queen says. He glares at you once more before taking off to the north. His escape makes little difference, it simply prolongs the inevitable. You will track him down and finally have his Song, before long.

The music of destruction sings in your ears. The crashes of buildings collapsing, fire licking against wood, burst pipes flooding the streets. It is all there, sounds on the breeze.

"Will you embrace me one last time, brother?" Oola says. Her expression is stoic as a placid sea. Then again, she was always the patient one.

"That is my line, sister." You step toward her, knife in hand. You can almost taste her power on your lips, she's so near. Her dark eyes shine, they remind you of Father's.

You startle. You hadn't thought of him in quite a while. But the memory is implanted within your mind now. Father and Mother teaching you and Oola to swim in the ocean. You were but tots then. Young and fresh and innocent.

You shake off the memory and regard her again. She has not moved, but you have taken another step forward.

"How does it feel?" she asks, voice low.

"How does what feel? Victory? I know it is not something you are much acquainted with." You are not trying to be smug. Much.

"No. Freedom."

You pause at that, at the wistful quality in her voice. Yllis, standing just next to her, is grim as ever. "My old friend," you call out warmly. What are grudges when victory is at hand?

He nods in acknowledgement, wary. Perhaps he has not forgiven you for killing him, but that is all water under the bridge as far as you are concerned.

"Freedom is the sweetest thing I've ever tasted. I shall not be imprisoned again." There is a warning in your voice.

Oola inclines her head slightly. "No, I should think not."

You step toward her, prodding at her shield, curious to know what she is feeling. All you want is a taste of her regret, her sadness, her disappointment at being bested. You do not remember her as a sore loser.

"My sister. There will be no hard feelings between us in the new kingdom I will create. There is even room for you."

"There is?" she asks, an eyebrow quirked.

"Of course. The bulk of my force stands now, awaiting my command. I do not have to destroy this city and everyone in it. I realize you are quite fond of them. I will give you them—the non-Singers—as a gift if you will just accept my rule."

You ready the knife. There is nothing she can do against your army once you give them the order to charge. You are obviously the victor here.

"Do you promise no hard feelings?" she whispers. Movement in your periphery catches your attention. The girl-queen. You will not make the same mistake twice where she is concerned.

"I promise."

A blast of Earthsong shoots toward you from the side. Potent but clumsy. You bat away the charge and give the girl-queen a withering glare.

"Your protégé could use some manners."

Oola lifts a shoulder. "She is young. And headstrong."

You sigh, and deflect new blasts from the child coming in a swift stream. The glint of a knife peeks out from Oola's fist. You can no longer read the expressions on her implacable face, but disappointment fills you. Her emotions are still well shielded, but—there. A glimpse of remorse in her eyes.

A vein in her neck pops forward as she tightens her fist.

"I will give you some more time to think on my offer," you say, taking a step back.

Surprise registers on her face. She expected you to strike.

And so you do, but not in the way she expects. A mental direction calls forth the regiment of waiting wraiths. They pour from their hiding places, racing down the gangplanks of ships and out of the shadows of destroyed buildings. Nearly one hundred strong, overwhelming the tiny force before you. Two Singers, Yllis—whose wraith form you cannot control, interestingly enough—and a handful of swarthy foreigners carrying oil canisters.

Pathetic.

As the wraiths converge, you lift yourself into the air on a controlled current of wind. Your sister spares you a glance before returning her focus to the battle before her.

Family has often been disappointing. But she will come around.

Once you are king again, she will have no other choice.

CHAPTER FIFTY-THREE

If Harmony were tangible, would you
embrace it?
Hold it to your bosom, safe and secure?
What we value, we protect,
and yet we continue to neglect
that which needs so much care and nurturing.

—THE HARMONY OF BEING

The new wraiths were motionless; the only sound coming from the cemetery was the whistle of a chilling wind. Goose bumps pebbled on Kyara's flesh.

Mooriah stepped up to her side. "The spirits are leaving other hosts to converge here," the woman said. "The Earthsingers will have no effect on these new things as they are not alive."

As if called by her words, Darvyn arrived, running with the wind at his back so he glided across the ground, nearly flying. He punched his arm forward, toward the waiting horde, and a red lightning strike shot out into a wraith standing fifty paces away. The thing did not react at all. It stood stone-faced, still waiting.

Darvyn attacked again and again, shooting blasts of energy into more of the creatures. Kyara sank into her other sight and redirected her avatar. It tore spirits from the unmoving bodies, releasing them from possession only to have the corpses retaken again and transform.

She opened her eyes again in the real world. "The selakki oil?"

Darvyn nodded and turned to grab a canister from a Raunian warrior, who led the group accompanying the Nethersingers. Kyara ejected another spirit and Darvyn let a stream of oil fly through the air to coat the body. The hovering spirit just darted away, toward the back of the cemetery to find another host.

"We don't have enough oil," the young man said. "Not for every corpse in that cemetery." The graves stretched out for thousands of paces. He was right.

The wraiths began to move, shuffling into a cluster at the edge of the burial ground. Whereas up until now, they'd all been foreign—Yalyish they'd assumed—now there were a startling number of Elsiran faces along with some Lagrimari.

"He's using our dead as well," she whispered, aghast. "Taking fresh spirits, not just ones waiting in the World After." For the True Father to control and manipulate their own dead—Kyara's heart dropped like a stone.

Darvyn took her hand. Fear welled deep in his eyes, mirroring her own.

"It's time to use the death stone," Mooriah said. "We cannot fight them. We need—" Her voice cut off, strangled as her face screwed up tight with pain. She wrapped her arms around her middle and moaned.

"What's happening?" Tana cried, reaching for the woman.

Kyara shook her head and used her other sight to find out. Mooriah's raptor shuddered, changing into its tiny bird form before it faded away to nothing.

In Kyara's normal vision, Mooriah's body fell to the ground and transformed. The dark cloud of the woman's spirit escaped with a *whoosh* and appeared to shiver.

Neither Kyara nor Tana had expelled Mooriah—one of the wraiths must have done this. Kyara's gaze darted to the amassing enemy, but each face was blank. She had no idea which one had targeted Mooriah, but that was the only explanation.

As the woman's spirit lunged for the body it had just vacated, a giant mirror hurtled through the air toward them. Kyara dragged Tana out of the way just in time. Glass cracked and splintered, hitting its intended target—the body Mooriah had just vacated.

The aged form of Kyara's former mistress and tormentor, Ydaris, lay crushed beneath the wreckage. Nethersong filled the woman immediately. She was dead.

More mirrors were vaulted their way by unseen hands in the midst of the crowd of wraiths, but this time Darvyn batted them away with winds.

Writhing with anger, Kyara struggled to focus, pointing her wildcat avatar into the opposing army, ejecting spirits left and right only to have them find hosts again almost immediately.

Her throat closed up. Her skin grew too tight against her muscles. She let go of her tight hold on Darvyn's hand and tried to catch her breath.

The Breath Father's words echoed in her head. *The Song of an ancient Nethersinger—it is mighty indeed . . . that power has grown beyond anyone's imagining.* Her vision swam and she stumbled in place. *Once you unleash what it holds, there is no going back. You have only to touch it to release its fearsome force into this world and become a goddess of death.*

The death stone was warm in her pocket and pulsing with purpose, like it wanted to be used. She fished the wrapped caldera from her pocket and held it in her shaking hand.

"That's it?" Darvyn said. She nodded, unable to speak.

Gingerly, she unwrapped the cloth from around the stone while not touching it. It was just a dull, red rock in her hand. Small and harmless in appearance. All she had to do was touch it, but she couldn't bring herself to.

Kyara's and Tana's avatars were still expelling spirits. Darvyn and the Raunians were manipulating the selakki oil, but a tiny corner of Kyara's mind was frozen. Immobilized by the decision before her.

She had no wish to be a goddess of death. But did she have a choice?

Tana's scream brought her back to the present.

"Papa!" the girl cried, sounding as though she was being murdered. "Papa!" She pointed a skinny, scarred arm toward one of the Elsiran wraiths who had moved to the front of the line.

"Benn?" Darvyn whispered with horror. "What? How?"

The man was as the other wraiths, impassive, sightless, waiting for instruction from their unseen master. Kyara's heart broke at the misery and grief coming from Darvyn and Tana.

Distracted as she was by the sight before her and the panic taking up all the space inside, she did not see Tana turn toward the stone. By the time she recognized the girl's intent it was too late.

Tana slapped her hand onto the death stone, which vibrated in response. Her small body convulsed in a seizure. Her eyes rolled back in her head and she started to fall.

There was no way she would be able to control the type of power the Breath Father said that the stone held. It already looked like it was killing her. Kyara grabbed the girl with her free arm. They both sank to the ground, Tana still attached to the death stone.

Tears filled Kyara's eyes. She looked up at Darvyn whose expression was full of confusion.

Her mouth opened, wanting to say something, but not wanting that something to be *Good-bye.*

In the end, she said nothing at all. Merely unwrapped her arm from around Tana and grabbed the death stone herself.

The last thing she saw was the man she loved, staring at her in shock as Kyara left the Living World.

Wherever she was felt like the stillness at the heart of the Mother. Kyara was disconnected from her body in the same way she had been inside the mountain, her awareness was now fixed on a glut of power surging just beyond her fingertips. Tana's presence was strong just outside the edge of Kyara's vision, and this power, this newly released Song of a long-dead Nethersinger was a formless entity trying to attach itself to the girl.

Kyara knew instinctively she had to wrench it away. She could not allow the burden to fall to a child. She reached for the wildcat tethered to her power.

"Find her dragon," she whispered, and the beast took off into the darkness.

The ancient Song was coalescing, its mist of energy taking on an avatar form and reshaping itself into some kind of large fish.

The animal floated in the darkness, needing no water, but looking far deadlier than she realized a fish could be. Sharp teeth elongated as the creature opened its mouth. A shark.

As Kyara set her sights on it, a storm began. Chilly winds battered her, attempting to separate flesh from bone, even if she had neither in this in-between place. Some instinctive knowledge took hold and she knew she had to capture and control this avatar in order to master its attached Song. It needed to become a part of her.

She was shaken like a rag doll by an intemperate toddler, smashed across invisible rocks by vicious waves. She could stand her ground no longer and sank to her knees, fearing that this wouldn't work at all. The Breath Father had been right and this was all too much for her.

He'd said she would need to be worthy, otherwise the death stone would be more dangerous than an army of wraiths. The battle to control the beast before her was certainly more intense than fighting the dead had been.

Exhaustion made her sag, but a cry in the distance—Tana's cry—caused her to rally. She braced herself, pulling forth the dregs of her energy and tried again. With every ounce of strength she possessed, she finally wrenched control of the ancient Song, bringing the creature to submission.

From out of the darkness her wildcat raced back, with Tana's dragon avatar on its heels. Then, shockingly, Mooriah's raptor plunged down—all three racing straight for Kyara. She braced herself for impact, squeezing her eyes shut.

An icy coldness overtook her that was soon chased away by an unendurable heat. Whatever was happening felt like it was tearing her apart.

And then the storm ended.

She gasped, opening her eyes to a new vision before her. An avatar hovered in place, one with a wildcat's paws and head, raptor talons, the body of a dragon, and the shark's tail and fin. The cat head opened its jaws wide and let out a roar. Fire escaped from its throat, illuminating the gloom. Kyara nearly stumbled from the deafening bellow and the heat.

This was a chimera avatar made of all the Songs of the Nethersingers linked, combined into one, and under Kyara's control.

She really was a goddess of death.

The beast lowered its head, glowing eyes regarding her with a modicum of respect. Then it winked out of existence, back to the fight in the real world. Kyara was only vaguely controlling it now, relying on her subconscious and the avatar's instinct for its mission and penchant for gobbling up Nethersong.

Tana's cries sounded from farther away. Kyara gathered herself and stumbled in their direction.

Darkness closed in around her, but as she moved toward the sound, a powerful light source bloomed. She felt more than saw it—or rather, she sensed its energy. As her awareness of it grew, it lit her from within and Tana became visible, not so far away at all. She stood turning in circles, shouting for her father.

"Papa! Where is he?" she screamed.

Kyara took a step toward her, but the girl slid away. "I'm going to bring him back," Tana said, tears streaming from her eyes. "Like how you brought back Queen Jasminda. I need to bring my papa back."

That's when Kyara realized they were in the World After. Was that where the heart of the Mother had lain all this time? It was a quick thought. Even quicker came the notion that Tana's father's spirit was already in the Living World. He wasn't here any longer to be brought back. She didn't get a chance to put this into words before Tana raced away, disappearing into the darkness.

Kyara gave chase, calling her name, but the World After did not follow normal rules, and as quickly as the girl had appeared, she was gone again. Kyara was only a few steps behind, but still lost her in the gloom. There were no footsteps to follow, the sound of her voice died out, and no path or trail made itself known. The girl had disappeared and Kyara was alone.

Only she wasn't. There was the light—or rather, the sense of light. And a voice calling her name. She stopped at the sound, so familiar.

Standing very still, she listened to the music of a child's voice—not Tana, but a girl of her age. A girl long dead. A girl she had killed.

Out of the surrounding shadows a small figure took shape.

"Ahlini?" Her friend glowed from within, the same as Kyara did, only her glow was much brighter. She was the source of this light that didn't seem to exist, but did.

And unlike when she'd seen Ahlini before in those dreams, the girl's eyes were clear. The dark brown irises meeting white. No longer blacked out by Nethersong—she no longer looked like one of Kyara's victims.

"Ahlini, why are you here?"

Her friend smiled beatifically. "I'm here to show you the Light."

As she spoke, the darkness lifted, and the light emanating from Ahlini became a brightness that overtook everything. It was as if Kyara was inside of something bright and beautiful and peaceful. Inside peace itself.

"What's happening? What is this place?"

"This is the Flame," her friend replied.

There was no heat, it was very unlike a flame, but Kyara felt the truth of the statement all the same.

"The Flame is the Light," Ahlini continued. "'The one who walks in the Dark will embrace the Light.'"

A prophecy from another time—Kyara barely remembered it. Others emerged from the darkness, people she recognized. Her victims, only they were no longer angry or pleading. They no longer bore the signature mark of her power. Their eyes were bright and now they were at peace.

"Am I . . . am I dead? Did I fail?"

Ahlini shook her head. "No. You still have work to do. You must wield the death stone's power."

"But the Breath Father told me that the death stone was too much for me. That I shouldn't use it."

Ahlini's serene face rippled and her body transformed into the wispy air-like image of the old man Kyara had known as the Breath Father.

"I told you its power was limited only by your imagination. You imagined the worst, and at the time it was what you needed to believe." His voice was once again the whisper of wind on tree branches. He changed back to Ahlini's small form.

"Wait! Has it been you this whole time? Was Ahlini never here?"

The childish voice spoke again. "I am one with the Flame. In the Flame, there are no individuals, only the collective. We are no one and everyone."

Ahlini changed again. She was the merchant's wife who had helped her after Kyara escaped the glass castle. Travelers she'd met along the road. Men and women who had been standing too close and been caught up in the release of her power. And then, once again, her friend.

Kyara was confused, but part of her also understood. "Why am I here? We're about to be destroyed. The True Father is winning."

"You are here, because you can control the dead. Use the power you have been given. You are stronger than he is, but you need help, warriors to fight. Here, you may find them."

The people who had gathered around her multiplied in number swiftly. They were her victims, but more than just those. She recognized the wizened face of the *ulla* of the harem's cabal. The *ulnedrim* guards who had been kind to her. A woman with a familiar face stood near the front of the growing crowd. One with a face so similar to Kyara's that she gasped. Some internal knowledge told her this was her mother.

Next to her stood a tall Lagrimari man. Her father, her real father—she didn't know either of their names, had never truly met them, but recognized them all the same. Not far away was a man who closely resembled Mooriah, one of her children? One of Kyara's great-grandparents? There were many more coming forward who felt familiar. Both Lagrimar and Elsiran.

A red-haired woman with eyes like Varten's and Roshon's stepped forward, too. Their mother.

"I thought that everyone was consumed by the Flame and reborn to different lives?" Kyara asked.

"We are all and we are one," Ahlini said. "We return here again and again. From death, life. We will be your army, we are ready to follow your command. Will you lead us?"

Kyara took a deep breath, staring at all the faces known and unknown. The Light around her extended on to infinity. There were more ancestors gathered here than she could fathom. What exactly were they? Beings? Spirits? Ghosts? She wasn't sure. Warriors she'd called them, that seemed like as good a name as any.

"Warriors. Please help me. Come and fight for the living."

She felt their acquiescence, their desire and their motivation. And then the archway appeared, visible in this field of Light just as it was in the darkness. The way back to the Living World was there.

Confident that her army was following, she walked through the archway.

CHAPTER FIFTY-FOUR

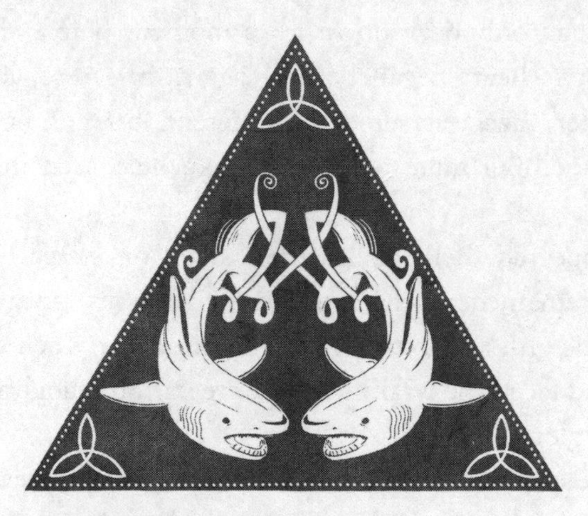

Without sorrow, grief would be a passing stain. An old scar with no power to cause pain. But sorrow's companion is misery. Its company is damaging, and woe is she who lets it settle and stay.

—THE HARMONY OF BEING

Darvyn wasn't sure if he should touch Kyara or not. She lay crumpled on the ground, hands entwined with Tana's. If they were somehow working Nethersong in this state, then he knew he couldn't interfere—Kyara was one of the only people in this world who could do him real damage with her abilities. But seeing her motionless on the ground like that made him uneasy.

And so he waited. It seemed that the battle was at a stalemate for the moment. Aside from the attack on Mooriah, the True

Father had yet to give a command to his amassed troops. He must still be locked in verbal warfare with his sister, the way they'd been when Darvyn had left them at the port.

Kyara had only been down for a moment before she stirred, and Darvyn's heart began beating again. She rose, looking up at him. Her gaze was somehow different. Something new was there—something more purposeful than he'd seen in her for a long while.

She appeared shell-shocked, but stood on stable legs. Tana, however, remained on the ground, unconscious. Kyara frowned down at the girl, a look of regret overtaking her. Then she firmed her jaw and faced the wraiths, who were still in a holding pattern. But not for long.

A dark spot in the sky grew in size as it drew closer. Darvyn's mouth dried as he saw the True Father approaching, flying through the air. Had he already taken Oola's or Jasminda's Songs? Guilt assailed him, he shouldn't have left, but he'd had to get to Kyara.

The True Father hovered, looking smug as he observed his army. He had every right to be, there was only Darvyn, whose Song had no effect on these new kind of wraiths, Kyara, and a dozen Raunians against thousands of the dead.

"The time has come." The floating man's voice echoed over the cemetery. "I will end this war once and for all. Leave no survivors but the Singers."

A screeching sound rang out and the wraiths lost their vacant expressions and snapped to attention. Darvyn clenched his fists. He'd been a soldier practically his whole life, fighting uphill the entire time and he would fight for as long as he could.

But Kyara caught his eye and shook her head slightly, the start of a sad smile on her lips. He frowned. "Embrace the Light," she whispered.

Overhead, the portal, dark and ominous, suddenly cleared of the spirits that were still pouring forth. The shimmering, dark tear in their world was pierced by a bright light.

Blinding and beautiful, it speared his retinas so that Darvyn could barely make out what was happening. But the solid beam began to quickly splinter into pieces. Arcs, like the Earthsong lightning Yllis had taught them to create, shot out of this new light and down toward the ground of the cemetery.

It was as though the sky had opened up and the darts of light rained down, just as the spirits had moments before. But there was much, much more light than there had been darkness.

Each ray hit a wraith and when it made contact, tiny explosions of light completely erased Darvyn's vision. He shut his eyes. Behind his lids the radiance intensified. It was like staring at the sun at noon. Brightness creeped into the corners of his eyes and he covered them with his hands to keep it out. Still it burned, not true pain, just an uncomfortable sensation that left him feeling buzzy. He winced, ducking his head into his elbow to avoid it.

And then it was done.

He actually felt the force retreat and blinked his eyes open, waiting for the afterburn to dissipate so that he could see again. What he finally saw made his jaw drop.

No wraiths. No spirits. The afternoon was gray again, the normal mundane clouds were pregnant with real rain. The cemetery was littered with corpses. Some recognizable as people, newly deceased. Some mere skeletons, with wisps of hair sticking to their skulls.

They had fallen where they'd stood; bones and decaying flesh stretching out as far as the eye could see.

Overhead, the portal was still there, a hole torn in the sky, but nothing emerged from it. Silently, it held the potential for doom, but for now remained empty. The True Father was nowhere to be seen.

Kyara stood beside Darvyn, gripping his hand in her own. He wrapped her in an embrace, squeezing her tight to him. He wasn't certain if it was relief he felt or more apprehension. But he forced himself into this present moment. Pulled himself back from Kyara to look at her face.

Her breathing was rapid, she had yet to come down from the adrenaline of battle—of whatever she'd just been through. But she held him tight and brushed her lips against his.

They kissed, grateful to be alive. While the hole in the sky looked down on them.

The ferocity of the wraiths that the True Father had unleashed upon the Earthsingers was even greater than before. Jasminda spun out of the way as a chunk from a ship hurled toward her.

The group of Raunian fighters engaged in hand-to-hand combat, forming a protective circle around Jasminda, Oola, and Yllis, but swarms of wraiths slipped through. The Raunians were quickly overwhelmed and began to fall, one by one.

Jasminda worked on healing them, in between fending off the volley of attacks, but splitting her focus was dangerous. Even with the massive power boost from the obelisk, pinpointing the Earthsong attacks so as not to hit one of their allies was difficult. As soon as she cast a wraith away from her, two more took its place. Her attention was drawn everywhere at once just to maintain her position, much less make any headway.

She gasped for breath and deflected a bombardment of wickedly sharp iron fence posts, when a sudden brightness in the sky stole her focus. Darts of light flooded her vision; she squeezed her eyes shut when it became too painful to keep them open. She couldn't say how long it lasted, but when the light receded and she opened her eyes, the wraiths were gone.

Dozens of bodies lay littered across the ground, transformed back into their original hosts. Mostly Elsirans, but some foreign-born residents of Portside had been caught by the spirits. Almost all were alive, but badly injured.

After another nervous glance at the sky, Jasminda hurried forward to heal them. Broken bones and internal injuries took up the most of the cases. She worked quickly, trying to get each person past the critical stage, knowing there would be others who could take the victims the rest of the way. An Elsiran woman had a severe head injury that was worrisome. Jasminda took an extra minute to ensure there wasn't further damage she'd missed, when a groaning man stole her attention.

He rolled over onto his back and Jasminda stumbled. Zann Biddell lay there, bleeding from his nose and mouth. She finished her work on the woman and moved to him. Crouching down, she assessed his damage. His eyelids fluttered before opening.

"Master Biddel, can you hear me?"

He moaned and held a hand up to his head.

"Be still, I'm going to see to your head."

"No." He batted her away. "Don't want any of your . . . witchcraft."

Jasminda sighed. "Very well then, there are others I can help." Annoyingly, Oola was not seeing to the other victims, instead She was staring up at the dark portal still hanging in the sky like a reverse moon.

"I will die . . . true to my principles," Zann Biddell said, breath rasping. "My people will know . . . that I was not moved."

Jasminda stood, her legs wobbly. "You will die a fool. And *your people* will not know anything. You think I will make you a martyr?" She shook her head and moved on to the next person needing aid.

"Tell them," Biddell wailed, his voice growing thin. He coughed blood and his body shuddered. "Tell them . . . please."

But Jasminda had already moved on.

After she'd seen to the worst cases, she stalked over to Oola. "Thank you for helping." Her sarcasm was lost on the woman, who hadn't yet stopped staring at the portal. "What do you think happened? With that light?"

"I do not know," She said, and launched into the air.

"Wait!" Jasminda cried.

There was another dark figure in the sky, heading north, and Oola followed it up the coastline. As Jasminda watched the Goddess disappear, Yllis stepped up beside her.

"You should go after Her. This is not over yet." His expression was contemplative, but worry settled in around his eyes. "There are Singers nearby who will help the rest."

Jasminda nodded and reached for the obelisk's power. Mastering the flying spell had never been on the top of her to-do list, but now with the additional focusing properties, she found it easier. Controlling the air currents to lift her into the air took concentration. She wobbled a bit as she rose one pace then two into the air. Quickly though, the freedom from gravity became liberating.

She moved slowly at first, testing herself before darting forward more quickly. "I understand why She likes it so much," she muttered.

Oola had flown north then west, headed toward the ocean. Jasminda went after Her, both chasing the initial figure who suddenly dropped from the sky like a missile. Oola dove for it with Jasminda steadily gaining speed behind Her.

The Goddess must have used Earthsong to catch the projectile before it hit the ground. The figure's descent slowed and it floated down to the beach on a cushion of air. As Jasminda reduced speed and grew closer to the ground she recognized the unconscious form of the True Father.

His face was placid, free of the anger and hatred and pain Jasminda had witnessed from him before. Her own landing left something to be desired. She sprawled in the sand, her knees and palms smarting, before righting herself and approaching Oola and Eero.

"What happened to him?"

Oola crouched next to Her brother. "He used up all the Songs he stole."

Eero's chest rose with his breath, and he roused. Jasminda readied herself for an attack. But the man simply opened his amber eyes to stare up at his twin sister.

"Have I done it? Have I won?" His voice was different, the signature rasp wasn't present. He almost sounded like a normal man.

Oola shook Her head. "No, Eero. You haven't." She stroked his wild hair away from his face, which was gaunt and drawn. Freckles peppered his skin, and deep lines framed his eyes.

A soft thud sounded just behind her and Darvyn was there with Kyara in his arms. He set her on her feet and the three of them peered down on the pathetic creature lying on the sand.

"What's happened?" Kyara asked.

"His power is drained." Jasminda loosened the grip of the knife she didn't remember palming. "The wraiths at the cemetery?"

"Gone." Kyara's voice cracked. "We had some unexpected help, but all the wraiths are gone everywhere."

Jasminda breathed deeply, though true relief was elusive. Eero still had the ability to steal his sister's Song. He needed to be watched closely since Oola's mindset was still uncertain where Her brother was concerned.

But Eero's hands were empty and tears filled his eyes. Jasminda was unmoved, but Oola cried with him. She leaned in to kiss his forehead and then stood, backing away.

"I love you, brother. Always remember that. And I will see you again in the next world." Then She spun around and walked off down the beach, turning Her back on them.

"What is She doing?" Jasminda asked.

Darvyn pursed his lips. "Coward," he said under his breath.

Realization dawned. She was leaving Eero's fate to them. A sharp pain blossomed in Jasminda's chest. "Could you kill your own brother?"

Darvyn's jaw was tense. "If it needed to be done? Yes."

Kyara placed a hand on his arm. "You may think that now, but don't be so sure. I once asked you to kill me to save others. Could you have done that?"

Pain shone in his eyes as he stared at Kyara. He dropped his head, shoulders slumping.

Jasminda turned back to the prone man. His eyes were vacant, staring up at the sky, not seeing or not caring, she had no idea.

"I'll do it," she said, the knife in her hand shaking. She had killed before, though not someone who appeared so helpless. She shook that thought off. She couldn't allow herself to be taken in by appearances. There could be no trial, no imprisonment—Eero was too dangerous. He'd proven it again and again. All he needed was a drop of blood to wreak havoc.

Her Song prodded at her, the life energy swirling in her veins funneled by the obelisk shuddered at the possibility of murder. But she was the queen, for better or worse. And she could not shy away from doing what was right for her people.

"No, I'll do it," Darvyn said. His fists were gripped tight. He looked just as torn as she was but also determined. He had suffered at Eero's hand as much as anyone had.

"It's already donc," Kyara whispered, her voice laced with misery. Her eyes were closed and a single tear slipped down her cheek.

"You said you never wanted to kill again." Darvyn was visibly holding himself back from reaching for her.

"I know. But it is what I was made to do."

Jasminda felt for the man's life energy, felt it peter out until it was no more.

His eyes remained open, staring at the hole in the sky. The whites filled with black and he saw no more.

Kyara lifted her head to the clouds, breathing deeply. Darvyn watched her carefully, broadcasting his pain and worry and care. He was strung so tight he might burst.

Jasminda looked into the distance at the figure retreating up the beach, leaving them all behind.

CHAPTER FIFTY-FIVE

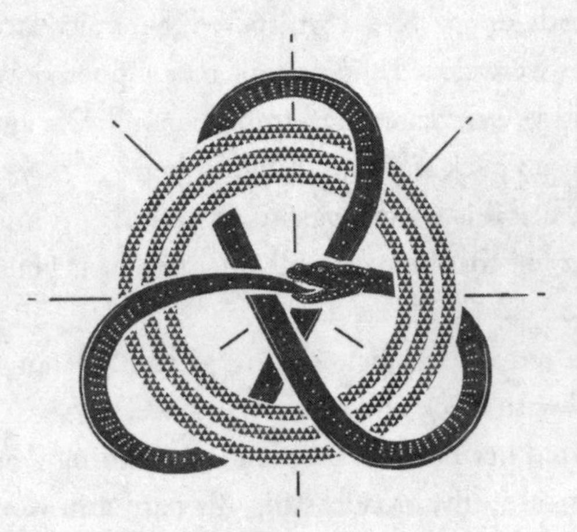

Do we only have one chance to join the refrain?
Or do opportunities come like the rain?
What's inside of you cannot forever be silent.
Whether in this lifetime or the next,
you will join the infinite choir.

—THE HARMONY OF BEING

The scent of smoke hung heavy in the air. Kyara wrinkled her nose, resisting the urge to sneeze. Clanging peals from the all-clear alarm rang for the second time, and people slowly trickled out of emergency shelters.

However, some were still trapped; the damage the wraiths had done to buildings had covered exits and buried basements under piles of rubble. As the streets gradually filled, people began banding together to dig out their neighbors. Lagrimari with their newly restored Songs worked alongside men and women with shovels and sticks to lever debris and create new paths underground to free the trapped survivors. The sight pierced the veil of Kyara's numbness just a little.

She'd left Darvyn with Jasminda at a sprawling hospital complex where they were coordinating recovery efforts and tending to the wounded.

"I just need to clear my head," she'd said. He'd understood.

As she walked, she lent aid where she could. Helping to push a half-crushed auto from the front of a building, pulling a woman away from a shower of bricks as a freestanding house collapsed, calming an agitated horse—she used her Song to weaken the beast so that its handlers could reattach the bridle. All the while, she tried to make sense of the swirling emotions within her.

The True Father's face at rest haunted her. After a lifetime of murder, why did this one affect her so deeply? But she knew the answer. Slaying the former king was the first time she'd consciously killed without the blood spell forcing her to, without any coercion whatsoever. It would stain her soul in a new way—even though it had been necessary.

Was he in the World After now, looking through some mirror at her, promising vengeance? She would do it again, a thousand times over, but that did not mean the stain would fade.

She paused in the middle of the sidewalk. Someone cursed softly, nearly bumping into her, then walked around, but her gaze was unseeing.

The World After. Tana.

She turned in a circle, disconcerted, then looked up to the portal hanging ominously overhead, quiet now, empty of spirits. She'd left Tana there. She'd have to go back and find her.

A woman on the other side of the street called out her name.

Kyara refocused and then cringed to find Ella running toward her. The woman's face was dirty, her dress ripped in places and blood was caked on her knuckles. But she smiled radiantly at Kyara when she stopped before her.

Then her smile turned to confusion as she looked around—searching for her daughter. Kyara's throat felt like someone had shoved hot spikes into it. She had no idea how to tell the woman that her husband was gone and Tana was somewhere in the World After chasing him.

But then Benn Ravel stepped to his wife's side, carrying Ulani on his hip. Kyara gasped.

"What's happened?" Ella asked, breathless. "Where is she?"

Kyara's gaze never left Benn, who was battered as well with a black eye blooming and a split lip. That's how she was sure he wasn't still a wraith. "You. You're alive?"

A dark bundle of fur rubbed up against her legs as Raven said his hello. Ella clutched Benn's free arm and the man nodded. "Feel like I was trampled by another runaway horse, but I'm still here. Where's my daughter?"

Ulani spoke up. "Papa was gone, but Tana brought him back." Raven gave a little *yip*, as if in agreement, and went to sit at Benn's feet.

"How did you know?" Kyara asked. Ulani shrugged.

Ella was growing frantic, and Benn had started breathing heavily. Kyara held up her hands. "She's in the World After. She went there to get you," she nodded at Benn, "and didn't return."

The girl's body—Kyara had become so distracted she hadn't thought to look after it. Likely it had been taken to a hospital. Tana wasn't dead, not really, but would anyone be able to tell?

Ella's growing horror was a punch to the gut. Kyara had promised this woman that she'd take care of her daughter and failed.

"I will go back and get her. I'll bring her back, don't worry. She's not in danger. It's just that the World After is . . ." She couldn't put into words the complex vastness of the place. She had no idea how large it was, had never navigated the place and didn't know where to begin, but she would bring Tana back no matter what.

Ella looked haunted. Benn's gaze held a misery that caused Kyara to take a step back. Guilt roared in her ears like an engine—one fueled by her lifetime of failures. It was so loud she almost didn't hear the bells.

Ulani's sudden smile seemed out of place. The girl was beaming at something just behind Kyara. She looked over her shoulder and squinted at the shine of golden light, like the sun had broken through the twilight gloom to shine its midday rays upon them.

And then Fenix was there.

He stepped out of a bright portal, which almost swallowed up the darkness of the place from where he'd emerged. And he carried something—no, someone—in his arms.

"Tana!" Ella cried, leaping forward. She brushed the girl's braided head and stroked her cheeks. Tana's eyes opened sleepily.

"Mama?" She yawned and stretched, looking around. Then her body seized as she caught sight of Benn. She clambered out of Fenix's hold to stand on shaky legs, then launched herself at her father, wrapping him and her sister in a hug.

Kyara's breathing restarted as the family reunited. She turned to Fenix, jaw agape.

"She got lost and needed a little help returning," the man said, "I happened to be headed this way when I sensed her."

"You sensed her in the World After?"

"We have tracking abilities." He said no more, leaving Kyara to wonder, not for the first time exactly what kind of power Fenix's people possessed. He was obviously able to cross between the worlds with ease, and with all she'd already seen him accomplish, what were his limits? It frightened her, but she was grateful to him.

"Thank you. I—" She shook her head. "I didn't end up taking very good care of her."

"As I understand it, children are rather difficult to look after. And you did a good job looking after this world." He lifted his arm, motioning to the shell-shocked survivors beginning to take stock of their homes and businesses. Everywhere she turned something had been damaged, if not destroyed outright. Buildings looked like they'd been bombed, power lines were down, a burst pipe two blocks over filled the street with water.

The reconstruction effort would take a long, long time. She may have been instrumental in saving the people, but she wasn't sure anyone would thank her. However, she didn't have the energy to contradict him.

"The portal is going to be a problem," Kyara said instead. "I don't think I can close it, or at least I don't know how to."

Fenix tilted his head up. The portal was stark against the darkening sky. She thought it would probably still be visible once it hit full dark.

"Where is Mooriah?" he asked.

"She was ejected from the body she'd been using. I haven't seen her since."

He closed his golden eyes and grew very still—not even appearing to breathe. "I know where she is."

They said their good-byes to the girls and their parents, then Fenix led Kyara back to the Portside Hospital, where Jasminda and Darvyn were out front overseeing the Earthsingers volunteering for healing tasks.

Jasminda had not met Fenix before. Though he'd tempered his

glow to appear more human, he still stood out and drew stares from those around them. Kyara made the introductions, but Fenix paid little attention to the Elsiran queen. His gaze had been captured by the crowd of bystanders gathered around the plaza.

The sea of people parted and Mooriah stood there, looking rather regal herself. Kyara wondered what body she was using, hoping it was not a corpse.

"Spirits cannot normally possess the dead," Fenix said, using that uncanny ability he had to read her thoughts. "It was the foul magic of the True Father's that made it possible. It cost him quite dearly. And I cannot read your mind, you just have a very expressive face." The hint of a smile danced on his lips.

Darvyn was suddenly next to her, speaking low in her ear. "Are you all right?"

She opened her mouth to answer, but nothing came out. She truly had no idea.

Mooriah paced toward them, scowling at Fenix. "Why haven't you closed the portal?"

"Hello to you, too," Kyara muttered, but Fenix's smile emerged full force.

"I will, but there's the matter of the sentinel to be decided."

"What is there to decide?" Mooriah snapped. "I have served the role all this time, I shall return again." At this, Fenix's smile slipped away.

"What is a sentinel?" Kyara asked.

"The barrier between worlds is still thin," Fenix responded. "No doubt some enterprising future mage will find a way to breach it again. The World After needs someone to watch over it, monitor the restless spirits, and give the living a warning the next time things go astray."

Kyara shuddered to think of a next time. She turned to Mooriah. "That's what you were doing for all that time? You were the sentinel?"

She lifted a shoulder. "Murmur told me that one was needed, and that was a role I was uniquely prepared to play."

"It needs to be a Nethersinger?" Kyara's chest grew tight. Darvyn stiffened beside her.

Fenix was grim. "Few others can survive in the World After."

"And that is why I will go back." Mooriah's expression was stoic, but Kyara sensed melancholy beneath the surface.

"You have served you time." Fenix crossed his arms, looking annoyed for the first time. "You committed no crime. And even if you had, surely the sentence has been paid."

"Who else then? This one and the girl have lives to live. I have already lived mine. You would ask one of these children to sacrifice so much?" Hurt laced her voice.

Fenix dropped his head, looking chagrined. "Of course not."

Kyara did not have to be an Earthsinger to sense the longing within Fenix for Mooriah. Centuries ago Mooriah had married another and raised a family, but there was obviously history between these two, even if it was complicated.

Mooriah reached for his hand. "Another lifetime. Is that not what I told you? Just, perhaps not this one."

Fenix remained silent, staring at the ground. Kyara closed her eyes, unwilling to see more. Darvyn's hand was solid at her back, a supportive presence. She kept her eyes shut as she spoke, unwilling to see what her words would do to him.

"It's my turn," she whispered, more breath than sound. Darvyn's hand gripped the back of her tunic, but she continued. "You've given up more than anyone could ever ask you to, Mooriah. It's my turn." She opened her eyes, still avoiding Darvyn.

Mooriah frowned. "I cannot ask you to do that."

"You don't have to. There's no place for me here, I've done too much that can't be forgiven. That shouldn't be forgiven. If this is penance, or punishment, or simply making amends. It must be me."

Tears welled in Mooriah's eyes. "This sacrifice you make, almost no one will know of it."

"I don't do it for glory. It's necessary, isn't it?"

Mooriah nodded slowly. Darvyn's hand was stone, still clutching the back of her clothing. She dared not look at him and flinched at the devastation in his voice when he spoke. "Is there any way I can go with her?"

"Darvyn, no!" She spun around to face him, but this time *he* ignored *her.*

"Fenix?" he pleaded. He was still as a statue, but cracks were already forming.

"The World After is for the dead," Fenix replied. Then he squinted and tilted his head to the side, peering at Darvyn. "But perhaps . . ."

"Perhaps what?"

"Perhaps if I unbind you . . ."

Darvyn's eyes widened. "I'm bound?"

"The powers you inherited from your father are buried within you. They would have been difficult for you to manage as a young child without training and so they retreated. Once they are unearthed, I see no reason for you not to be able to survive between worlds. You could go with her if you chose to."

Darvyn stopped breathing. Kyara was afraid he might have had a stroke. This was a lot of information to absorb all at once. A look was shared between the two men. Darvyn's lips moved, mouthing the word, "Please."

Kyara had no time to object to his giving up his life as well. Before she could form the words to protest, there was a flash of light, almost imperceptible it went by so quickly. In its wake, Fenix observed Darvyn expectantly.

"It's done?" he asked.

"It's done," Fenix said.

Darvyn stretched out his arms and turned his hands palm up, then down. "I don't really feel any different."

Fenix chuckled. "Give it time, give it time."

He truly didn't seem any different to her eyes, however, sinking into her other sight made things clearer. Instead of the barely visible speck of Nethersong he usually manifested as, Darvyn was present. Not quite the substantial form Fenix displayed, more like a ghostly apparition of himself.

Kyara shuttered her vision, focusing back in on the real world. "Darvyn, I—I'm not asking you to do this with me."

"You don't have to. There's no place for me here," he echoed her words from a few moments ago. "Not without you."

She grabbed Darvyn's hand and pulled him closer. "Are you sure you want this? It won't be life the way you know it. I'm not sure it will really be life at all."

He palmed her cheek with a hand. "But it will be with you. And that's all that matters."

Loss and pain, that was almost all she'd ever known. But she knew love now, too. Her Song had brought nothing but misery for so long, now it gave her a purpose beyond just taking life, she could help to protect it.

Tears filled her eyes as Darvyn wrapped his arms around her. Though she couldn't imagine what her existence in the World After would be like, at least she would not be alone.

CHAPTER FIFTY-SIX

Loneliness and heartache tend to swell
when the clamor of the solo drowns out the
polyphony. You would do well to bid them both
farewell.
And lift your voice.

—THE HARMONY OF BEING

Mooriah was not good with good-byes. As Kyara and Darvyn explained to the others where they planned to go and why, she had no desire for a drawn-out farewell. King Jaqros had arrived with all the desperation of a man separated from his wife during a calamity. He was also a longtime friend of Darvyn's and was having trouble understanding where his friend was headed and why he had to leave at all. Mooriah left it to the others to fill him in; she wandered to the side of the plaza out of earshot of the rest of them.

One wing of the hospital was discharging funnels of smoke. Someone—a wraith no doubt—had thrown a truck into the side of the building and while the fire had been put out, the wreckage smoldered on. The rest of the building was usable, though without electricity. However, it would be empty soon as Earthsingers were still filing in, volunteering to heal the injured.

The uncomfortable press of this modern city had not grown any easier for Mooriah to manage. She'd spent weeks back in this world and part of her had actually been eager to return to the meditative stillness of the World After. Though having someone to share it with like Kyara did would have been agreeable.

Her dear husband had passed into the Flame, as he should have. Now he was at peace. She would not have asked him to forego that on her account, though he no doubt would have.

She stood at the edge of a concrete barrier, separating the plaza from the street several steps below. Her back was to the hospital and though she did not hear the footsteps approaching her, she felt his presence when he arrived. For a long time, he just stood behind her, observing the city or observing her, she could not say.

"Will you go to the Flame now?" Fenix finally asked.

"The Flame holds as little appeal to me as it ever did. But I have no other options. I cannot resist for much longer. Its pull grows stronger now that peace has returned and my reasons for fighting it are gone."

"Hmm." The centuries had not changed the annoying habit he had of humming in response to things. But she'd taken note of other changes. He was not the same irreverent, headstrong, selfish man she'd once helped escape captivity. Part of her missed that version of him, but he had come into the potential she'd seen in him all those years ago, and for that she was grateful.

"Speak plainly, man," she snapped to hide the burst of sentimentality she could not acknowledge.

He chuckled. "You have grown, too. No longer a shrinking violet."

She spun around. "I was never a shrinking violet."

"Yet you weren't always this shrewish harridan."

She narrowed her eyes, and he smiled. She turned away again, hissing under her breath.

"What if there was another way?"

She clucked her tongue. "There is death and the Flame, what other way?"

"You could come with me." He spoke so quietly she wasn't certain she'd heard him properly. He stepped fully into her periphery.

"To your world? How?"

"There are ways."

"But I remember you saying—"

"I know. It will not be easy but it is possible." He was quiet for a time, letting her consider before speaking again. "Is that something you would want?"

She had seen little of the world in her lifetime, and while she had no regrets for the life she had led, the possibility of the unknown still pulled at her, just as it always had.

Could she take what he offered?

"Your parents have arrived," Fenix said. She turned around to find Oola and Yllis clustered with the others.

Mooriah sighed and made her way back to the group, Fenix's

offer ricocheting around her brain. It would cost him something to take her with him—cost him any chance of returning to this world, she suspected. Would it be worth it?

Oola and Yllis stood side by side amidst the chatter and tears of Kyara and Darvyn's explanations. The two were studiously ignoring one another, though their shoulders were touching.

Mooriah chuckled at the sight of them. Stubborn until the end. "Can you bring them, too?" The words were spoken before she'd considered the implications, but they felt right. She hadn't had the chance to get to know her mother. Or her father for that matter. Not really. And the two of them had been torn apart by war and guilt and probably other things she had no idea of. None of them belonged in this world any longer—their jobs here were done. If their options were the Flame or Fenix's mysterious home, then the choice was infinitely easier. What he was really offering was more time.

"Is my mother bound in some way, too? Could she survive the trip?"

"Not in her current form, but as a spirit she could—the same as you." Fenix's gaze was a physical force on her skin, but she still avoided looking directly at him.

"Would it . . . harm you to bring them?"

He paused. "There would be no permanent damage." So, yes. But he would if she asked.

Oola looked over at her, a question in the woman's gaze. Mooriah faced Fenix, standing just out of earshot of the group. His intense attention burned into her, sparking like a fireball. "And you do not mind?"

"I have waited lifetimes for you. The cost is nothing in comparison."

"Neither of us are the same people we once were. We would need to get to know one another again."

"In this new lifetime."

She swallowed as something in her middle fluttered. She turned away, cheeks hot. It looked like she would have to say her good-byes after all.

CHAPTER FIFTY-SEVEN

It is enough to just be
quiet
and
listen.

—THE HARMONY OF BEING

The number of people pressed into Rosira's northern temple must be in violation of some sort of fire code. Zeli stood at the front of the only Sisterhood temple still standing in the city—the southern one had been destroyed by terrorists and the eastern one pulled down by the hands of the wraiths. The joyous anticipation inside the walls was like effervescence, popping and fizzing in the air. She inhaled it deeply.

"Who are all of these people?" Varten whispered to her, craning his neck to take in the crowd.

She shrugged. "It was an open invitation, and everyone needs a reason to celebrate."

The audience had dressed in their finest clothes to come here today and experience some joy again. On the raised platform in front of them was a table holding several tiny glass bowls and a larger empty one. A small candle flickered inside one of the smaller bowls. Varten had described the Elsiran marriage ceremony to her and she liked the symbolism of it all.

Only a handful of Sisters stood behind the platform. The order had been devastated by the questions about the Goddess Awoken and Her possible allegiance to the True Father. Her disappearance after his death had made the rumors swell. That added to the imprisonment and upcoming execution of the former High Priestess had left the organization in shambles. Zeli was not certain they would survive—but maybe out of it something new would be born.

A hush came over the crowd and then a low chant began. All the Raunians in attendance—and there were so many she wondered if there was anyone left on the island at all—began to sing, their voices rising in a lilting melody. Ani emerged from a door behind the platform and climbed the short steps. She was radiant in a voluminous gown made of iridescent blue material that left her arms and shoulders bare.

She wore a matching glove on her single hand, and a ribbon tied around her other arm where it ended below the elbow. Roshon approached the platform from the opposite direction, grinning from ear to ear. He wore a sharply cut formal suit and looked comfortable in it. Queen Jasminda and King Pia arrived last, making the small stage quite crowded.

Darvyn and Kyara had agreed to delay their departure until after the nuptials. They stood with Dansig, King Jaqros, Tai, and Lizvette in the front row.

Tears formed in Zeli's eyes, she loved weddings. The Elsiran and Raunian ceremonies were held simultaneously. The Elsiran one involved transferring the contents of each small bowl into the larger one. The Raunian service involved lots of knot tying and a series of call and responses in their language—some of which involved the whole audience. Zeli stumbled over the pronunciations of the words, without any clue as to what she was saying, but the love and hope of everyone present rippled through her Song.

When it was done, the bride and groom stayed at the front to receive their guests, another Raunian tradition. Their families were at the front of the line, and she followed Varten, who hugged his brother and new sister fiercely before stepping back.

Zeli placed a wrapped gift into Roshon's hand. Wedding presents weren't part of Elsiran custom, but they were important in Lagrimar.

"Open it," Varten said, grinning. His brother peeled back the paper and opened the box to reveal the little figurine of two boys with their arms hooked into one another's—the same one the twins had been fighting over when Zeli met them.

"I decided you can have it," Varten said.

"*I* decided that it would be a good wedding gift," Zeli said, elbowing him. Varten shrugged and chuckled.

"Thank you," Roshon said, holding it gently, and Ani beamed.

"Maybe we'll give it back to you when you two get married," she said.

Zeli's face grew hot. From the corner of her eye she saw Varten's jaw drop then snap shut. He nodded. "Deal."

Then he grabbed Zeli's hand and moved off, allowing the next person in line their chance to greet the newlyweds. She had questions, lots of questions, but she couldn't voice them as they worked their way through the throng and to the temple's exit.

Outside, masses of people queued up to get their chance to greet the prince and princess.

"Marriage?" she finally asked, brows raised as they stood on the temple's front steps.

He looked sheepish. "Well, you know . . . I mean that is if you want . . . Well, the thing is. I love you, Zeli. And I do want to marry you. If you'll have me. One day. I mean we—"

She silenced him with a kiss, reaching up to wrap her arms around his neck and pull him down. His arms encircled her waist and for a moment, she forgot where she was. Though the air was frigid, Zeli was quite warm. She breathed him in, losing herself in the softness of his lips, and the heat of his body pressed against hers.

Finally she pulled away and gasped for breath. "I love you, too, Your Grace. And I would be delighted to marry you."

Varten blinked slowly. "Really? Maybe once all the hubbub dies down. Wouldn't want to steal any of their thunder, you know?" He gave her a cautious glance. "I mean, Ani and Roshon were engaged for years, so there's no rush. Unless you wanted to rush. Or not."

She kissed him again, delighting in the feel of him against her. She was so full of hope and joy, it was very possible she might burst.

A chattering trio of women moving past bumped into Zeli, reminding her that they were still on the temple's front stairs. She took Varten's hand and they descended.

At the bottom of the steps, a small group of women in Sisterhood robes appeared to be arguing with a couple of rough-looking Elsiran men. Zeli tugged on Varten's hand and motioned toward the commotion. In wordless agreement, they approached.

"The Goddess abandoned us," one of the men spat, flinging his arms wide. "Why don't you take those robes off and admit the truth—She was just a charlatan, a hypocrite witch who didn't give a rat's arsehole about any of us."

The half-dozen women being accosted looked weary. Though they still wore the uniform, they seemed lost—Zeli's Song revealed deep wells of emptiness and sorrow within them. Like they were just going through the motions without any other notion of what to do. She recognized most of them—once she'd hoped they'd be her family, now she felt sorry for them.

"The Goddess's teachings are still a balm in times of need," one Sister was saying. "They are timeless and Her presence or absence makes little difference in their power."

The Elsiran man shook his head, grumbling along with his fellows. "I went to temple every week for practically my whole life. Thirty-five years of faith, of believing in Her. And now what? Now we're left with nothing." His anger masked deep hurt and loss. Zeli could understand his grief—it was shared by so many of the faithful. What to do when that faith is betrayed?

She moved closer. "What was it about being a follower of the Goddess that brought you comfort?" she asked the man.

The entire group looked at her sharply, surprised at her interruption. She didn't feel the need to apologize for intruding, the desire to help was strong within her. "All of Her wisdom, all of Her guidance, it hasn't gone anywhere. It wasn't even unique or specific to Her. Who among you had the Dream?" Two of the men nodded as well as one of the Sisters.

"Was what She told you in the Dream so profound? Or was it your belief in Her and your joy at being one of the chosen that made it all the more impactful?"

The faces staring at her frowned with confusion. "I served the Goddess, too. I believed in Her. But now I look back and wonder, what exactly was it that we believed in?" She turned to the lead Elsiran man.

"What was it that made you go to the temple every week?"

His brow wrinkled. "Faith. Duty."

"Anything else?"

"My family." He shrugged. "Our neighbors. It's what we did, slept there once a week, hoping for a Dream."

"Did it make you feel like you belonged to something bigger? Like you had a way of battling hardships and pain?"

He thought for a moment and then agreed. "It brought me peace."

"And where did the peace come from?" Zeli pushed.

He shook his head.

"Where has it gone?" she asked. She took in the gathered group, which seemed to have grown. "Inside of you. It's all there. That's where all feelings come from. Having a Song means that I can sense your despair and your delight, and everything in between. I can feel it growing and shrinking, and I promise you that these emotions don't originate from anywhere other than inside each of you."

Her listeners were rapt. "There is a voice within you that whispers quietly. It causes your skin to pebble when you walk a dark alley alone. It resonates with accomplishment when you help a neighbor to bear a burden. It sings in harmony when you meet the love of your life. We are very, very good at not listening to this voice. We want verification from outside of us—from goddesses or queens. We are convinced that someone knows better, that we cannot trust ourselves and so we turn without when we should look within.

"The Goddess's teachings struck a chord with that inner voice. It is what made you feel that creating community with your family and neighbors brought joy. That giving to charity and helping those in need was the right thing to do. *The Book of Her Reign* may say, 'It is no burden for those with plenty to spread their excess among those who lack' but you believe it because of that voice inside. If the book told you that stabbing your mother was the way to achieve the Dream would you have done it?"

The man recoiled. Several others grumbled, affronted at the thought. Zeli spread her hands. "You don't have to be lost. You just have to find yourself."

One of the Sisters turned to her, appearing pensive. "I know your voice, it's so familiar."

Others murmured in agreement and Zeli pressed her lips shut. Should she reveal that it was her voice in their heads during the attack? They'd all heard her, but she wasn't certain she should bring it up. Perhaps that should continue to be a mystery.

An Elsiran woman who had wandered over spoke up. "What do you call these teachings?"

Zeli's brows climbed. "They're not teachings. They're just . . . I don't know, just thoughts."

"I'd like to hear more," a young man said from the back of the group. It had definitely doubled in size since she'd been speaking.

She shook her head, perplexed. She turned to Varten, widening her eyes and silently asking for his help.

"You could tell them about sacrifice," he said, voice low. "About trust and strength and courage." His eyes were smiling at her, and the admiration and love in his gaze settled her confusion. "You've learned a lot that you can share. And I think . . . I think a lot of people would want to hear it. Not all of us have Songs, but we can all learn to live in harmony. With each other and with ourselves."

She swallowed and glanced back at the receptive faces turned her way. "Maybe that's what I could call it? Harmony?"

His eyes crinkled as he smiled. "The Harmony of Being."

Zeli filled with a new kind of warmth. One that was full of purpose. Her head swam, she had not intended to become a teacher of any kind, but the people's need for comfort pulsed through her Song. This was something she could do, at least. Something good.

"Why don't we head to the park," Varten called out. "And she'll tell you more about it."

Murmurs of agreement rippled through the group. Varten squeezed her hand. "It's okay, you can do this," he whispered.

And she believed him.

EPILOGUE

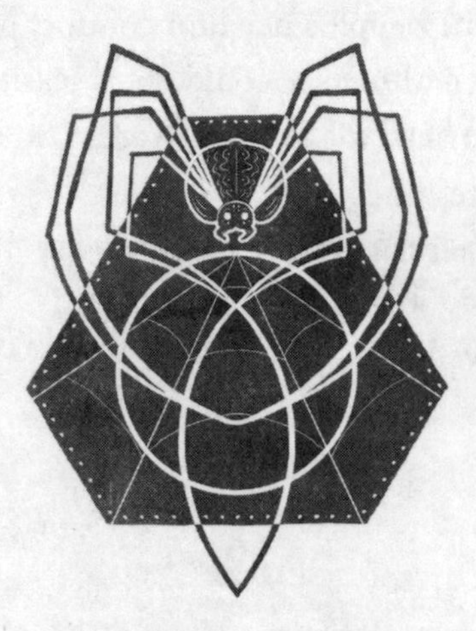

We sing because while blood flows in our veins
we are alive and we have voices
and songs
that must be heard.

—THE HARMONY OF BEING

Jasminda faced the eastern mountain range, its snowcapped peaks so familiar, but no longer home. It felt like a million years since she'd last seen them—could it have only been months? These mountains formed an unbroken chain from north to south except for this one place—Breach Valley. An innocuous patch of land, brown and crisped with a thin layer of snow lying atop it.

Kyara stepped to her side, her braids undone, hair crinkling around her face. *Cousin,* Jasminda thought. *I wish we could have had more time.*

As if she'd heard her thoughts, Kyara turned and smiled. Jasminda could not recall ever seeing the woman do so before.

"You leave today?" Jasminda asked.

Kyara nodded. "Darvyn wanted to see this, to help in the transition." She turned and motioned behind her toward the organized chaos occurring on this side of the range.

Dozens of buses that had carried the Lagrimari across the country were refueling at the eastern army base, preparing for the trek across the border and into the neighboring land. Now that they had their Songs back, the Lagrimari had decided to return to their homeland and rebuild it. Working together, linking their Songs, they would transform the desert into arable land, much as their ancestors had done.

Jack, Darvyn, and Papa stood to the side chatting with a group of older men—former prisoners of war whom they'd known for years. An air of melancholy clung to the scene—so many changes all at once. Jasminda shivered, drawing her coat tighter.

"We can come back," Kyara said. "If you ever need us. If there is another threat, we'll be here. Mooriah was not able to return at will since she was truly dead, but Darvyn and I don't have that restriction." A peace had settled upon her, one which had removed the ever-present strain around her eyes.

"Thank you, and I am sorry that you all will have to make this sacrifice."

Kyara shook her head. "It isn't sacrifice, it's purpose. I welcome it. It's better this way."

"Your Majesty," a gravelly voice called from behind them. They turned to find Turwig and Rozyl. The old man bowed but Rozyl merely raised a brow. Kyara smiled at them in greeting and then retreated to where Darvyn was.

"You don't need to bow to me anymore," Jasminda said. "I'm no longer your queen."

"You will always be our queen," Turwig replied solemnly.

Looking upon the buses and the folks gathered there, her eyes misted. "I suspect the time for kings and queens is nearing an end," she whispered, echoing Oola's words from not long ago. "The will of the people is not necessarily what we would expect. The referendum taught me that."

Turwig nodded. "I suppose you're right."

"What will you do?"

"For now the elders of the Keepers will serve as a ruling council. We'll need to wrest control of some territories from warlords who have cropped up and work on cleaning up the mess of the past five hundred years." He should have sounded overwhelmed, but excitement was the primary emotion brushing her Song.

"And what of the Sons of Lagrimar?" she asked.

Rozyl tensed. "We will have to contend with them, for better or worse. They have a seat at the table and will not relinquish it."

"This will of the people you speak of can be unpredictable and they are considered heroes by many," Turwig added.

Terrorists or freedom fighters, the distinction between them depended much on your perspective. Jasminda shook off a chill.

"Can we count on your aid with transforming the land?" Rozyl asked. "You may be the strongest Singer now that Darvyn is leaving."

"Of course I will help. But I suspect that once the people get used to singing again, things will go a bit faster. And our nations will need to remain strong allies, what better way to strengthen the ties?"

Turwig hummed in approval.

"Good luck to you," Rozyl said, tears filling her eyes. Jasminda pulled the woman into a hug and received several hard thumps on the back in return.

"And you as well," she whispered.

Rozyl pulled away and marched off without another word. Turwig gave her another bow before following. The two Keepers boarded a bus that would take them back across the border.

Jasminda's gaze was drawn back to Jack and the others. Papa's expression was jovial as he joked around with the group of men. Both were too far away to easily scan their emotions—she could have stretched just a bit to do so, but decided not to push. It would be clear soon enough.

A short figure marched toward her, tight steely curls bouncing with each step. Jasminda's eyes widened but she stood her ground. One of her Guardsmen moved to intercept the newspaperwoman, but Jasminda waved him off.

"It's all right, let her through. How can I help you, Mistress Harimel?" Wariness made her skin feel tight.

"Your Majesty." Hazelle Harimel dipped into a slight curtsey once she'd reached Jasminda's side. "I wanted to get your reaction to the exodus of the Lagrimari. What do you think the future holds for the two lands?"

There was no obvious vitriol in the question, though Jasminda didn't let her guard down. "I certainly hope that the future is one of mutual benefit. We intend to be close allies and leave the hurts of the past behind."

"Do you forsee that the open border will cause challenges?"

Jasminda blinked, unsure of what to make of this nearly pleasant woman. "I do not. Open travel will be important since so many Lagrimari have chosen to stay in Elsira and pursue visas as we rewrite the immigration laws. And the Keepers have been actively recruiting Elsirans with a variety of skill sets to emigrate and assist the new government with updating infrastructure and modernizing the land. There are great opportunities for both peoples and the king and I are determined to assist Lagrimar in any way we can."

Hazelle Harimel scribbled in her notebook. Jasminda resisted the urge to peek to see if her words were being transcribed correctly. She brushed against the woman's emotions to find them . . . calm. Determined as ever but without any malice present. What had happened to her?

"I'd like to take a moment, off the record, to thank you for your leadership during the Wraith War." Sincerity bled from the reporter. It took all of Jasminda's will not to stumble in shock.

"I myself was. . . . possessed by a wraith." The words were difficult for her to utter. "Afterward, a Lagrimari girl healed me. I . . ." She looked toward the buses, to the people boarding them, ready to go and reclaim their land, make the desert farmable, and take back their lives. "I can imagine that it has not been easy, being in your position, Your Majesty. But I'm grateful that you're here. I know our people owe you a great debt."

The tears she hadn't allowed to fall before broke through and tracked Jasminda's cheeks. She struggled to gather herself in order to answer. "I'm not sure what to say. Thank you, that means a lot." And it did. Hazelle Harimel nodded and concluded her interview before taking her leave.

Jasminda was still reeling when Jack came up to her. "Is that woman still bothering you?"

"No, she's actually not." She sniffed and turned her back to the crowd to blow her nose. Jack slipped a hand around her waist and she leaned into his warmth.

"Said all your good-byes?" she asked.

"Good-byes for now. But not forever."

"And has Papa decided what he's going to do?"

"I think he's vying for the role of ambassador."

She raised a brow. "I never pegged him for a diplomat."

"Really? He dealt with a lot of abuse for many years without losing his cool or retaliating. He raised some incredible children amidst it all. I'd say he's perfect. He's got my vote."

Jasminda chuckled. The sound of an engine starting made her turn back. The first bus had shut its doors and pulled onto the road. She held her breath as it passed where she and Jack stood. The pavement ended on what had always been a battlefield. Across the border, the roadway started again, the hard-packed dirt leading to Lagrimar's Great Highway.

Papa came up to them and she put her free arm around him. "I never thought I'd live to see the day," he said, voice full of wonder. Whether he meant that the Mantle was down or that free Lagrimari people were returning to their land with hope in their hearts, she wasn't sure. Perhaps both.

"Me, neither," she said. "But I think we will both live long enough to see many amazing things."

Jack chuckled and her Song lit up at the sound. The joy and hope from those who waited eagerly for their homecoming combined. If she stretched far enough, she would be able to sense the relief of those who'd known so much war—those on both sides of the border.

She gave in to the urge and let her power soar, riding on the wings of a lifetime of longing and drawing in the energy of all. She sucked it all into her Song, allowing it to fill her until she was full. Life flowed all around her, flowed through her, and back out into the world.

ACKNOWLEDGMENTS

Ending a series is like completing a marathon. Not that I've ever run a marathon—or run at all outside of mandatory gym classes—but in my mind, they're much the same. Painful and difficult, but ultimately rewarding efforts that take a physical and mental toll and yield benefits that last a lifetime.

Getting to the final chapter of the final book in the series I began eight years ago is like no other accomplishment I've ever achieved. It wasn't very long ago that I couldn't conceive how anyone could complete a whole novel. Now, I've written four fairly long ones—though looking back, I'm still not sure how I got to the finish line. Certainly, it wasn't accomplished without a small army of people along the route, cheering me on.

Huge thanks to my writing community and every critique partner and beta reader who has helped me shape my words, including the homies Nakeesha Seneb, Cerece Rennie Murphy, Denny S. Bryce, and Ivy Spadille.

To Danielle Poiesz, who never fails to ask the questions I hadn't thought of, even when I've tried to think of everything. She always makes my writing more coherent and has improved my craft exponentially over the years.

To my agent, Sara Megibow, who is a constant source of knowledge, encouragement, insight, and optimism. I'm very grateful to be a part of the crew.

To my team at St. Martin's Press, including Meghan Harrington, Beatrice Jason, Mara Delgado Sánchez, and everyone whose name I don't know: I deeply appreciate all of your efforts to bring my words to the world.

And to my editor, Monique Patterson, whose support and belief in me and my work has been life-changing.

To the readers, the bloggers and tweeters and Bookstagrammers, everyone who has read and enjoyed and shared my stories, along with all of My Imaginary Friends—I owe you all of my gratitude. I would be a tree on the ground in the forest with no one to know or care without you all.

To the singer Jamila Woods for the *LEGACY! LEGACY!* album, which was the soundtrack of my life during the writing process of this novel and whose words and music made the presence of the ancestors clearer in my mind.

And finally, to my family. My brother, my mother, my father (whose presence never fades), and my husband, who all surround me with love and support. They allow me to delve into the dark places where creativity sometimes takes me and make it possible for me to leave it all on the page when I emerge.

About the Author

Valerie Bey

L. Penelope has been writing since she could hold a pen and loves getting lost in the worlds in her head. She is an award-winning fantasy and paranormal romance author. Equally left- and right-brained, she studied filmmaking and computer science in college and sometimes dreams in HTML. She lives in Maryland with her husband and furry dependents. Sign up for new release information, exclusives, and giveaways on her website: lpenelope.com.